paper
books

Titles available in this series:

Lionel Abrahams
The Celibacy of Felix Greenspan

David Adey
Under the Southern Cross

Phyllis Altman
The Law of the Vultures

Jane Austen
Northanger Abbey

Ken Barris
Small Change

Michael Chapman and Tony Voss
Accents

Michael Chapman
and Achmat Dangor
Voices from Within

Michael Chapman
The Paperbook of South African English Poetry

John Cleland
Fanny Hill

Joseph Conrad
Heart of Darkness and Typhoon

John Conyngham
The Arrowing of the Cane

Stephen Gray
Market Plays

Janet Hodgson
Princess Emma

Steve Jacobs
Diary of an Exile

Steve Jacobs
Under the Lion

Dan Jacobson
The Price of Diamonds

Henry James
Washington Square

Henno Martin
The Sheltering Desert

Sarah Gertrude Millin
God's Stepchildren

Bloke Modisane
Blame me on History

Sisa Ndaba
One Day in June

Digby Ricci
Reef of Time

Sheila Roberts
Jacks in Corners

Olive Schreiner
The Story of an African Farm

Olive Schreiner
The Woman's Rose

Martin Trump
Armed Vision

Russell Vandenbroucke
Truths the hand can touch

Peter Wilhelm
Some Place in Africa

Peter Wilhelm
The Healing Process

RAISING THE BLINDS

A Century of
South African
Women's Stories

Introduced and edited by
Annemarié van Niekerk

AD. DONKER PUBLISHER

AD. DONKER (PTY) LTD
A DIVISION OF JONATHAN BALL PUBLISHERS (Pty) Ltd
P O Box 33977
Jeppestown
2043

First Published 1990
Reprinted 1996

ISBN 0 86852 181 7

For my sisters, Christine and Ilse
. . . in memory of our Mother

Typeset by Book Productions, Pretoria
Printed and bound by National Book Printers,
Drukkery Street, Goodwood, Western Cape

Contents

Acknowledgements

The editor would like to express her very special thanks to Andries W. Oliphant for his interest, his assistance with the concept of the anthology, the choice of the title and his involvement and concern.

The editor and publisher would like to express their thanks to all concerned for permission to reproduce the material contained in this anthology:

The Library of the University of Cape Town for Pauline Smith's 'The Sisters'. 'The Nuisance' from *This Was the Old Chief's Country* by Dorris Lessing, copyright 1951 Doris Lessing – Reprinted by permission of Jonanthan Clewes Ltd, London on behalf of Dorris Lessing.

Society to Help Civilian Blind for Sarah Gertrude Millin's 'A Pair of Button Boots' from *Two Bucks Without Hair*.

Nadine Gordimer for 'Good Climate, Friendly Inhabitants' from *Not for Publication*.

Juta and Company Ltd for 'The Silent Song' by E.N. Jonsson from *The Silver Sky and Other Stories*.

Sheila Roberts for 'The Touch of your Hand' from *Outside Life's Feast*.

Cherry Clayton for 'The Sisters'.

E.M. MacPhail for 'Still Life with Peach and Ashtray' from *Falling Upstairs*.

Ellen Palestrant for 'Six Free Pulls' from *Nosedive and Other writings*.

Gcina Mhlophe for 'Nokulunga's Wedding'.

Rose Zwi for 'A Lonely Walk to Freedom'.

Amelia Blossom (Pegram) House for 'Conspiracy'.

Jayapraga Reddy for 'Friends' from *On the Fringe of Dreamtime and Other Stories*.

Zoë Wicomb for 'When the Train Comes'.

Margaret Roestorf for 'The Very Quick Man' from *The Dog of Air*.

Maud Motanyane for 'Two Minutes'.

Pnina Fenster for 'Dreams of Golden Beauty'.

Dina Lefakane and Serita sa Sechaba for Kefiloe Tryphinah Mvula's 'The Naked Night'.

John Johnson (Authors's Agents) Ltd for Bessie Head's 'The Lovers' from *Tales of Tenderness and Power*.

Shelley Power Literary Agency Ltd for Gladys Thomas's 'The Promise'.

Maureen Isaacson for 'I Could Have Loved Gold'.

Joan Baker for 'Undercover Comrade'.

Skotaville Publishers for Noorie Hammond's 'An Act of Love' from *The AWA Collection* and Ponkie Khazamula's 'I Won't Be Moved', from *One Never Knows*.

Although every effort has been made to trace copyright holders, this has not always been possible. Should any infringement have occurred the editor and publisher apologise and undertake to amend these omissions in the event of a reprint.

Introduction

I

The history of cultural domination in South Africa has, within the sphere of literature, resulted in a situation where race, gender and class factors adversely affected the literary production of women. Within this context *Raising the Blinds* focuses on short stories produced by South African women. The title signifies a gesture of raising the blinds of a dark and shut-in interior, exposing it to light. This involves the exposure of an already existing, but previously obscured interior. It is a deliberate ending of a division between an enclosed space and its environment to enable a free interchange between these dimensions. As a narrative project this anthology is aimed at ending the confinement and culturally induced blindness concerning women as storytellers and writers in South Africa.

As the subtitle indicates, the collection is specifically aimed at shedding light on the short fiction of South African women of all races, over the past century. It is achieved by the inclusion of acknowledged writers, and the rediscovery of those whose writings have been submerged, silenced and ignored for decades. Generally speaking, white middle and upper class women featured fairly prominently, though never fully representatively in the sphere of South African fiction. Until very recently, however, black working class and peasant women have been systematically marginalised and obscured for political as well as cultural factors. In addition it is also oriented towards introducing currently emergent voices.

In this introduction I will briefly outline the motivation and methodology behind compiling the anthology before outlining the nature of the selection.

The anthology is a representative selection of work by women narrators from the country's wide spectrum of social and cultural positions and endeavours to compare divergent and interrelated themes, and the various narrative forms and styles. This book is therefore also an account of the differentiated and changing gender statuses in respect of class and race within the colonial and apartheid history of the country, as manifested in the stories.

Rather than isolating fiction as an autonomous aesthetic phenomenon, by amputating narratives from their social context, the anthology is an exploration of the interrelationship between narratives and the context of production. This overview is oriented towards illuminating the extent to which the historical context is embedded in and constitutive of the narrative artifacts. This also shapes the productivity of women writers including the nature and type of literature they produce, its thematic, structural, stylistic and linguistic features. It also enables us to highlight which sector of South African women is productive during a specific period. Finally, it also enables us to comprehend the reception and aesthetic evaluation.

II

As a point of departure it is essential to indicate briefly how South African society divided women amongst themselves within a male dominated context by stratifying them in relation to each other over the past century.

White women were part of the dominant race group which frequently correlated with a privileged class position. Despite this they were still subject to the sexist prescriptions of a patriarchal society. Consequently, at the end of the nineteenth century, which is the starting point of this anthology, white women were by and large restricted to the domestic sphere. Socially and psychologically this tied them to the roles of wives and mothers. Accordingly, women's main value was derived from the male conceptualized 'femininity' of their 'womanhood' and the functional purposes it represented. These roles, it was argued, did not require any advanced education for women. Education, it was feared, would interfere with and change the circumscribed role of women and enhance the possibility of escape from the domestic sphere. Women's subordinate and restricted position, Coward asserts, denied them, 'benefits in their own right as individuals, but only as dependents of men, or as women who have lost the support of men.'[1] This resulted in women's economic discrimination outside and within the domestic sphere, thus decreasing the chances of escaping male domination or challenging the social evaluation scale.'

In the course of this past century however, the more privileged white women, advanced considerably in their education. Black domestic workers, initially black males, and later during the rapid industrialization in the 1930s when men were absorbed in the new factories, black women increasingly contributed to making the advancement of white women possible. They relieved white women of most of their domestic and child minding duties freeing them to devote more time to self-development. This included leisure time for writing. Thus, the white woman's social advance resulted from the black woman's disadvantage.

Despite the increased opportunities to acquire knowledge, develop writing skills and pursue professions white middle class women continued to encounter literary prejudices. The themes, styles, structure and language of their writings were confined by mainstream literary traditions. At the end of the nineteenth and beginning of the twentieth century critics openly applied different criteria to women's writing. From their critiques it is evident that women were expected to write in a 'feminine' way, and that their writing could only be evaluated according to this criterion. Amongst other things this was, for example, characterised by emotional or passionate language, a sweet tone and a light and tender style. 'Feminine' themes centered around domestic and moral issues, interpersonal relationships, focusing especially on portraits of kind, self-sacrificing women, while so-called 'universal' themes were reserved for male writers. Ironically women's writing was mostly regarded as 'strong' literature if it remained within these boundaries, demarcated according to male conceptions of woman's weakness. Iain Lang in a review of Pauline Smith's *The Little Karoo*, 'Strength out of Sweetness', published in 1925, remarks: 'No recent collection of short stories has shown steadier emotional power ... Miss Smith's main affirmation of goodness lies in her portraits of women, humble, loving wives or daughters, whose silent self-sacrifices make the themes of a great many of the stories ... Here lies the woman writer's distinctive power; and of Pauline Smith we may say – reversing Samson's riddle – "Out of sweetness comes forth strength".'[2] Commenting on the same collection, Herman Charles Bosman remarked in 'The Truth of the Veld', in 1945, that 'Pauline Smith's knowledge of her subject is profound and penetrative and strong, passionately so, and her approach is essentially feminine. Her stories are pure with light and very tenderly told and brave. One requires nothing more than this from a woman story-teller. But, also, one demands nothing less.'[3]

These prejudices are further manifested in male authors' domination in short story anthologies. A random overview of a selection of South African short story compilations substantiates this assertion. Jean Marquard's *A Century of South African Short Stories* (1978) reveals how literary discrimination has been internalised and perpetuated by women themselves. Marquard's anthology includes twenty-five stories by men and eleven stories by women. Except for one story by Bessie Head, all other black women writers are excluded.

Likewise, Stephen Gray's *Modern South African Stories* (1980) consists of twenty-one stories by men and seven by women; *Under the Southern Cross, Short Stories from South Africa* (1982), compiled by David Adey, includes twenty stories by men and nine by women; Mothobi Mutloatse's *Reconstruction* (1981) includes only fiction written by men; and *Armed Vision* (1987), the collection of translated Afrikaans short stories, edited by Martin Trump, includes twenty stories by men and two by women. No black women writers are included in this collection. Apart from privileging of stories written by men, all these anthologists, excluding Jean Marquard, are male.

A more recent compilation, *The Drum Decade, Stories From The 1950s* (1989) edited by Michael Chapman discloses how the sexism of the 1950s is perpetuated in an anthology almost forty years later. This selection of thirty-one stories does not include a single female writer. Although Chapman makes provision for narratives other than the conventional realist fiction of the time, he failed to include any of the experiential material by women published in *Drum*, in his selection.

When scrutinizing literary curricula at school or university level it becomes clear that work by male writers constitutes the main literary references. This domination also prevails in institutions responsible for determining aesthetic criteria such as publishing houses, educational institutions, editorial boards of journals, literary critics and reviewers.

Investigating the editorial staff of journals alone provides ample evidence of South Africa's male dominated literary front. For example, in 1976 *Contrast* had three women and thirteen men on its editorial staff; the *'80–'82 Quarry*, one man; a 1981 *Bloody Horse*, one woman and twelve men; a 1985 *Standpunte*, one woman and fourteen men; a 1987 *New Coin*, one man; a 1988 *Sesame*, one man; a 1990 *Tydskrif vir Letterkunde*, five women and ten men; a 1990 *New Contrast*, two women and thirteen men. On *Staffrider's* editorial board, which consists of eight men and three women, Gcina Mhlophe is the only black woman. She is also the only black woman editorial member of all the magazines referred to above.

To anyone with even the most superficial knowledge of South African society, it must be evident that black and working class women have been far more severely oppressed than white middle, and even white working class women. In the precapitalist societies before colonialism, black women mainly served as domestic and agricultural workers and the reproducers of human life and society, including the necessary labour force. Despite this they had an important status as bearers of fertility and performed a central role as performers of the oral narratives practied in these societies. With the advent of colonialism a very small percentage of black women were gradually exposed to missionary education. This was purely aimed at socialising them into colonial society as subordinates in all social respects. Apart from race and class prejudices, the education transmitted Western christian values, which devalued traditional culture. It resulted, in conjunction with economic changes, in the gradual dissolution of traditional society and the further weakening of the position of African women. Young women trained in missionary institutions often ended up as domestic workers in the colonial homes.

The forceful penetration of capitalist economy into a rural economy, in the course of the eighteenth and nineteenth centuries, destroyed the African peasantry and forced black men to migrate to industrial areas. Influx control measures ensured that most women remained in the rural areas, cultivating land while facing ever greater problems of land shortage, lack of labour and insufficient capital. Poverty and insecurity, nevertheless, forced a large percentage of women to join the workforce in urban areas. But since black women have been the last group to become wage labourers in industries, it has placed them in the most disadvantaged position within the working class. The suffering experienced by women living and working in exploitative environments, where they did not have any substantial rights, has been immense.

These oppressive social conditions have had disastrous consequences for the general advancement of black women. In the years following the rise to power of Afrikaner nationalism, those who found access to education, were subjected to the menace of Bantu Education. Educational deprivation within this intricate tissue of political oppression and economical exploitation has lead to racialistically distorted conceptions of the intellectual potential of black women. This is of course part of the general discrimination against women's intellects, knowledge and experience in male dominated societies.

The unrepresentative nature of institutionalised South African literature is evident in its exclusion of, for example, the widely practised indigenous oral narratives. These narratives have been denigrated due to the collective and non-individualised nature of their origin. A similar marginalisation has affected the historical-documentary literature produced by black women as a means of providing social and historical perspectives of their lives and experiences. In these personal accounts, the absence of fictional devices which transform the raw material of personal experience into imaginative or symbolic narratives, conventionally associated with the short story, disqualifies them for consideration as fiction. This anthology sets out to break these restrictive aesthetic categories, within the sphere of women's writing. It is done by including, for example, oral narratives and stories of social and historical nature. Examples of the latter are Johanna Masilela and Anna Mazibuko's life stories. These narratives can easily be accommodated within the genre of the short story.

Stylistically and thematically the short story displays great diversity as a literary form and it is difficult to define according to any single inherent criterion. This would imply restricting and narrowing the genre according to arbitrary boundaries. J.A. Cudden remarks that the classification of the short story is extremely difficult. He further stresses the formal diversity of the short story which derives from other forms such as myths, legends, fables, parables, fairy tales, anecdotes and even the essay: 'In the end the form has shown itself to be so flexible and susceptible of so much variety that its possibilities seem almost endless'.[4] Accordingly, as J.C. Lawrence asserts, the short story could be told historically, dramatically and didactically.[5] Against this background it should be clear that the privileging of any single definition of the short story at the expense of others is likely to result in a subtle process of exclusion and marginalization. Within a multi-linguistic and diverse cultural context the dangers of a monolithic definition should be avoided.

This diversity should also be kept in mind when dealing with the workers' literature produced by black women. Like the other forms of literature produced by black women, the prevailing literary tradition frowned upon this too because of the themes of worker resistance and the aesthetic incompatibilities with dominant notions which stress the autonomy of fiction. It is telling that Elsabe Brink is one of the first critics to illuminate the writings of the Garment Workers produced between 1929 and 1945. Considerable documentation of contemporary women workers' narratives still remains to be undertaken.

Recently some publishing houses and individual editors have started correcting the under representation of the black woman in the South African literary canon by collecting and publishing the work of women writers. Most of these anthologies are collected short stories, but some also include poetry and historical documentations. *Lip, From Southern African Women* (1983), *Vukani Makhosikazi, South African Women Speak* (1985), *Sometimes When It Rains, Writings by South African Women* (1987), *Women In South Africa, From The Heart* (1988), and

One Never Knows, An Anthology of Black South African Women Writers in Exile (1989) are examples of this corrective approach. Even though these anthologies rightly represent those voices which have traditionally been silenced, it is still a way of entrenching racial division between South African women writers, as most of these only include writings by black women. This anthology, however, intends to bring together a representative selection of all the South African women short fiction writers, disregarding their race and class or the dominant aesthetic tradition.[6]

III

The stories in this anthology are presented chronologically according to their publishing dates in collections, journals, magazines or newspapers from which they were selected. This provides some perspective on the nature, directions, and curves in the general development of South African fiction by women. The selection covers the late nineteenth up until the late twentieth century and enables the reader to trace and analyse the complex relationship between the tides of history and literature.

The anthology begins with the precolonial period illustrating the oral tradition, practised by the indigenous peoples and transmitted to contemporary times. This is followed by the late nineteenth and early twentieth century period dominated by white colonial fiction. The next phase is represented by a mid-twentieth century period, more specifically the 1950s and 1960s, during which prominent white voices emerged, reflecting on and challenging the newly instituted apartheid regime, while writing by black women was still submerged in the sexism of the *Drum* decade. The seventies, characterised by the advent of the Black Consciousness Movement and the emergence of English short fiction writing by black women, dealing both with rural life and the township context is next in line. The eighties, dominated by black voices, and from which an analytical awareness of women's position in society is evident, concludes the sequence which more or less covers a century.

The oral narratives, translated from five representative indigenous languages, which open the anthology display the translinguistic nature of their themes. These are the earliest known forms of southern African narrative, dating from precolonial communal rural societies. The process of transference within and between communities has stretched over many centuries to the extent that these narratives are still told today and have influenced the structure, style, themes and tone of a writer such as Bessie Head. It therefore remains a vital factor within the formation of

South African narratives of the past century and needs to be placed in relation to the literature that followed it.

These oral narratives are included in an anthology of women narrators since most story tellers in precolonial communal societies were women. Harold Scheub specifically mentions the role of women in the production of this narrative form, which also implicates the status of women in these societies as intellectuals, artists, educators and preservers of the social order. With reference to the Xhosa *ntsomi* he observes: 'The *ntsomi* is an organic extension of the culture from which it springs; it is the image of the perfect society, preserved through the years and daily renewed in performance. The performer is the intellectual in this oral society, she is the educator. But she is also an artist, and she desires to project an image that is at once a reaffirmation of her own inherited ideals, an extension of her culture, and – most important – a thing of beauty. These cannot be separated in performance ... The *ntsomi* performance is not only a primary means of entertainment and artistic expression in the society, it is also the major educational device.'[7]

When reading these narratives, it is important to keep in mind that the written texts are only shadows of the original multi-textured productions. According to Scheub rather than expressing herself analytically and descriptively in the words only, the performer prefers to make ample use of body movements, gesture, vocal dramatics, song, and an over-all rhythmic framework, which can never be captured by the written representation.[8]

The narratives reproduced here, and those in other languages, mostly deal with mother-children relationships and wife-husband interaction, which are related to the productive and reproductive role of women in these societies. These relations, in which the control and appropriation of the productive and reproductive capacity of women were central, explain the thematic concerns of the narratives. In this respect Jeff Guy has pointed out why marriage and infertility were incompatible concepts.[9] This is portrayed for example in the Southern Sotho oral narrative, 'The Child With A Moon On His Chest'. Production shortage which often caused tension between husband and wife, is central to the Venda story, 'Hearts Which Are Alike'. In 'Two Girls Encounter A Murderer' it is also not coincidental that evil and danger are represented by the woman who, instead of producing children, consumes them.

But in all five stories it is evident that women do possess some power and status within these societies. This is primarily attributable to the integrity and value of the possessor of fertility. Guy asserts that the 'value attached to fertility gave the possessors of that fertility social standing and social integrity'.[10] These early gender relationships, he further mentions, still await sensitive analysis, based not only on documentary sources but also on language, idiom, oral history and personal testimony.

The small percentage of black women who were drawn into Western-style education of mission institutions during the nineteenth century, received a gender-specific education, directed towards the linking of their sex, class and race attributes to domesticity and subordination in the colonial households. These domestic spheres of society bordered on slavery, and totally excluded any possibility of serious writing. It has resulted in an enormous gap in our knowledge of how black women experienced this period. The only women's short fiction writing to go by is that written by white middle class women, mainly alienated from the experiences of black women.

The most prominent published short story writers from the first half of the twentieth century are Olive Schreiner, Pauline Smith and Mary Byron. In very diverse ways they all relate to the role of women in late nineteenth and early twentieth century South African society. It was a period during which European immigrants flowed into the country bringing with them the influences of European social movements and ideas. These gradually influenced South African thought on the established social hierarchies. Olive Schreiner, for example, was one of the highly prominent women who spoke and wrote about the whole spectrum of social inequalities, as reflected in 'Three Dreams In A Desert', included in this anthology. In this story which consists of a succession of three dreams, the narrator refers to woman as a beast of burden on which 'the Age-of-dominion-of-muscular-force ... put his burden of subjection'. To this state of affairs a liberal-feminist conclusion of hope for the future is offered: 'And on the hills walked brave women and brave men, hand in hand. And they looked into each other's eyes, and they were not afraid. And I saw the women also hold each other's hands.'

Pauline Smith, on the other hand, focuses sympathetically on rural Afrikaners and their uncritical acceptance of power hierarchies. The story, 'The Sisters', portrays the sisterhood between women subjected to severe oppression, caused by men's urge to have power over women and land by means of a process of possession and exploitation. Though Smith's women characters are mostly suffering, they have internalized a Biblical doctrine of acquiescence to subordination. Instead of militating against their oppression, both Marta and Sukey resort to the Biblical phrase: 'Who am I that I should judge him?'

Mary Byron, again, heavily influenced by her colonial heritage, uncritically focuses on the lives of colonial English women after the Boer

War, and their problems of adapting to their new circumstances. Byron's stories encode attitudes of British and white superiority and condescendence towards black people. After elaborating on the 'intolerable weight of the incapacity of natives' in 'Neighbours' the narrator remarks: 'That the woman can and does rise above these disabilities and gradually and with laughter transform a hovel to a home is one of the wonders of our unconquerable race.'

Though Goudvis's anthology of stories was only published in 1956, she wrote most of her stories during the 1940s. Sarah Gertrude Millin's Alita stories, dealing with maid-madam situations, also started appearing in journals during the 1920s, but were collectively published only in 1957. This explains why these stories display affinities with the earlier twentieth century rather than the period of publication.

Goudvis's story included in this anthology, 'The Apostasy Of Carlina', relates to a central concern of intercultural contact in a time when many black women were incorporated into colonial society. An important aspect of this incorporation was the coupling of Christianity and so-called 'civilization' as agents of Western culture. This process included the teaching of the virtues of faithfulness, trust, obedience and loyalty, with the aim of moulding good servants, and is clearly portrayed in Goudvis's story. It centers around the madam's concern about the apostasy of her domestic worker, but the last sentence of the story discloses that she is firstly concerned about losing a good servant, and secondly, that her class and race position blinds her to her own sexism: 'I'll never get another girl like Carlina'.

These early twentieth century stories thus reflect some of the dominant, but diverse features of gender and race relations within the Afrikaner and English communities. Aesthetically, most of the early stories by women writers can be characterised in terms of a realist tradition. Taking Shipley as a point of departure, realism can be loosely defined as a form of literary and artistic representation in which the writer consciously strives to render what is regarded as social, human and natural reality in terms of a faithful verisimilitude. This convention, based on a theory of knowledge which stresses objective sensory perception free of subjective and moral judgements, occupies a central place in local literary aesthetics.[11] Olive Schreiner, however, has an ambivalent relationship to realism. In conjunction with her critical approach towards social hierarchies and the perpetuation of social myths, which often characterise the realist writing of the other women from this period, she challenges conventional formal criteria. This, according to Clayton, is done by employing other formal devices such as allegorical and symbolic representations which draw on the material of dreams to subvert social realism: 'The intertwining of dream life with real life ... sets timelessness against chronological sequence, reverie against causality, dream/imagination against action'.[12]

Though black women's writing in English is still absent during this period, it has to be noted that the first woman writer in Zulu, Violet Dube, debuted in 1935 with a collection of short stories, *Woza Naso*, which are based on traditional narratives.

The period of the 1950s brought about crucial historical changes in the country, which especially influenced internal race relations. The National Party rose to power in 1948. Their ideology of ethnic nationalism and racial supremacy was enforced through a series of apartheid laws, such as the Population Registration and Group Areas Acts of 1950, the Bantu Education Act of 1953, the Pass Laws of 1958, and the Homelands Policy. Along with these oppressive laws, the South African Communist Party, the ANC and Pan Africanist Congress were banned.

During the mid-twentieth century women's short fiction writing in English became more prominent, but still remained largely white. Seminal South African voices emerged in this period. Amongst them were Doris Lessing and Nadine Gordimer. Lessing, after becoming involved in radical politics in Salisbury emigrated to Britain. It was after she left Southern Africa, that a collection of her short stories was published. Nadine Gordimer, on the other hand, remained in the country, but wrote to expose the atrocities of apartheid policy. In her story, 'Good Climate, Friendly Inhabitants', she presents a complex combination of race and gender relations. While Gordimer perfected the realist form of the short story, Lessing experimented with a variety of forms. The story by Lessing included here, however, is related to the realistic tradition.

The first short story by a black woman included in *Raising The Blinds* is a confessional narrative from *Drum* magazine. This publication, as Michael Chapman remarks in *The Drum Decade*, was 'the substantial beginning, in South Africa, of the modern black short story'.[13] According to him, most of the fiction writers associated with the magazine were 'concerned with what was happening to their people and, in consequence, with moral and social questions.' However, as critical as this magazine, and its fiction, was of apartheid politics, as uncritical was it of gender relations. It more than often perpetuated the idea that women existed for sexual consumption by men. An awareness of this notion is clearly reflected in the short stories by women that were published in the magazine, all of which deal exclusively with love affairs. 'I Broke Their Hearts', in which Doris Sello tells the story of a woman who wants to take revenge on men for the suffering they cause women, eventually presents a romantically harmonious ending when she meets 'the right man'. A critical reading, however, exposes that she has been caught in her own trap.

After the few *Drum* stories of the fifties, another long period of silence followed during which hardly any black women short story writers, apart from Bessie Head, emerged. This can, amongst other things, be attributed to harsher measures of repression in the country during the sixties, which resulted in renewed revolt in black communities in 1976.

Even though Bessie Head's first collection of short stories, *The Collector Of Treasures*, was only published in 1977, her stories started appearing in *The New African, Transition, Classic, Freedomways, New Statesman,* and other magazines from the early 1960s. *The New African* in particular, provided an important forum for African culture, together with its political, social and economic analysis and comment. A great amount of poetry and short stories by black writers appeared in this magazine, amongst which Head's work was one of the only women's voices.

The Collector of Treasures was the first anthology of short stories in English produced by a black woman in South Africa. In her stories Bessie Head achieves an unique and harmonious combination of the indigenous oral storytelling tradition and Western literary conventions. 'The Lovers' (from *Tales Of Tenderness And Power*), included in this anthology, is a fine example of this trans-traditional approach. Although Head's work is not reducible to any single ideology, her writing implicitly embodies the African values cherished by the Pan Africanist Congress and the later Black Consciousness Movement of the seventies. Her rediscovery of and critical view on indigenous traditions give her work a complexity which resists simplification.

'The Lovers', for example, narrates the story of two young people who, by rebelling against the tradition of arranged marriages, have to face the retribution of the community. It serves the purpose of exposing oppressive traditions, and on a more subtle level is an enactment of how these traditions and power structures in general, are socially kept in tact. For this, the short story adopts a central function of traditional storytelling, namely myth creation and transference. As a transitory figure, Head's stories provide a vital link between the oral tradition and the eurocentric tradition of a large proportion of South African writing.

This period delivered another of South Africa's most outstanding, but often neglected, short story writers, Sheila Roberts. In 1975 her first collection, *Outside Life's Feast*, awarded the Olive Schreiner Prize, was published. Roberts' writing expanded the new direction brought about by Gordimer and Lessing, who, like Schreiner before them, introduced in short fiction by women a critical look at race, class and gender inequalities. Whereas Gordimer focuses more on South African racism, Roberts' stories illuminate the consequences of a class society for white urban working class characters. Roberts' often stated familiarity and proximity to the white working class have produced an ironically critical, but sensitive, look at the South African white working class. An interesting comparison with this aspect in Roberts' narratives, is Pauline Smith's identification and sympathy with white labour tenants while herself being an outsider to this class. Roberts, writing in the realist tradition, portrays the hardships of women from this unprivileged class and a generally unsympathetic society. Nicol remarks that Roberts has the ability to portray a character and make her 'instantly recognizable in extremely economic terms'.[14]

The effect of the Black Consciousness Movement of the seventies on the short fiction writing of black women only becomes evident in the late seventies and eighties, when many of the stories written during the previous decade were published. This movement consciously provided a positive definition of being black in all fields of society, but especially on the cultural front. Steve Biko defines this movement as follows: 'It seeks to demonstrate the lie that black is an aberration from the 'normal' which is white ... It seeks to infuse the black community with a new-found pride in themselves, their efforts, their value systems, their culture, their religion and their outlook in life.'[15] During this time, on 16 June 1976, the Soweto uprisings occurred, whereafter, in 1977, all black oppositional organizations were banned. The emphasis on black cultural identity, however, gave rise to a strong literary movement.

With Head as an important forerunner, the eighties was a vital period for the emergence of black women voices. A few factors, following from the conscientisation of the seventies, urged this on. Andries Oliphant points to the important role played by magazines such as *New Classic* and *Staffrider*, which gave black writers opportunities to publish.[16] The writings of Jayapraga Reddy and Miriam Tlali, for example, gained prominence through *Staffrider*.

In 1981, after the dissolution of the Johannesburg branch of the non-racial, international writers' association, PEN, the African Writers' Association was constituted according to the principles of black self determination. The following year Skotaville was established, which was the first black South African publisher. This was followed by the black women's publishing house, Seriti sa Sechaba in 1987. The non-racial Congress of South African Writers, founded in 1987 and its different regional magazines, literary workshops, and Women's Forum, together with the upsurge in trade unions' cultural activities, stimulated cultural developments over a wide spectrum of the South African population.

These alternative cultural formations, along with intellectual initiatives, have registered the necessity to emphasize feminist issues. This is evident in COSAW's conference on women and writing and the subsequent publication of *Women Speak* (1989) and COSATU's organization regarding women's rights and the subsequent publication, *Women And The Living Wage Campaign* (1989). From the universities a number of critical studies emerged. Cherry Clayton's *Women and Writing in South Africa*, published in 1989 and the feminist issues of *Journal of Literary Studies*, published in March 1988, along with various feminist conferences are some examples of the present upsurge in feminist discourse locally.

In relation to this Oliphant mentions that the two dimensions that gained prominence in the eighties, namely that of a popular inclusive non-racial approach and the workers' perspective, gave new direction to contemporary literature.[17] This change of direction is also clearly noted in women's writing, which, in this period, registers a sudden flourishing of work produced by black women. Since E.M. Macphail's *Falling Upstairs* in 1982 and Ellen Palestrants's *Nosedive And Other Writings* in 1983 there have been no short story anthology debuts by white women in English, apart from Margaret Roestorf's collection of tales and paintings, *The Dog Of Air*. These tales with their fantastical quality stylistically represent a refreshing change from the predominant realist conventions deployed by the majority of white women writers in South Africa.

The general emergence of writing by black women in the eighties resulted in the publication of several short story collections. In 1987, Jayapraga Reddy's *On the Fringe of Dreamtime and Other Stories* and Zoë Wicomb's *You Can't Get Lost In Cape Town* appeared. In the following year Farida Karodia's *Coming Home and Other Stories*, and in 1989 Miriam Tlali's *Footprints In The Quag* and Bessie Head's posthumous collection *Tales of Tenderness and Power* were published. Numerous stories by black women also appeared in other collections.

Jayapraga Reddy is one of the first Indian woman short fiction writers to publish a collection of short stories in South Africa. Her narratives reflect a far greater awareness of the dynamics operating within gender, race and class intersections than the early white women short fiction writers. She positions her characters in confrontational relations, but analytically examines the nature of this interaction, instead of blindly reproducing dominant ideology. 'Friends', included in this anthology, for example, reveals that oppression is not a two-dimensional white-black opposition. It also explores the class aspects and the gender implications, in which race hierarchies are reinforced by internal stratifications in oppressed communities themselves. The story is a fictional illustration of the practical operation of overlapping and interacting power hierarchies by demonstrating how oppressed people are often co-responsible for keeping the chain of oppression intact by co-operating, instead of breaking the chain. Although Reddy explores some aspects of South African Indian culture, hardly any traces of oriental narrative conventions appear in her stories, which can be formally placed within a social realist tradition.

In the same year Zoë Wicomb's *You Can't Get Lost In Cape Town* (1987) appeared. Wicomb, living in England since 1970, remarkably reflects on the oppressed status and complex identity of black women in South African society as suggested by the title of the title story. It ironically refers to the mountains of racist and sexist laws and attitudes in the country, complicating the lives of black women, making it almost impossible not to 'get lost'. The stories in Wicomb's collection encode an autobiographical impulse which transcribe the experiences of a young, so-called coloured woman in the South African context. As a result of this autobiographical dimension Wicomb's writing partly blends in with the South African black woman's literary tradition. Even though the historical documentary nature of, for example, Bessie Head and Miriam Tlali's writing is not characteristic of Wicomb's work, her narratives are shaped by the relationships and experiences within a specific spatio-temporal moment which reflect on prominent incidents in South African history. However, her skilful creative transformation of this material should prevent critics from marginalizing it as mere historical or cultural documentation.[18] Her stories further display a profound awareness of the extent to which linguistic deprivation lies at the heart of cultural and gender oppression in societies characterized by domination. The subtle and refined feminist perspective which informs her work renders it unique within the corpus of South African writing by women. Despite this, her work has received scant attention in South Africa.

Miriam Tlali, the first published black woman novelist inside South Africa to write in English has also been neglected. Cecily Lockett observes that white critics in South Africa have found Tlali's work problematic since they judged it in terms of 'inappropriate Anglo-American or European critical paradigms'.[19] Lockett also emphasizes Tlali's rejection of 'intellectualism' by according little respect to traditional generic conceptions of 'novel' and 'short story'. She proceeds to characterize Tlali's work as 'a loosely-woven rendering of the fabric of black experience from the perspective of a black woman', which is important in any evaluation of Tlali's work. It is in this regard noteworthy to point out that Ndebele also faults Tlali's aesthetics from a fairly narrow realist perspective, which privileges the ordinary and subjective experiences as the appropriate mode of representation as opposed to the social reportage which Tlali favours.[20]

Tlali mainly deals with the consequences of a racist, capitalist structure for black women in urban township settlings. In this way the story 'Mm'a-Lithoto' illustrates how black women are effected by traditional patriarchy in a township environment where women are repressed in their womanhood, as well as in their wider social roles.

Thematically the stories by black women, included in this anthology, relate to a vast spectrum of experiences familiar to black women in South Africa. This includes forced marriages, pass law problems, madam-maid relationships, racial prejudice, poverty, forced removals, domestic and social violence and motherhood during times of youth resistance against the school system. When scrutinizing the themes covered by white women, the difference in the experiences of women from different races in the country is evident. They generally focus on issues like problematic domestic workers, sexual violence, inter-personal relationships and other middle class concerns such as personal appearance and beauty. Many of the stories in this anthology provide an ironical or critical analysis of these concerns. This notwithstanding, there are also thematic overlaps in the writings of both black and white women, for example, illegal abortion, breeching of the Immorality Act, sexual harassment and other related moral themes. In exceptional cases such as Gordimer and Zwi the themes which preoccupy black women writers are also to be found in their work.

IV

This overview attempted to suggest that the production of literature by South African women has been undeniably impaired by the nature of South African society from which it arose. In addition the dominant aesthetic prejudices and cultural colonization affected the appreciation of their work. Women, compared to men, never had equal access to the cultural field and South African women amongst themselves still do not have equal access to the means of literary production. This contributed to the destruction of a homogeneous group of women and complicated the struggle for the liberation of women in general, and within the cultural and literary sphere in particular.

This signals the need for strong action towards the creation of unity amongst women. On the cultural front it implies an unanimous resistance against the enforcement of a single, so-called neutral, universal and undifferentiated aesthetic system. Coupled to this, a total reassessment of literature, and a reconstruction of the literary tradition as well as the rewriting of a literary history is required. While extensive work still needs to be done in the broad areas of cultural production, this anthology is a step towards the creation of such a South African culture, beyond the damaging forces of sex, race and class prejudices through which aesthetic judgements are filtered.

Annemarié van Niekerk
Johannesburg, 1990

NOTES

1. Rosalind Coward, *Patriarchal Precedents: Sexuality and Social Relations* (London: Routledge & Kegan Paul, 1983) p. 285.
2. Iain Lang, 'Strength out of Sweetness: Genius of a New Woman Writer'. In *T.P.'s and Cassell's Weekly* (London, 28 March 1925) p. 88.
3. Herman Charles Bosman, 'The Truth of the Veld: *The Little Karoo* by Pauline Smith'. In *The South African Opinion* (Johannesburg, April 1945) p. 99.
4. J.A. Cuddon, *A Dictionary of Literary Terms* (Harmondsworth: Penguin Books, 1970) p. 623.
5. James Cooper Lawrence, 'A Theory of the Short Story'. In *North American Review* (No. 205, February 1917). Reprinted in *Short Story Theories*, ed. May, pp. 274–286.
6. The frequent compartmentalisation of South African literature according to language barriers should also be challenged. Accordingly, the initial conceptualisation of this anthology included translated short stories by Afrikaans writers, in order to provide a more complete overview of the traditions of short fiction by women in South Africa over the past century. It was, however, suggested by my publisher that the focus of this anthology should be on stories in English in order to keep the book within a reasonable size.
7. Harold Scheub, *The Xhosa Ntsomi* (Oxford: Clarendon Press, 1975) p. 88.
8. Ibid., p. 45.
9. Jeff Guy, 'Gender oppression in southern Africa's precapitalist societies'. In *Women and Gender in Southern Africa to 1945*, ed. C. Walker. (Claremont: David Philip Publishers, 1990) p. 41.
10. Ibid., p. 46.

11 Joseph T. Shipley, *Dictionary of World Literature* (New Jersey: Littlefield, Adams & Co., 1972) pp. 335–336.

12 Cherry Clayton, 'Olive Schreiner: Paradoxical Pioneer'. In *Women and Writing in South Africa*, ed. C. Clayton (Marshalltown: Heinemann, 1989) p. 55.

13 Michael Chapman, 'More Than Telling a Story: *Drum* and its Significance in Black South African Writing'. In *The Drum Decade*, ed. M. Chapman (Pietermaritzburg: University of Natal Press, 1989) p. 183.

14 Mike Nicol, 'A new tradition of realism'. In *To The Point* (25 July 1975) p. 31.

15 Steve Biko, *I Write What I Like* (London: Heinemann, 1978) p. 49.

16 Andries W. Oliphant, 'Swart Literatuur in Suid-Afrika'. Due to be published shortly in *Glossarium van Suid-Afrikaanse Literatuur*, ed. T.T. Cloete (Pretoria: Haum Literêr, 1990).

17 Ibid.

18 Annemarié van Niekerk, Review of *You Can't Get Lost in Cape Town* by Zoë Wicomb. In *Staffrider* (Vol. 9, No. 1, 1990) p. 94.

19 Cecily Lockett, 'The Fabric of Experience: A Critical Perspective on the Writing of Miriam Tlali'. In *Women and Writing in South Africa*, ed. C. Clayton (Marshalltown: Heinemann, 1989) p. 276.

20 Njabulo S. Ndebele, 'Turkish Tales and Some Thoughts on South African Fiction'. In *Ten Years of Staffrider*, ed. A.W. Oliphant and I. Vladislavic (Johannesburg: Ravan Press, 1988) pp. 336–339.

A SAN ORAL NARRATIVE

The Origin Of Death

from *Specimens of Bushman Folklore* by W.H.I. Bleek and L.C. Lloyd (1968)

We, when the Moon has newly returned alive, when another person has shown us the Moon, we look towards the place at which the other has shown us the Moon, and, when we look thither, we perceive the Moon, and when we perceive it, we shut our eyes with our hands, we exclaim: '*!kábbĭ-ă* yonder! Take my face yonder! Thou shalt give me thy face yonder! Thou shalt take my face yonder! That which does not feel pleasant. Thou shalt give me thy face, — which thou, when thou hast died, thou dost again, living return, when we did not perceive thee, thou dost again lying down come, — that I may also resemble thee. For, the joy yonder, thou dost always possess it yonder, that is, that thou art wont again to return alive, when we did not perceive thee; while the hare told thee about it, that thou shouldst do thus. Thou didst formerly say, that we should also again return alive, when we died.'

The hare was the one who thus did. He spoke, he said, that he would not be silent, for, his mother would not again living return; for his mother was altogether dead. Therefore, he would cry greatly for his mother.

The Moon replying, said to the hare about it that the hare should leave off crying; for, his mother was not altogether dead. For, his mother meant that she would again living return. The hare replying, said that he was not willing to be silent; for, he knew that his mother would not again return alive. For, she was altogether dead.

And the Moon became angry about it, that the hare spoke thus, while he did not assent to him (the Moon). And he hit with his fist, cleaving the hare's mouth; and while he hit the hare's mouth with his fist, he exclaimed: 'This person, his mouth which is here, his mouth shall altogether be like this, even when he is a hare; he shall always bear a scar on his mouth; he shall spring away, he shall doubling come back. The dogs shall chase him; they shall, when they have caught him, they shall grasping tear him to pieces, he shall altogether die.

'And they who are men, they shall altogether dying go away, when they die. For, he was not willing to agree with me, when I told him about it, that he should not cry for his mother; for, his mother would again live; he said to me, that, his mother would not again living return. Therefore, he shall altogether become a hare. And the people, they shall altogether die. For, he was the one who said that his mother would not again living return. I said to him about it, that they (the people) should also be like me; that which I do; that I, when I am dead, I again living return. He contradicted me, when I had told him about it.'

Therefore, our mothers said to me, that the hare was formerly a man; when he had acted in this manner, then it was that the Moon cursed him, that he should altogether become a hare. Our mothers told me, that, the hare has human flesh at his *kátten-ttŭ*; therefore, we, when we have killed a hare, when we intend to eat the hare, we take out the 'biltong flesh' yonder, which is human flesh, we leave it; while we feel that he who is the hare, his flesh it is not. For, flesh belonging to the time when he formerly was a man, it is.

Therefore, our mothers were not willing for us to eat that small piece of meat; while they felt that it is this piece of meat with which the hare was formerly a man. Our mothers said to us about it, did we not feel that our stomachs were uneasy if we ate that little piece of meat, while we felt that it was human flesh; it is not hare's flesh; for, flesh which is still in the hare it is; while it feels that the hare was formerly a man. Therefore, it is still in the hare; while the hare's doings are those on account of which the Moon cursed us; that we should altogether die. For, we should, when we died, we should have again living returned; the hare was the one who did not assent to the Moon, when the Moon was willing to talk to him about it; he contradicted the Moon.

Therefore, the Moon spoke, he said: 'Ye who are people, ye shall, when ye die, altogether dying vanish away. For, I said, that, ye should, when ye died, ye should again arise, ye should not altogether die. For, I, when I am dead, I again living return. I had intended, that, ye who are men, ye should also resemble me and do the things that I do; that I do not altogether dying go away. Ye, who are men, are those who did this deed; therefore, I had thought that I would give you joy. The hare, when I intended to tell him about it, — while I felt that I knew that the hare's mother had not really died, for, she slept, — the hare was the one who said to me, that his mother did not sleep; for, his mother had altogether died. These were the things that I became angry about; while I had thought that the hare would say: "Yes; my mother is asleep." '

For, on account of these things, he (the Moon) became angry with the hare; that the hare should have spoken in this manner, while the hare did not say: 'Yes, my mother lies sleeping; she will presently arise.' If the hare had assented to the Moon, then, we who are people, we should have resembled the Moon; for, the Moon had formerly said, that we should not altogether die. The hare's doings were those on account of which the Moon cursed us, and we die altogether; on account of the story which the hare was the one who told him. That story is the one on account of which we altogether die and go away; on account of the hare's doings; when he was the one who did not assent to the Moon; when the Moon intended to tell him about it; he contradicted the Moon, when the Moon intended to tell him about it.

The Moon spoke, saying that he (the hare) should lie upon a bare place; vermin should be those who were biting him, at the place where he was lying; he should not inhabit the bushes; for, he should lie upon a bare place; while he did not lie under a tree. He should be lying upon a bare place. Therefore, the hare is used, when he springs up, he goes along shaking his head; while he shakes out, making to fall the vermin from his head in which the vermin had been hanging; while he feels that the vermin hung abundantly in his head. Therefore, he shakes his head, so that the other vermin may fall out for him.

A XHOSA ORAL NARRATIVE

Two Girls Encounter A Murderer

from *The Xhosa Ntsomi* by H. Scheub (1975)

Now for a *ntsomi*.

There were two girls. They said to their mother, 'We want to go to our uncle's home.'

The mother agreed. Provisions and other fitting things were prepared for them, and the day of their journey arrived. As they prepared to travel, their mother told them the way they should travel: they should not take the path that leads westward, but should take the one going to the east.

They agreed, and off they went. They travelled and travelled and travelled, they travelled until they came to a fork in the path.

The younger one said to the elder, 'Mama said that we should take the path going west.'

The elder one said, 'Mama said that we should travel on the path going towards the east.'

They quarrelled until the sun was about to set. Then the older one said, 'I, Xhentsiwe, am annoyed! You've upset me. You go by that path, and I'll take this one of mine. We'll meet further ahead.'

So she took the path going eastward, and the younger one took the one going west. They travelled and travelled, they travelled on those paths of theirs. It happened then that the elder one, as she continued on her way, discovered that she had to travel through fearful forests. So she turned around and returned to where she had come from, then she took the path the younger sister had taken. She travelled and travelled, she travelled until she found her on the path. Then both of them travelled. They travelled and travelled and travelled, they travelled until they came to a certain homestead. The sun was down now, so they requested a place at this homestead. They found a girl there.

She said, '*Ko!* Where have you come from? Nobody comes here, because my mother is a murderer — she eats people!'

The girl gave them some food, and told them to eat quickly, her mother not yet having arrived.

'Because if she does come, she'll eat you!'

They ate their food hurriedly, then the girl took them and put them into another house. She closed it up. Just as she finished putting the girls into that house, she heard a voice calling out.

'Nomahamle! Have you smeared the floor?'

'Yes, Mama!'

'Oh, Nomahamle! Oh, Nomahamle! My child!' And again, she said, 'Nomahamle! Have you gathered wood for me?'

'Yes, Mama!'

'Oh, oh, Nomahamle! Oh my child, Nomahamle!'

Finally, she arrived, and when she had arrived, she put her load down — it was a dead person!

She said, 'What's in the house, Nomahamle?'

Nomahamle answered, 'No, Mama, there's nothing here!'

The mother was quiet. She got her things ready, pots in which she would cook that 'small animal' of hers.

She again asked, 'Nomahamle, what is that smell? There's the slight odour of humans here today!'

Nomahamle said, 'No, Mama, there's nothing like that!'

The mother cooked then, and ate that meat of hers. Then she went to sleep. That night, the mother went out to the house that contained these two children. She found that a dog was sleeping at the entrance to that house, and it would not get up. She was angry. She said, 'You must get up from the entrance! I see some cockroaches of my house.' But the dog refused to get up from the entrance. So she went back and slept. She returned again some time later, but the dog refused to get up from the entrance. She said, 'You must get up! I see some cockroaches of my house!' But the dog refused to get up. So she again went back and slept.

She was overcome by sleep, and when she was in that state, Nomahamle went out. She came to that house, and successfully got the girls out without her mother seeing them. She said that they should go and hide themselves, because her mother would eat them.

When the murderer was awake, she returned once more. She said, 'You must get up from the entrance! I see some cockroaches of my house!' The dog got up, and she went into the house. She found that there was no longer anyone in the house. She was angry.

So she went to Nomahamle, and said, 'Nomahamle, where have those small animals gone? I sensed that they were here in the house.'

Nomahamle said, 'There's no small animal here, Mama!'

She said, 'I'll beat you now!' But she didn't beat the girl after all.

They travelled and travelled, Xhentsiwe and Nomasimi travelled. They found that their journey to their aunt's home was a long one. They travelled and travelled. They travelled, passing by mountains and crossing streams, journeying in dreadful forests. Finally, they had been travelling on the path three days. On the fourth, they saw a homestead far off in the distance.

One of them said, 'It's possible that that's our uncle's place over there. Even though I've never come this way, from what Mama said, I think that this is probably the place.'

They travelled and travelled and travelled then. And when they were close, the murderer suddenly appeared, following their trail! She appeared, coming now with dogs, and she was very angry by this time!

The girls ran, and found a tall tree. They climbed up into this tree — the murderer was close now — the girls climbed this tree, and shouted towards the homestead that they had seen. The murderer arrived, carrying an axe. She cut, she cut the tree. When the tree was about to fall, a bird appeared, saying,

'Ntengu, Ntengu, little wood-chips!
Do you know that these children are people?
What have they done?'

The tree stood straight then.

Then the murderer returned, and angrily started again. When the tree seemed as if it would fall, the bird returned, and said,

'Ntengu, Ntengu, little wood-chips!
Do you know that these children are people?
What have they done?'

During this time, people from their aunt's place were coming. They finally arrived and drove the murderer away. The children came down from the tree.

They travelled then, going to their aunt's place. They told about this ugly journey of theirs, how they had travelled. Those at their aunt's home praised them for their escape from that murderer, praising them because they had not been killed by her.

The *ntsomi* is ended, it is ended.

A ZULU ORAL NARRATIVE

Unanana-Bosele

from *Nursery Tales, Traditions, And Histories Of The Zulus* (Vol. 1)
by H. Callaway (1970)

There was a woman who had two young children; they were very fine; and there was another child who used to stay with them. But that woman, it is said, had wilfully built her house in the road, trusting to self-confidence and superior power.

On a certain occasion she went to fetch firewood and left her children alone. A baboon came and said, 'Whose are those remarkably beautiful children?' The child replied, 'Unanana-bosele's.' The baboon said, 'She built in the road on purpose, trusting to self-confidence and superior power.'

Again an antelope came and asked the same question. The child answered, 'They are the children of Unanana-bosele.' All animals came and asked the same question, until the child cried for fear.

A very large elephant came and said, 'Whose are those remarkably beautiful children?' The child replied, 'Unanana-bosele's.' The elephant asked the second time, 'Whose are those remarkably beautiful children?' The child replied, 'Unanana-bosele's.' The elephant said, 'She built in the road on purpose, trusting to self-confidence and superior power.' He swallowed them both, and left the little child. The elephant then went away.

In the afternoon the mother came and said, 'Where are the children?' The little girl said, 'They have been taken away by an elephant with one tusk.' Unanana-bosele said, 'Where did he put them?' The little girl replied, 'He ate them.' Unanana-bosele said, 'Are they dead?' The little girl replied, 'No. I do not know.'

They retired to rest. In the morning she ground much maize, and put it into a large pot with amasi, and set out, carrying a knife in her hand. She came to the place where there was an antelope; she said, 'Mother, mother, point out for me the elephant which has eaten my children; she has one tusk.' The antelope said, 'You will go till you come to a place where the trees are very high, and where the stones are white.' She went on.

She came to the place where there was the leopard; she said, 'Mother, mother, point out for me the elephant which has eaten my children.' The leopard replied, 'You will go on and on, and come to the place where the trees are high, and where the stones are white.'

She went on, passing all animals, all saying the same. When she was still at a great distance she saw some very high trees and white stones below them. She saw the elephant lying under the trees. She went on; when she came to the elephant she stood still and said, 'Mother, mother, point out for me the elephant which has eaten my children.' The elephant replied, 'You will go on and on, and come to where the trees are high, and where the stones are white.' The woman merely stood still, and asked again, saying, 'Mother, mother, point out for me the elephant which has eaten my children.' The elephant again told her just to pass onward. But the woman, seeing that it was the very elephant she was seeking, and that she was deceiving her by telling her to go forward, said a third time, 'Mother, mother, point out for me the elephant which has eaten my children.'

The elephant seized her and swallowed her too. When she reached the elephant's stomach, she saw large forests, and great rivers, and many high lands; on one side there were many rocks; and there were many people who had built their villages there; and many dogs and many cattle; all were there inside the elephant; she saw too her own children sitting there. She gave them amasi, and asked them what they ate before she came. They said, 'We have eaten nothing. We merely lay down.' She said, 'Why did you not roast this flesh?' They said, 'If we eat this beast, will it not kill us?' She said, 'No; it will itself die; you will not die.' She kindled a great fire. She cut the liver, and roasted it and ate with her children. They cut also the flesh, and roasted and ate.

All the people which were there wondered, saying, 'O, forsooth, are they eating, whilst we have remained without eating any thing?' The woman said, 'Yes, yes. The elephant can be eaten.' All the people cut and ate.

And the elephant told the other beasts, saying, 'From the time I swallowed the woman I have been ill; there has been pain in my stomach.' The other animals said, 'It may be, O chief, it arises because there are now so many people in your stomach.' And it came to pass after a long time that the elephant died. The woman divided the elephant with a knife, cutting through a rib with an axe. A cow came out and said, 'Moo, moo, we at length see the country.' A goat came out and said, 'Mey,

mey, at length we see the country.' A dog came out and said, 'At length we see the country.' And the people came out laughing and saying, 'At length we see the country.' They made the woman presents; some gave her cattle, some goats, and some sheep. She set out with her children, being very rich. She went home rejoicing because she had come back with her children. On her arrival her little girl was there; she rejoiced, because she was thinking that her mother was dead.

A SOUTHERN SOTHO ORAL NARRATIVE

The Child With A Moon On His Chest

from *The Form, Content And Technique Of Traditional Literature In Southern Sotho* by S.M. Guma (1980)

It is said it was a great chief, Bulane. He had two wives. Now one of them did not have any children, while the other one had them. This chief had a moon on his chest. One of these women was very much loved by Bulane; it is the one who had children. He ill-treated the one who was without children.

After a short while, the childless woman conceived. A few months passed and it was time for her to be confined. The woman who had children came and helped her. She gave birth to a child who had a moon on his chest. Now the midwife took it, and threw it behind the pots in the cupboard. A mouse quickly took it, and went into its hole with it. The baby's mother was unconscious. The midwife quickly went outside. She found a puppy in a hen's nest, and quickly returned with it and put it next to the child's mother. Then she shook her. 'Wake up and see; you have given birth to a dog.' And this childless woman was disappointed when she found she had given birth to a dog.

Then this midwife quickly went outside to Bulane and said, 'Your wife has given birth to a dog.' Bulane was greatly disappointed. He said, 'Go and take that dog and throw it away.' They took it and threw it away. And the poor little woman came out of her hut disappointed.

A few days passed and Bulane's (senior) wife came to that hut. She found the mouse having taken out the child with a moon on his chest and playing with it. She was shocked and said, 'I thought that child had died!' Then she quickly went out and said to her husband, Bulane, 'You can see, my lord, I am really ill. Diving bones say before I can get well, you must burn down your wife's hut, this one who has just given birth to a dog.' Bulane answered his wife and said, 'It is well that it should be burnt down,' because he loved her very much. Now this woman thought that if the hut were burnt down, the child would die, the mouse would also be burnt by the fire, and she would no longer see this child with a moon on his chest, because she wanted to destroy it.

The mouse overheard the secret of the senior wife and the chief, and quickly left the hut with the child with a moon on his chest, and went into a culvert with it. The chief went out the next day and burnt that hut. The *mofumahadi* was convinced she had destroyed the child and the mouse, and would not see them again.

A few days passed and the *mofumahadi* went to get cow-dung from the cattle-kraal. She found the child with a moon on his chest sitting under a cow. She was shocked and said, 'What can I do to kill him?' When she left the cattle-kraal, she moaned aloud and said she was very sick. The chief asked her, 'What are you suffereing from? What can I do that you should be well again?' She said, 'Divining bones say you should pull down your cattle-kraal. It is only then that I shall get well.'

The mouse overheard the secret of the chief and the senior wife. It went out with the child and took him to a house of traders, *bahwebi*. When the cattle-kraal was pulled down, the child with a moon on his chest was not there. The mouse parted with him there, and went to its home. One day certain people went to exchange goods, *bapatsa*. Now a certain man from Bulane's village also went there to buy. He found this young man, who had something shining on his chest. He returned home and told Bulane about the handsome young man he had seen with a moon on his chest. Bulane left there and then to go and see him. On arrival, he asked him, 'Whose child are you? How did you come here?'

The young man with a moon on his chest explained to him and said, 'My mother gave birth to me, and my father's wife threw me into a cupboard, *mohaolwana*. Then the mouse received me, went with me into its hole and there looked after me. My father's wife took a dog, and said my mother had given birth to it.' Bulane started examining him closely, *qamakisisa*, and remembered that his senior wife had said the other wife had given birth to a dog. Now the child with a moon on his chest told him how he had gone to the cattle-kraal, until the mouse fled with him, and took him to the house of traders.

Then his father opened his chest, in order to see whether he was really the child with a moon on his chest. He found that it was the child with a moon on his chest. He took him and went home with him. He hid him in his hut. He called a big *pitso*, and invited all his people to it. Cattle were slaughtered and numerous pots of beer brewed. He said they should spread mats on the ground from where he had hidden the child with a moon on his chest. Then he took him out and brought him to this great *pitso*. He showed him to the people and explained how his senior wife had treated him (Bulane) in a treacherous way. Then the mother of the child with a moon on his chest was made to take off her rags and was dressed in beautiful clothes. And the child with a moon on his chest was made a chief by his father. As for the woman who had children without a moon on the chest, it was said she is a wicked person, *molotsana*. She was given her belongings, *thepa,* and it was said she must leave and return to her original home.

A VENDA ORAL NARRATIVE

Hearts Which Are Alike

from *Some Venda Folk-Tales* by G.P. Lestrade (1942)

Famine was once great in the land. Now in those days a certain man and his wife were living in their village, they two. For them their life there at home was difficult, because they did not get on with each other on account of the famine. While the one said: 'You are finishing the food for me', the other said: 'It is you, you always eat a lot.'

This man was a great hunter of guinea-fowl. In his wife's cooking-hut there were placed hanging-poles which were hung full of bodies of guinea-fowls. In those days they were living on guinea-fowl meat. But though meat was plentiful, they continually kept on not getting on with each other.

It happened that, one day, the man took down one guinea-fowl from the platform, and gave it to his wife so that she might cook it, and it would constitute supper.

Well, the guinea-fowl was put on to the hearth, and the man went out, and went to hunt.

When the man had gone away, and the hearth had started roaring, the woman, taking the lid off that pot which was on the hearth, found that meat already done, and she spoke, and said: 'Seeing that the day is still so much in the midday, let me take this guinea-fowl out of the water, and let me put in another. My husband, since I know that he has gone to hunt, will not come back soon: he will find this other one already done, and will not know that it is not the same.'

Right then that woman took that guinea-fowl out of the water, and put in another one there into the pot.

Now there in the cooking-hut there was a large clay grain-bin into which, when the land was peaceful they regularly poured eleusine. It was then that the woman said: 'Let me hide carefully behind it, so that even if the man comes back while I am still busy eating he may not quickly see me.' So things were, and she hid herself behind the grain-bin.

Right then the man also arrived, looking about in the courtyard and in the cooking-hut, saw the woman was not to be seen, spoke in his heart, and said: 'My wife has gone to the river: let me take that guinea-fowl out of the water, eat it, and put another one into the pot, since a good deal of the day is still there; and also since my wife, when going to the river or to gather wood, does not return soon. She will find this other one already done, and will not know that it is not the same.' He also said further: 'On the other hand, perhaps she may have been gone a long time, she may already be coming back; and if she finds me eating, she will scold me. Let me hide behind the grain-bin, so that she shall not find me.

Now when he says: 'I am going to squat down behind the grain-bin to hide', he finds his wife squatting right there behind the grain-bin, and eating another guinea-fowl.

The man was greatly surprised, spoke to his wife, and said: 'My wife, but indeed our hearts are alike. I intended to hide from you, and you intended to hide from me. Let us come out there outside, my wife, so that we may eat properly seated.'

Right then those people, both of them, the man and the woman, began a new life. They no longer troubled each other, they diligently searched for food during that famine, and the land was again at peace.

OLIVE SCHREINER

Three Dreams In A Desert

from *Dreams And Dream Life And Real Life* (1893)

As I travelled across an African plain the sun shone down hotly. Then I drew my horse up under a mimosa-tree, and I took the saddle from him and left him to feed among the parched bushes. And all to right and to left stretched the brown earth. And I sat down under the tree, because the heat beat fiercely, and all along the horizon the air throbbed. And after a while a heavy drowsiness came over me, and I laid my head down against my saddle, and I fell asleep there. And, in my sleep, I had a curious dream.

I thought I stood on the border of a great desert, and the sand blew about everywhere. And I thought I saw two great figures like beasts of burden of the desert, and one lay upon the sand with its neck stretched out, and one stood by it. And I looked curiously at the one that lay upon the ground, for it had a great burden on its back, and the sand was thick about it, so that it seemed to have piled over it for centuries.

And I looked very curiously at it. And there stood one beside me watching. And I said to him, 'What is this huge creature who lies here on the sand?'

And he said, 'This is woman; she that bears men in her body.'

And I said, 'Why does she lie here motionless with the sand piled round her?'

And he answered, 'Listen, I will tell you. Ages and ages long she has lain here, and the wind has blown over her. The oldest, oldest, oldest man living has never seen her move: the oldest, oldest book records that she lay there then, as she lies here now, with the sand about her. But listen! Older than the oldest book, older than the oldest recorded memory of man, on the Rocks of Language, on the hard-baked clay of Ancient Customs, now crumbling to decay, are found the marks of her footsteps! Side by side with his who stands beside her you may trace them; and you know that she who now lies there once wandered free over the rocks with him.'

And I said, 'Why does she lie there now?'

And he said, 'I take it, ages ago the Age-of-dominion-of-muscular-force found her, and when she stooped low to give suck to her young, and her back was broad, he put his burden of subjection on to it, and tied it on with the broad band of Inevitable Necessity. Then she looked at the earth and the sky, and knew there was no hope for her; and she lay down on the sand with the burden she could not loosen. Ever since she has lain here. And the ages have come, and the ages have gone, but the band of Inevitable Necessity has not been cut.'

And I looked and saw in her eyes the terrible patience of the centuries; the ground was wet with her tears, and her nostrils blew up the sand.

And I said, 'Has she ever tried to move?'

And he said, 'Sometimes a limb has quivered. But she is wise; she knows she cannot rise with the burden on her.'

And I said, 'Why does not he who stands by her leave her and go on?'

And he said, 'He cannot. Look——'

And I saw a broad band passing along the ground from one to the other, and it bound them together.

He said, 'While she lies there he must stand and look across the desert.'

And I said, 'Does he know why he cannot move?'

And he said, 'No.'

And I heard a sound of something cracking, and I looked, and I saw the band that bound the burden on to her back broken asunder; and the burden rolled on to the ground.

And I said, 'What is this?'

And he said, 'The Age-of-muscular-force is dead. The Age-of-nervous-force has killed him with the knife he holds in his hand; and silently and invisibly he has crept up to the woman, and with that knife of Mechanical Invention he has cut the band that bound the burden to her back. The Inevitable Necessity is broken. She might rise now.'

And I saw that she still lay motionless on the sand, with her eyes open and her neck stretched out. And she seemed to look for something on the far-off border of the desert that never came. And I wondered if she were awake or asleep. And as I looked her body quivered, and a light came into her eyes, like when a sunbeam breaks into a dark room.

I said, 'What is it?'

He whispered, 'Hush! the thought has come to her, "Might I not rise?" '

And I looked. And she raised her head from the sand, and I saw the dent where her neck had lain so long. And she looked at the earth, and she looked at the sky, and she looked at him who stood by her: but he looked out across the desert.

And I saw her body quiver; and she pressed her front knees to the earth, and veins stood out; and I cried, 'She is going to rise!'

But only her sides heaved, and she lay still where she was.

But her head she held up; she did not lay it down again. And he beside me said, 'She is very weak. See, her legs have been crushed under her so long.'

And I saw the creature struggle: and the drops stood out on her.

And I said, 'Surely he who stands beside her will help her?'

And he beside me answered, 'He cannot help her: *she must help herself*. Let her struggle till she is strong.'

And I cried, 'At least he will not hinder her! See, he moves farther from her, and tightens the cord between them, and he drags her down.'

And he answered, 'He does not understand. When she moves she draws the band that binds them, and hurts him, and he moves farther from her. The day will come when he will understand, and will know what she is doing. Let her once stagger on to her knees. In that day he will stand close to her, and look into her eyes with sympathy.'

And she stretched her neck, and the drops fell from her. And the creature rose an inch from the earth and sank back.

And I cried, 'Oh, she is too weak! she cannot walk! The long years have taken all her strength from her. Can she never move?'

And he answered me, 'See the light in her eyes!'

And slowly the creature staggered on to its knees.

And I awoke: and all to the east and to the west stretched the barren earth, with the dry bushes on it. The ants ran up and down in the red sand, and the heat beat fiercely. I looked up through the thin branches of the tree at the blue sky overhead. I stretched myself, and I mused over the dream I had had. And I fell asleep again, with my head on my saddle. And in the fierce heat I had another dream.

I saw a desert and I saw a woman coming out of it. And she came to the bank of a dark river; and the bank was steep and high. And on it an old man met her, who had a long white beard; and a stick that curled was in his hand, and on it was written Reason. And he asked her what she wanted; and she said, 'I am woman; and I am seeking for the land of Freedom.'

And he said, 'It is before you.'

And she said, 'I see nothing before me but a dark flowing river, and a bank steep and high, and cuttings here and there with heavy sand in them.'

And he said, 'And beyond that?'

She said, 'I see nothing, but sometimes, when I shade my eyes with my hand, I think I see on the further bank trees and hills, and the sun shining on them!'

He said, 'That is the Land of Freedom.'

She said, 'How am I to get there?'

He said, 'There is one way, and one only. Down the banks of Labour, through the water of Suffering. There is no other.'

She said, 'Is there no bridge?'

He answered, 'None.'

She said, 'Is the water deep?'

He said, 'Deep.'

She said, 'Is the floor worn?'

He said, 'It is. Your foot may slip at any time, and you may be lost.'

She said, 'Have any crossed already?'

He said, 'Some have *tried!*'

She said, 'Is there a track to show where the best fording is?'

He said, 'It has to be made.'

She shaded her eyes with her hand; and she said, 'I will go.'

And he said, 'You must take off the clothes you wore in the desert: they are dragged down by them who go into the water so clothed.'

And she threw from her gladly the mantle of Ancient-received-opinions she wore, for it was worn full of holes. And she took the girdle from her waist that she had treasured so long, and the moths flew out of it in a cloud. And he said, 'Take the shoes of dependence off your feet.'

And she stood there naked, but for one white garment that clung close to her.

And he said, 'That you may keep. So they wear clothes in the Land of Freedom. In the water it buoys; it always swims.'

And I saw on its breast was written Truth; and it was white; the sun had not often shone on it; the other clothes had covered it up. And he said, 'Take this stick; hold it fast. In that day when it slips from your hand you are lost. Put it down before you; feel your way: where it cannot find a bottom do not set your foot.'

And she said, 'I am ready; let me go.'

And he said, 'No — but stay; what is that — in your breast?'

She was silent.

He said, 'Open it, and let me see.'

And she opened it. And against her breast was a tiny thing, who drank from it, and the yellow curls above his forehead pressed against it; and his knees were drawn up to her, and he held her breast fast with his hands.

And Reason said, 'Who is he, and what is he doing here?'

And she said, 'See his little wings ——'

And Reason said, 'Put him down.'

And she said, 'He is asleep, and he is drinking! I will carry him to the Land of Freedom. He has been a child so long, so long, I have carried him. In the Land of Freedom he will be a man. We will walk together there, and his great white wings will overshadow me. He has lisped one word only to me in the desert — 'Passion!' I have dreamed he might learn to say 'Friendship' in that land.'

And Reason said, 'Put him down!'

And she said, 'I will carry him so — with one arm, and with the other I will fight the water.'

He said, 'Lay him down on the ground. When you are in the water you will forget to fight, you will think only of him. Lay him down.' He said, 'He will not die. When he finds you have left him alone he will open his wings and fly. He will be in the Land of Freedom before you. Those who reach the Land of Freedom, the first hand they see stretching down the bank to help them shall be Love's. He will be a man then, not a child. In your breast he cannot thrive; put him down that he may grow.'

And she took her bosom from his mouth, and he bit her, so that the blood ran down on to the ground. And she laid him down on the earth; and she covered her wound. And she bent and stroked his wings. And I saw the hair on her forehead turned white as snow, and she had changed from youth to age.

And she stood far off on the bank of the river. And she said, 'For what do I go to this far land which no one has ever reached? *Oh, I am alone! I am utterly alone!*'

And Reason, that old man, said to her, 'Silence! what do you hear?'

And she listened intently, and she said, 'I hear a sound of feet, a thousand times ten thousand and thousands of thousands, and they beat this way!'

He said, 'They are the feet of those that shall follow you. Lead on! make a track to the water's edge! Where you stand now, the ground will be beaten flat by ten thousand times ten thousand feet.' And he said, 'Have you seen the locusts how they cross a stream? First one comes down to the water's edge, and it is swept away, and then another comes and then another, and then another, and at last with their bodies piled up a bridge is built and the rest pass over.'

She said, 'And, of those that come first, some are swept away, and are heard of no more; their bodies do not even build the bridge?'

'And are swept away, and are heard of no more — and what of that?' he said.

'And what of that——' she said.

'They make a track to the water's edge.'

'They make a track to the water's edge——. And she said, 'Over that bridge which shall be built with our bodies, who will pass?'

He said, *'The entire human race.'*

And the woman grasped her staff.

And I saw her turn down that dark path to the river.

And I awoke; and all about me was the yellow afternoon light: the sinking sun lit up the fingers of the milk bushes; and my horse stood by me quietly feeding. And I turned on my side, and I watched the ants run by thousands in the red sand. I thought I would go on my way now — the afternoon was cooler. Then a drowsiness crept over me again, and I laid back my head and fell asleep.

And I dreamed a dream.

I dreamed I saw a land. And on the hills walked brave women and brave men, hand in hand. And they looked into each other's eyes, and they were not afraid.

And I saw the women also hold each other's hands.

And I said to him beside me, 'What place is this?'

And he said, 'This is heaven.'

And I said, 'Where is it?'

And he answered, 'On earth.'

And I said, 'When shall these things be?'

And he answered, 'IN THE FUTURE.'

And I awoke, and all about me was the sunset light; and on the low hills the sun lay, and a delicious coolness had crept over everything; and the ants were going slowly home. And I walked towards my horse, who stood quietly feeding. Then the sun passed down behind the hills; but I knew that the next day he would arise again.

PAULINE SMITH

The Sisters

from *The Little Karoo* (1925)

Marta was the eldest of my father's children, and she was sixteen years old when our mother died and our father lost the last of his water-cases to old Jan Redlinghuis of Bitterwater. It was the water-cases that killed my mother. Many, many times she had cried to my father to give in to old Jan Redlinghuis whose water-rights had been fixed by law long before my father built his water furrow from the Ghamka river. But my father could not rest. If he could but get a fair share of the river water for his furrow, he would say, his farm of Zeekoegatt would be as rich as the farm of Bitterwater and we should then have a town house in Platkops dorp and my mother should wear a black cashmere dress all the days of her life. My father could not see that my mother did not care about the black cashmere dress or the town house in Platkops dorp. My mother was a very gentle woman with a disease of the heart, and all she cared about was to have peace in the house and her children happy around her. And for so long as my father was at law about his water-rights there could be no peace on all the farm of Zeekoegatt. With each new water-case came more bitterness and sorrow to us all. Even between my parents at last came bitterness and sorrow. And in bitterness and sorrow my mother died.

In his last water-case my father lost more money than ever before, and to save the farm he bonded some of the lands to old Jan Redlinghuis himself. My father was surely mad when he did this, but he did it. And from that day Jan Redlinghuis pressed him, pressed him, pressed him, till my father did not know which way to turn. And then, when my father's back was up against the wall and he thought he must sell the last of his lands to pay his bond, Jan Redlinghuis came to him and said:

'I will take your daughter, Marta Magdalena, instead.'

Three days Jan Redlinghuis gave my father, and in three days, if

Marta did not promise to marry him, the lands of Zeekoegatt must be sold. Marta told me this late that same night. She said to me:

'Sukey, my father has asked me to marry old Jan Redlinghuis. I am going to do it.'

And she said again: 'Sukey, my darling, listen now! If I marry old Jan Redlinghuis he will let the water into my father's furrow, and the lands of Zeekoegatt will be saved. I am going to do it, and God will help me.'

I cried to her: 'Marta! Old Jan Redlinghuis is a sinful man, going at times a little mad in his head. God must help you before you marry him. Afterwards it will be too late.'

And Marta said: 'Sukey, if I do right, right will come of it, and it is right for me to save the lands for my father. Think now, Sukey, my darling! There is not one of us that is without sin in the world and old Jan Redlinghuis is not always mad. Who am I to judge Jan Redlinghuis? And can I then let my father be driven like a poor white to Platkops dorp?' And she drew me down on to the pillow beside her, and took me into her arms, and I cried there until far into the night.

The next day I went alone across the river to old Jan Redlinghuis's farm. No one knew that I went, or what it was in my heart to do. When I came to the house Jan Redlinghuis was out on the *stoep* smoking his pipe.

I said to him: 'Jan Redlinghuis, I have come to offer myself.'

Jan Redlinghuis took his pipe out of his mouth and looked at me. I said again: 'I have come to ask you to marry me instead of my sister Marta.'

Old Jan Redlinghuis said to me: 'And why have you come to do this thing, Sukey de Jager?'

I told him: 'Because it is said that you are a sinful man, Jan Redlinghuis, going at times a little mad in your head, and my sister Marta is too good for you.'

For a little while old Jan Redlinghuis looked at me, sitting there with his pipe in his hand, thinking the Lord knows what. And presently he said:

'All the same, Sukey de Jager, it is your sister Marta that I will marry and no one else. If not, I will take the lands of Zeekoegatt as is my right, and I will make your father bankrupt. Do now as you like about it.'

And he put his pipe in his mouth, and not one other word would he say.

I went back to my father's house with my heart heavy like lead. And all that night I cried to God: 'Do now what you will with me, but save our Marta.' Yes, I tried to make a bargain with the Lord so that Marta might be saved. And I said also: 'If He does not save our Marta I will know that there is no God.'

In three weeks Marta married old Jan Redlinghuis and went to live with him across the river. On Marta's wedding day I put my father's Bible before him and said:

'Pa, pray if you like, but I shall not pray with you. There is no God or surely He would have saved our Marta. But if there is a God as surely will He burn our souls in Hell for selling Marta to old Jan Redlinghuis.'

From that time I could do what I would with my father, and my heart was bitter to all the world but my sister Marta. When my father said to me:

'Is it not wonderful, Sukey, what we have done with the water that old Jan Redlinghuis lets pass to my furrow?'

I answered him: 'What is now wonderful? It is blood that we lead on our lands to water them. Did not my mother die for it? And was it not for this that we sold my sister Marta to old Jan Redlinghuis?'

Yes, I said that. It was as if my heart must break to see my father water his lands while old Jan Redlinghuis held my sister Marta up to shame before all Platkops.

I went across the river to my sister Marta as often as I could, but not once after he married her did old Jan Redlinghuis let Marta come back to my father's house.

'Look now, Sukey de Jager,' he would say to me, 'your father has sold me his daughter for his lands. Let him now look to his lands and leave me his daughter.' And that was all he would say about it.

Marta had said that old Jan Redlinghuis was not always mad, but from the day that he married her his madness was to cry to all the world to look at the wife that Burgert de Jager had sold to him.

'Look,' he would say, 'how she sits in her new tent-cart — the wife that Burgert de Jager sold to me.'

And he would point to the Zeekoegatt lands and say: 'See now, how green they are, the lands that Bürgert de Jager sold me his daughter to save.'

Yes, even before strangers would he say these things, stopping his cart in the road to say them, with Marta sitting by his side.

My father said to me: 'Is it not wonderful, Sukey, to see how Marta rides through the country in her new tent-cart?'

I said to him: 'What is now wonderful? It is to her grave that she rides in the new tent-cart, and presently you will see it.'

And I said to him also: 'It took you many years to kill my mother, but believe me it will not take as many months for old Jan Redlinghuis to kill my sister Marta.' Yes, God forgive me, but I said that to my father. All my pity was for my sister Marta, and I had none to give my father.

And all this time Marta spoke no word against old Jan Redlinghuis.

She had no illness that one might name, but every day she grew a little weaker, and every day Jan Redlinghuis inspanned the new tent-cart and drove her round the country. This madness came at last so strong upon him that he must drive from sun-up to sun-down crying to all whom he met:

'Look now at the wife that Burgert de Jager sold to me!'

So it went, day after day, day after day, till at last there came a day when Marta was too weak to climb into the cart and they carried her from where she fell into the house. Jan Redlinghuis sent for me across the river.

When I came to the house old Jan Redlinghuis was standing on the *stoep* with his gun. He said to me: 'See here, Sukey de Jager! Which of us now had the greatest sin — your father who sold me his daughter Marta, or I who bought her? Marta who let herself be sold, or you who offered yourself to save her?'

And he took up his gun and left the *stoep* and would not wait for an answer.

Marta lay where they had put her on old Jan Redlinghuis's great wooden bed, and only twice did she speak. Once she said:

'He was not always mad, Sukey, my darling, and who am I that I should judge him?'

And again she said: 'See how it is, my darling! In a little while I shall be with our mother. So it is that God has helped me.'

At sun-down Marta died, and when they ran to tell Jan Redlinghuis they could not find him. All that night they looked for him, and the next day also. We buried Marta in my mother's grave at Zeekoegatt ... And still they could not find Jan Redlinghuis. Six days they looked for him, and at last they found his body in the mountains. God knows what madness had driven old Jan Redlinghuis to the mountains when his wife lay dying, but there it was they found him, and at Bitterwater he was buried.

That night my father came to me and said: 'It is true what you said to me, Sukey. It is blood that I have led on my lands to water them, and this night will I close the furrow that I built from the Ghamka river. God forgive me, I will do it.'

It was in my heart to say to him: 'The blood is already so deep in the lands that nothing we can do will now wash it out.' But I did not say this. I do not know how it was, but there came before me the still, sad face of my sister, Marta, and it was as if she herself answered for me.

'Do now as it seems right to you,' I said to my father. 'Who am I that I should judge you?'

MARY BYRON

Neighbours

from *Dawn And Dusk In The Highveld* (1931)

Ours is becoming a populated area. A large estate has been subdivided and these smaller farms, we learn, have already been sold. From our house on the hill of observation, we see repairs going on above the rough-hewn stone of the dilapidated little houses, deserted since the Boer war. The hammering on corrugated iron sounds and re-echoes from the distance; driving past we see the crude paint upon new doors.

Further on a rich man's hobby brings surveyors and builders busy on a big enterprise. The wide veld over which one could ride night-long, day-long, to the rainbow's end, is scored across and across with wire fencing. Bungalows appear as in a night with pleasing red roofs that some day, one pictures, will nestle in the foliage of the now foot-high trees. Smoke rises from a dozen chimneys, neighbours come together in friendly fashion — but ah, for the wild freshness of morning when the world was ours!

To the red-roofed houses come strange occupants, come and pass away. Advertisements in England must have implied to their understanding a new and simple way to 'get rich quick.' Else one wonders what could have been the lure that drew men from Penge and Peckham Rye to the depths of the veld.

'I like it well enough meself' says one — 'public-house' is written all over him — 'but the missis don't seem to settle down. You see she has been that used to just settin' and reachin' 'er 'and for a bottle o' beer when she felt like it.'

Another talks of the cramped space in his little house. 'It doan't seem to me as us could get a coffin not in nor out of them awkward passages,' he complains.

One more, as we have seen, comes equipped for life in the veld with a piano and a French chef, a fourth grows more fearful of the required deeds of daring among fierce savages. No doubt from a youth he has revelled in wild cowboy tales, but he feels it a different matter to live them.

His train arrives late, so the agent supplies blankets and gives him permission to sleep in the dwelling of his fancy. In the morning no one can get into the house. Handles are turned, windows shaken, all are fast shut. The agent grows nervous. 'There's something wrong,' he says. 'Whoever locks a house in the veld?' and redoubles his banging. At last a sleepy head comes to the window.

'Oh, is it you?' says a drowsy voice and a door is unlocked. Boxes or wedged workmen's tools hold fast the other doors and windows, and the agent sees a revolver close by the bed. 'Sorry I overslept myself,' explains the occupant, 'I'd been awake watching most of the night, since I heard the blacks shouting. I didn't guess I'd have to spend the night here by myself. Takes some pluck,' he adds with pride, 'to sleep alone with all those natives around.'

But though Basutos do not lurk in secret places with tomahawk and scalping knife — never was there so easy-tempered and happy-go-lucky a race — yet in their very quality of casual good temper, lies the tragedy for many a woman pioneer. Here is the case of the bride just below us in the rough little house with its new tin roof. She has come — as she thought — most carefully prepared for her new life. She has had a course of domestic science, she can cook an excellent dinner, her own fingers have stitched most of the pretty lingerie of her trousseau, her dresses are an elaborate simplicity, she has a nice taste in china and in silken hangings and cushions. It is her first home and she fills it with the pleasant memories of long shopping hours and the kindness of friends. And she is practical, too. There are sets of shining saucepans and labour-saving devices. She can launder her silk blouses and her husband's shirts. She has, one would think, every equipment for success — and the end of a month finds her in despair.

Here is no stove with its thermometer and regulated gas jets such as she found at her training college, yet even so she might have managed if an unexpected downpour had not soaked her only available fuel — the mud and cow-dung slabs stacked on the kraal wall — if the piccanin had not spilt the soup on top of the stove, then snatched from her newly-piled linen a teacloth of damask with which to wipe it up; if Paulina, shrilly expostulating, had not so roughly dragged the iron rings from the stove to clean them that two fell on the hearthstone and were cracked across.

The gleaming saucepans have been lowered into the flames to speed the cooking and nothing will ever remove their burnt-in coating of black nor mend the double saucepan that has been put on the fire empty of water. Her labour-saving devices, where are they? The potato-peeler, the blade forced the wrong way, is now useless, her bread-maker has been worked with such violence that its clamp has broken off.

This is the history of everything — brute force, often aided by the poker, has forced into unholy union parts meant to be as divergent as the poles — broken, bent, useless. It applies to all — to the teacups chipped or handleless, to the frocks rubbed into rags on stones, and my friend has gone down under the intolerable weight of the incapacity of her natives, blanket-clothed, somnolent, now leaning on the sun-warmed walls of the kraal and carrying on a languid, unending conversation with the ploughboy half a mile away.

The mud floor is worn into holes where the heavy bare feet stumble and spill water, but the very thought of the required 'smearing' with bullock's blood and manure fills my friend with such loathing that even the holes seem better.

This is no overdrawn picture. Some of us have been through it, all of us have seen it. That the woman can and does rise above these disabilities and gradually and with laughter transform a hovel to a home is one of the wonders of our unconquerable race.

What then must be added to our learning? Must we know all the mysteries of life and death, we women of the lonely places? Here is another bride, poor little Sally Brent (such a baby she seemed, fresh from her English home) called from her warm bed one wild night of wind.

'Mrs Brent! Mrs Brent! For God's sake come with me. Poor Agnes' trouble is on her. I've told my boy to go for the doctor but he's half the night finding his horse and then it'll take two or three hours.'

'I'll inspan my nags and go over and fetch the doctor,' says Sally's husband, hurrying into his clothes. 'Cheer up, old man, I'll go like hell.'

Poor little Sally, shivering, dazed with sleep, tripping over her long coat as she climbs into the cart!

'What do you want me to do? What can I do?' she asks with chattering teeth.

'It's coming too soon. Why, the nurse isn't due for a week. I woke up hearing her moaning. She didn't want to wake me. She put her head under the pillow. Oh, my poor old Agnes.'

Clop, clop, go the horses' feet, the cart heaves and jolts over the rough and lonely road where no landmarks stand out for guides. There are no other houses for half a dozen miles. Grey road, indistinguishable from grey veld, grey ant-heaps to capsize the unwary driver. A moon flickers now and then through the race of the clouds and one sees the black wavering line of the donga, here and there taking a part of the road in its sweep, encroaching with its dangerous overhanging banks until the cart is forced on to the clods of the rough-ploughed land. The tent of the cart shakes above their heads; one curtain, torn loose, flaps in sudden cracks like a whip-lash. Trees leap up suddenly in the flashes of light with curious flat effect of cardboard stage-properties. Sally has found herself almost enjoying the rush of the wind that shakes her hair into waving plumes, the eerie feeling of the night, the bell-call of the frogs in the dam. They have reached the quince hedge and turned into the drive before the horror of her errand bursts on her again. From the stoep she can hear the groans of the unfortunate sufferer. God! what was she going to do? She trembles from head to foot as she pushes at the door where a line of light gleams, then draws a breath of relief. Nothing very sensational after all, just a figure lying quiet in the bed. The groans have ceased. The lamp is set in a corner out of the draught and the room seems very dimly lit at first as she stoops over the bed. In the grey face lined deep with pain she hardly recognizes her friend. A ghost of a smile is on the pinched lips.

'How good of you, Sally,' and presently, 'Wrap yourself in the rug. It is so cold, so cold,' she shivers.

The girl makes a great effort to brace herself and force her mind to think of the simple things. The husband has come to her help and together they build the fire. He brings her fuel and water, moving with nervous eagerness. She fills the hot-water bottle, sets the can of milk to heat, forces a calm into her movements, but each groan from the next room sets her nerves quivering and brings a lump into her throat.

'I can't bear it,' she tells herself, 'when, oh when, will the doctor come?'

Her tasks ended there is nothing left, nothing to divert the fearful apprehensions ... The hours pass. Sometimes the woman is easier. She talks to Sally, tells her where to find things when the doctor shall come. 'He'll tell you what to do,' and how she must wash the baby and of its pretty clothes waiting in the long drawer.

'Don't worry, Sally,' she says, then pain seizes her again and Sally shrinks away and longs to block her ears from those heart-breaking moans. The husband comes and goes.

'Stick it out, old girl,' he says. 'The doctor must be here soon.' And still the endless time goes on. There is a faint grey in the sky, for which did they but know it, the doctor too has prayed, that he may see to splice up that broken buggy-pole in the maze of veld and donga.

Sally cannot be still. She drags off her shoes and on stockinged feet creeps from room to room, bends over the woman, now a huddled heap in the bed, tiptoes back again. By the window the husband stands, tense, staring at the dawn, his hands gleam white where he clutches the back of a chair. Agnes sees no one, a sharp sob joins now and again to the wail of the wind.

'God, O God!' she gasps.

'God,' echoes the girl, and wonders. Can that help? They pray for them in chruch, she remembers, 'for all women labouring of child, all sick persons and young children ... all women labouring' — she wants to scream. How will prayers help? It is action, action that is wanted and she can do nothing.

There is a lull in the wind and silence, then suddenly on their frantic ears rings shriek upon shriek. The man knocks his chair clattering to the ground as he rushes from the room. He has stood by many a suffering animal in the long nights and helped it bring to birth, but this he cannot face.

'Damn that bloody doctor,' he screams, and the girl sees him running up the road stumbling like a drunken man.

'Agnes,' cries the girl in an agony, 'tell me what to do, only tell me what to do!'

And so the doctor finds her when he comes at last, crouched in the chair, hands clutched before her face, rocking to and fro, a trembling figure half distraught, and on the bed a new-born infant and a mother who has bled to death.

DORIS LESSING

The Nuisance

from *This Was The Old Chief's Country* (1951)

Two narrow tracks, one of them deepened to a smooth dusty groove by the incessant padding of bare feet, wound from the farm compound to the old well through half a mile of tall blonde grass that was soiled and matted because of the nearness of the clustering huts: the compound had been on that ridge for twenty years.

The native women with their children used to loiter down the track, and their shrill laughter and chattering sounded through the trees as if one might suddenly have come on a flock of brilliant noisy parrots. It seemed as if fetching water was more of a social event to them than a chore. At the well itself they would linger half the morning, standing in groups to gossip, their arms raised in that graceful, eternally moving gesture to steady glittering or rusted petrol tins balanced on head-rings woven of grass; kneeling to slap bits of bright cloth on slabs of stone blasted long ago from the depths of earth. Here they washed and scolded and dandled their children. Here they scrubbed their pots. Here they sluiced themselves and combed their hair.

Coming upon them suddenly there would be sharp exclamations; a glimpse of soft brown shoulders and thighs withdrawing to the bushes, or annoyed and resentful eyes. It was their well. And while they were there, with their laughter, and gossip and singing, their folded draperies, bright armbands, earthenware jars and metal combs, grouped in attitudes of head-slowed indolence, it seemed as if the bellowing of distant cattle, drone of tractor, all the noises of the farm, were simply lending themselves to form a background to this antique scene: Women, drawing water at the well.

When they left the ground would be scattered with the bright-pink, fleshy skins of the native wild-plum which contracts the mouth shudderingly with its astringency, or with the shiny green fragments of the shells of kaffir oranges.

Without the women the place was ugly, paltry. The windlass, coiled with greasy rope, propped for safety with a forked stick, was sheltered by a tiny cock of thatch that threw across the track a long, intensely black shadow. For the rest, veld; the sere, flattened, sun-dried veld.

They were beautiful, these women. But she whom I thought of vaguely as 'The cross-eyed one', offended the sight. She used to lag behind the others on the road, either by herself, or in charge of the older children. Not only did she suffer from a painful squint, so that when she looked towards you it was with a confused glare of white eyeball; but her body was hideous. She wore the traditional dark-patterned blue stuff looped at the waist, and above it her breasts were loose, flat crinkling triangles.

She was a solitary figure at the well, doing her washing unaided and without laughter. She would strain at the windlass during the long slow ascent of the swinging bucket that clanged sometimes, far below, against the sides of naked rock until at that critical moment when it hung vibrating at the mouth of the well, she would set the weight of her shoulder in the crook of the handle and with a fearful snatching movement bring the water to safety. It would slop over, dissolving in a shower of great drops that fell tinkling to disturb the surface of that tiny, circular, dully-gleaming mirror which lay at the bottom of the plunging rock tunnel. She was clumsy. Because of her eyes her body lumbered.

She was the oldest wife of 'The Long One', who was our most skilful driver.

'The Long One' was not so tall as he was abnormally thin. It was the leanness of those driven by inner restlessness. He could never keep still. His hands plucked at pieces of grass, his shoulder twitched to a secret rhythm of the nerves. Set a-top of that sinewy, narrow, taut body was a narrow head, with wide-pointed ears, which gave him an appearance of alert caution. The expression of the face was always violent, whether he was angry, laughing, or — most usually — sardonically critical. He had a tongue that was feared by every labourer on the farm. Even my father would smile ruefully after an altercation with his driver and say: 'He's a man, that native. One must respect him, after all. He never lets you get away with anything.'

In his own line he was an artist — his line being cattle. He handled oxen with a delicate brutality that was fascinating and horrifying to watch. Give him a bunch of screaming, rearing three-year-olds, due to take their first taste of the yoke, and he would fight them for hours under a blistering sun with the sweat running off him, his eyes glowing with a wicked and sombre satisfaction. Then he would use his whip, grunting savagely as the lash cut down into flesh, his tongue stuck calculatingly between his teeth as he measured the exact weight of the blow. But to watch him handle a team of sixteen fat tamed oxen was a different thing. It was like watching a circus act; there was the same suspense in it: it was a matter of pride to him that he did not need to use the whip. This did not by any means imply that he wished to spare the beasts pain, not at all; he liked to feed his pride on his own skill. Alongside the double line of ponderous cattle that strained across acres of heavy clods, danced, raved and screamed the Long One, with his twelve-foot-long lash circling in black patterns over their backs; and though his threatening yells were the yells of an inspired madman, and the heavy whip could be heard clean across the farm, so that on a moonlight night when they were ploughing late it sounded like the crack and whine of a rifle, never did the dangerous metal-tipped lash so much as touch a hair of their hides. If you examined the oxen as they were outspanned, they might be exhausted, driven to staggering-point, so that my father had to remonstrate, but there was never a mark on them.

'He knows how to handle oxen, but he can't handle his women.'

We gave our natives labels such as that, since it was impossible ever to know them as their fellows knew them, in the round. That phrase summarized for us what the Long One offered in entertainment during the years he was with us. Coming back to the farm, after an absence, one would say in humorous anticipation: 'And what has the Long One been up to now, with his harem?'

There was always trouble with his three wives. He used to come up to the house to discuss with my father, man to man, how the youngest wife was flirting with the bossboy from the neighbouring compound, six miles off; or how she had thrown a big pot of smoking mealie-pap at the middle wife, who was jealous of her.

We grew accustomed to the sight of the Long One standing at the back door, at the sunset hour, when my father held audience after work. He always wore long khaki trousers that slipped down over thin bony hips and went bare-chested, and there would be a ruddy gleam on his polished black skin, and his spindly gesticulating form would be outlined against a sea of fiery colours. At the end of his tale of complaint he would relapse suddenly into a pose of resignation that was self-consciously weary. My father used to laugh until his face was wet and say: 'That man is a natural-born comedian. He would have been on the stage if he had been born another colour.'

But he was no buffoon. He would play up to my father's appreciation of the comic, but he would never play the ape, as some Africans did, for our amusement. And he was certainly no figure of fun to his fellows. That same thing in him that sat apart, watchfully critical, even of himself, gave his humour its mordancy, his tongue its sting. And he was terribly attractive to his women. I have seen him slouch down the road on his way from one team to another; his whip trailing behind in the dust, his trousers sagging in folds from hip-bone to ankle, his eyes broodingly directed in front of him, merely nodding as he passed a group of women among whom might be his wives. And it was as if he had lashed them with that whip. They would bridle and writhe; and then call provocatively after him, but with a note of real anger, to make him notice them. He would not so much as turn his head.

When the real trouble started, though, my father soon got tired of it. He liked to be amused, not seriously implicated in his labourers' problems. The Long One took to coming up not occasionally, as he had been used to do, but every evening. He was deadly serious, and very bitter. He wanted my father to persuade the old wife, the cross-eyed one, to go back home to her own people. The woman was driving him crazy. A nagging woman in your house was like having a flea on your body; you could scratch but it always moved to another place, and there was no peace till you killed it.

'But you can't send her back, just because you are tired of her.'

The Long One said his life had become insupportable. She grumbled, she sulked, she spoilt his food.

'Well, then your other wives can cook for you.'

But it seemed there were complications. The two younger women hated each other, but they were united in one thing, that the old wife should stay, for she was so useful. She looked after the children; she did the hoeing in the garden; she picked relishes from the veld. Besides, she provided endless amusement with her ungainliness. She was the eternal butt, the fool, marked by fate for the entertainment of the whole-limbed and the comely.

My father referred at this point to a certain handbook on native lore, which stated definitively that an elder wife was entitled to be waited on by a young wife, perhaps as compensation for having to give up the pleasures of her lord's favour. The Long One and his ménage cut clean across this amiable theory. And my father, being unable to find a prescribed remedy (as one might look for a cure for a disease in a pharmacopoeia) grew angry. After some weeks of incessant complaint from the Long One he was told to hold his tongue and manage his women himself. That evening the man stalked furiously down the path, muttering to himself between teeth clenched on a grass-stem, on his way home to his two giggling younger wives and the ugly sour-faced old woman, the mother of his elder children, the drudge of his household and the scourge of his life.

It was some weeks later that my father asked casually one day: 'And by the way, Long One, how are things with you? All right again?'

And the Long One answered simply: 'Yes, baas. She's gone away.'

'What do you mean, gone away?'

The Long One shrugged. She had just gone. She had left suddenly, without saying anything to anyone.

Now, the woman came from Nyasaland, which was days and days of weary walking away. Surely she hadn't gone by herself? Had a brother or an uncle come to fetch her? Had she gone with a band of passing Africans on their way home?

My father wondered a little, and then forgot about it. It wasn't his affair. He was pleased to have his most useful native back at work with an unharassed mind. And he was particularly pleased that the whole business was ended before the annual trouble over the water-carrying.

For there were two wells. The new one, used by ourselves, had fresh sparkling water that was sweet in the mouth; but in July of each year it ran dry. The water of the old well had a faintly unpleasant taste and was pale brown, but there was always plenty of it. For three or four months of the year, depending on the rains, we shared that well with the compound.

Now, the Long One hated fetching water three miles, four times a week, in the water-cart. The women of the compound disliked having to arrange their visits to the well so as not to get in the way of the water-carriers. There was always grumbling.

This year we had not even begun to use the old well when complaints started that the water tasted bad. The big baas must get the well cleaned.

My father said vaguely that he would clean the well when he had time.

Next day there came a deputation from the women of the compound. Half a dozen of them stood at the back door, arguing that if the well wasn't cleaned soon, all their children would be sick.

'I'll do it next week,' he promised, with bad grace.

The following morning the Long One brought our first load of the season from the old well; and as we turned the taps on the barrels a foetid smell began to pervade the house. As for drinking it, that was out of the question.

'Why don't you keep the cover on the well?' my father said to the women, who were still loitering resentfully at the back door. He was really angry. 'Last time the well was cleaned there were fourteen dead rats and a dead snake. We never get things in our well because we remember to keep the lid on.'

But the women appeared to consider the lid being on, or off, was an act of God, and nothing to do with them.

We always went down to watch the well-emptying, which had the fascination of a ritual. Like the mealie-shelling, or the first rains, it marked a turning-point in the year. It seemed as if a besieged city were laying plans for the conservation of supplies. The sap was falling in tree and grass-root; the sun was withdrawing high, high, behind a veil of smoke and dust; the fierce dryness of the air was a new element, parching foliage as the heat cauterized it. The well-emptying was an act of faith, and of defiance. For a whole afternoon there would be no water on the farm at all. One well was completely dry. And this one would be drained, dependent on the mysterious ebbing and flowing of underground rivers. What if they should fail us? There was an anxious evening, every year; and in the morning, when the Long One stood at the back door and said, beaming, that the bucket was bringing up fine new water, it was like a festival.

But this afternoon we could not stick it out. The smell was intolerable. We saw the usual complement of bloated rats, laid out on the stones around the well, and there was even the skeleton of a small buck that must have fallen in in the dark. Then we left, along the road that was temporarily a river whose source was that apparently endless succession of buckets filled by greyish, evil water.

It was the Long One himself who came to tell us the news. Afterwards we tried to remember what look that always expressive face wore as he told it.

It seemed that in the last bucket but one had floated a human arm, or rather the fragments of one. Piece by piece they had fetched her up, the Cross-eyed Woman, his own first wife. They recognized her by her bangles. Last of all, the Long One went down to fetch up her head, which was missing.

'I thought you said your wife had gone home?' said my father.

'I thought she had. Where else could she have gone?'

'Well,' said my father at last, disgusted by the whole thing, 'if she had to kill herself, why couldn't she hang herself on a tree, instead of spoiling the well?'

'She might have slipped and fallen,' said the Long One.

My father looked up at him suddenly. He stared for a few moments. Then: 'Ye-yes,' he said, 'I suppose she might.'

Later, we talked about the thing, saying how odd it was that natives should commit suicide; it seemed almost like an impertinence, as if they were claiming to have the same delicate feelings as ours.

But later still, apropos of nothing in particular, my father was heard to remark: 'Well, I don't know, I'm damned if I know, but in any case he's a damned good driver.'

DORIS SELLO

I Broke Their Hearts

from *Drum*, September (1953)

My story is, in a way, a wicked one. But I hope you will understand what led me to it — and be happy with me for not having totally ruined my life with the lives of the men I took my revenge out on.

I was working for a burial society in my home town, Krugersdorp. There was a local boy Henry, there too working as chief canvasser. He was an ambitious man with big dreams for the future. He took me out a lot, and within two months madly in love. My college days had not conditioned me for this type of emotion, I found out. I loved him; and he told me hundreds of times that he loved me too.

One day he walked home with me, and on the way almost broke my heart.

'I've got great news, Cynthia,' he said happily. 'The boss says he's opening a branch-office in Springs and he wants me to go over and run it.'

My heart went cold.

'Oh, Henry! Then when will I see you? I'll miss you so!'

'Don't you worry, Cyn; I've got it all worked out. I can come home on week-ends, and baby, when I've fixed things there and I'm made the manager, we're going to get married! How do you like that?'

My heart was full of joy.

He was so keen on the job that, after those few first months, when he began coming home once a month or so and hardly phoning me, I believed his preoccupied excuse that the job was coming on fast and he had to devote most of his time to me.

Some of the times I saw him he was so moody and quiet I began fearing he was straining himself. But, my heart sang, he would soon be settled down enough to marry me. And then I could help him and he wouldn't be so moody all the time.

And then came the blow that completely hardened my heart and made me curse men; all men. There was a rumour that he would soon be marrying a Springs girl! I couldn't believe it; and I wouldn't believe it. How could he after all those promises? Then came the confirming blow. His unknowing sent me an invitation card to the wedding!

Yes. I attended the wedding. I wasn't even envious of the pretty bride in her misty veil. I was too bitter for that. I made a vow at that bridal table. I vowed I would break men's hearts as mine had been broken. Not one man; but as many men as I could cram into the time I was still young, pretty and desirable to them. Yes. I would break all their hearts. Revenge will be sweet! I thought.

It wasn't long before I had my first chance. There was a good-looking boy teaching in one of the primary schools. He'd been trying to date me the whole year, but I hadn't encouraged him with my mind full of the unfaithful Henry.

But now I encouraged him. He was so happy when we were together, I wondered if he ever taught his school-classes anything! I encouraged him to think I loved him. We did everything together: bioscopes, dances, parties and picnics. And I tempted him all I could with all my charms.

Some days I would kiss him and he would try to tell me he loved me, but I would stop him by talking of something else. Other days I would refuse to kiss him; gently so that he would not give up hope. I did my best to deepen his love for me. And I think I did.

I watched him closely, and when his eyes changed from shining stars to brooding discontent, I knew I almost had him. For the following week I let him kiss me as much as he pleased or had the opportunity to. And I would put as much love into the kisses and caresses as I could. But when he began saying:

'Cynthia. Listen to me my darling! I—'

I would interrupt him with a kiss and say 'Not now, Freddy. Not now!'

Then on Sunday morning he came to my home when all the family had gone to church. After the usual remarks about the weather he didn't waste time.

'Cynthia,' he said, moving to the sofa where I was seated. 'Cynthia! I've been trying to tell you this for weeks. Now you must listen to me my darling! I love you. I love you Cynthia and I want to marry you.'

For a moment I was silent. My heart was full; too full for words. At last. At last my revenge was come! I drank in the sweetness of the moment and almost forgot his presence.

'Speak Cynthia!' He begged me, holding my hand. 'Tell me you love me... and will marry me!'

It was then I laughed. Laughter filled the room. His hurt and surprised expression made me laugh all the harder. He must have thought I was going mad. It was a dry, hoarse laugh that, I am sure, was not reflected in my hate-filled eyes.

'Love you! Me love you? Never! I shall never love a man again! They'll give me their hearts and I'll wring all the love and blood out of them! Go! Go you poor foolish man! Go, for your purpose is over and you must give way to another! I shall have my full revenge! Ah, revenge is sweet; isn't it, Henry?' And I looked up to the photo of my old Henry hanging on the wall.

He slunk out of the house. I never saw him again. He left that evening on some pretext that his mother in Pretoria was ill. And he never came back.

He was only the first. Many others followed.

There was Jerry Lerato, the young and temperamental medical student from the university, who would come all the way from Johannesburg as often as he could to see me. I heard he almost committed suicide when I told him off. There was the jealous Danny Mahlaba, who nearly throttled me to death ... oh, there were many; and they all went the same way. I made quite a reputation for myself. And I thought I was happy. My bitter heart took in all these men's heartbreaks as a sweet salve for my own once-broken heart.

Then he came to our location. Jeffery Modise. He came from Pretoria like my first 'lover', and he also came here to teach. He was a quiet, kind and handsome young man who had a few of the girls gossiping.

I met him formally when he had been a month here. It was at a birthday party. We were introduced, and he was very nice to me. He was so gentle, and his eyes shone with confidence and understanding of the world's troubles; not mine, though, I thought.

He'd heard about me, of course, but during the weeks that followed he didn't act like he had. He, I thought, with everybody else who noticed, was to be my next victim!

We saw a lot of each other, and had quite a bit in common. For the first month he visited me often at home, and we would sit and discuss films, books, songs, politics and any other subject under the sun we knew anything about. Anything but love, because he never mentioned it or acted like any of my past victims.

In the second month he began taking me out to the bioscope in Johannesburg and to parties and other functions. I liked him and respected him; but I would not stop from treating him the same as the others at the end! All men were like Henry; and they all had to suffer.

He began to follow the usual line, suggesting we go to community picnics. But this was going to be different, I thought. He had wasted a lot of time already; I would have to push him on to his destruction. I refused to go to these, and suggested that instead we take my gramophone, our favourite records and a few other things that would make a 'picnic for two' enjoyable.

With a funny look in his eyes, he agreed.

I wore a tight, little sleeveless jacket and a round-pleated skirt with sandals. I had always drawn attention with this outfit before, and hoped it would help me catch this different fish faster.

We went by train to Witpoortje. It could have been a most enjoyable picnic if I hadn't been scheming all the time. With the passing hours I would playfully wrestle with him and press my soft body into his. We played cards for kisses, but he only gave me light smacks on the cheek — and I made sure I lost often so I could get a chance to complete the temptations with my lips.

But no. He wouldn't be tempted. Some moments I would think he was breaking, but he would pull himself together and just smile his funny smile.

We had a few more picnics like this one until I became annoyed. How could a young man like him resist my temptation so long? I began asking myself. Is there anything wrong with him — or with me?

Then one day, after two months of sulking and refusing most of his dates, he suggested we go for a late-afternoon walk into the hills behind the location. Ah, I thought, now he is beginning to miss our picnics. Today I shall surely thaw him out!

We walked hand in hand into the hills, talking of anything — but love. We sat and watched the sun set over the silvery mine dumps. We sat and watched the moon come up from the east. We lay side by side in the tall grass ...

Everything was perfect for romance. And he began reciting love-poems for me; softly and in a rhythmic voice that almost made me forget my scheming. I caressed his arm, and he would now and again pat my hand ... They were beautiful poems, and he said them marvellously. He said them fluently in his dreamy voice, and a feeling began taking hold of me. My face slowly and unconsciously moved closer to his, and I only realised this when he moved his away.

That almost spoiled the evening, but he went on in that dreamy voice as if nothing had happened. At last we stood up to go. He stood holding me round the waist, and, looking at the sky with a smile on his face, said a poem by Byron I slightly knew. These lines I still remember:

Though the night was made for loving,
The day returns too soon ...

The sword outwears its sheath,
And the soul (or was it heart?) wears out the breast ...

Then we walked home saying very little. I had lost all idea of time, and scarcely knew my own home when we got there. At the gate, he stopped and, turning me towards him said, 'Good night, Cyn. It was a lovely evening.'

'Yes,' I heard my voice stammer. 'It was.'

My face was looking up at him, and I thought he was going to kiss me; but with that funny smile that was now familiar he said 'good night' and walked away.

I thought a lot about him from that night. Unknowingly I was beginning to yearn for his kisses, his embraces and love. But they were not for me, it seemed.

About a month later we went out on another stroll. This time he did not talk much, and I hardly noticed the glances he stole at me. I was yearning for him with my whole body. I had many times been angry with myself for this, but now with him so near me I could not resist the yearning wiping everything else out of my mind. If only he would kiss me!

We sat again under the moon and stars. Tonight he did not recite love poems. Instead he sang me two songs: 'Cynthia' and 'Blue Moon.' He began with 'Cynthia', which had a special meaning for me, I later found out. The lines which go

Cynthia ... I'm glad your lovely dream came true,
For I'm the boy who worships you ...
My Cynthia's in love ... and so in love!

still ring in my ears every time he smiles at me.

'Blue Moon' was the climax. When he came to

And then there suddenly appeared before me,
Someone my arms could never hold.
And then somebody whispered 'Please forgive me,'
And when I looked up, the moon had turned to gold!

he stopped and looked up at me with a smile full of love.

'Will you forgive me, Cynthia?' he asked.

'What?' I heard my voice ask.

His answer was to sweep me into his arms and kiss me ... I never before in my life returned a kiss with such power; the power of my whole yearning body. He loves you, he loves you raced through my mind. And I knew I loved him, too!

He had been too clever for me. I had started out to steal his heart, but he had instead stolen mine by creating a curiosity that turned into a longing, yearning and love in me.

And now I am the proud, and no more hard-hearted, mother of his son. OUR son!

BERTHA GOUDVIS

The Apostasy Of Carlina

from *The Mistress Of Mooiplaas And Other Stories* (1956)

Carlina was the prize girl of the Roumelian Mission.

The Roumelians were the only sect sufficiently enterprising to build a Native church in our village, and when the Reverend Nansen, a meek little man with a big wife, came to take charge of it there was some excitement in Native circles. The other denominations were only represented by Bantu evangelists and these were not of much account in the opinion of the neighbouring heathen.

Carlina was once a member of another church, represented in our village by a Native preacher named Penyati. His wife had the habit of organizing tea parties when members and their friends could have light refreshments and the joy of singing hymns in unison for the payment of one shilling. At one of these affairs Mrs Penyati had affronted Carlina, so the girl went over to the Roumelians after the Nansens came to start their Mission.

The Nansens were pleased with their convert, for Carlina was a well conducted girl and possessed the unusual qualification of a sweet soprano voice. She led the choir in a manner which gave the little mission church quite a musical reputation, and her attendance at church and class was regular and punctual.

Mrs Parsons, the storekeeper's wife, who employed Carlina, was proud of her maid and often remarked that although she did not hold with missionaries as a rule she really believed that they had made a Christian of Carlina.

This happy state of affairs lasted for quite a long time. Carlina had no followers and was decorum personified. She was a quiet girl and seldom had much to say for herself, a fact on which Mrs Parsons commented with pleasure. Then Mangwani, the dashing Native police sergeant, was seen to be hanging around the girl. His fine figure, smart uniform and swaggering gait had won the hearts of many maidens, but no one thought that he had a chance with Carlina. He used to attend the girl on her way from evening classes, but it was not until their friendship had continued for some weeks that we noticed it, although there was already much gossip and innuendo about the pair in Native circles.

Some time elapsed before the state of affairs was brought to Mrs Parsons' notice. I went into the store one day and found her leaning over the counter in earnest talk with the missionary's wife. She said to me by way of explanation: 'We're talking about Carlina and that sergeant fellow. You never heard of such goings-on. I saw them last night through the kitchen window. He was sitting down on one of my chairs with his arm round her waist, and she was plaiting his beard for him. You know those spiky little plaits he has sticking round his chin. I marched straight in but never said a word — just stood there and looked at them. Then Carlina gave a silly sort of laugh and moved away and began to wash up the supper things which were still lying dirty on the table. He stood up and said "Inkosigaas." Then I let them have it. "Well I never thought it of you Carlina, a decent Christian girl like you," I said. "You know he's a married man, and very much married, too," I said. "We all know he's got two wives already, and a fine lot of piccaninnies." ' She stopped for a moment to get her breath.

Mrs Nansen looked much disturbed. 'And what did Carlina say to all that?' she enquired.

'She only giggled and went on with the washing up — never a word did I get out of her. He stood there, pulling at those little plaits of beard and then I gave it to him hot. "You get out of my kitchen," I said, "and leave my girl alone. Go back to the wives you've got already and let them plait your beard for you. If you come into my house again the Baas will give you sjambok." '

'Did he understand all that?' asked Mrs Nansen.

'Did he understand?' rejoined Mrs Parsons with scorn. 'He understood what I meant by sjambok, for out he slunk without a word, and if he comes with his games in my kitchen again, sjambok he'll get, if I have to give it to him myself.'

When Mrs Parsons stood like that, with her hands on her hips and her black eyes alight, she looked as if she meant it.

'I've always hoped that Carlina would marry one of our evangelists,' said Mrs Nansen. 'She seemed so fond of her religion and anxious to lead a Christian life. Of course, we knew her father wouldn't let her go without getting the cattle for her, but when one of our men marries he pays for his wife just like any other Native — but they get married in Church and live like Christians afterwards, and he knows that he can never take another wife. My husband and I will talk to Carlina. She knows that Mangwani has two wives already, and I hope she will have no more to do with him.'

One evening a week later we were having a quiet game of bridge with the schoolmaster and the magistrate's clerk, who had dropped in for a rubber, when there came the sound of psalm singing from the kitchen.

'I wish you would make them stop that caterwauling,' remarked the head of the house with some irritability. I had put down a dummy of which the highest card was the knave of diamonds, but if he would persist in a no-trump call without assistance he had only himself to thank.

I went down the corridor to the kitchen, where I found Carlina and my own maid, Maria, busy with their sewing, singing as they worked. From the chair in the corner rose the stalwart form of the sergeant of police, with his hand raised in salute.

A fine soldierly fellow was this Mangwani in his smart uniform. The firelight shone on his brass buttons and the buckles of his broad leather belt. I wondered whether our sex's well-known predilection for a uniform extended to the demure Carlina. She was bending attentively over her work, her head bound with a scarlet kerchief. Maria was brown-complexioned with a squat nose and thick lips, but Carlina was as dark as night, with finely chiselled features. As she sat there in her clean light frock and scarlet doek I admired her myself. I told them that the Baas was not inclined for music that evening. They were all so well behaved that I saw no reason for further interference, but the next day I remarked to Maria that considering the much-married state of the sergeant I was surprised that Carlina encouraged him. Maria said that she was surprised too, and thought that the sergeant must have put the tagata on her friend.

'Why Maria, I thought that you, a Christian girl, did not believe in such nonsense,' I exclaimed, but Maria only shrugged her shoulders.

A few days later Mrs Parsons stopped me in the street.

'What do you think?' she said. 'Carlina's given me notice.'

'Has she really?'

'That she has. She says she is sick and wants to go home, but it's all nonsense. I've heard that story before. I've given her castor oil and Epsom salts and made her a mustard plaster, but there's no gratitude in them. She's never been the same since I turned Mangwani out of the kitchen and it's my opinion that she's no better than the rest of them, although she always seemed so meek and mild.'

A few weeks later Maria told me that she had heard bad news of Carlina. 'She's going to be married,' she continued.

'But there is nothing so dreadful about that,' I said.

'But she is going to marry the sergeant, and missis knows that he's got two wives already. He has given Carlina's father five cows and he must give five more. Carlina will be no more Christian girl, for Christian girl can't marry man with wives.' Maria went on to say that the missionary people were very sorry about Carlina. They had talked to her but she wouldn't listen. She would only listen to Mangwani.

I knew then that the mission church would soon lose its soprano. I saw Carlina with the sergeant in the Parsons' store one morning. They were buying beads at the Native counter. Carlina still wore civilized attire and seemed quite unabashed. She showed all her ivory teeth as she bade me good morning. The sergeant lolled over the counter pulling his little plaits of beard. Mrs Parsons at the opposite counter sniffed audibly, but Carlina did not seem to mind. It was Mrs Parsons who described the final scene of Carlina's apostasy.

'I went to see the wedding for I've always wanted to see a Native wedding as you know, but something always came between. This one was nearby — just down the hill. It happened on a Sunday, too, so I tramped down there with the old man. Such a crowd you never saw — all dancing and going on like mad. The girls were on one side, naked most of 'em as God made them, save for a tiny bit of petticoat and a string of beads, but some were togged up fine, with coloured handkerchiefs or striped towels and thing-um-me-bobs in the hair. The men danced opposite them. I felt queer at first to see all those naked savages twirling their shields and assegais. They had rows and rows of little cones round their ankles, and after jumping and dancing they would take a tremendous leap and come down with a bound, and all the cones would clatter. It was a sight, I can tell you. And there was Carlina in the middle of the girls, holding a big knife, and going on like any savage of them all. To think that was the decent quiet girl who used to go so regular to church and sing in the choir. I only wish the Nansens had been there to see her. Then there came along three big fellows with great black feather things on their heads, and the middle one was Mangwani himself, the scamp. He looked very different from what he does in uniform, and then he started to leap about and enjoy himself. I suppose the other wives were looking on and the children, too. A fine crowd, the lot of them. Well, I wonder what Mrs Nansen thinks of her Christian girls now? And what I'm to do, the Lord only knows, for that Topsy isn't a bit of good — as lazy as they make 'em and cheeky too. I'll never get another girl like Carlina.'

SARAH GERTRUDE MILLIN

A Pair Of Button Boots

from *Two Bucks Without Hair And Other Stories* (1957)

Some time ago Alita brought me a letter to read to her. Alita is my native cook and I am her secretary. This is the letter:

To Mrs Alita Itumeleng
From Miss Emily Itumeleng
My Dear Mother
I am taking this short delightful for to acknowledge to you about my life on earth I am still well under the mercy of our Lord No complains indeed about me. Hoping to hear the same from you
Oh mammy I am shame for the people I have no close to wear All the girls is got bottanes boots I go naked Oh mammy you did say you will give me a piano Please send bottanes boots

Your everlasting child
MISS EMILY ITUMELENG

PS Big size 5

Let me say at once that the opening paragraph of Miss Emily's letter is a formula which means nothing. But the letter itself, the second tightly packed paragraph, might not suffer by a little annotation. For instance, 'bottanes' boots — what are 'bottanes' boots? And what is all this about a piano?

I will explain.

Alita, on her salary, which is not as large as that of, say, the latest cinema favourite, supports the following:

Her aged mother, the guardian of her family.
Her son, Sydney, in the fourth standard.
Her daughter, the aforesaid Miss Emily, aged eighteen.
Miss Emily's daughter, Josephine.
Mr No Pass, who has no other name but Mr No Pass because, as Alita

remarked at the time, he came into the world without a pass.

And Mr No Pass's baby sister.

These last two are the offspring of a sister of Alita's who has recently taken a new husband and discarded the fruits of former unions. Alita has also a brother, who having gone to the German war with the Native Labour Contingent has now come back consumptive. And then she has a crippled husband.

Alita herself was sent to me from Bloemfontein. I was to recognise her on Johannesburg station by a red rosette. I had been led to expect a light-coloured graduate from a domestic school. But a dark, middle-aged woman with red cheeks and anxious eyes, was leaning well out of a third-class window, and her bosom was covered with an enormous arrangement in red.

That was Alita — a pioneer to the Rand, where wages are great and passes for females non-existent.

On the first of every month Alita takes her whole earnings to the post-office and sends them to her mother. Her own needs are met by tips and perks. An occasional gift, and a commission on what she can dispose of to old clothes men, on the one hand; and the sale of bones, papers and bottles, on the other hand. Lately, by the way, the fluctuations in the bottle market — from a penny to sixpence, and suddenly down to threepence again — have greatly upset Alita's equilibrium. She had been holding six bottles against a rise. When the market dropped to threepence, she had obstinately refused to let go her stocks. And now, as I warned her, she would, in the way of all gamblers, go on holding them until they were practically worthless again ...

During the last few months all these profits had been going to swell a certain fund. We called it the shawl fund.

2

It was like this:

On Sundays all Alita's friends wear to church a black cashmere shawl with long, elegant fringes. Among them walked Alita, clad only in her blue dress with the little white spots. You would never have guessed from her gallant bearing and animated conversation that she was suffering great shame. But Alita's animation was only the pride of defiance.

She had explained it to me with passion (I am translating from our medium of Afrikaans).

'It is not right for a woman of my age to go like this (she drew up her unshawled shoulders) to church. All the other women are dressed as married women should be dressed. Only I go meanly in the face of the world.'

Poor Alita! In twenty years of married life she had never attained the dignity of a black cashmere shawl. And this although she had once got as far as buying one. But then she had ended by giving it to her mother, who had accidentally burnt her own. And her further savings had always found an outlet elsewhere.

It was after this outburst of Alita's that we hit on the special shawl fund idea. On the day she received this letter from Miss Emily the fund stood at thirty-seven shillings. A black cashmere shawl of passable quality, with fair fringes, could, in those times, be obtained for not less than forty shillings.

Forty shillings was our mark.

3

But I still have to explain away that letter.

For instance, the piano. You would hardly think that Alita was in a position to buy pianos. Nevertheless, a piano is one of Miss Emily's most constant demands. I suppose it must have reference to some old childhood promise: 'If you are good, I will give you a piano.'

But, unfortunately, neither in the conventional nor in any other sense has Miss Emily been 'good'. There is, to begin with, the matter of Josephine. Josephine is not an authorised version ...

And about the 'bottanes' boots.

I have known now for a long time that high button boots are to the young native girl of Bloemfontein what furs and diamonds are to the favourites of the footlights. They are not only a possession, they are a symbol. In the native location in Bloemfontein high button boots stand for smartness, for affluence, for social position.

But in those days of leather-shortage, to demand 'bottanes' boots!

Alita almost wept.

'But, Alita,' I remonstrated, 'it's so hot in Bloemfontein. Emily doesn't really need high button boots.'

'Missis,' said Alita despairingly, 'all the girls will have high button boots for Christmas. Only my child must go about like an orphan because her father is broken and her mother must be the man of the family. As I sit here, the only one among all the women without a black shawl, so Emily must sit naked in the house while her friends go around in button boots.'

Knowing the Christmas weather in Bloemfontein, I myself would have preferred not only metaphorical, but actual, nakedness to high button boots; but it was not a question of comfort, it was a matter of principle. Meat was dear, meal was prohibitive, money had not half its ordinary value, but Miss Emily had to have bottanes boots. So much, at least, had European culture taught her.

4

And Alita was being torn by a double sorrow. Constant demands for bottanes boots for Christmas (or, alternatively, a piano). A sudden cessation in the letters of the consumptive brother.

And then there came a letter from Miss Emily which set her on fire.

If Miss Emily did not get bottanes boots in time for Christmas, she would sell the baby!

'But what nonsense!' I said.

'No,' said Alita, 'she means it. She will sell the baby. And who will carry water for me in my old age?'

'But she can't sell the baby. No one would buy it.'

Alita shook her head. Who was I to understand the charms of Josephine, the temptation she might be to someone?

Next day she came to me, haggard.

'I want the money, missis.'

'What for, Alita?'

'For the boots.'

'Oh, Alita, not *that* money.'

'Yes, please, missis.'

I refused peremptorily.

'The shawl money? No!'

Another few days passed.

And then I came upon Alita weeping silently in a corner.

'What is it, Alita?' I asked. But, of course, I knew.

'All the girls will go to church in stiff white dresses — wip, vip' (unconsciously Alita swaggered her shoulders and hips) '— with high button boots, and my child will stay naked at home. Oh, missis, give me the money.'

I brought it out.

'Here, take it. But I am angry with you, Alita.'

Alita was smiling through her tears. She handed me the money back.

'Missis must buy the boots, please. For thirty-seven shillings. Let it be the best boots in Johannesburg!'

Little Alita knew the price of best boots in Johannesburg! But I got her some wonderful boots, for all that. Not only with buttons, but with four holes to lace at the top as well.

Alita was delighted. She tried them on in front of a wardrobe looking-glass.

'Such boots no other girl in Bloemfontein has,' she sighed with satisfaction.

'But, Alita, your shawl?'

'God will send it,' said Alita. But her voice lacked conviction.

5

And yet — He did send it!

There came a wire, a letter, a parcel. The wire was from Cape Town. The consumptive brother of the Labour contingent, lost, unheard of, was on his way home. To die; but we did not know that at the time.

A few days later came a letter and a parcel from Bloemfontein.

And, in the parcel was a shawl, with long, long fringes.

Alita threw it over her shoulders, and walked from the kitchen to the fowl-run, turning her body from side to side in deliberate triumph.

'I will wear this to church on Christmas Day. And thank the Lord that he sent back my brother. And all the women will say "Aie-e, Alita!" '

She put her head against the glory of her shoulder.

'My everlasting brother!' she said, in English, in deepest tenderness. 'My everlasting brother!'

NADINE GORDIMER

Good Climate, Friendly Inhabitants

from *Not For Publication* (1965)

In the office at the garage eight hours a day I wear mauve linen overalls — those snappy uniforms they make for girls who aren't really nurses. I'm forty-nine but I could be twenty-five except for my face and my legs. I've got that very fair skin and my legs have gone mottled, like Roquefort cheese. My hair used to look pretty as chickens' fluff, but now it's been bleached and permed too many times. I wouldn't admit this to anyone else, but to myself I admit everything. Perhaps I'll get one of those wigs everyone's wearing. You don't have to be short of hair, any more, to wear a wig.

I've been years at the garage — service station, as it's been called since it was rebuilt all steel and glass. That's at the front, where the petrol pumps are; you still can't go into the workshop without getting grease on your things. But I don't have much call to go there. Between doing the books you'll see me hanging about in front for a breath of air, smoking a cigarette and keeping an eye on the boys. Not the mechanics — they're all white chaps of course (bunch of ducktails they are, too, most of them) — but the petrol attendants. One boy's been with the firm twenty-three years — sometimes you'd think he owns the place; gets my goat. On the whole they're not a bad lot of natives, though you get a cheeky bastard now and then, or a thief, but he doesn't last long, with us.

We're just off the Greensleeves suburban shopping centre with the terrace restaurant and the fountain, and you get a very nice class of person coming up and down. I'm quite friends with some of the people from the luxury flats round about; they wouldn't pass without a word to me when they're walking their dogs or going to the shops. And of course you get to know a lot of the regular petrol customers, too. We've got two Rolls and any amount of sports cars who never go anywhere else. And I only have to walk down the block to Maison Claude when I get my hair done, or in to Mr Levine at the Greensleeves Pharmacy if I feel a cold coming on.

I've got a flat in one of the old buildings that are still left, back in town. Not too grand, but for ten quid a month and right on the bus route ... I was married once and I've got a lovely kid — married since she was seventeen and living in Rhodesia; I couldn't stop her. She's very happy with him and they've got twin boys, real little toughies! I've seen them once.

There's a woman friend I go to the early flicks with every Friday, and the Versfelds' where I have a standing invitation for Sunday lunch. I think they depend on me, poor old things; they never see anybody. That's the trouble when you work alone in an office, like I do, you don't make friends at your work. Nobody to talk to but those duckies in the workshop, and what can I have in common with a lot of louts in black leather jackets? No respect, either, you should hear the things they come out with. I'd sooner talk to the blacks, that's the truth, though I know it sounds a strange thing to say. At least they call you missus. Even old Madala knows he can't come into my office without taking his cap off, though heaven help you if you ask that boy to run up to the Greek for a packet of smokes, or round to the Swiss confectionery. I had a dust-up with him once over it, the old monkey-face, but the manager didn't seem to want to get rid of him, he's been here so long. So he just keeps out of my way and he has his half-crown from me at Christmas, same as the other boys. But you get more sense out of the boss-boy, Jack, than you can out of some whites, believe me, and he can make you laugh, too, in his way — of course they're like children, you see them yelling with laughter over something in their own language, noisy lot of devils; I don't suppose we'd think it funny at all if we knew what it was all about. This Jack used to get a lot of phone calls (I complained to the manager on the quiet and he's put a stop to it, now) and the natives on the other end used to be asking to speak to Mpanza and Makiwane and I don't know what all, and when I'd say there wasn't anyone of that name working here they'd come out with it and ask for Jack. So I said to him one day, why do you people have a hundred and one names, why don't these uncles and aunts and brothers-in-law come out with your name straight away and stop wasting my time?' He said, 'Here I'm Jack because Mpanza Makiwane is not a name, and there I'm Mpanza Makiwane because Jack is not a name, but I'm the only one who knows who I am wherever I am.' I couldn't help laughing. He hardly ever calls you missus, I notice, but it doesn't sound cheeky, the way he speaks. Before they were allowed to buy drink for themselves, he used to ask me to buy a bottle of brandy for him once a week and I didn't see any harm.

Even if things are not too bright, no use grumbling. I don't believe in getting old before my time. Now and then it's happened that some man's taken a fancy to me at the garage. Every time he comes to fill up he finds some excuse to talk to me; if a chap likes me, I begin to feel it just like I did when I was seventeen, so that even if he was just sitting in his car looking at me through the glass of the office, I would know that he was waiting for me to come out. Eventually he'd ask me to the hotel for a drink after work. Usually that was as far as it went. I don't know what happens to these blokes, they are married, I suppose, though their wives don't still wear a perfect size fourteen, like I do. They enjoy talking to another woman once in a while, but they quickly get nervous. They are businessmen and well off; one sent me a present, but it was one of those old-fashioned compacts, we used to call them flapjacks, meant for loose powder, and I use the solid kind everyone uses now.

Of course you get some funny types, and, as I say, I'm alone there in the front most of the time, with only the boys, the manager is at head office in town, and the other white men are all at the back. Little while ago a fellow came into my office wanting to pay for his petrol with Rhodesian money. Well, Jack, the boss-boy, came first to tell me that this fellow had given him Rhodesian money. I sent back to say we didn't take it. I looked through the glass and saw a big, expensive American car, not very new, and one of those men you recognize at once as the kind who move about a lot — he was poking out his cheek with his tongue, looking round the station and out into the busy street like, in his head, he was trying to work out his way around in a new town. Some people kick up hell with a native if he refuses them something, but this one didn't seem to; the next thing was he got the boy to bring him to me. 'Boss says he must talk to you,' Jack said, and turned on his heel. But I said, you wait here. I know Johannesburg; my cash-box was there in the open safe. The fellow was young. He had that very tanned skin that has been sunburnt day after day, the tan you see on lifesavers at the beach. His hair was the thick streaky blond kind, waste on men. He says, 'Miss, can't you help me out for half an hour?' Well, I'd had my hair done, it's true, but I don't kid myself you could think of me as a miss unless you saw my figure, from behind. He went on, 'I've just driven down and I haven't had a chance to change my money. Just take this while I get hold of this chap I know and get him to cash a cheque for me.'

I told him there was a bank up the road but he made some excuse. 'I've got to tell my friend I'm in town anyway. Here, I'll leave this — it's a gold one.' And he took the big fancy watch off his arm. 'Go on, please, do me a favour.' Somehow when he smiled he looked not so young, harder. The smile was on the side of his mouth. Anyway, I suddenly said okay, then, and the native boy turned and went out of the office, but I knew it was all right about my cash, and this fellow asked me which was the quickest way to get to Kensington and I came out from behind the desk and looked it up with him on the wall map. I thought he was a fellow of about twenty-nine or thirty; he was so lean, with a snakeskin belt around his hips and a clean white open-neck shirt.

He was back on the dot. I took the money for the petrol and said, here's your watch, pushing it across the counter. I'd seen, the moment he'd gone and I'd picked up the watch to put it in the safe, that it wasn't gold: one of those Jap fakes that men take out of their pockets and try to sell you on streetcorners. But I didn't say anything, because maybe he'd been had? I gave him the benefit of the doubt. What'd it matter? He'd paid for his petrol, anyway. He thanked me and said he supposed he'd better push off and find some hotel. I said the usual sort of thing, was he here on a visit and so on, and he said, yes, he didn't know how long, perhaps a couple of weeks, it all depended, and he'd like somewhere central. We had quite a little chat — you know how it is, you always feel friendly if you've done someone a favour and it's all worked out okay — and I mentioned a couple of hotels. But it's difficult if you don't know what sort of place a person wants, you may send him somewhere too expensive, or on the other hand you might recommend one of the small places that he'd consider just a joint, such as the New Park, near where I live.

A few days later I'd been down to the shops at lunch hour and when I came by where some of the boys were squatting over their lunch in the sun, Jack said, 'That man came again.' Thinks I can read his mind; what man, I said, but they never learn. 'The other day, with the money that was no good.' Oh, you mean the Rhodesian, I said. Jack didn't answer but went on tearing chunks of bread out of half a loaf and stuffing them into his mouth. One of the other boys began telling, in their own language with bits of English thrown in, what I could guess was the story of how the man had tried to pay with money that was no good; big joke, you know; but Jack didn't take any notice, I suppose he'd heard it once too often.

I went into my office to fetch a smoke, and when I was enjoying it outside in the sun Jack came over to the tap near me. I heard him drinking from his hand, and then he said, 'He went and looked in the office window.' Didn't he buy petrol? I said. 'He pulled up at the pump but then he didn't buy, he said he will come back later.' Well, that's all right, what're you getting excited about, we sell people as much petrol as they like, I said. I felt uncomfortable. I don't know why; you'd think I'd been giving away petrol at the garage's expense or something.

'You can't come from Rhodesia on those tyres,' Jack said. No? I said. 'Did you look at those tyres?' Why should *I* look at tyres? 'No-no, you look at those tyres on that old car. You can't drive six hundred miles or so on those tyres. Worn out! Down to the tread!' But who cares where he came from, I said, it's his business. 'But he had that money,' Jack said to me. He shrugged and I shrugged; I went back into my office. As I say, sometimes you find yourself talking to that boy as if he was a white person.

Just before five that same afternoon the fellow came back. I don't know how it was, I happened to look up like I knew the car was going to be there. He was taking petrol and paying for it, this time; old Madala was serving him. I don't know what got into me, curiosity maybe, but I got up and came to my door and said, how's Jo'burg treating you? 'Ah, hell I've had bad luck,' he says. 'The place I was staying had another booking for my room from today. I was supposed to go to my friend in Berea, but now his wife's brother has come. I don't mind paying for a decent place, but you take one look at some of them ... Don't you know somewhere?' Well yes, I said, I was telling you that day. And I mentioned the Victoria, but he said he'd tried there, so then I told him about the New Park, near me. He listened, but looking round all the time, his mind was somewhere else. He said, 'They'll tell me they're full, it'll be the same story.' I told him that Mrs Douglas who runs the place is a nice woman — she would be sure to fix him up. 'You couldn't ask her?' he said. I said well, all right, from my place she was only round the corner, I'd pop in on my way home from work and tell her he'd be getting in touch with her.

When he heard that he said he'd give me a lift in his car, and so I took him to Mrs Douglas myself, and she gave him a room. As we walked out of the hotel together he seemed wrapped up in his own affairs again, but on the pavement he suddenly suggested a drink. I thought he meant we'd go into the hotel lounge, but he said, 'I've got a bottle of gin in the car,' and he brought it up to my place. He was telling me about the time he was in the Congo a few years ago, fighting for that native chief, whats's-name — Tshombe — against the Irishmen who were sent out there to put old what's-name down. The stories he told about Elisabethville! He was paid so much he could live like a king. We only had two gins each out of the bottle, but when I wanted him to take it along with him, he said, 'I'll come in for it sometime when I get a chance.' He didn't say anything, but I got the idea he had come up to Jo'burg about a job.

I was frying a slice of liver next evening when he turned up at the door. The bottle was still standing where it'd been left. You feel uncomfortable when the place's full of the smell of frying and anyone can tell you're about to eat. I gave him the bottle but he didn't take it; he said he was on his way to Vereeniging to see someone, he would just have a quick drink. I had to offer him something to eat, with me. He was one of those people who eat without noticing what it is. He never took in the flat, either; I mean he didn't look round at my things the way it's natural you do in someone else's home. And there was a lovely photo of my kid on the built-in fixture round the electric fire. I said to him while we were eating, is it a job you've come down for? He smiled the way youngsters smile at an older person who won't understand, anyway. 'On business.' But you could see that he was not a man who had an office, who wore a suit and sat in a chair. He was like one of those men you see in films, you know, the stranger in town who doesn't look as if he lives anywhere. Somebody in a film, thin and burnt red as a brick and not saying much. I mean he did talk but it was never really anything about himself, only about things he'd seen happen. He never asked me anything about myself, either. It was queer; because of this, after I'd seen him a few times, it was just the same as if we were people who know each other so well they don't talk about themselves any more.

Another funny thing was, all the time he was coming in and out the flat, I was talking about him with the boy — with Jack. I don't believe in discussing white people with natives, as a rule, I mean, whatever I think of a white, it encourages disrespect if you talk about it to a black. I've never said anything in front of the boys about the behaviour of that crowd of ducktails in the workshop, for instance. And of course I wouldn't be likely to discuss my private life with a native boy. Jack didn't know that this fellow was coming to the flat, but he'd heard me say I'd fix up about the New Park Hotel, and he'd seen me take a lift home that afternoon. The boy's remark about the tyres seemed to stick in my mind; I said to him: That man came all the way from the Congo.

'In that car?' Jack said; he's got such a serious face, for a native. The car goes all right, I said, he's driving all over with it now.

'Why doesn't he bring it in for retreads?'

I said he was just on holiday, he wouldn't have it done here.

The fellow didn't appear for five or six days and I thought he'd moved on, or made friends, as people do in this town. There was still about two fingers left in his bottle. I don't drink when I'm on my own. Then he turned up at the garage just at the time I knock off. Again I meant to look at the tyres for myself, but I forgot. He took me home just like it had been an arranged thing; you know, a grown-up son calling for his mother not because he wants to, but because he has to. We hardly spoke in the car. I went out for pies, which wasn't much of a dinner to offer anyone, but, as I say, he didn't know what he was eating, and he didn't want the gin, he had some cans of beer in the car. He leaned his chair back with all the weight on two legs and said, 'I think I must clear out of this lousy dump, I don't know what you've got to be to get along here with these sharks.' I said, you kids give up too easy, have you still not landed a job? 'A job!' he said. 'They owe me *money*, I'm trying to get *money* out of them.' What's it all about, I said, what money? He didn't take any notice, as if I wouldn't understand. 'Smart alecks and swindlers. I been here nearly three lousy weeks, now.' I said, everybody who comes here finds Jo'burg tough compared with their home.

He'd had his head tipped back and he lifted it straight and looked at me. 'I'm not such a kid.' No? I said, feeling a bit awkward because he never talked about himself before. He was looking at me all the time, you'd have thought he was going to find his age written on my face. 'I'm thirty-seven,' he said. 'Did you know that? Thirty-seven. Not so much younger.'

Forty-nine. It was true, not so much. But he looked so young, with that hair always slicked back longish behind the ears as if he'd just come out of the shower, and that brown neck in the open-neck shirt. Lean men wear well, you can't tell. He did have false teeth, though, that was why his mouth made him look hard. I supposed he could have been thirty-seven; I didn't know, I didn't know.

It was like the scars on his body. There were scars on his back and other scars on his stomach, and my heart was in my mouth for him when I saw them, still pink and raw-looking, but he said that the ones on his back were from strokes he'd had in a boys' home as a kid and the others were from the fighting in Katanga.

I know nobody would believe me, they would think I was just trying to make excuses for myself, but in the morning everything seemed just the same, I didn't feel I knew him any better. It was just like it was that first day when he came in with his Rhodesian money. He said, 'Leave me the key. I might as well use the place while you're out all day.' But what about the hotel, I said. 'I've taken my things,' he says. I said, you mean you've moved out? And something in his face, the bored sort of look, made me ask, you've told Mrs Douglas? 'She's found out by now,' he said, it was unusual for him to smile. You mean you went without paying? I said. 'Look, I told you I can't get my money out of those bastards.'

Well, what could I do? I'd taken him to Mrs Douglas myself. The woman'd given him a room on my recommendation. I had to go over to the New Park and spin her some yarn about him having to leave suddenly and that he'd left the money for me to pay. What else could I do? Of course I didn't tell *him*.

But I told Jack. That's the funny thing about it. I told Jack that the man had disappeared, run off without paying my friend who ran the hotel where he was staying. The boy clicked his tongue the way they do, and laughed. And I said that was what you got for trying to help people. Yes, he said, Johannesburg was full of people like that, but you learn to know their faces, even if they were nice faces.

I said, you think that man had a nice face?

'You see he has a nice face,' the boy said.

I was afraid I'd find the fellow there when I got home, and he was there. I said to him, that's my daughter, and showed him the photo, but he took no interest, not even when I said she lived in Gwelo and perhaps he knew the town himself. I said why didn't he go back to Rhodesia to his job but he said Central Africa was finished, he wasn't going to be pushed around by a lot of blacks running the show — from what he told me, it's awful, you can't keep them out of hotels or anything.

Later on he went out to get some smokes and I suddenly thought, I'll lock the door and I won't let him into the flat again. I had made up my mind to do it. But when I saw his shadow on the other side of the frosty glass I just got up and opened it, and I felt like a fool, what was there to be afraid of? He was such a clean, good-looking fellow standing there; and anybody can be down on his luck. I sometimes wonder what'll happen to me — in some years, of course — if I can't work any more and I'm alone here, and nobody comes. Every Sunday you read in the paper about women dead alone in flats, no one discovers it for days.

He smoked night and day, like the world had some bad smell that he had to keep out of his nose. He was smoking in the bed at the weekend and I made a remark about Princess Margaret when she was here as a kid in 1947 — I was looking at a story about the Royal Family, in the Sunday paper. He said he supposed he'd seen her, it was the year he went to the boys' home and they were taken to watch the procession.

One of the few things he'd told me about himself was that he was eight when he was sent to the home; I lay there and worked out that if he was thirty-seven, he should have been twenty in 1947, not eight years old.

But by then I found it hard to believe that he was only twenty-five. You could always get rid of a boy of twenty-five. He wouldn't have the strength inside to make you afraid to try it.

I'd've felt safer if someone had known about him and me but of course I couldn't talk to anyone. Imagine the Versfelds. Or the woman I go out with on Fridays, I don't think she's had a cup of tea with a man since her husband died! I remarked to Jack, the boss-boy, how old did he think the man had been, the one with the Rhodesian money who cheated the hotel? He said, 'He's still here?' I said no, no, I just wondered. 'He's young, that one,' he said, but I should have remembered that half the time natives don't know their own age, it doesn't matter to them the way it does to us. I said to him, wha'd'you call young? He jerked his head back at the workshop. 'Same like the mechanics.' That bunch of kids! But this fellow wasn't cocky like them, wrestling with each other all over the place, calling after girls, fancying themselves the Beatles when they sing in the washroom. The people he used to go off to see about things — I never saw any of them. If he had friends, they never came round. If only *somebody* else had known he was in the flat!

Then he said he was having the car overhauled because he was going off to Durban. He said he had to leave the next Saturday. So I felt much better; I also felt bad, in a way, because there I'd been, thinking I'd have to find some way to make him go. He put his hand on my waist, in the daylight, and smiled right out at me and said, 'Sorry; got to push on and get moving sometime, you know,' and it was true that in a way he was right, I couldn't think what it'd be like without him, though I was always afraid he would stay. Oh he was nice to me then, I can tell you; he could be nice if he wanted to, it was like a trick that he could do, so real you couldn't believe it when it stopped just like that. I told him he should've brought the car into our place, I'd've seen to it that they did a proper job on it, but no, a friend of his was doing it free, in his own workshop.

Saturday came, he didn't go. The car wasn't ready. He sat about most of the week, disappeared for a night, but was there again in the morning. I'd given him a couple of quid to keep him going. I said to him, what are you mucking about with that car in somebody's back yard for? Take it to a decent garage. Then — I'll never forget it — cool as anything, a bit irritated, he said, 'Forget it. I haven't got the car any more.' I said, wha'd'you mean, you mean you've sold it? — I suppose because in the back of my mind I'd been thinking, why doesn't he sell it, he needs money. And he said, 'That's right. It's sold,' but I knew he was lying, he couldn't be bothered to think of anything else to say. Once he'd said the car was sold, he said he was waiting for the money; he did pay me back three quid, but he borrowed again a day or so later. He'd keep his back to me when I came into the flat and he wouldn't answer when I spoke to him; and then just when he turned on me with that closed, half-asleep face and I'd think, this is it, now this is it — I can't explain how finished, done-for I felt, I only know that he had on his face exactly the same look I remember on the face of a man, once, who was drowning some kittens one after the other in a bucket of water — just as I knew it was coming, he would burst out laughing at me. It was the only time he laughed. He would laugh until, nearly crying, I would begin to laugh too. And we would pretend it was kidding, and he would be nice to me, oh, he would be nice to me.

I used to sit in my office at the garage and look round at the car adverts and the maps on the wall and my elephant ear growing in the oil drum and that was the only place I felt: but this is nonsense, what's got into me? The flat, and him in it — they didn't seem real. Then I'd go home at five and there it would all be.

I said to Jack, what's a '59 Chrysler worth? He took his time, he was cleaning his hands on some cotton waste. He said, 'With those tyres, nobody will pay much.'

Just to show him that he mustn't get too free with a white person, I asked him to send up to Mr Levine for a heachache powder for me. I joked, I'm getting a bit like old Madala there, I feel so tired today.

D'you know what that boy said to me then? They've got more feeling than whites sometimes, that's the truth. He said, 'When my children grow up they must work for me. Why don't you live there in Rhodesia with your daughter? The child must look after the mother. Why must you stay here alone in this town?'

Of course I wasn't going to explain to him that I like my independence. I always say I hope when I get old I die before I become a burden on anybody. But that afternoon I did something I should've done long ago, I said to the boy, if ever I don't turn up to work, you must tell them in the workshop to send someone to my flat to look for me. And I wrote down the address. Days could go by before anyone'd find what had become of me; it's not right.

When I got home that same evening, the fellow wasn't there. He'd gone. Not a word, not a note; nothing. Every time I heard the lift rattling I thought, here he is. But he didn't come. When I was home on Saturday afternoon I couldn't stand it any longer and I went up to the Versfelds and asked the old lady if I couldn't sleep there a few days, I said my flat was being painted and the smell turned my stomach. I thought, if he comes to the garage, there are people around, at least there are the boys. I was smoking nearly as much as *he* used to and I couldn't sleep. I had to ask Mr Levine to give me something. The slightest sound and I was in a cold sweat. At the end of the week I had to go back to the flat, and I bought a chain for the door and made a heavy curtain so's you couldn't see anyone standing there. I didn't go out, once I'd got in from work — not even to the early flicks — so I wouldn't have to come back into the building at night. You know how it is when you're nervous, the funniest things comfort you: I'd just tell myself, well, if I shouldn't turn up to work in the morning, the boy'd send someone to see.

Then slowly I was beginning to forget about it. I kept the curtain and the chain and I stayed at home, but when you get used to something, no matter what it is, you don't think about it all the time, any more, though you still believe you do. I hadn't been to Maison Claude for about two weeks and my hair was a sight. Claude advised a soft perm and so it happened that I took a couple of hours off in the afternoon to get it done. The boss-boy Jack says to me when I come back, 'He was here.'

I didn't know what to do, I couldn't help staring quickly all round. When, I said, 'Now-now, while you were out.' I had the feeling I couldn't get away. I knew he would come up to me with that closed, half-asleep face — burned as a good-looker lifesaver, burned like one of those tramps who are starving and lousy and pickled with cheap booze but have a horrible healthy look that comes from having nowhere to go out of the sun. I don't know what that boy must have thought of me, my face. He said, 'I told him you're gone. You don't work here any more. You went to Rhodesia to your daughter. I don't know which place.' And he put his nose back in one of the newspaper he's always reading whenever things are slack; I think he fancies himself quite the educated man and he likes to read about all these blacks who are becoming prime ministers and so on in other countries these days. I never remark on it; if you take any notice of things like that with them, you begin to give them big ideas about themselves.

That fellow's never bothered me again. I never breathed a word to anybody about it — as I say, that's the trouble when you work alone in an office like I do, there's no one you can speak to. It just shows you, a woman on her own has always got to look out; it's not only that it's not safe to walk about alone at night because of the natives, this whole town is full of people you can't trust.

E.N. JONSSON

The Silent Song

from *The Silver Sky And Other Stories* (1974)

You may think it odd, that I who so loved Aunt Julie, should have been the cause of her death; and yet, looking back through the years to our brief companionship, I can see all the happiness we had together leading to that strange fulfilment — as though it was right that I, the only human being she had ever loved, should have given her her freedom.

The farm at M'Mahlope was a grim place when I arrived there as a little boy of nine after the sudden death of my parents in an accident. My grandparents lived alone save for poor Aunt Julie — the only child left to them. Disheartened by their long struggle to wring a meagre living from their almost barren land bordering the Kalahari Desert which year by year inched its relentless way into the farm, they had grown like the land, dour and uncompromising, and at the death of my father, their only son, they had withdrawn even deeper into their tight-lipped silence. Though to them Aunt Julie was alien — her simpleness a punishment meted out to them by a stern God for some unknown crime they had committed — to me, a frightened little boy, she spelled enchantment — an escape from the terrifying realities of life at M'Mahlope. The desolate little house with mud floors and a sagging roof, was a place of unbelievable horror to me whose short life had been spent in the soft green midlands of Natal where my father had been employed in a factory in the little town of Lowick. Noise had surrounded me. The perpetual blare of the radio which my mother switched on as she dressed in the morning — the shouts of children in the nearby cottages — the rush of cars on the main road a few yards away and the wail of the factory siren. Noise to me meant security, and the silence of this vast desert world paralysed me.

Aunt Julie must have been about thirty when I arrived at the farm, and though she could neither read nor write, the ways of the animals, the birds and the flowers were an open book to her. She showed me the tiny flowers that blossomed un-noticed in crevices of the rocks, taught me to quench my thirst during our long walks by eating the wild tsama melons as the animals did, and taught me to understand the signs of weather changes by watching the flight of the birds in a torrid sky.

Sometimes, in a burst of resentment, my grandparents would give her a hoe telling her harshly to go and work instead of idling — then her eyes would grow dark with bewilderment as she walked to the maize field, dragging the hoe behind her, her beautiful bare feet scuffing listlessly in the dust. Then — suddenly — a bird or a butterfly would catch her eye and work would be forgotten.

The hours that I spent walking with Aunt Julie in that desert world are still fresh in my memory. We would walk for miles, stopping each yard or so to examine fresh wonders — spiders' webs bright with dew drops, hanging from the twisted bushes — the footprints of hares and mice and tortoises across the sandy paths, a lizard bright eyed and watchful, sunning itself on a stone — and looking up we watched the birds flying in formation across the sky, and she told me the ways of them all, though she knew few of their names.

Life was so simple for Aunt Julie. 'We will take a tin with us when we go out this morning,' she would say sometimes, 'The honey bird is going to lead us to honey ...' She was always right — as soon as we got out of sight of the house we would find a honey guide waiting for us impatiently, and as it saw us it would fly to us and then flutter on ahead, looking back anxiously and calling with an odd chattering cry which changed to a contented chirping as we reached the bee's nest, and Aunt Julie lit little twists of grass to smoke the bees out. She always shared the honey carefully, putting a comb containing grubs on a branch for the little bird who watched us so anxiously from a short distance, 'We must always share, Davey,' she said, smiling at my eagerness and the bird's bright-eyed watchfulness.

In that arid and drought-stricken country where the river beds were sandy wastes during the greater part of the year, and the buck and other wild animals lived on the tsama melons and the only water that we had was dragged from a deep and reluctant borehole, rain was the most important thing in life. A week after a good rain the whole of the land under the scrub bushes was covered with luxuriant grass growing inches in an hour; and so, at the first sign of clouds gathering in the distance, hopes ran high and anxious eyes watched the horizon. I remember one day when the purple storm clouds were banking over the brooding desert and the darkened sky was split by vivid lightning as the thunder rolled and echoed from the stony hills, my grandmother called out to us as we set out to walk to the river bed, 'The rains are coming — you must not go out,' she called. It was the first time I had heard any emotion in her flat monotonous voice, but Aunt Julie shook her head. I can see her now, standing there against the sombre background, her flute-like voice clear above the thunder, her face showing surprise and bewilderment, 'But the rains are not coming,' she said, 'They will not come for many days,' and I can see too my grandmother's face as life and hope left it. She knew that Aunt Julie spoke the truth, and yet at that moment I think she hated her. She turned without a word and went back into the dreary little tumble-down house, and Aunt Julie and I continued on our way.

A week or two later when we were returning, under a cloudless sky, from one of our expeditions, Aunt Julie stopped suddenly and clapped her hands, 'The rains are coming — the rains are coming,' she sang, and like leaves in an autumn breeze we danced home, her slim legs and arms dryadlike against the background of brown earth and scrub bushes, her pale hair floating out round her paler face which neither the harsh winds of the Kalahari nor the scorching sun could ever burn.

Often at dusk we watched the spring hares come out of their holes which they had dug deep underground. First a nose would appear, then two great eyes, then like a jack-in-the-box the spring hare would leap straight up into the air. 'Why does he jump so high when he comes out of his hole?' I asked, the first time I saw this happen. And aunt Julie's eyes filled with tears, 'He is afraid of leopards and jackals and people — he is afraid of people ...' I saw a slow tear trickle down her cheek and I put my hand into hers, 'You are afraid of people too — aren't you?' I asked and she nodded her head in silence. One evening when we were sitting watching the sunset deepening from orange to scarlet over the Kalahari and the spring hares silhouetted against the horizon were dancing with wild abandon, I saw that she was swaying, her bare feet moving in the hot dry sand as though she too was dancing with them. 'What are you doing Aunt Julie?' I asked impatiently and she looked at me in wonderment, 'Can't you hear the music Davey? Can't you hear the music and the singing? Listen carefully ... listen ... listen Davey ...' But no music came to me, I could only hear the sighing of the evening breeze and the distant hooting of an owl.

'But *who* do you hear? Who sings and plays the music?' I persisted, and she looked round before she answered in a low whisper, 'The little golden people — this land belongs to the little golden people, Davey.' We looked at each other guiltily because this was a subject that my grandparents would never allow her to mention. At the words 'Little golden people,' my grandfather would frown at her angrily, 'You are lying Julie,' he would say sternly, 'There are *no* little golden people,' —

then the shut out look of fear and bewilderment would come into her dark eyes and she would cover her mouth with her hands as though afraid that words might slip out in spite of her fear, and with bent head she would sit trembling until something happened to catch her vagrant attention — a dancing sunbeam or a bumble bee — it needed so little to bring the gentle smile back to her pale face.

We were sitting by the dry river bed one morning, leaning against the warm trunk of the baobab tree, watching a tortoise crawl slowly up the bank, when I asked her suddenly about the golden people, '*Who* are they Aunt Julie?' I asked urgently. 'Who are the little golden people — why mustn't you talk about them?' She looked round as though she feared that even in that lonely spot my words could be heard; and sat in silence for several minutes, dragging reluctant thoughts from her shadowed brain, then she got up with a sudden determination quite foreign to her. 'Come and I will show you something,' she said, and very quietly we began to walk up a small stony hill. As we neared the top she stopped as though undecided whether to go on or not. She stood looking down over the flat country studded with scrub, broken only by the winding rift of the dry river bed and a thin column of smoke rising from the farm house chimney. I think in some way the smoke made her uneasy, recalling to her troubled mind her parents and some words or orders of theirs which she could never remember clearly for very long. She sighed and brushed her eyes with her hand, then turning, led me to a spot where the overhanging rocks made a natural shelter.

'Look up Davey,' she said, and looking up I cried out in amazement at the paintings of eland and giraffe and leaping buck pursued by a dozen or more small running figures, whilst in a corner, as though forgotten in the chase a zebra turned its striped neck in amazement.

I remembered then that my father had shown me a similar picture in an old magazine and had told me that there were pictures just like that in a rock shelter on his father's farm, and that they had been painted by Bushmen many years ago before the farmers had killed them all for stealing their cattle, 'But these are Bushmen paintings Aunt Julie — my father told me about them — he said there were some on the farm — Bushmen painted them.'

'Bushmen,' she repeated vaguely, 'Why do you call them Bushmen Davey? They live in caves ...'

'But they don't live anywhere now Aunt Julie,' I persisted, 'They have all been killed.'

Her pale face grew paler still and her eyes widened with horror, 'Oh no Davey, don't say that — please don't say that — they are here always, the little golden people, when I come here alone they talk to me and play their music for me — who would kill my little golden people Davey — who would do this — no, no, Davey, no, no . . .'

Seeing her so distraught I was afraid and hastened to comfort her in the only way that I could think of, 'The Bushmen are dead Aunt Julie,' I said, 'Only the Bushmen — not your little golden people —' though in my heart I knew the two were the same. 'Bushmen,' she said her face clearing, 'I don't know about Bushmen Davey;' she repeated the unfamiliar name several times then she smiled, her fears forgotten as she noticed a bat hanging dimly high up in a corner of the shelter. 'Look at his wings Davey,' she said, 'they are folded so close now but when night comes they will open so wide — so wide — as he flies away to look for his supper', and as she spoke she stretched out her arms as though she too would fly away.

There was a gossamer air of unreality about Aunt Julie and I held her dress tightly in my hand half afraid that like the bat and the birds she loved so well she would spread her wings and fly away from me . . .

We often went to the shelter after that, though we never mentioned it to my grandparents, and I came to believe that some of the little people must still be alive as she talked about them so often, dancing to the music that I could never hear, and singing me the songs that she had learned from them during all the lonely years before I came to M'Mahlope. The paintings covered the whole of the flat rock which roofed the shelter and the facing of the rock on the right of the entrance, but a small rock on the left was smooth and bare. 'I wonder why they did not paint pictures on this rock too Aunt Julie?' I asked and she answered without hestitation that they would one day, 'One day we will come here and find a picture Davey,' she said. I half believed her but as the weeks passed without anything happening, I lost interest and was no longer disappointed when we came to the shelter and found the stone bare.

We always came home before darkness fell and I think my presence eased some worry from my grandparents' shoulders — they were thankful to know that their strange and elfin daughter was no longer always alone, and thankful too that she seemed able to provide me with the companionship they were too old and discouraged to give me.

We had finished our supper of mealie-meal porridge and milk one evening and my grandfather was reading a chapter from the Bible which ended each day for us, when I heard Aunt Julie, who had slipped unnoticed from the room, singing softly outside the window. She was singing one of the little high-pitched haunting songs with a monotonous refrain which I heard her sing so often when we were alone, and as I looked up in surprise I caught the look of fear that passed between the old people, and my grandmother got up stiffly and hurried from the room, her veldschoens flapping softly on the earthern floor. My grandfather and I sat waiting tensely until a moment later she returned, leading Aunt Julie, white and tearful by the hand. After the Bible reading they led her to her room and I heard the sound of the bolt on the outside of her door being fastened and Aunt Julie's terrified sobbing as she beat on the door begging to be released ...

'Let her out — please let Aunt Julie out,' I begged, her terror of confinement attacking me as I looked at the set faces of my grandparents and heard her frantic screams above the frenzied beating of her fists on the door. My grandfather rose to his feet and put his hand on my shoulder, 'Go to bed Davey,' he said sternly, 'This is none of your business — go to bed.'

My stretcher was on the verandah, and long after I lay down I heard Aunt Julie's terrified sobbing and the beating of her hands on the door, but only when I heard the sound of my grandparents' snores did I dare to move. The brilliant moonlight flooded the country with a light almost as bright as day as I crept to her room and with shaking fingers drew the bolt of the door aside. She was standing there paler than ever in the moonlight coming through the barred window, shaking from head to foot, her hands clasped to her mouth — like a wraith she slid past me and through the open door into the living room and out across the yard. For a moment I hesitated, terrified at what I had done, then I ran out after her and caught her up as she turned down the path that led across the river bed and on towards the hill. As I reached her she turned and smiled, the events of the last hour already forgotten — 'I always love the moonlight Davey — I always love the moonlight' she said and began to sing again the song she had sung outside the window. Years later I realised that my simple grandparents had been terrified of what they thought was 'Moon madness' and so would never allow her to go out if they could prevent it, but I know that it was only the fact that everything was bright outside — like daylight — that made her so restless; she could never bear to be in the house when it was light outside.

It was the first time in my life that I had been out in the moonlight and I was amazed to see that the whites and in the dry river bed had turned to silver, and that the baobab cast long shadows although there was no sunshine. We felt the warmth of the tree's garnered sunshine as we sat down and leaned against the great trunk, and watched an owl float past us on muted wings — the moonlight turning his eyes to bright lanterns. We sat there for some time and then I burst into tears, overcome by the night's happenings and the loneliness of the desert spread out before us, 'I want my mother,' I sobbed.

Aunt Julie took my hand in hers hesitantly. Any display of affection was hard for one who had been rebuffed through all her timid childhood. She hated to see me cry, but to her the word 'Mother' conjured up a grim figure whose grudging care had not concealed her impatient dislike. She sighed — bewildered — unable to respond to an emotion she herself had never experienced. We sat for a long time until my sobs subsided and then we started off again without speaking, across the river bed and up the path towards the Bushman shelter.

Aunt Julie saw the leopard first. It was lying on a high rock near the entrance to the shelter, its coat luminous in the moonlight.

'Look Davey,' she said over her shoulder as she walked forward slowly, 'Look how beautiful.' I am sure that nothing would have happened if she had been alone — no animal was afraid of her, but sensing my alien presence it stiffened, looking right past her to me — a growl rumbling in its throat ... Then I screamed and it launched itself into the air ... It must have been the first time in her life that Aunt Julie acted quickly — some primitive instinct of protection made her throw herself in the animal's path, and as I turned to run I saw her thin arms go round its neck and saw her fall to the ground with the weight of its body and heard her scream as her head hit the rock at the left of the entrance.

Panic fear gripped me as I ran screaming down the path, and when I eventually reached home it was some time before my hysteria subsided enough for me to tell my grandparents what had happened. Woken so suddenly from their sleep they tried to soothe me and piece my story together, and after they had dressed hurriedly, my grandfather's hands trembled so much that he found it difficult to load the rifle he had not used for so long a time.

I went with them — afraid to go but still more afraid to remain alone in the house, and we hurried over the rough ground the silence broken only by my sobbing and the harsh breathing of the old couple. As we rounded the corner near the top of the hill, we found Aunt Julie lying with her arms stretched out just as she had stretched them when she showed me how the birds and the bats flew. Her pale hair was spread out on the ground and her lips were parted in a smile of utter peace and contentment. The leopard had not mauled her and her death had been caused by the force with which her head had struck the rock as she fell. We knelt beside her, a stricken group, and then I rose to my feet and looked down on the old couple kneeling there in silent tears — 'She has gone — she has gone —' I sobbed, 'You can never shut her up again — Aunt Julie has gone away — you can't shut her up any more ... Aunt Julie has gone away ...'

* * *

My grandparents sent me away to a distant relative shortly afterwards — they could not bear to have me near them after what had happened and I myself was so distraught with loneliness that I must only have been a burden to them. It was forty years before I visited M'Mahlope again as my grandparents had died soon after Aunt Julie and the farm was sold to a neighbouring farmer — the small sum going towards giving me a start in life. It was a long way from where I had been educated and made my life and for years I had no reason to go there though I had always had a longing to return to the country that Aunt Julie had loved so well, and so, being by an unexpected chance on business in that district, I got permission from the owners to go over the old farm.

The house had long since disappeared into the ground from which it had sprung, but the baobab tree still stood near the river bank. I walked up and laid my hand on it, but the warmth had gone from it and my questing hand was covered with a soft grey powder — the tree was disintegrating and soon the hot winds would scatter its dust to mingle with the harsh sands of the Kalahari. I walked over the familiar ground thinking of Aunt Julie, and yet I felt no sadness, only a strange feeling of fulfilment. Each yard of the way held memories for me — this was her country — here she had lived and here she had died — quickly and mercifully amongst all the things that she had loved — What terrible fate would have been hers if she had outlived her parents? At the thought of what she had been spared I felt only gratitude that I had been guided to do what I had done that night so long ago — to open the door for her and give her her freedom.

When I reached the rock shelter I stood as I had stood so often with her, looking down over the dry river bed and the vast waste of the desert, then I turned and went into the shelter and looked again at the drawings of the animals — the buck and giraffe and the zebra and all the little running figures and I remembered her talking of 'The little golden people.' As I left the shelter I glanced at the rock whose smooth surface had been left untouched, and there, painted in pale yellow ochre, was the crude figure of a woman — a woman with pale hair flowing round her face — and hands of the same pale colour stretched out stiffly towards the flying figure of a leopard leaping towards her in mid-air . . .

I can give no explanation at all. People thought that all the Bushmen round there had been wiped out years ago, my grandfather having played a major part in the slaughter when he was quite a young boy. Whether a small elusive band had survived, or whether it was only the spirits of the little golden people with whom Aunt Julie had communed, learning their long forgotten songs, who had returned to pay her a last tribute, I do not know. All I know is that there on the rock is the picture of her as I had seen her last — with her arms outstretched to save me.

The painting was crude but the slender elongation of the arms gave the impression of wings, and I remembered how often she had spread her arms in pretence of flying, and how, when I had seen her lying dead, my anguish had been more for my own loss than for her dying — young as I was then I had sensed a strange feeling of release — that with outstretched arms and pale hair flying, Aunt Julie had escaped and was happy listening to a silent song and dancing to an unheard tune . . .

SHEILA ROBERTS

The Touch of Your Hand

from *Outside Life's Feast* (1975)

January. Perspiration and diesel fumes. Old suspected-dead emotions waft into consciousness bringing restlessness and tension. But in the crowded lunch-time streets of Johannesburg one is only aware of a fleeting pulse-ache, like the conditioned tightening of muscles under an unpredictable robot which one is not really concentrating on. Memories come and disappear, disturbing like the traffic, but not experienced with the full being until an ache with multiple throbbing points insists on attention. It screams like an insanely driven motor-cycle along the congested highways where memories travel to and fro between the unconscious and full awareness. Because it is January my carapace of indifference constructed over years cracks; the weak places in its walls make me shiver. I am sensitive to eyes looking in, to questions. Living is a torture of anticipating pain.

But these undermining memories will recede, because that is according to their very nature — they must recede to return; then when they go my armour pieces together and imperviousness reassures me. Like the dried branch in the vase of blooms, I do not exude, express or visibly alter. I am I, integrated, unified, unadaptable, separated from my own kind. It is desires which make human beings secrete those sticky filaments which adhere to others, until they tangle each other with a miriad infinitesimal tentacles. When I am not remembering I do not desire. But while my nerves still feel jellied from the influence of the memory, I must relive.

I am again too young to fit with ease into an unpliable adult world. I walk the same streets, see without seeing the same haze and prying sunlight flatten the contours and fade the colours of Eloff Street. The lunch-hour pedestrians are again to me like automatons controlled by their wrist-watches and sensitive to the changing flashes of the traffic lights. I hate them because they seem hostile and I, not quite eighteen, am going to have a child, so I am told.

When I am alone I squeeze and knead my abdomen with my hands to find this thing — pregnancy. But my body feels the same. I am not sick in the mornings nor have I put on weight. It is too soon, of course. In any case, I have only the doctor's word. Yet I am changed. I wonder whether the soul of the minute blob of mucus within me is clinging monkey-like to my own soul, making it shrivel and droop under the burden. I tell myself that the explanation must be that my soul is too undeveloped as yet, like my mind and body, and that it cannot support this parasite. I weep for us, but only down my throat, swallowing the tears like one swallows catarrh.

So as to escape the inactivity and my own kneading hands, I walk. I walk each day from one to two in the afternoon, and when the flats of Hillbrow look phantasmal, the only time of the day that they do, at about seven-thirty in the evening. They become tinged with peach and turquoise and the lights are crisp and stellular, even promising. That part of my brain which registers tunes repeats mournfully 'Oh, star of wonder'. The faces of the people milling in the streets buying bread, milk and food in plastic bags are softened. I try to compose explanations to the conglomeration of cells with me why I cannot be its mother. I try to convince myself that it is only a conglomeration of cells, but I cannot. Its father is trying to arrange to have me 'fixed up', he calls it. When I see him and he spews words which hover in the air, unabsorbed by my mind because their meaninglessness renders them impermeable and solid, I am emptied of all feeling, retaining only this potential infant and its adhesive soul. I look at him. He is frightened but mouths manfully and I see a vision of a tiny spidery-limbed creature clinging, clinging.

In order to inject some reality into my visions, I buy a book containing diagrams illustrating the stages of growth of the foetus. The little monkey creature of my nightmares now assumes the face of a chameleon with blue-lidded eyes and bulging temples.

Somehow, with help from pals, he arranges it. An ageing doctor in an older suburb agrees to examine me, which he does without the usual rubber glove. As I lie on the stretcher, which is covered with only a blanket, with my knees wide, I imagine the minute creature protests as it is prodded. The slight pain makes me nauseous. As I sit up, aware of my vaselined loins, the yellow glare of the consulting room, like slime on my retinas, causes my body to cool rapidly and to sweat. The instruments under the glass casing look so well used, that I look around for disposal bins, trying to visualize their interiors, filled with bloody swabs and foetuses.

The old doctor gives me an injection designed to budge pregnancies. If not, two more will follow. He blows his nose. The gesture is too human, and I must reassess him, but the incongruity causes my diaphragm to jerk with amusement. The alchemist's cave of steaming sterilizers and framed, hanging formulas cannot rationally be the haunt of a little, bald, moustached daddy with a maroon striped tie. It is too absurd.

At home I dry the dishes automatically, drugged by my mother's chatter and my own repetitive inner life droning in silent vociferousness, droning, droning ... will get you out of it water surrounded for forty weeks ...

Don't take two at a time; they'll slip life felt at fourteen weeks don't worry just about every fellow I know my responsibilities

Must get the man to see the washing machine so much vaseline why no sheet often injections do the trick

All you do is dream little hands claw hanging on not easy to kill how many already in bin I didn't mean this to happen a fellow can make a slip all steaming needles and pliers stab it out

Never hear a word I say worse than birth I've heard injection burning

Hurry with those forks, then just wipe the sink must walk to think ... think ...

The injections are not effective. Nor are the tablets he laid hands on through a friend of a friend. I lie unmoving in bed listening to the last cars howl round the corner and watching the sliding light patterns formed by the headlights on the ballooning curtain. My brain seems to toss and turn as the images follow now in succession now jumbled idiotically together — sometimes a slug-like creature beating off with tiny flippers the noxious fluids injected into my system which threaten to drown it; its tenacious adherence to my innards; sometimes the ordinary face of the doctor shining jaundiced under the tubular lights, and the hot, roaring, hooting, jamming, beating streets, hot and throbbing, hot like the gusts which bloat the curtains, like the wet dishes in my sweating hands and like my head.

He has the money the doctor demanded and we go for the fourth time to the smudged and shabby consulting room. He stays in the car. It is early evening, long-shadowy. Workers returning home communicate their relief to the air and to the conforming poplars growing out of circular spaces in the pavements, but not to me. There are no patients in the waiting room, only a white-overalled woman reading a periodical, who nods me towards the consulting room without even focusing her eyes in interest. I am hardly able to walk normally, but shift my legs forward, left, right, left, right; they have lost all obedience to my brain. Only my wet hands and tight throat assure me that I am alive. The doctor is peering into the bubbling box, extracting long steely things. I mumble something about trying further injections but my voice dries up like a burning leaf and I taste the ashes as I obey the doctor's instructions.

It is not really painful like a beating or a burn, but I try to stop the room from swaying by clutching the sides of the stretcher bed. Whatever is inside me is being jabbed with efficient cruelty and I tell it sorry sorry sorry. I don't know that I am crying until the doctor tells me to sit up and I find that my cheeks and ears are wet. I have an unbearable impulse to grab the doctor with my clawing hands but I am too weak. I stand and my knees wobble because my bones and muscles are transformed into some foul liquidity which oozes through my pores and rocks my stomach. I succeed in reaching the door by concentrating desperately on reproducing the familiar walking movements by means of memory and will.

He starts the car when he sees me and we drive several blocks in silence. He puts his hand on mine and I look at his face to mark the surprise and disgust he must register as a result of contact with my skin. I feel I am encased in a moist, tough sheath like a reptile. There is no reaction. That was the first time that I noticed with bewilderment that my quivering, repelled response to human contact was not perceived by the other person. As these occasions increased in number over the years, my bewilderment decreased and I tried to reduce these tactile experiences. Now I have ensured their complete discontinuance. I know my carapace is invisible and intangible, but it is so sensitive to touch, and triggers off an internal nausea so uncontrollable, that I want always to be alone.

It is dark when I arrive at our Berea flat. My mother is annoyed because she has had to delay dinner for me. She says I am all she has, so she encourages herself to be eternally irritated by me. We sit at table and I try hard to eat and listen, but my attention is like a floodlight turned on my uterus. My eyes search through mental pictures for the right one, but they cannot escape a *mise en scène* of a dark, spongy cavern with porous walls containing a mangled ball of membrane-covered spittle. My mother lectures me for my frequent absences, my lack of affection for her, my pallor. Too frequent outings at night will undermine my health, she says, and it's not right for a girl just out of school, so I promise her to stay in more often. I need not have promised as I soon found that staying in was the easiest way to avoid other people and their bodies, no matter how brief or slight the contact was.

I half awake from sleep, my consciousness held back by a dream of mud, cold and sucking, in which I am sitting, playfully rolling my legs. I try to lift myself out of it, but am drawn back with clammy insistence.

Then I wake completely knowing that my thighs and the sheets are wettish, more gummy than liquid. I switch on the lamp and examine what looks like chewed, raw liver, which is smeared here and there. I leap horrified to the floor, holding my nightie well up and keeping my legs apart. I am so frightened I cannot act practically. I am praying, praying that I will not see IT or parts of IT. I cannot bear to see it; I will go insane with horror and remorse. I hobble to the toilet and sit there, pressing, pressing, and continually flushing the water. I am out of my mind because the little thing must be dead and its remains are leaving me reluctantly. I am crying noisily, crazily, like a child about to have a fit, and can only scream go away, go away, when my mother's pale, puckered face looks into the lavatory, her eyes unadapted to the light, wide, innocent and disturbed.

'What's the matter, are you sick?'

'Yes, sick. Go away, will you!'

She withdraws slowly and I hold back my raucous wheezing to listen for the direction of her slippered footfalls. She seems to be hesitating as she flip-flops up the passage. She stops and moves on, then stops again. I clench my jaw and fists in shame as I understand that I must have splotched blood in the passage. I rise, flush the toilet without looking, and follow her to my room. She is looking at my sheets.

'Sit down. No, lie down, dear.' She seems worried and pitying.

'Tell Mom all. Who did this to you?'

'This?'

'Tell me who the swine is. I suppose he thought you have no one to defend you just because your father's dead, well ...'

'Defend me? What are you talking about?' I lie back helpless in an overwhelming sensation of distance. My own mother is like a monstrous talking toy, wound up, and repeating well-worn phrases.

'You can't say I didn't warn you about men *and* warned you to be careful. You know what they are. And, I told you, no decent man will marry a girl that's ... Did he take you to a midwife? I hope *you* didn't have to pay anything.' Then she brushes my hair off my forehead tenderly and I wince.

'No, it was a doctor. Please just forget about it Mom, it's all over.' I am lying. It will never be over. I wish it was only a nightmare, but because she is there I know it is not. She gets up to fetch her eternal cigarettes. I turn my face to the wall and long for oblivion to shut out the recurring visions. All the diagrams I had gazed at float before my eyes. I ache to cradle the funny tadpole body with its large head in my hands. The smell of nicotine helps me back and I try to listen to what she is saying.

'Why didn't you tell me before? It always helps to confide in someone, especially your own mother, you know. It's not a nice thing to go through. I know, I know. Ah, you are surprised, I can see. Well I have been through it, twice in fact. You can't teach your mother anything. Your poor father never wanted children you know; said the world was too wicked. I was going to take you away too, but then he had that accident and I couldn't think straight after that, and then it was too late. But the second one was already three months. Imagine how sore that was, and then it was nearly formed. A perfect little boy.'

I try to sit up. I must get out of the room. For the love of God, leave me, I beg her. My face must frighten her, because she gets up and leaves the room telling me to call her if I want anything.

I creep along the wall back to the lavatory and then gaze in the basin, which is clear. I am going mad and cannot stop myself because of the thought that IT is rushing along the sewers with all the filth. My little one.

Now, I live alone, so does my mother, but she has her friends. People I work with think I am odd. Perhaps I am. Mostly I do not suffer, but when the summer is at its fiercest I cannot retain my normal, comforting emptiness, and seem to fill inwardly with a pain-infused kernal too large for my shell to contain. I also cannot bear to see small babies, especially their little fists, and always cross the road if I see a pram-wheeling mother approach. At night in January, I lie awake, without bedclothes, gazing at the curtain which is sometimes sucked against the burglar guards and sometimes bunched joyfully out.

CHERRY CLAYTON

Sisters

from *Quarry '78–'79* (1979)

She had first seen Sarah running along the road outside the new house, along the high eastern ridge of Johannesburg which dipped into steep tree-filled valleys on both sides. She was running and singing in an aimless way, when, conscious of the knot of white people gathered outside the front gate and speaking about her, she turned her head to give them her full, white-toothed, ridiculously happy smile. She was very young.

'Please look after Sarah,' said the woman who was moving out, in a spasm of warmth, confidingly, 'we've grown so fond of her.'

'Of course we will,' said Alice, a little annoyed that the request should be considered necessary. Were they not most evidently a liberal, even faintly radical, couple?

So they settled down together, Alice and Brian adapting to the shape and feel of the cool, old-fashioned house, living in their careless, untidy way; Sarah in the small white-washed room behind the garage, with pictures torn off calendars, a scrap of lace curtain, and an old chest of drawers littered with lotions and skin-lighteners. Once a month a tiny old Jewish merchant arrived at the back-door with a magic suitcase crammed with pills, laxatives, remedies, cheap jewellery, potions and creams. Sarah and the old man would squat with equal interest over the open suitcase, absorbed as children, haggling. Afterwards Alice would tease her about buying love-potions. Her only answer was to laugh, but it was a full enough reply. She and Alice liked each other, though they seldom spoke. Alice left her domestic rituals intact, which gave a familiar pattern to the week, became the grid on which their lives rested.

There was not much housework. Sarah stuffed the washing in a big damp bundle into the passage cupboard, put Brian's socks in Alice's wardrobe, and left her duster forgetfully in odd corners, while she played with the kittens. Sometimes she spoke to Alice in her high sweet elocution about her friends, her brothers and sisters, her plans for further education. She seemed happy.

Then things changed. They began to have burglaries at the house, which opened onto the street on two sides, over long dark stretches of lawn, and a frail fence. Besides, they were careless. They left windows open. There was no burglar proofing or alarm, standard equipment for the other houses in the areas. Sometimes, as Alice was in the act of closing a window, the wail of a neighbouring burglar alarm would begin, a blood-chilling siren as inhuman as the police siren it was meant to summon, like two mating banshees speeding avidly toward each other for a mechanical fuck. She would pause at the window, frozen in the moment of the shriek. Often there was complete silence afterwards; whoever attended to the alarm, or cared if it had been accidentally sounded, remained a mystery.

Their own burglaries were frequent: their clothing disappeared out of cupboards; they would come home and find an empty wardrobe, a swinging door, and the vague, lingering unease of another presence in the house, the smell and shadow of the burglar.

One night Alice was woken by a repeated scream, and she met Sarah in the passage as she was still pulling on a dressing-gown. She was shaking; her face was paler than any skin-lightener would ever make it. Her head was unfamiliar without her usual scarf or beret. She oozed terror. It was a strong smell about her; she had brought the raw fear of the backyard into the house.

'Call the master ... call the master. It was a man. In my room. He had his hands on my neck ...' She put her own hands to her throat in imitation and protection, reviving her terror. She shivered uncontrollably. Alice and Brian calmed her, told her to sleep in the spare room. They searched the back garden. Nothing but a breeze, ruffling glimmering night-time shrubbery.

The next day Alice bought steel bars to protect the window of the outside room. It was a bright, still autumn day. Peace lay thick on the ground with the fallen leaves, which Alice had raked into brittle, shifting heaps. She stood on a rickety kitchen chair in the tiny room. Her husband stood next to the chair, steadying it, passing her the nails, occasionally putting his hand up between her legs to caress the skin of her thighs, or the pout of female flesh higher up. She giggled and dropped the hammer. They were happily childish together while they did the work. It was not a very good job. But it would keep out intruders.

There seemed to be no further trouble. No more burglaries, no more night-time visitors. Things became peaceful again. A year later Alice and

Brian moved away, to a house in the north of Johannesburg. Sarah did not want to leave her family and friends, so they said good-bye, told her to visit. Occasionally she did, for a formal tea-time call, sitting on her hands on a dining-room chair, asking one by one after the family, later after Alice's little boy when he was born, a special visit then with a rattle of pink and blue plastic, two hemispheres joined by a rough ridge. Then the visits tailed off. They had been uncomfortable occasions.

About a year later, dropping into the busy, preoccupied stream of their lives, Sarah arrived at the kitchen door. She seemed to have grown heavier, the girlish outline blurred by an older, thicker shape. She wanted a job. 'All right,' said Alice, tired of a series of temporary servants who never spoke in the house or looked at her, hating her as much as she was irritated by them.

The little boy got on with Sarah, though she was not as playful as before, and the open gaiety of her face had gone.

A few weeks after she had started work, she came into the sitting-room where Alice sat reading. She obviously had something to say.

'Do you know I'm going to have a baby?' she said, smiling in embarrassment. 'No Sarah,' said Alice, taken aback. How could she not have noticed? She thought, guiltily, that she seldom really looked at Sarah properly. Now she did.

'Can I have the baby while I'm here?' she said, very nervously. Now Alice understood it all: why she had come back, why she had waited a while before speaking, why she had left the other job, why she was standing there now in an agony of self-consciousness, twisting her skirt in her hand. And with understanding, suddenly throwing its broadening, retrospective light on how much had been concealed, out of fear, came a pang for a life led in such anxious dependency, moving in and out of strange backyards in a maze of motives and needs largely thwarted and unfulfilled. It was a moment of pure sympathy: 'Of course you can stay. Of course you can have the baby here.'

Later she thought, in a more generalized pang: so much for the barred window, for the girlish terror, and felt some of the sadness attendant on all breakthroughs of that kind, of barred windows, of the veined membrane of flesh that protects the soft, dark, inner chamber from the male intruder.

The sympathy did not last very long as Sarah became more pregnant, subject to nervous tremors and moods. Alice disliked seeing her own confinement repeated at such close quarters; the girl mirrored and parodied her own sense of entrapment. The kitchen seemed too small. Sarah would stand at the stove, stirring her porridge, then leaving it to breathe and puff at the lid like a live thing, while Alice prepared the evening meal, looking at the huffing, dribbling pot in distaste, as if it represented, in cartoon form, a disgruntled baby and the annoyance it was causing. And then Sarah would forget her food on the stove; suddenly one of them would have to run to rescue a scorched mess. This issue escalated between them until it reached epic proportions, like the minor incidents, unreceived telegrams, that can eventually precipitate a divorce, or a world war. Alice became a silent bully: the more Sarah feared her arbitrary madam's anger, the more she was drawn by a nervous response to do precisely those things that would bring down Alice's full displeasure. A network of complicated malice and dislike grew up between them. They seemed to have no control of the intimate emotions that jounced around between them, following their own involuntary paths.

Then one morning the baby came. Very early in the morning Sarah appeared at their bedroom door, her arms folded over her belly. She had been walking up and down in the garden until it seemed a decent hour to wake white people in order to take a black one to the doctor. She was trembling with the involuntary shudder that sometimes sets in with labour, her teeth chattering. She was frightened. Alice took her to the doctor, began the procedure that they had previously arranged to get her to the hospital.

At the doctor's they had to wait in a small chilly parlour, with potplants and plastic furniture, Sarah shivering and Alice trying to comfort her, patting her shoulder, saying: 'It's all right, Sarah. They'll look after you.' But the trembling and the shuddering went on. The tiny cold green room became a locus of female fear, as Alice remembered her own onset of childbirth, the haemorrhage that began pumping bubbles of blood out from between her legs, as though some monstrous death machine had been switched on inside. And she, too, had lain there shivering in that impersonal spasm when the body enters some crisis and starts to behave according to its own laws, heedless of whoever lives inside it.

As she drove home from the doctor, Alice regretted that she had been so impatient with Sarah: she was so vulnerable. She had the double vulnerability of being a woman, and black, in a society that existed mainly for white men.

As if in confirmation of this thought, the telephone was ringing when Alice reached the house: it was her husband's mistress. She was a great telephoner. The telephone had become a black instrument out of which, like a surreal painting, sprouted the cancerous flower that her marriage had become. She had always preferred to know and confront her husband's women, though it was a form of emotional crucifixion. The first glimpse of pain had always made her rush to meet it, to know it all, to pull it free of the integument of concealment and deceit that had kept it from her for a while, as if pain was her right, as if she and it were old lovers running to embrace one another at a railway station, cutting a clean line through crowds and pressure. Meeting pain head-on, you could sometimes win through to stillness, find the pain sending out stray off-shoots of compassion.

And yet, as Alice heard the high-pitched voice at the other end of the line, she wanted to bang her head against the wall and howl. Instead, she rested her cheek against the cool plaster and listened to the hysterical gabble: 'You'd be much better off without him. He makes promises that he can't keep, that he doesn't ever intend keeping. He'll just let you down time and again. I know his kind.' The voice went on and on. There was no stopping it once it was in full spate. Alice thought dully: 'Why do I have to sit here listening to my husband's mistress complaining to me about feeling forsaken and bereft?' At the same time she felt an odd impulse to defend him against this arraignment: surely he wasn't that monstrous?

The voice rose another octave: 'You must talk to me. After all, I'm not the Whore of Babylon you know.'

'I know,' said Alice, but was tempted to an inappropriate snigger. The springs of her mind seemed to be giving somewhere.

'And we're all sisters under the skin.'

'Of course,' but she thought I'm not your sister you fucking stupid neurotic bitch. I'm not in the least like you.

But she could not say that. At least not aloud. And it wasn't even true.

During the next few weeks Alice had reports from Sarah's family about her condition: she had had a little boy by Caesarean section: everybody was fine. Sarah's elder sister Elizabeth, matronly and capable, came to work in the house until Sarah was able to return to work. Then, Alice heard, Sarah had gone to the location to stay with her mother.

Months passed. No particular news, though Elizabeth mentioned once that Sarah was sick. One night Alice was standing at the kitchen window, her arms in the sink, when she became aware of people moving in the dark backyard. She adjusted the range of her vision, trying to peer through the reflection of her own image and the bright kitchen into the darkness beyond. Then she made out Elizabeth and another of Sarah's endless sisters, Florence. They came into the kitchen, serious and troubled. Elizabeth did the talking.

'Sarah. She's very bad, mam. Thin like a bone. You won't know her. I say to her: Sarah, Sarah, but she don't know me.'

'But what's happened? What's wrong with her? Why didn't you tell me before?' Alice could feel anger rising: why had they left things so late? It was a conspiracy of silence. They turned their heads away, were silent.

'She go funny, mam. She run mad.' Elizabeth said 'mad' like 'mat.' 'She's screaming nonsense and banging the walls. His mother,' she slipped into the masculine pronoun that she often used, 'she like the witchdoctor.' They both smiled. Alice felt a wave of pure aversion. Stupid rubbish. Sarah could die and they would still be sniggering about the witchdoctor and swallowing his poison.

'We'll go tomorrow and take her to the hospital,' said Alice, but she felt dispirited. You could not get to the bottom of these wells of superstition and reticence. Something at the very end always resisted you, held out against you, would not give.

'I will take you, mam. I will show you the way.'

In the late afternoon of the next day they left their peaceful suburb and drove through the stillness of late autumn, along avenues of trees with untidy droppings of leaves beneath them. They passed onto the loops of a brief, complicated junction, which rolled them down and around its concrete curves, like a ball-bearing in a child's toy, onto the motorway. At the other end, after the high rush of powerful cars against the Johannesburg skyline of towerblocks, and mine-dumps appearing like hallucinations around unexpected ramps and corners, they joined the main road south. The workers were sifting out of the central city area, and Alice found her car caught up in a miraculously controlled maelstrom of bodies and vehicles, all moving in the thin, golden-reddish mining air of the south. Green and white single-decker buses were crammed with bodies, faces at the dusty rear windowpane; shark-finned cars with men in zoot-suits and hats blared hooters and jumped the queue at incredible risk. Alice was part of a huge, lively, good-tempered flow that grew blacker as it moved further south, depositing the last white sediment in the final ring of shabby poor-white suburbs, as if purifying itself toward essential blackness. Then the road curved a little, past giant billboards with eternally smiling, light-skinned partygoers radiant over their COKE, towards the huge black city of Soweto, with its satellite townships like a rash around a larger sore. One of these smaller townships was their destination.

Elizabeth sat next to Alice, her human passport in an unfamiliar country. Alice was aware of moving against the official currents of the city, caught surprised children's glances at a white face behind the wheel as they penetrated further into black territory. Elizabeth kept directing her from large traffic arteries to smaller and still smaller roads. This pattern set up a rhythm for their journey that felt internal, as if it were an exact replica of a bodily system, and Alice was moving along her own blood and nerves towards some vital knot of her own being.

They turned from smooth tar onto narrower, older roads, with giant bluegums at intervals, large pieces of their dry bark ripping downward under their own weight, exposing pale new skin. Then they were on gravel, on a muddy road with deep dongas and rusted car-hulks, on a path, and at the house. It was one of the tiny domino houses of the location, ridged by subdivision; children carrying tins and Fanta bottles of water yelled as they drew up at the house. There was a flurry inside; relatives milled about; everybody smiled. There was much goodwill and little communication.

Then Alice saw Sarah. She lay in a bundle of grey blankets against the wall, her eyes closed. She was emaciated, and had blackened sores around her mouth. Her thin arms were free above the blankets, and she kept moving them in slow, weird undulations, like an underwater plant miming distress.

They put her on the back seat, and Elizabeth supported her with an arm. All the way to the hospital Alice could see her head, the sickness coiled in the dusty little plaits of her hair, bobbing like a sad apple in the rearview mirror.

At the hospital the rhythm of their progress changed. They were still moving, but in slow-motion: move and wait, move and wait, like a ship moving through canal locks. They became passive and stupid as the hospital took charge of them. They were given a number for Sarah, a name-bracelet for her arm as if she were a newborn infant and might be taken home by the wrong mother. Then she was on a trolley, and they were her porters.

It was the evening supper hour for the staff; dusk was drifting into the building, filling it softly like a cup. People were changing shifts, preparing for the long hospital night ahead.

They waited in a corridor. Nurses in crisp uniforms passed them, looking like adverts in a career guide for black schoolgirls; children in laughing gangs clattered along, all holding hands like a paper cutout. Orderlies rode empty trolleys down the polished corridor with practised speed. Once a woman came up the corridor howling in grief. She had obviously had news of a death. She reeled, drunk with sorrow. She stopped sometimes to hang onto a pole, and bang her head with her fists, and increase the volume of her scream. Alice and Elizabeth watched her politely.

Eventually Alice was conducted to a screen at the end of a ward. Here she would find out what she had come for: this was the destination of the journey. She saw Sarah on the bed where she had been examined, a doctor holding up an arm on either side of her, the lank, thin body half-raised, so that her head lolled. Alice saw with a shock the furred pubic crest of bone, exposed where the blanket had fallen back. There were a few weals on her legs where purplish flesh had burst through the skin. The dry skin of her feet was pulling away from pale footpads, and looked dusty, as though it had turned to an inorganic substance.

'Well, what is it?' said Alice, feeling an obscure tide of resentment rising in her as she saw the casual way they handled the girl, stroking her arms to determine texture.

'We can't really tell you much now,' said the young Indian doctor. 'She's mostly suffering from neglect and dehydration. One can't tell with these toxic cases ... We'll see in a few days.'

'But is it very serious?' said Alice, wanting something more, something to take back to the family.

'Well, she's not going to die in the next ten minutes,' said the Indian doctor, smiling. 'The arm movements are not important. It seems to be more ...' he paused and made small circular movements with a finger at his temple, 'psychological. It could be post-natal disturbance. It often happens, you know.' He smiled again. The white doctor gave a soft chuckle. Alice stumbled back, stunned by the crude gesture and the laugh, which seemed to flash a livid imprint of insanity into her own brain. She turned and left.

They had not gone far from the hospital when they saw the parallel lights of the motorway ahead, like a runway. 'Look, Elizabeth,' said Alice with relief, 'it's the M1.' She felt a stab of sudden love for her husband and child, one of those involuntary visitations of intense feeling that occur at irrelevant moments, as one changes gear, or opens a door.

'We people don't know this highways, mam,' said Elizabeth. She spoke gently. There was a little closeness between them. They had done something together. Sarah was safe in the hospital. She would be looked after. Yet Alice still had in her clothing the warm, smoky smell of black bodies, the sweet, defeated smell of waiting, expecting nothing. And remembering the slack, dangling body on the bed, the female cavity that must have been opened and probed into slow pleasure in that small outside room, and that was now so like a wound, she thought: it is you who are my sister. My victim. My sister. My shadow. My self.

E.M. MACPHAIL

Still Life With Peach And Ashtray

from *Falling Upstairs* (1982)

Mr. Polkinghorne, having been married for so long, was unprepared for falling in love. When he was young he had often been in love, sometimes as often as two or three times a day, that is if he had gone out to the shops during his lunch hour or had walked home through the park instead of taking the tram.

In the shops he could rely on falling in love at JEWELLERY where young women used to choose strings of coloured glass beads to wind around their necks. Also at the perfume counter where the young women who had grown tired of the necklaces were dabbing scent on their wrists from sample bottles. The scent alone would have been enough and so was the counter which wasn't called anything, but where there were bins of pale coloured silky things watched over by a grey haired lady wearing a black dress with a white collar.

When the supply of young men who came into the drawing office straight from school dried up because they went into the army instead, Mr Polkinghorne was told that until other arrangements could be made he would have to manage on his own. This meant the night-watchman, who waited until the security gate staff arrived, would let him in through the side door in the early mornings.

Mr. Polkinghorne's skin took on the same papery look and colour as the plans which he pored over all day and the tin lids scattered about the drawing office on window-sills and filing cabinets were filled with the stubs of cigarettes which he squashed out while lighting up again. Although he often felt like a pet rat or hamster which has been presented with an exercise wheel, he didn't altogether miss the company of the young men who, being undecided after leaving school, had spent a month or two in the drawing office because their fathers thought they might as well have a shot at draughting plans and that sort of thing. They had not been unlike his own sons. Given to sudden shouts of laughter; asking if it would be possible to leave a bit early (and not once in a while either); leaning out of the windows and whistling between two fingers in a way which startled a nerve in Mr. Polkinghorne's temple and then in the afternoons, when they became restless, chewing bits of tracing paper which they flicked at each other with setsquares.

Pandora came to work in the drawing office. Also because her father thought it would be a good idea. Old Polkinghorne, now that the young men were away, would look after her and teach her some draughtsmanship which might be useful to her later on.

Pandora was born when her parents had least expected her, when they had given up hope and when the garden and pets took up all the time left over from their work and friends. As often happens to such parents she was an exceptional baby. They would watch her for hours, remarking that she wasn't at all red and crumpled like other babies shown to them in the past by their more fortunate friends. Her features were formed; she had her mother's nose; her father's chin; she would be tall but not too tall; her hands were those of an artist or pianist and her father took the day off from work when her mother phoned to say that she thought Pandora had smiled for the first time. They found homes for the dogs; the cat left of its own accord. And they deliberated over their baby's name. Not for her, this treasure, Jane or Betty or Susan. Rosebud fitted exactly but of course could become inappropriate. And then together at the same moment — they were great readers — inspiration came to them, as one hears, like a divine message: Pandora. That was it. A treasure chest of their hopes and love and other feelings they weren't quite sure about. And Panny, while she was a little girl, had an unusual, a sweet sound.

Falling in love for Mr. Polkinghorne was like the starting up of a piece of abandoned machinery of which all the parts are present though locked by the dust of disuse, rusted or jammed with grease, and when the switch is pressed, effort is transmitted through the fulcrum to the load. Axles, wheels, cogs, shafts move slowly at first — sometimes there is the squealing noise of metal on metal — but as they warm up the machine starts to pulsate and throb. It vibrates but not rhythmically as when it was new.

If someone had asked Mr. Polkinghorne to describe his assistant, Pandora, he would have said that her hair was sort of dark, her skin fairish, her eyes more or less blue, her legs sound and her figure — clearing his throat — quite good. But if it had been possible for the someone to have been curled up inside that part of Mr. Polkinghorne which controlled his hands, the someone would have known that his fingers longed to dip into her hair. It reminded him of clear deep water pouring over smooth rocks.

When it parted — he had not realised that hair could be heavy since Mrs. Polkinghorne wore a hairnet — to show the back of Pandora's neck as she lay stretched across a plan, his hands trembled. When he managed to get his cigarette alight at last, he took a breath at the wrong moment and coughed and spluttered and wheezed for some time. Although he was fairly certain about the colour of her eyes, he discovered that the pupils could dilate and change to the prismatic brilliance of the Fox Glacier, a picture of which he had seen once in the National Geographic magazine. He might have been better able to describe her hands if only because he became more used to looking at them than any other part of her; as he showed her how to place the tracing paper and secure it; how to use a protractor; or when she took from him the cup of tea he had poured and carried to her — so that hardly any of it was in the saucer. The backs of her hands might have reminded him of the top of the milk in the jug after it had been left standing for a few hours; her palms had the unexpectedness of the underside of a shell picked up on the beach. The colour of her fingernails changed almost from day to day, salmon or carmine, silver and a deep maroon which, the first time he saw them, made Mr. Polkinghorne put his hands in his pockets.

When Pandora's father had come to arrange for her to work for him Mr. Polkinghorne had said that seeing she was a young lady it might be better perhaps if she wore trousers because of having to stretch across the plan tables and so on. He of course was used to the young men in their denims, faded and frayed at the edges, and although Pandora sometimes wore denim she also wore the trousers which were presently in fashion. Narrow and short to the ankle with which went high spikey-heeled sandals showing her carmine or silver or salmon or maroon toenails. The tight waist-band gripped what Mr. Polkinghorne would have described as folds which, when she bent to pick up something from the floor, opened and spread in a way which made him wonder if she had bought them in a hurry and that they weren't meant for bending down. They were of a thin material and in the different colours of ice cream. The trousers, the sandals and the T-shirts which had two little buttons imprisoned on either side sometimes kept Mr. Polkinghorne in his glass box office until he had smoked three cigarettes in succession, after which he would come out, his shoulders hunching forward in his grey-brown tweed jacket, his elbows pressed in to his sides as though to hold up his trousers.

'Good morning, Panny,' he would say. She had told him when she started not to call her by her surname. 'And how are we today?'

If she didn't answer he soon discovered it was best not to try again until she came over for a cigarette. Then he would offer her one of the long filter-tipped ones she liked. Having lit it and one of his own plain ones, he knew she would settle down and have a little chat.

'And has your father agreed to let you go to the party on Saturday?' Mr. Polkinghorne asked.

'Sure,' answered Pandora, her chin tilting upwards as she blew a plume of smoke from her kissing-pursed lips which matched her toenails. It was a maroon and ice cream-pink day.

'But you told me he'd said you were still too young to go out with boys.'

'But I'm not going out with a guy,' replied Pandora. 'I'm going out with an old school friend. I've told you before I wasn't allowed to go to a mixed school, so I'm going with one of the girls from my class.'

'And there'll only be girls at the party?' asked Mr. Polkinghorne.

'Only girls,' answered Pandora. 'That's what my father wants, so there'll only be girls. But what do you think, Polky? Do you think I look as though I'd want to go to a party where there'd be only girls?'

Pandora stubbed out the last half of the cigarette and then, uncrossing her ankles, which rested on the edge of the plan table, she stood up. He watched her walk away and he noticed that the pink trousers were caught in the crease of her sit-upon.

All the parts of the once forsaken machine were working now in a synchronization of a sort and Mr. Polkinghorne bought a new tie to match his tweed jacket on which, if one looked closely, could be seen a tiny orange bird hidden in the intricacy of the pattern of grey-brown branches. He also bought some stuff called Brut from the chemist shop, in a strange-shaped bottle and two beige slim-line shirts with a small black rose embroidered on one side at waist level.

The days were lengthening and he waited for the first peach to swell into a perfect sphere, for its skin to flush to the colour of early dawn. He had thrown a net over the tree to prevent the birds from attacking the fruit and in the evenings he picked Mrs. Polkinghorne's sweetpeas, hiding them in a jam jar behind the garage so that they would stay fresh overnight. The peach would be picked first thing in the morning, wrapped in tissue, his hand holding it safely in his pocket while he listened to his wife's instructions before leaving.

He still came to his office early enough for the night-watchman to let him in at the side door, but now the extra time in the mornings was taken up with transferring the flowers into the vases he had bought during his lunch hour, placing one on the sill nearest to the cupboard in which Pandora kept her things, and trying to make up his mind where to put the other one. On the plan table where she would be working? Perhaps not, it might get in her way. The peach he placed in a saucer on his desk, waiting for the right moment. He would sit quietly smoking until it was almost time for Pandora to arrive, when he would empty the tin lid with the few stubs into the bin in the passage, open the windows to air the room and try to concentrate on the newspaper.

Peeling the peach was, in itself, not difficult, Mr. Polkinghorne having waited for it to ripen exactly to the point that his penknife would slit the membrane without damage to the luscious globe. The difficulty was knowing when Pandora would want to eat the peach. If he peeled it too soon, it would turn brown and she would say 'Ye-ugh'; and if it wasn't ready she might say, 'I think I'll have a cuppa and a ciggie instead.' But he came to recognise the signs for when he should start peeling the peach. She would stand back from the table, stretch her arms upwards, cradling the back of her head between her interlocked fingers, the two buttons inside her T-shirt protruding as she flexed her back. Then he would slip the knife beneath the suede-like skin, lifting it gently, holding it against the blade with his thumb and tearing it downwards slowly, his fingers sure of themselves until the peach, in its juicy translucence, sat in the middle of the saucer. As he carried it over to her it wobbled slightly.

He hadn't looked so well for years, people told Mr. Polkinghorne, adding that a bit of weight off the middle made such a difference and that hard work never killed anyone. He couldn't bring himself to contradict them about working harder, recalling the new plans still unrolled and hidden in the back of the tall cupboard.

Although he came to the office as early as ever, he was returning home later than usual if there was the chance of giving Pandora a lift home, despite the heavy traffic, in the opposite direction to which he lived. Nevertheless, there were long periods during the day when he waited to peel the peach or light her cigarette or for the chance to stretch out beside her across the plan table, standing on tiptoe so that his grey-brown tweed shoulder was level with her apricot tanned upper arm. Then he was able without turning his head to watch the pulse at the bottom of her throat, to smell her hair, to feel her slight warmth, while he explained some of the principles of orthographic projection. It was while he was answering her question about why right angles were so important that she turned to him suddenly and said, 'You know something, Polky? I think I'd like to eat a peach.' He hurried off to his office.

Pandora said she would keep an eye on the step-ladder while he climbed up, the new globe in his pocket to replace the other, the smoke from the freshly lit cigarette between his lips making him blink as he unthreaded the screws on the round white bowl. Placing it carefully on the small shelf at the top of the ladder, he looked down at Pandora as she opened her mouth, the peach held between her fingers tipped with the same colour as the inside of her mouth. Perhaps it was the smoke, or dust that made him cough. Holding onto the top of the ladder, guarding the lamp bowl, undecided about flinging away his cigarette without dropping it onto Pandora, he became enveloped in a paroxysm of wheezing and strangled spluttering. Pandora was absorbed with the peach, pursing her mouth after each bite, the tip of her rosy tongue licking a dribble of juice from the side of her mouth.

When Mr. Polkinghorne's false teeth castanetted across the plan table, teetered on the edge for a moment and dropped to the floor, she placed the pip carefully in a tiny shell-shaped ashtray and stood up, sucking the ends of her fingers. Her faceted aquamarine eyes followed Mr. Polkinghorne as he climbed slowly, reluctantly, backwards down the ladder, the pockets of his tweed jacket hanging down as though weighted. Stepping down from the last rung, he turned, his hand in front of his mouth. Pandora, pointing with her salmon-tipped toe to the denture, on the domed surface of which was gummed the remains of the afternoon tea biscuit, said, her mouth stretched into a smile shape, 'There they are. You'd better pick them up.' Mr Polkinghorne bent down, as though genuflecting.

One of the wheels failing to engage with another from which the cogs had been stripped continued spinning under its own momentum for a few seconds until the connecting rod slowed and stopped and the pistons subsided.

ELLEN PALESTRANT

Six Free Pulls

from *Nosedive And Other Writings* (1983)

I turned up the volume:

'They say somewhere in Africa something is happening that has never happened before.

'They say somewhere in Africa something is being built that has never been built before.

'Somewhere in Africa something very exciting is being created that has never been created before.'

'Somewhere in Africa
Somewhere in Africa ...'

SUN CITY
SUN FUN CITY
SUN CITY
SUN CITY
SUN CITY

I switch off the video recorder and mount the staircase of the stage. Walk to the microphone:

'Ladies and Gentlemen, I hope you enjoyed our Sun City documentary. We are now going to spin the Sun City Wheel of Fortune and who knows, any one of you people seated in front of me might be sitting on a LUCKY CHAIR. Yes — a LUCKY CHAIR for if the wheel lands on a number which corresponds with the number on your chair, *you* will be the LUCKY WINNER.

'Furthermore, there isn't merely one lucky chair, but three lucky chairs for three lucky winners! During the next forty-five minutes

Ladies and Gentlemen, I am going to spin the Sun City Wheel, not once, not twice but *three times*.

'Okay let's go!'

I beckon to Mary, who is standing next to the mobile wheel to switch it on. She tosses her hair back, protrudes her chest and smiles. The wheel rings out harsh and starts to spin.

The wheel builds up momentum. It spins faster and faster.

'Watch it spin Ladies and Gentlemen! Watch it spin! Round and round it goes. Round and round.'

The audience seated on the rows of chairs in front of me stare ahead self-consciously. They attempt to look excited for after all something IS happening. They look at Mary. She is still smiling. They look at me. Quickly I smile.

'Watch it spin Ladies and Gentlemen! Watch it spin! Round and round it goes. Round and round.

'Do you know that any three of you thirty-six lucky people seated in front of me might win a fabulous prize: A Bus Package Trip to Sun City. Return fare as well. Entrance to the Casino. And the Disco. Even Dinner. Or The Extravaganza. Or Dinner and The Extravaganza. Or The Extravaganza, Dinner and the Casino or . . .'

I'm hating this. What am I doing here? I'm embarrassed. What am I doing here! 'It's a job,' I tell myself. 'You've taken it on — voluntarily. So deal with it.'

'Watch it Ladies and Gentlemen! The Wheel of Fortune is about to stop. It's stopping! It's stopping! It's stopping on number 19. No — 20! No — 21! 21 it is! Number 21 will you please come up and receive your prize.

'Let me open the envelope. My what have we here? The LUCKY WINNER of seat 21 has won — just wait for it Ladies and Gentlemen — has won 6 FREE PULLS ON THE ONE ARM BANDIT! Congratulations!'

The winner stands in front of me. She is bewildered. She giggles. I hand her the envelope and she claps her hands and says, 'Thank you Madam'.

She places the envelope in the pocket of her white starched apron, lace trimmed, and pulls at the side seams of her pale green overall.

She returns to her seat. She works in the flatlands of Killarney. So do most of the audience seated in front of me. They wear overalls of all colours — pink, yellow, blue, green, floral, checked. There is also a group wearing white overalls trimmed with red — they work at the local supermarket. Word has spread that there are prizes to be won — free trips to Sun City.

The maids are cleaning up today. They are beating their madams hollow. They have been winning since we began this morning for they occupy the majority of seats. Only a handful of seats are occupied by the madams. They wear sunglasses. It is sunny.

'Ladies and Gentlemen, we will have two more spins of the Wheel of Fortune. Who will be the lucky winner of a trip to the getaway playground of Bophuthatswana? To the fabulous, glamorous, exciting Sun City of Africa?

'Okay Mary, let the wheel go! Round and round it goes. Round and round.'

I can't believe I'm doing this. Actually doing this. Disassociate — that's what I must do. Remove myself. Regard today as experience. As input. Look at the people. Study them. Perceive.

I look but all I see are many overalls and blank faces. Blank faces of the Mall. They have been trapped. We have trapped them. If they want to take part in the spin they have to watch the documentary. That's the rule. Some have watched it five times! They dare not leave their seats for others standing around will snatch them up. After all, there are prizes to be won.

Someone has just won!

'Number 11 it is! Come up and receive your prize. My Goodness! You have won — Return Fare, Casino, Extravaganza and Dinner for Two!'

He comes up to receive his prize. He wears dark navy overalls with the name GLENGARDENS, stamped in red on both sleeves. He wears knee pads. They smell of Cobra Floor Polish.

I switch on the video. The documentary offers to take the audience on a lightning visit to the great Sun Cities of the world starting in 'Gay Paris, where it all began,' and ending where it has 'all been built under the blazing sun of Africa'.

Somewhere in Africa.

Somewhere in Africa something is happening that has never happened before.

And somewhere in Killarney I am making a fool of myself.

GCINA MHLOPHE

Nokulunga's Wedding

from *Lip* ed. by S. Brown, I. Hofmeyr, S. Rosenberg (1983)

Mount Frere was one of the worst places for a woman to live. A woman had to marry whoever had enough money for lobola and that was that. Nokulunga was one of many such victims whose parents wholeheartedly agreed to their victimisation. She became wife to Xolani Mayeza.

By the time Nokulunga was sixteen years old she was already looking her best. One day a number of young men came to the river where she and her friends used to fetch water. The men were strangers. As the girls came to the river, one of the men jumped very high and cried in a high-pitched voice.

'Hayi, hayi, hayi!
Bri — bri mntanam uyagula!'

He came walking in style towards the girls and asked for water. After drinking he thanked them, went back to his friends and they left. This was not a new thing to Nokulunga and her friends, but the different clothes and style of walking left them with mixed feelings. Some were very impressed by the strangers but Nokulunga was not. She suspected they were up to something but decided not to worry about people she did not know. The girls lifted their water pots onto their heads and went home.

In late February the same strange men were seen at the river, but their number had doubled. The day was very hot but they were dressed in heavy overcoats. Nokulunga did not see them until she and her friends were near the river. The girls were happily arguing about something and did not recognise the men as the same ones they had seen before. Only when the same man who had asked for water came up to them again did they realise who the strangers were. Nokulunga began to feel uneasy.

He drank all his water slowly this time, then he asked Nokulunga if he could take her home with him for the night. She was annoyed, and filled her water pot, balanced it on her head and told the others she had to hurry home. One of her friends did the same and was ready to go with Nokulunga when the other men came and barred their way.

Things began to happen very fast. They took Nokulunga's water pot and broke it on a rock. Men wrapped Nokulunga in big overcoats before she could scream. They slung the bundle onto their shoulders.

The other girls helplessly looked on as the men set off. The men chanted a traditional wedding song as they quickly climbed the hillside, while many villagers watched.

Nokulunga twisted round, trying to breathe. She had witnessed girls being taken before. She thought of the many people in the neighbourhood who seemed to love her. They couldn't love her if they could let strangers go away with her without putting up a fight. She felt betrayed and lost. She thought of what she had heard about such marriages. She knew her mother would not mind, as long as the man had enough lobola.

The journey was long and she was very hot inside the big coats. Her body felt so heavy, but the rhythm of her carriers went on and on ... her lover Vuyo was going back to Germiston to work. He had promised her that he would be away for seven months then he would be back to marry her. She had been so happy.

Her carriers were walking down a very steep and uneven path. Soon she heard people talking and dogs barking. She was put down and the bundle was unwrapped. A lot of people were looking on to see what the newcomer looked like. She was clumsily helped to her feet and stood there stupidly for viewing. She wanted to pee. For a while no one said anything, they all stood there with different expressions on their faces. The children of the house came in to join the viewing one by one and the small hut was nearly full.

She was in Xolani, her 'husband's' room. She was soon left alone with him for the night. She sat down calmly, giving no indication that she was going to sleep at all. Xolani tried to chat with her but she was silent, so he got undressed and into the big bed on the floor. He coughed a few times, then uneasily invited her to join him. She sat silent. He was quiet for a while, then asked if she was going to sleep that night. No. For a long time she sat staring at him. She was watchful.

But Nokulunga was tired. She thought he was sleeping. Xolani suddenly lunged and grabbed her arm. His eyes were strange, she could not make out what was in them, anger or hatred or something else.

She struggled to free her arm, he suddenly let go and she fell. She quickly stood up, still watching him. He smiled and moved close to her. She backed off. It looked like a game, he following her slowly, she backing round and round the room. Each round they moved faster. Xolani decided he had had enough and grabbed her again. She was about to scream when he covered her mouth. She realised it was foolish to scream, it would call helpers for him.

She still stood a chance of winning if they were alone. He was struggling to undress her when Nokulunga went for his arm. She dug her teeth deep and tore a piece of flesh out. She spat. His arm went limp, he groaned and sat, gritting his teeth and holding his arm.

Nokulunga sat too, breathing heavily. He stood up quickly, cursing under his breath and kicked her as hard as he could. She whined with pain but did not stand up to defend herself.

Blood was dripping from Xolani's arm and he softly ordered her to tear a piece of sheet to tie above the bite. She did it, then wiped blood from the floor. Xolani got under the bedcovers in silence. Nokulunga pulled her clothes together. She did not dare to fall asleep. Whether Xolani slept or not, only he knows. The pain of his arm did not make things easier for him.

Day came. Xolani left, and Nokulunga was given a plate of food and locked in the room. She had just started eating when she heard people talking outside. It sounded like a lot of men. They went into the hut next to the one she was in and came out talking even louder. They moved away and she gave up listening and ate her food, soft porridge.

The men sat next to the big cattle-kraal. Xolani was there, his father Malunga and his eldest brother Diniso. The rest were uncles and other family members. They were slowly drinking their beer. They were all very angry with Xolani. Malunga was too angry to think straight. He looked at his son with contempt, kept balling his hands into fists.

No one said anything. They stole quick glances at Malunga and their eyes went back to stare at the ground. Xolani shifted uneasily. He was holding his hurt arm carefully, his uncle had tended to it but the pain was still there. His father sucked at his pipe, knocked it out on the piece of wood next to him, then spat between his teeth. The saliva jumped a long way into the kraal and they all watched it.

'Xolani!' Malunga called to his son softly and angrily.

'Yes father,' Xolani replied without looking up.

'What are you telling us, are you telling us that you spent all night with that girl and failed to sleep with her?'

'Father, I . . . I . . .'

'Yes, you failed to be a man with that girl in that hut. That is the kind of man you have grown into, unable to sleep with a woman the way a man should.'

Silence followed. No one dared to look at Malunga. He busied himself refilling his pipe as if he was alone. After lighting it he looked at the other men.

'Diniso, are you listening with me to what your brother is telling us? Tell us more Xolani, what else did she do to you, my little boy? Did she kick you on the chest too, tell me, father's little son?' He laughed harshly.

An old man interrupted. 'Mocking and laughing at the fool will not solve our problem. So please, everyone think of the next step from here. The Mjakuja people are looking for their daughter. Something must be done fast.' He was out of breath when he finished. The old man was Malunga's father from another house.

The problem was that no word had been sent to Nokulunga's family to tell them of her whereabouts. Thirteen cattle and a well-fed horse were ready to be taken to the family, along with a goat which was called imvula-mlomo, mouth opener.

The sun was about to set. Nokulunga watched it for a long time. She was very quiet. She stared at the red orange shape as it went down into the unknown side of the mountain.

By the time the colours faded she was still looking at the same spot but her eyes were taking a look at her future. She had not escaped that day. She felt weak and miserable. A group of boys sat all day on the nearby hill watching her so that she did not try running away. She was there to stay.

She did not know how long she stood there behind the hut. She only came to when she heard a little girl laughing next to her. The girl told her that people had gone out to look for her because they all thought she had managed to get away while the boys were playing. She went back into the house. Her mother-in-law and the other women also laughed when the little girl said she'd found Nokulunga standing behind the hut. More boys were sent to tell the pursuers that Nokulunga was safe at home.

She hated the long dress and doek she had been given to wear, they were too big for her and the material still had the hard starch on it. The people who had gone out to look for her came back laughing and teasing each other about how stupid they had been to run so fast without even checking behind the house first.

Nokulunga was trembling as it grew dark. She knew things would not be as easy as they had been the night before. She knew the family would take further steps although she did not know exactly what would happen.

She was in her husband's room waiting for him to come in. The hut suddenly looked so small she felt it move to enclose her in a painful death. She held her arms across her chest, gripping her shoulders so tight they ached.

The door opened and a number of men about her husband's age came in quietly. They closed the door behind them. She watched Xolani undress as if he did not want to. His arm did not look better as he stood there in the light of the low-burning paraffin lamp. She started to cry.

She was held and undressed. Her face was wet with sweat and tears and she wanted to go and pee. The men laughed a little.

One of them smiled teasingly at her and ordered her to lie down on the bed. She cried uncontrollably when she saw the look on Xolani's face. He stood there with eyes wide open as if he was walking in dreamland, his face had the expression of a lost and helpless boy. Was that the man she was supposed to look upon as a husband? How was he ever to defend her against anything or anyone?

Hands pulled her up and her streaming eyes did not see the man who shouted to her that she should lie like a woman. She wiped her eyes and saw Xolani approaching her.

She jumped and pushed him away, grabbed at her clothes. The group of men was on her like a mob. They roughly pulled her back onto the bed and Xolani was placed on top of her. Her legs were each pulled by a man. Others held her arms.

Men were cheering and clapping hands while Xolani jumped high, now enjoying the rape. One man was saying that he had had enough of holding the leg and wanted a share for his work. Things were said too about her bloody thighs and she heard roars of laughter before she fainted.

'The bride is ours
The bride is ours
Mother will never go to sleep
without food
without food

The bride is ours
The bride is ours
Father will never need for beer
will never want for beer . . .'

The young men were singing near the kraal. Girls giggled as they sang and did Xhosa dances. Soon they would be expected to dance at Xolani's wedding. They were trying new hairstyles so each would look her best. The young men too were worried about how they would look. Some of them were hoping for new relationships with the girls of Gudlintaba.

That place was known for the good-looking girls with their beautiful voices. Others knew too that some relationships would break as a result of that wedding. Everyone knew the day was in their hands, whether fighting or laughter ended the day.

Women prepared beer and took turns going to the river for water, happy and light-footed in the way they walked. Time and again a woman would run from hut to hut calling at the top of her voice, ululating joyfully:

'Lililili . . . lili . . . lili . . . liiiiii!

To give birth is to stretch your bones!

What do you say, woman who never gave birth?'

Nokulunga spent most of the time inside the house with one of her friends and her mother's sister tending to her face. They had a mixture of eggs and tree bark as part of the concoction. All day long her face was crusted with thick liquids supposed to be good for her wedding complexion. Time and again her mother's sister would sit down and tell her how to behave now that she was a woman. How she hated the subject. She wished days would simply go by without her noticing them.

'Ingwe iyawavula amathambo'mqolo.

The leopard opens the back bones.'

She heard the girls happily singing outside. She hated the bloody song. The only thing they all seemed to care about was the food they were going to have on that day she never wanted to come. Many times she would find herself sitting there with her masked face looking out of the tiny window. She hated Xolani and his name. She felt that he was given that name because he would always do things to hurt people, then he would keep on apologising and explaining. Xolani means 'please forgive'.

The day came. Nokulunga walked slowly by Xolani's side with lots of singing and laughing and ululating and clapping of hands around her. She did not smile, when she tried only tears came rolling down to make her ashamed.

It was the day of his life for Xolani, such a beautiful wife and such a big wedding. He was smiling and squeezing her hand when Nokulunga saw Vuyo. He was looking at Xolani with loathing, his fists very tight and his lips so hard. She pulled her hand from Xolani's and took a few steps. She began to cry. Xolani went to her and tried to comfort her. A lot of people saw this, they stood watching and sympathising and wondering . . .

Months passed. Nokulunga was sitting by the fire, in her arms a five-day-old baby boy was sleeping so peacefully she smiled. Her father-in-law had named it Vuyo. How thankful she had been to hear that, she would always remember the old Vuyo she had loved.

Nokulunga now accepted that Xolani was her lifetime partner and there was nothing she could do about it. Once she saw Vuyo in town and they had kissed. It had been clear to them that since she was already pregnant, she was Xolani's wife, and Vuyo knew he would have to pay a lot of cattle if he took Nokulunga with the unborn baby. There was nothing to be done.

SHARYN WEST

Beds

from *Lip* ed. by S. Brown, I. Hofmeyr, S. Rosenberg (1983)

The earliest memory I have is of being in my cot. The nappies hanging around me were still wet. They shut out the light. My father was out there somewhere. I knew my mother was not. This became a pattern of my knowing, growing childmind. When she was there it was often behind the bathroom door bleeding and bruised.

Years later I slept in the corner behind a curtain hung to carve a triangle of my own space. The room was cluttered and the dust on the carpet was generations thick. We did not clean that room thoroughly in our haste to move in and hide our possessions. The boarding house was the only place to move into. My father had not worked in the years after my mother had left and it was all we could afford. Slowly my Gran's savings had dwindled and disappeared. Her pension could not pay rents. We were lucky to find that room. Although it was small it had a balcony that we would use for a kitchen.

There was the first bed that I really became attached to. The curtain and the pile of sheepskins were the first materials I used to make a world for myself in which to enjoy the night time. I had a body that was growing and the need to feel it. I knew my dreams were different since I had kissed Jennifer Letts on the corner. Before, my Gran, my sister and I had slept in a big double bed. The warmths not the bed were important.

High school was a procession of different beds in different dormitories of the Girls' Hostel. That's when bed became territory and night was of supreme importance. Lights-off returned me to myself and solitude. I recall a tent made of blankets over the bedstead and the books I made my accomplices. The giggles of close friends slipping into sleep in each others' beds were an achievement I could not risk. Free schooling paid for in timid quiescent days over years. The sharing and the daring had to wait.

At university, the term-time-residence-rooms had a bed that was separate and alone. Months of vacation spells spent on lounge floors, sofas and in spare rooms of friends' homes gave me companions. No one I knew had to work their free days to go to school.

Sleeping alone was my only escape from loneliness. My wages couldn't pay for boarding in the residences and I couldn't afford to value the lifestyle. Forced to look for other space I also found my own. What brought the change? Was it meeting her, hours undisturbed in my room at the bottom of a garden, giggling until dawn and long kisses led us into sleep. My work record had been strong. But I missed classes, assignments and even exams. We had to live at night in secret and in guilt. A need for night stalked my mind in the day and kept me distracted. I could no longer simply open a door and walk in, I carried too much of my night with me to feel clear, and my life in bed seemed to follow me down all the corridors I walked.

When I failed we moved to another city, another college. Beds on the floors of communal houses became a lifestyle, we stole our time in the moments between people. Family and friends hated our closeness and punished us for our visible love. The world was our bed wherever we came to lie.

I abandoned the bed we built when I left. It held too many shattered achievements. Besides I didn't know how to use all that space. Months you had lain there also not believing your illness, believing they would help us in our home. How was I to know what you did not tell me and I would not see? How was I to know they would not believe your illness until I had to carry you to the lavatory? Two months I visited your hospital bed. Five days longer your cold hands were all I could touch behind sterile doors. I was without fear but clumsy in my gloves and gown of intensive-care-green. How was I to know they hated our love more than they loved your life? I didn't know them then.

When I visited my gran to tell her of your death, she too lay dying in a fully, mechanised hospital bed. Cranking her head and shoulders into a sitting position made me cry. She could not console me and I had not wanted her to try. She wouldn't lie about the pain of staying when lovers go. She did give me your ring though, and her hanky to blow my nose.

And I think of you still. Beds and closed doors are more welcome in my life again. Often I lie and grin in the night, knowing what I cannot see. Sometimes I giggle to think of the things you said about people in the daylight. I wish we could have had womanspace. Maybe the daylight would also have been our friend.

ROSE ZWI

A Lonely Walk To Freedom

from *Lip* ed. by S. Brown, I. Hofmeyr, S. Rosenberg (1983)

The heavy wooden door shut quietly behind her. She heard the peephole slide open then snap shut again. She was free. A wave of panic washed over her and she leaned against the door, her eyes shut. She wanted desperately to bang on the door. What would she say when they opened it? I'm feeling faint? I've left something behind? I'm not ready to leave yet? She felt like a snail without its shell. Slowly the mist before her eyes cleared and she saw two rows of Africans, men and women, flanking both sides of the steps that led to the door. She took a deep breath, picked up her suitcase and started to walk down the steps. No one responded to her tremulous smile. They stood huddled in the cold morning air, clutching parcels wrapped in newspaper, cartons of milk and unwrapped loaves of bread. They had a long wait before them: visiting time was hours away.

She put her case down on the pavement and looked about her in bewilderment. The Fort stood on a high point and she could see the greater part of the city. Most of the old landmarks, the highest buildings, were now dwarfed by new structures which were still being built. Enormous cranes hovered over them and the sky was full of movement. To her left, over the new highway which was streaming with four rows of cars speeding towards the city, was a large corrugated iron fence which closed off the excavations. She strained to remember what had stood there before. Then she recalled walking past the Fort on her way to University, past the small semi-detached houses, the grubby children and the women with curlers and doeks on their heads. All gone. A builder's notice announced that this was the site of the new civic centre.

Judith watched the cars rush past. The early morning sun reflected off their sleek, shiny surfaces blinding her. She must buy sunglasses. Behind their tinted lenses the world might not look so large, so threatening. Perhaps she would feel less vulnerable. A young student on his way to University smiled at her, drawing her into contact with people again. She picked up her case and walked in the direction of Hillbrow.

There was a rawness in the morning air. She detected the honey smell of blossoms though there were none in sight. Perhaps they were imprisoned behind the high walls of the Chief Warder's house which stood next to the prison. The plane trees had put out their first green leaves and she stopped to touch a horny tree trunk. Enclosed by rings of concrete paving, these trees still responded to some law which bade them sleep in winter and put out buds in spring. Perhaps she too would breathe and stretch and grow again despite the rings of steel which cramped her being. Perhaps her numbness would melt in the warmth of spring.

After previous absences from Johannesburg everything had always looked smaller, dingier. When she had returned from her visit to England seven years ago, Johannesburg had seemed like a provincial backwater. Today everything looked larger, newer and brighter than she could remember. Perhaps it was. Or perhaps it only seemed so because she was accustomed to confined spaces.

All night she had lain awake in her cell, listening to the sounds of freedom outside. She heard cars change gear as they pulled up the steep hill on which the Fort stood. With a high-pitched groan they reached the top of the hill, then gradually faded away as they drove down towards the city. They were going to the cinemas, the theatres, to restaurants. After Saturday night, Wednesday was the most popular night for going out in Johannesburg. Several times she heard the sirens of ambulances as they drew up at the Non-European Hospital over the road from the Fort, or at the Fever Hospital to its left, or at the General Hospital just one block away. On Hospital Hill one expected to hear such sirens, yet every wail set her heart hammering in agitation. It was almost dawn before she fell asleep.

Her cell was identical to the one where she had spent the five weeks before and during her trial. It had been like coming home again. The cell was small, with room enough for a bed, a tiny locker and a sanitary bucket at the foot of the bed, but it had a large, barred sash window that looked onto the courtyard. She preferred the Fort to the other prisons — over the years she had become a connoisseur. She had hated Barberton where she lost three years of her life. Pretoria Central was sinister, frightening, and she had abhorred that dreadful dank cell in the jail outside of Pretoria where she had spent fifty-eight days in solitary confinement. The thought of that tiny, evil-smelling cell with its high, barred and netted window still brought on attacks of claustrophobia. She had torn her nails in her efforts to reach the window which looked onto the exercise yard.

That had also been the period of interminable interrogation. She remembered the glow of triumph on Lieutenant Van As's face when he told her that Ralph Ferguson had turned state witness and that she might as well make a statement. She had not believed him. Interrogators told such lies in order to extract confessions, to turn prisoners against their friends. Only when she was finally brought to the Fort did she realise that Van As had not been lying. She had spent those weeks awaiting trial in front of the large barred sash window, drawing the warm rays of the late winter sun into her numbed body.

She crossed the street carefully when the traffic light turned green and found herself outside the nursing home where she'd had her abortion; Ralph had insisted on it. Her suitcase containing two changes of clothing, a few books and her banning orders, now felt unbearably heavy. She put it down and stared into the entrance to the nursing home. Of all the tapes they had made her listen to, the one in which she had discussed her pregnancy with Ralph had been the most painful. Van As had looked sanctimonious while the young sergeant made obscene remarks. She had flushed and paled with humiliation.

What should have been a walk to freedom was becoming a series of halts along her personal Via Dolorosa. Only there was no one to wipe her brow or adjust her cross. Neither had anyone wiped her brow in that hospital room on the fifth floor.

If I'm to survive, Judith thought, lifting the case which seemed lighter again, I'll have to root myself firmly in the present and fill the void by reading the newspapers of the past three years.

She would have to relearn how to live an ordinary life and draw all the threads together. Above all she had to stay sane, knowing how near breakdown she was. If her incipient madness were detected she would be locked up again, this time in a mental home. But anxieties were embedded in even the most ordinary things. Where she would live, for example. Nathalie had written to her in jail saying she could not have her in her home — her father was politically opposed to Judith's ideas. Nathalie was her closest friend in Johannesburg. But Kathy Nathanson, whom she had met several times at Nathalie's house, had offered to put her up. Judith replied as cheerfully as she could, thanking Kathy. It would have been easier in every way to live with Nathalie in Johannesburg. Kathy's house was outside the Johannesburg municipal boundary and she would have to get special permission to come into town. Accessibility of newspaper files had become an obsession with her. Except for an occasional article in one of the women's magazines which had been allowed to them in jail, Judith had little idea of what had been happening in the outside world. An uncensored sentence in one of Nathalie's letters had remained a mystery to her.

'Where's Biafra?' she had asked the girls in her cell.

But she would cope with the difficulties as they arose. In the meantime, she'd better relish every moment of her morning in Johannesburg. It might be the last few hours she would ever spend there. She walked into a large pharmacy opposite the nursing home. Her first purchase would be a pair of sunglasses.

There was a marvellous smell of soap, perfume and powder in the shop. Judith looked about her. Pottery, wooden bowls, copper vases, kitchenware in bright oranges, blues and greens. She had forgotten such things existed. She walked towards a stand displaying sunglasses. New shapes and colours. She took a pair off the hook. It cost twice as much as her monthly chemist's allowance in jail. There two rand had to cover things like creams, soap, toothpaste, sanitary towels. The tooth powder they provided in jail had made her gag, and the red soap they made on the premises was fat and greasy. 'Rich white ladies,' they had told one another guiltily when they ordered their own toothpaste and a cake of soap, knowing that the black prisoners could not afford such luxuries.

'Have you any cheaper glasses?' Judith asked the well-groomed assistant who approached her. She cleared her throat; her voice sounded so strange to her.

'This is our cheapest line,' the assistant answered brusquely. 'Try the bazaars.'

Judith smiled as the assistant turned her back on her and continued dusting the shelves. Adjustment number one: she belonged to the income group which could not afford to buy glasses in glossy pharmacies. She had worked out her budget last night at the Fort. Out of a total of one hundred and fifty rand, the remains of her last salary cheque which Nathalie had deposited for her in the building society, she had to pay for a single sea voyage to England and for her keep in Johannesburg for two months. She could make do with the clothes she had, but she would have to shorten all her dresses, she thought, looking at the miniskirted assistant who found it difficult to bend without revealing a large section of her upper thigh. Not as short as that, of course. With her long thin legs she would look like a secretary bird.

The streets were filling up with shoppers and with people on their way to work. As Judith walked among them her haziness and anxiety began to wear off. No one took notice of her. She caught a glimpse of herself in one of the long mirrors in the corner of a window: Her old-fashioned suit hung loosely from her shoulders and her skirt covered her knees. Her blonde hair had become dull and lifeless and streaked with grey.

Some people paid to have grey highlights put into their hair; she had earned hers.

In the bazaar she bought herself a pair of cheap sunglasses which the saleslady assured her were good enough to read with. Then she stopped at the small tobacconist next door and bought several packets of cigarettes. She had actually enjoyed the bite which brown paper gave to pipe tobacco. In jail she had become expert at rolling her own cigarettes but she could hardly do that at the Nathansons'. She lit a cigarette eagerly and inhaled the smoke deeply into her lungs. She sighed. It was easy getting used to luxurious things.

On a street corner she bought a newspaper, her first in three years. She lingered for a while over the English and Afrikaans papers which were laid out on the pavement with small piles of coins next to them. She was equipped to make her long-awaited pilgrimage to the Florian.

For years she had dreamed of sitting on that open balcony on the first floor, in the sun. She had even planned in detail what food she would order on her first visit. In the general bleakness of prison life, swamped by deprivations of every kind, her emotional life had become centred around food. She remembered drawing up as many as eleven different menus for her first visit to the Florian. Because so much of her life had been bound up with that café, she had forgotten that it in fact served up indifferent food. One went there primarily to meet one's friends, to kibbitz over a game of chess, to look at and listen to other people. From the other world, however, the remembered meals had glowed with culinary genius.

About a block away from the café Judith stopped suddenly and looked into the window of a music shop. With the sixth sense she'd developed over the years, she felt she was being followed. She casually turned her head from the window in the direction from which she had come. For a moment she saw only the milling crowds. Then she picked out a tall young man in a navy blue suit standing at the cinema about thirty feet away, examining the stills of the forthcoming film. Her mouth felt dry and her knees began to shake. Nonsense. What purpose was there in tailing her on the first morning of her release? What could she communicate, and to whom? She hurried on towards the café, her lighter mood destroyed.

Before she walked into the Florian, she turned around again; the young man had disappeared. The window of the café held an abundance of almond tarts, cheese cakes, yeast buns, Danish pastries and an assortment of biscuits. A warm vanilla smell wafted through the door onto the pavement, luring buyers. Judith felt more relaxed as she walked into the shop. At the far end of the counter stood Mrs Lonsdale, an elderly woman who for years had kept a 'special' almond tart for her on Friday evenings.

'Miss Fletcher!' she called out happily. 'My dear Miss Fletcher! Where have you been all this time? Overseas again? How naughty of you not to say goodbye. But you're so thin, my dear. And so pale. Not much sun over there, I suppose. This is still the best country in the world.'

Was it possible that she did not know, Judith wondered. But she responded gratefully to Mrs Lonsdale's warm hug. Judith had heard that there had even been a photograph of her in the *Daily Mail* during the trial.

'I've been away,' she confirmed.

'So you have, so you have. I'll speak to you later, my dear. Go upstairs and have yourself a nice cuppa.'

'Could I leave my suitcase with you until lunch time?'

'Of course. Here, let's put it behind the counter. Goodness, you travel light! When I go to Durban for a few weeks I've always got trunks of useless baggage with me. Leave it right here.'

Judith walked up the familiar stone stairs. The first five feet of wall was panelled with wood and the rest covered with faded wallpaper that had hung there for as long as Judith could remember. At the top of the stairs were two green doors marked 'Ladies' and 'Gentlemen'. The main room of the restaurant was empty. Five rows of ceramic-tiled tables stretched away across the long room towards the veranda where a few people sat eating breakfast. A stuffed antelope's head looked down onto the empty room. The sun streamed through the east windows.

I hope this building will never be pulled down, Judith thought, as she went outside. Today, more than ever, the Florian seemed the one unchangeable element in Johannesburg. Two elderly ladies were having tea and buttered buns. On different parts of the balcony sat three men with their newspapers open on their tables. There was no one Judith knew or recognised.

The tables standing in the direct sunlight were empty. Judith chose one facing Twist Street. It was dusty and weather-worn; the chairs were faded and peeling. Even the tin ashtrays had not changed, though they were grubbier and more dented. They were hot to the touch from the sun.

'Good morning, Miss Fletcher,' a deep African voice said at her side. 'What will you have for breakfast?'

'Iphraim!' she cried, stretching out her hand. She withdrew immediately he averted his eyes from it. 'How nice to see you again.'

'How is Miss Fletcher?' he asked, looking at her carefully. 'You've been away a long time.'

'I'm better now, thank you. How is Phillip?'

Phillip was his only son. She had taught him at night school several years ago. He should be writing his matriculation exam at the end of the year, she calculated.

'Phillip was arrested five months ago. Tsotsis chased him one night on his way from school. He jumped into a car, to hide away. The tsotsis ran past him and the boss came out of the house. Phillip was arrested for trying to steal the car. He got eighteen months.'

'Iphraim! Didn't he have a lawyer?'

'It didn't help, ma'am. It was Phillip's word against the white man's.'

Judith looked down at the sugar basin Iphraim had put in the centre of the table.

'Hey, boy! Waiter! My bill!' one of the men called out to Iphraim.

Nothing changes. Judith looked across the road at the building activity, at the cranes swinging precariously across the busy street, at the white foremen directing black workers. Beneath the surface prosperity, the delirious construction, the busy, hustling crowds, Johannesburg was the same as ever, drawing anything sane and wholesome into its murky depths.

'The same, Miss Fletcher?' Iphraim asked when he returned to her table.

'Do you know, Iphraim, I've forgotten what "the same" is. I've thought so often of what I would order when I came back here that I don't remember what I used to have.'

'A glass of milk with anchovy toast, madam,' Iphraim said.

'Let's be different today. I'll have toasted cheese with a cup of real coffee. The coffee at my hotel was terrible.'

'Phillip says they don't even get coffee.'

'I know, Iphraim, I know.'

Judith sat in the sun for two hours. By the time she rose to leave she felt warmed through and slightly lethargic. She left her paper on the table. There was not a single item in it, including many of the advertisements, which she had not read. She took up her bag and said goobye to Iphraim. As she stepped onto the covered part of the veranda she saw the tall young man in the navy blue suit sitting at a table, reading a newspaper.

AMELIA HOUSE

Conspiracy

from *Unwinding Threads* ed. by C.H. Brunes (1983)

Pretoria: Immorality Act: 1957 Session of Parliament increased the maximum penalty for illicit carnal intercourse between whites and non-whites to seven years imprisonment. It also became an offence to conspire to commit an act.

Amy stared at the window high in the wall. The row of windows met the ground level of the basement room. Through the ivy she watched the feet of passing students. A starling pecked at the window. The University of Cape Town nestled against the slope of the mountain at Rondebosch. The marble pillars of Jameson Hall shone out over the ivy covered walls. Amy liked to stop at the entrance of Jameson Hall where she could look back and take a full view of the campus. All those steps leading up from the road — she always meant to count and never did: the student residences (for Whites Only); the playing fields (for Whites Only); and then she let her gaze go out to the horizon across the Cape Flats. This panorama she enjoyed again and again. Amy usually enjoyed working in the archives, but today she felt trapped inside the mountain.

As she sat trying to imagine from the books what the Cape looked like when Simon van der Stel was Governor, the view from the top of the steps kept obtruding. She could sit in this room undisturbed because not many students came to this section.

'How much would I have to pay to know those deep and profound thoughts?' Saimon broke into Amy's reverie.

'You shouldn't creep up on me like that. Me heart can't stand it.'

'Admit it's my presence that sends your heart pounding. This six-foot Adonis makes his little five-foot and-a-dot mere mortal woman tremble.'

'The conceit of the cave man — not god. How did you know I was here?'

'Don't I always know where to find you? I changed into a butterfly and peeped in at each window. You waved to me when I fluttered by five minutes ago.'

'A butterfly? Why not just send your spirit to inhabit Prof. Grayson's poodle? It gets all over campus.'

'I know you like butterflies better. You'll try to catch me and stroke my wings. You stroking my body — what a thought!'

Saimon held Amy's hands and kissed her forehead, her eyelids, each cheek and then took her in his arms as she turned up her mouth to respond to his kiss.

'Enough. I might just forget how immoral we are and let you kiss me the rest of the morning.' Amy broke away hurriedly. Looked up at the windows. Only the passing feet; no eyes peering in. Even the starling had flown away.

'I managed to get two tickets for the Roman Catholic Students' Annual Ball. So here, Miss Baptist, is yours, and this one is for Mr Jew. I bet we'll be the most devout Catholics present. I've also thought of a plan for us to meet on my parents' boat.'

'Kristina and John are going to the dance. I can arrange for John to take me and you can escort Kristina. Nothing more respectable — a coloured couple and a white couple — no immorality there.'

'You've become quite a schemer too. Want to see more of me, hey? Not content with kisses in the archives and pecks behind the book stacks? I'll have to watch it. I think my downfall is being plotted.'

'I don't have to take risks for you, Saimon Zolkov. There are any number of safe dates I can have.'

'Only joking, my little black bird.'

'An English literature major resorts to clichés. Even your Romantic poets could give you a better image. Black bird. Be careful where you call me that name. I've already been told not to allow myself to be insulted. You never forget my colour.'

'Why so touchy today? You know it was your raven black curls that first caught my eye. Shall I say, my little raven black bird?'

'I wish I was thousands of miles from this place. I want to laugh and run across a sunny beach with you. Not sneak around. A peck on the cheek behind the Social Science book stack. A quick squeeze near Humanities. I could write a paper on a catalogue of our courtship.'

'It's hard for me too. We're not ashamed. But we have to behave as if we are. Please, Amy, don't get bitter. Soon our exams will be over. Graduation will be over and we'll have a honeymoon on the Costa

Brava.' Amy was almost smiling. 'We can't feel the warm sands of *these* beaches between our toes,' Saimon pulled Amy close to him. 'But I promise you, my little Amy, we'll run across the beaches of Spain.'

'And no looking around for policemen to spring out like cockroaches from any crack.'

'Mr and Mrs Zolkov in sunny Spain.'

'I didn't even want to think about that. I'm glad your mother approved of me and will let you go to England. But then there's still your father.'

'Amy, with him it's not colour. It's religion. You know that. He probably has a good Jewish girl in mind for me.'

'I accept that. My mother is anxious to see me leave here. I don't suppose she'll ever sleep easy until I'm safely out of Cape Town.'

'I forgot to ask. How did your passport interview go?'

'If Prof. Inskip were handing out acting awards, I could've won it for the acting I did at that interview. I was ever so humble and my mother did herself proud too. She went on about how she kept money from my late father's insurance to send me on this trip and what a good girl I was and how I deserved a nice holiday and I would be back to teach our coloured children. Our schools need good children and teachers. She went on and on. There the old man was, with his broken-down typewriter trying to fill in responses to his set questions: 'What do you know about Communism? Do you belong to any banned organization? Why are you going? How long will you stay? How much money have you got?'

'You're not serious, are you? All those questions just to get a passport?'

Amy sat still a second or two. It struck her that Saimon really knew very little of the life of coloureds. Very little of her life.

'An interview at the main police station, Caledon Square, no less. You ought to have seen the poor old *Boer* trying to type with two fingers. I could hardly keep a straight face.'

'A no-laugh pantomime, hey?'

'I wanted to laugh, but couldn't risk one slip. I was desperate for that passport and had to give all the correct responses. There was me, a History major, saying "Communism? I have no time to read rubbish!" with raised eyebrows and a suitably disgusted expression.'

'Why didn't you give him a lecture on the ideological differences between Marx and Lenin?'

'He probably hadn't ever heard of those two gentlemen. I played it straight. I had a good rehearsal. John went for his interview last week. He briefed me. I passed, I guess, because the *Boer* said he would see that I get the passport as soon as I have my return ticket. My mother went to buy it today. I sail on the Windsor Castle seven days after Graduation.'

'I don't suppose you realize that I first declared my love to you one year ago today.'

'Declared your love, no less. I'll excuse you that quaint expression considering you are busy with a paper on the Romantic Poets. Yes. I do remember being caught on the top gallery behind the History books. I also remember you stared at me a whole year during English II classes.'

'But you stared back, you bold hussy.'

'You found a timid little black bird behind the bold hussy.'

'Not timid. Bold and ready to hold on to the worm she caught.'

'I didn't see the worm putting up any fight. He was only too willing to be carried off to be devoured.'

'I do believe there is something metaphysical about that image, or is it a metaphor?'

'A final year English student, doubting his images and metaphors?'

'Gosh. It's time for our lecture. We'll have a lecture on Revenge Tragedy if our dear Prof. remembers his topic.'

'You go first. I'll follow later. I can't face any suspicious looks from our librarian.'

'Will you be back here this afternoon?'

'No. I'll see you tomorrow in my History tutor's office. She'll give me a key. I don't want us to meet here anymore. I feel we're being watched. Kristina says to watch out for Mr Alex.'

'Mr Alex?'

'You know him. The coloured man who sits at the back of the class.'

'Oh yes, that old man. What about him?'

'Don't you wonder why he's taken six years for a three-year course?'

'I know he's been around a long time, but judging by the questions he asks, I didn't wonder why he took two years for each course.'

'That's all part of his act. Do you know what his major is? He's a government agent. Kristina told me. She should know. You know who her father is, don't you?'

'Yes. Chief of Police. But I also think you mustn't imagine surveillance. He's probably here to report on the political opinions of the students.'

'No, Saimon. I'm not going to take a chance on that. Even if it's not Mr Alex watching us, I feel somebody is.'

'Okay. We'll be careful.'

'Remember my History tutor's office tomorrow.'

'See you then. Don't forget the big ball. Save a few dances for me. The last dance. I'll catch Kristina later. See her after class. Kolbe House at eight. Don't fly away.'

'Stomp on any cockroaches you see.'

John and Amy joined the other students gathered around the two fountains in the centre of the ballroom. Every year the engineering students rigged up a unique way of serving the wine. The previous year a big steam engine puffed away burning brandy. After the remarks about the waste, the planning committee promised to make every drop available for drinking. This year they had constructed two fountains — one spouting red wine and the other white wine. Mugs hung around the base of each fountain. Although John and Amy were as intrigued as the other students by the beautiful fountains, they were both more interested in trying to locate Saimon and Kristina.

Amy wore a long yellow organza sheath dress. Huge butterfly sleeves were an eye-catching feature. She had tied her waist-length black curls together at the nape of her neck with a big yellow bow. She wore no make-up and no jewellery. She was aware that she was getting second glances from many of the men.

'Ladies and Gentlemen, dinner is served. Stand not on the order of your seating, but be seated or words to that effect. As a Law student I'm allowed to misquote Shakespeare,' boomed out Bertram Davidson, the President of the Roman Catholic Students' Union.

Katrina and Saimon sat at the other end of the table from John and Amy. Neither couple paid much attention to the speeches and food. They waited for the dancing to begin.

'As President of the Union, I wish to welcome all members and friends. Tonight we say farewell to Father McInnis who helped to keep Kolbe House truly Catholic and not just Roman Catholic. This is the only place at the University of Cape Town where everybody, regardless of colour and creed can mix freely. As we are here for festivities, I don't intend making a political speech, but I would like everybody to be reminded of the greatness of Kolbe House. As a non-white on this campus, I know what it feels like to pay recreation fees for tennis courts and swimming pools I'm not allowed to use. Not to be welcomed at the Freshmen's Ball because my colour denies me the right to a ticket. So I wish to propose a toast to Kolbe House, Father McInnis, and all true Catholics among us.'

'Hear, hear. Long live Kolbe.'

'I wish to thank all our friends for their continued support. Now to the dancing.'

John and Amy hurried to the ballroom and swung into a quick-step. Although they had to continue to be absorbed in each other, both looked around for Saimon and Kristina. Although Kolbe House boasted its liberal attitudes, all the mixed couples knew they had to tread softly. Spies and cockroaches hide in cracks.

'Good evening, Kristina, Saimon. Glad you could make it. Hope you enjoy yourselves. As a Roman Catholic member with a Baptist partner, I would like to welcome my Jewish friend with his Dutch Reformed partner. As our President said — a truly Catholic gathering. Could I have the next dance with your lovely partner?'

'Only if I'm allowed a dance with your lovely partner.'

Amy floated in Saimon's arms totally oblivious to anybody or anything around her. To be held by him for such a long time sent a chill of fear and excitement through her.

'What's that shiver for? Not scared again? You look so beautiful, I can't bear to see you hanging on John's arm. That was the longest dinner I've ever had to sit through. I don't know what I ate.'

'John is jealous of Katrina on your arm and so am I and I daresay Katrina doesn't like me with John — but we have to fool the cockroaches.'

'Kolbe House will be seeing a lot of us. I've agreed to join a symposium on Comparative Religions next week. They might convert me yet.'

'I'm glad you'll be there. I offered to help Francis with the catering. See you there.'

'John invited Katrina and me to join the two of you on a tour of the grounds in half-an-hour. It's the best time to go into the woods to see Father McGeown's ghost.'

Amy became vaguely aware of other couples dancing around her. Some of them she had suspected of going together. She felt safer, knowing there were others like her and Saimon, but she could never shake off the deep fear of knowing what the penalty was if she and Saimon were ever caught.

Saimon returned a dazed Amy to John.

'Saimon, Katrina has agreed to view the ghost. We'll meet you on the back verandah. Meanwhile the key word is, circulate. Nobody sticks to his partner so move around. Don't forget to stomp the cockroaches!'

The game had to be played convincingly. Each one had to appear to be completely unattached and ready to play the field. Katrina and Amy did not see John and Saimon during the next hour. They were constantly claimed for one dance after the other.

'Time for a breath of fresh air, Amy,' John announced when he returned. 'The ghost will be walking soon. Not scared I hope?'

Saimon watched John and Amy leave the ballroom hand in hand. He caught the pained expression on Katrina's face.

'We can go out the front door and walk around the side of the house. There seem to be many interesting nooks to explore,' said Saimon as he led Katrina outside.

Chinese lanterns swung in the breeze on the front verandah. Bright coloured lights glowed in the two big oak trees at the gate. Katrina and Saimon were anxious to get out of the light to the dark side of the house.

'A bit spooky this old house. I won't venture upstairs,' remarked Katrina.

'Won't venture upstairs. A little spooky. But willing to see Father McGeown's ghost walking in the woods?'

'I'm not afraid when I'm with John.'

'Thanks, kind lady. I thought all women felt protected in my presence.'

'Be serious. You know what I mean. In case I forget — thanks for escorting me here. It means so much to get to be alone with John.'

'No thanks necessary, Katrina. That score is even. You and John — Amy and me.'

Saimon and Katrina wondered who was left in the ballroom since they seemed to stumble over one couple after another, until their eyes got used to the dark. The back of the house was not lit at all.

'Thought you'd eloped with my girl. Amy is no company out here under the stars when all she talks about is Saimon, her man,' John teased. 'We four have to go into the woods together and then we can pair off. Saimon, you'll have to watch for a light in that top window. It's Father McInnis' signal for everybody to return to the ballroom. I'll escort Amy back in, okay?'

'Thanks, John. Long live Kolbe. Come, my little black bird, off to the woods to build a nest.'

'Stomp the cockroaches,' John and Saimon chorused as they parted company ... seven years imprisonment ... offence to conspire to commit an act ...
conspire to ...
conspire to ...
offence ...

Amy approached the gate at the Table Bay Yacht Basin with outward defiance. She gave an extra tug at the turban she had tied around her head to hide her long curls. She hoped her old, lace-up brown brogues looked shabby enough. She made certain that her floral overall was longer than her coat. Although she never smoked, this afternoon she dangled a cigarette from the corner of her disguise, but she could not relax until she was past the guard and on the yacht.

'Where do you think you're going? No hawkers allowed here. What're you selling? I have to inspect that basket,' the guard growled at Amy.

'No, Baas, I'm not selling nothing. Young Master Zolkov's having a party tonight on the boat. I have to clean up the rooms and prepare the table.'

'They usually send their houseboy. And they always let me know who's coming.'

'The boy is busy at the house. The old Master and Madam is having a dinner. I work by the family next door. I said I would help Young Master Zolkov. Which boat is it?'

'The white and blue one second on the left. I'll have to ask Mr Zolkov not to forget to let me know who's coming to the party. Security is my job.'

'Yes, Baas. You do you job good.'

Amy lifted her basket and tried to seem not too eager to get to the boat. As she reached the gangway, she noticed Saimon sunbathing on deck. She hoped he would not laugh at her disguise.

'Master Saimon. Security wants to know about your guests tonight,' she shouted. She made certain the guard heard.

'Go tell him I'll be down later with the list. He was at lunch when I came through,' Saimon shouted back, hardly looking at Amy.

She did not really want to face the guard again but she had to obey her 'Master Saimon.'

When Amy returned, Saimon had gone below. As she descended the stairs into the galley, Saimon doubled up with laughter.

'I'll close my eyes and open my arms. I think I could kiss you if I keep my eyes closed.'

'No, Master Saimon, no kisses. I have to go up and clean the deck. I don't want the Security to worry. No, no, Master Saimon, don't forget about the Immorality Act. If the police catch you kissing a coloured girl who will be arrested?' Amy acted the shocked servant pushing off her boss's advances. 'Patience, Saimon. I have to clean the decks first. The guard might come around to see what's happening. I'll have to keep on my beautiful outfit.'

Amy collected the bucket of water and brooms and clattered up the stairs. She set to work with loud mumblings about having to waste her time cleaning when all those wild young people would only be messing everything with wine tonight.

Saimon returned from his talk with the Security Officer and started up the engine.

'Hey, Master Saimon, I'm not working on no moving boat. I don't swim. Where're you going?' Amy tried to sound indignant.

'I'm taking it around to False Bay to meet the Shapiros. You can work on the way.'

'Master Saimon, your mother said nothing about no trip. I'll work inside while we go. No big wave is gonna knock me off the top. I'm going to ask for danger money.' Amy shouted as she hurried below. She collapsed on the nearest bunk, grateful that she need no longer play a role.

'Shouldn't you be navigating this vessel, Master Saimon? We can't risk running aground.'

'Don't worry. Zolly is at the helm. He was in the shower when you arrived so you didn't notice. Now don't get upset. Zolly has known about us even before I was brave enough to approach you. He has a girl-friend of colour too (as our Prime Minister says). Zolly knows how we feel.'

Amy stiffened for a moment but then relaxed as Saimon pulled off the turban.

'Let's get the real Amy out from under all this. Everything off — including that hideous lipstick.'

Saimon took off Amy's overall, while she untied her shoes. Both shivered with excitement. Amy wore a bikini under her overall. As soon as Saimon got the overall off, he started kissing her all over.

'I still have to remove my hideous lipstick, remember?'

'To hang with the lipstick. We've waited too long to be together like this. We've waited. A whole year sneaking kisses behind book stacks and accidental hand brushing. This is our day.'

'Slowly. Have you forgotten the Roman Catholic Students' Ball? What happened under the willow between a certain Jew and a Baptist?'

'We're alone here and nothing to stop us.'

'Police patrol in boats too. I can't help feeling a little afraid.'

'Zolly will signal long before any Coast Guard can come near.'

Saimon had removed the top of her bikini. Amy instinctively pulled her long, black curls over her breasts. Even if she was in love with Saimon and knew she wanted him to touch her, all the guilt of her strict Baptist upbringing caused her to stiffen in his embrace.

'I'm sorry, Saimon. I'm just too scared. No. I can't think straight: guilt, fear, love. I want you. But I'm scared to go all the way. Let's just stop right now. I'm bound to mess things up. Saimon, please don't be angry. We can wait another three months. London doesn't seem so far off. Graduation — London — us together without fear. Right now I'm scared stiff and that's not how I want the first time to be. Please understand.'

'Speech over? We've had all the academic discussions about your virginity. I respect your views. So relax, little Amy. I'll know when to stop. Just let's enjoy what we can of each other.'

Amy relaxed as best she could with half an ear open for a Coast Guard whistle.

'Time to stop, Saimon. Have you forgotten the Shapiros don't know about us? Can't take any chances. I'd better get into my work clothes and finish the cleaning.'

'Okay. You get the food and table organized. I'll check everything above.'

'Yes, Sir. Right, young Master Saimon.'

Maximum penalty for illicit carnal intercourse between whites and non-whites increased to seven years' imprisonment ... also an offence to conspire ...

'A gathering of the penguins,' Amy bounced into Miriam's room. There were eight others in the room, all trying to freshen up their make-up and comb their hair. All wore white dresses and black graduation gowns.

'What a day! I thought the graduation ceremony would never end. Especially as I was almost last. Miriam and Saimon Zolkov bringing up the rear.'

'Although Amy Abrahams went up first, I just wanted it to be all over. I only waited to see you and Saimon,' Amy remarked.

'I looked at that piece of neatly, rolled-up paper and couldn't believe that that was what the three years of slogging was all about.'

'The great anti-climax is what graduation is all about,' remarked another girl.

'Maybe we will all feel less cynical tomorrow.'

'Tomorrow, tomorrow. I wonder how I will feel after tonight,' Amy thought out aloud.

'Cheer up, Amy. What about three weeks from tomorrow?' Miriam tried to be cheerful. 'By the way, Linda, what did Prof. Smit find to talk about at dinner? You hung on his every word,' Miriam added trying to distract attention from Amy and her problems.

'He invited me to see his etchings.'

'That old line!' chorused all the girls.

'Miriam, why has Saimon decided to fly to London this evening instead of Sunday?'

'Yes. Isn't that a sudden change?'

'Nothing sudden or sinister. The 10:30 tonight makes it more convenient for my uncle to meet him tomorrow evening instead of Monday. We'd better join the rest of the party now,' Miriam replied.

'I'll be out in a moment. I need to repair my slip strap. Do you have a little pin for me, Miriam?' asked Amy.

'Be right with you. I'll take everybody else in first to meet Mummy and Daddy.'

Amy sat down at the dressing table recalling the day's events. Graduation, lunch with the English Faculty, tea with the German Faculty, dinner with the History Faculty and now Saimon's farewell. Such a short one.

'Now let's fix that non-existent broken slip strap. Since I'm soon to be your big sister, you might as well use my shoulder to cry on,' Miriam spoke as she came into the room.

'Do you think that we're panicking for nothing? Saimon and I haven't been alone at any time for the past two weeks. Do you think the police are still suspicious? Must he leave tonight? Can't the 10:30 go without him? Will he be waiting for me in London?'

'Amy, you know you can't take any chances. You'll only be separated for three weeks. We have our spies too. We've been assured that the police are on to your involvement with Saimon.'

'I'm sure Kristina told her father when John broke off with her. She's so bitter against coloureds now. The Chief of Police's daughter crazy about coloureds!'

'No. It's not Kristina. She's also meeting John overseas. The break-off was a front.'

'So who could have spied on us? Oh, yes I know. It's that old man, Mr Alex. He told me he was a Government Investigation Officer. "A fancy name for a spy", I said. I'm sure I made him angry. You know the one that has been at 'varsity goodness knows how long and nobody can figure out what his major is. How long does it take for a major in spying to graduate?'

'Amy there's no use upsetting yourself like this. You are wasting precious time. Let's join the party. Saimon leaves here for the airport in two hours. Don't you want to be near him?'

'I'm sorry, Miriam. Parting is such sweet sorrow and yet I can't say goodbye till it be morrow. We won't even be alone before he leaves.'

'Cheer up. Good news. Join the party, then we can slip away down to the end of the garden to Isaac's studio. I'll show you his latest canvas until Saimon can get away.'

'You mean Isaac has decided to accept me into this family?'

'Everybody is batting for you. Saimon wants to tell Daddy tonight, but I think he shouldn't. Mummy also wants him to wait until after the wedding. Daddy will accept the deed done.'

'I'm ready to join the mob.' Amy bit back some tears. She hurried over to the bar. A drink would be something to hang onto. Only when she reached the bar, did she notice Saimon there. A slight panic made her pull up short. Above all, she must avoid obvious contact with him. There could be a spy at the party. Now she was face to face with him, she had to behave as casually as possible.

'Glad to see you here. I didn't know whose party you were going to first. Did you hear I'm leaving for London this evening?'

'Miriam told me. She told me to come here first. I've three other parties tonight. Mine is tomorrow. We'll have a week of parties if I survive tonight.'

'You can drink my health at some of those parties. I'll be busy with interviews. I hope I get into Cambridge.'

'I thought you were going to get a job on your uncle's newspaper.'

'No. He wants me to study at a British University for at least a year first.'

Amy had heard this all before, but she and Saimon had got used to this special casual public conversation.

'I have to go now. I see Miriam signalling to me. She's going to show me Isaac's new painting. I'm so excited. If you have to go before I get back in, I wish you all the best. Good luck in England. I'll be in England in three weeks' time. Might bump into you at Speakers' Corner or the Tower of London. One never knows,' Amy threw over her shoulder as she hurried to join Miriam.

Amy did not really see any of the pictures. It seemed like hours before Saimon came.

'No, Miriam. No need for all the lights. Light the lamp,' Saimon suggested.

'I'll light some candles instead.'

As soon as one candle was lit, Miriam switched off the lights and hurried back to the house.

'My little Amy Abrahams. Three weeks hence, little Amy Zolkov.' Saimon held her close. 'Shaking all over as usual. Still. Quiet, little black bird.'

'I'm trying not to cry. Tonight one-and-a-half hours and then nothing. Nothing for three weeks. Saimon, you're sure you'll be waiting for me?'

'Don't doubt me now, Amy. Our love is the only thing that has meaning in this crazy country. My eyes can tell colours apart, but not my heart.'

'I wish I could fly away tonight too. I'm so very, very scared.'

'Come here. Sit on the floor. Can't cast shadows on the windows then.'

'You're still scared too, aren't you, Saimon? Just hold tight. I don't want you to let go of me.'

Amy responded to Saimon's kisses as she had never done before. For the first time she wanted to give herself to him completely. She took off her graduation gown and spread it on the floor.

'Tonight I can't believe in my Baptist doctrine. I might never see you again. I can't help feeling as if you're going off to war. You might be killed on duty. Separation. Death. It's the same.'

'I'll be waiting. I'll be at Southampton when the Windsor Castle docks. My wife.'

Saimon blew out the candles then returned to their place on the floor.

'Come here, my wife.'

'Yes. Your wife. I'll be that tonight. I'm not scared anymore. We can stay in this studio for an hour at the most and you're not going to forget this hour ever.'

'Promises. Promises.'

Amy stopped any further remarks from him by kissing him. She wrapped her tongue around his. Tickled his palate. Ran her tongue along his gums. Gently sucked his tongue into her mouth.

'I'm not dreaming still, am I? My little Amy, you do surprise me.'

'I'd better stop, if you object.'

'More. More ...'

'Well, I must live up to the idea of being a hot, black woman. Isn't that why you fell for me? For the promises?' Amy tried to be flippant.

'Amy, my Amy, I love you. We don't have time for analysis now. Don't ever forget I love you — not because of colour. I love you — you the person — my little black bird.'

'Deep down I know that. Sometimes I just can't think it's all true. I believe in my love for you. Yes. I do believe in your love.'

Saimon ran his fingers over her face and down her arms. Clasped her hands between his and kissed each cheek. Soon Amy had discarded her white dress and Saimon was in his underwear. Amy felt free, but still afraid to enjoy her freedom. 'I'm frightened. Will it hurt? I want you. I'm not cheap. I love you. Love you ... love you. Don't hurt me.'

'You know I'll be gentle.' Saimon suddenly became very quiet as he tried to make certain he had not heard some movement outside.

'Somebody's outside, isn't there?' Amy could hardly get the words out.

'No. It's just the dog. Relax, Amy, relax.'

Amy lay still for a few moments to reassure herself that there was nobody out there.

'You have to relax, little bird. There will be some pain when I go in, but not much if you relax.'

'Pain. A sweet pain. I want to be your wife tonight. You believe me, don't you?' Amy tried to reassure herself. She had been running her tongue over his body but stopped suddenly. 'I don't know now though. Perhaps we should wait another three weeks,' Amy mused for a second or two. 'No. No. It's right for it to be now. You love me? Don't you? Saimon?'

Saimon sat up because he thought he had heard some steps on the gravel. He crawled over to the window, tried to peer outside. He could see the party guests in the house and on the porch dancing, eating and laughing.

'Nobody anywhere near here. Miriam will see to that. I see her on the porch.'

Saimon and Amy settled back on their spot. Amy felt the need to keep talking. 'Wait until you're married. The man will lose respect for you.' She pictured her mother giving her that oft-repeated advice. 'If he loves you, he'll wait. You have to be extra certain, remember he might be playing a trick on a coloured girl. They use you, but they marry their own kind.' Amy recalled her mother's very earliest remarks. Does he really love me? She lay with her legs tight together, but as he rolled onto her, he pushed them apart without resistance from her. She was not going to allow herself to be haunted. Saimon was in no hurry. He wanted Amy to be at ease. The music from the party drifted down to them. They were far from the crowd. They had time just to explore each other.

Saimon was ready. He thrust, deep. Beautiful pain. Amy yelled. Flashlights. Flashlights through the window. The door kicked open. Lights ... more lights. Saimon and Amy lay in the middle of a sea of brilliant lights. Their world caving in around them. Two very tiny people viewed by giants in boots. Lights. Policemen everywhere like cockroaches. Even more lights. More cockroaches.

Saimon could hear his mother and Miriam screaming down the path. The music from the party drifted on. Saimon tried to wrap Amy in the cloak as he grabbed his clothes.

The shiny 10:30 South African Airways bird left for London on time. One passenger did not make it.

ANNA MAZIBUKO

There You Are Under The Cows

from *Vukani Makhosikazi* ed. by J. Barrett, A. Dawber, B. Klugman, I. Obery, J. Shindler, J. Yawitch (1985)

'The first place I worked was on the farms. I worked in Amersfoort [South Eastern Transvaal] in the yard of Jan Niekerk. I was 12 years old and my job was to look after the children of the nonatjie — his wife. But at that time I didn't earn any money. I just worked for a plate of food.

'Then my family moved to Morgenzon in the Eastern Transvaal. It is near Standerton. I was 14 then. I worked on a farm and we used to plough there. We didn't earn wages then. That was the time when you got some of the crop, but there was no crop that year, so we moved after six months. There was no crop because there was no rain.

'I ran away from the farms and went to the town of Morgenzon and worked for a doctor. I earned R3 a month. I left that job because the missus was very mean. I was then 15 years old.

'So I went to look for work with other whites and found a job with a woman. But she was very poor. Her floors were made from cow dung. She paid me five shillings a month. But she made me a pretty dress so I had something to wear. She made it with her own hands.

'But I only stayed four months and then I went to some others called Groenewald. There I did everything — wash, cook, clean the house. There I earned R3 a month. I stayed there for six months and I left and went off again.

'So then I went to Holmdene [Eastern Transvaal] and stayed with my sister on a farm. That man's name was Swanepoel. I was paid R4 a month doing lots of different jobs. I was expected to work as hard as an adult but very quickly. I had to weed, thresh the mielies, and bind the mielies into bundles. I really worked there For every sack of mielies I got five cents. It had to be absolutely full, and white inside.

'In the farms you work very hard — even today people still work like that. I lived with my sister in Holmdene for a year. The boss we were working for left and so we went to Standerton when the family home moved there from Morgenzon. This was after my father died.

'I lived in Standerton with my brothers for a while. I worked for Mr Viljoen who is now a very important man in Pretoria. He is now called Doctor Viljoen. He was the superintendent of the township in Standerton. Then he went to Ermelo, and then to Nelspruit. He was the superintendent and so his job was to smash down the townships and make them pretty. He spoke very good Zulu. He had four children, but I've forgotten their names. I used to look after them.

'He demolished Ermelo location and made Phumule. And in Standerton he demolished all our tin houses and made "Losmachine". In this way he progressed eventually to Pretoria.

'He was never a doctor of bodies. He was a doctor of demolition. He's got old now. I used to wash and clean and cook. I earned R8 a month from Mr viljoen. In that time everything went according to permission. I didn't have permission from the farm I was born on to work in the town. Dr Viljoen fixed me up and got the permission.

'After Dr Viljoen I worked for another household. But that woman was impossible. She was really kwaai [angry]. So I left there. I ran away. I ran away from a lot of places. I'm not prepared to work for whites who make me cross.

'So then I worked for another boss in Standerton — also earning R8 a month. I left that place properly, because my permission had expired. So I left and went back home.

'When I went home I had a baby. She only lived one year and a month. She died. So I left.

'I decided it was the time to get married, so I set off to find a man. The one I found was no good, but I had many of his children. I had nine, but five died. I still have four children. They were all the children of the man I married. Three of them were boys.

'That man was from Standerton. He's from the farms, and he's there until today. I couldn't agree with him so I left. Last week I went to look for my children. I found the youngest who is ten. The only one I have with me is my daughter. The three boys are with him. I am separated now from that man. But I said to him he should keep the children, because I knew when I left I'd be very poor.

'Life on the farms is very hard. It's very heavy. In Standerton where I lived with the father of my children we would get up at six in the morning. The woman of the family (that is I), would have to start cooking and the man would have to start milking. Even now he's still milking at six.

'After cooking for the children and my husband I would go to the farmhouse and do the cooking and cleaning. I earned R12 a month — working for Mr Human and his wife and daughter-in-law.

'At the farms there's a lot of ploughing. If it does not rain you're in a lot of trouble. My husband has always earned R30 a month and a bag of meal. And he would get the corners of the fields (the agterskot), after the reaping. So if the crop died you died.

'The white farmer never gave us extra. And yet he knew my husband was a man with a wife and children. In the years when there was no rain, those were the years when our children died.

'My husband used to have two cattle. I am not sure if he still has them.

'He had three wives. The first one left in 1969. She couldn't bear it. The first wife lasted for eight years. I stayed for 17 years. I realised I could never bear the way of life on the farms. I'd rather work for R40 a month and know that I'll get clothes and food. But there you never know.

'Even now that man is still milking at six o'clock. Every afternoon at 4pm he calls them in again to the shed and sits down beneath them and starts again to milk. That's the law of the whites. Whatever the weather, wherever you are. There you are under the cows.

'In the morning after the milking he must go out and plough the fields on the tractor, skoffel [weed and hoe the fields], start again to plough the fields, skoffel the fields ... and at four o'clock he must get off the tractor and get under the cows.

'Next morning same thing. Then when you've finished ploughing and skoffeling, back to the cows. After you've milked the cows you must go to make cream on the machine. And after the cream he can go home. That was his life. Day in and day out.

'As for me, my life was a white lady's kitchen — day in and day out. All for that R12.

'There were only two black households on the farm. That boss was dirt poor. His father died and he had to take over the farm. Before that he lived in a caravan, going from place to place with his children. When he got here to the farm he found us already here.

'That first year we certainly ploughed. We got 1800 bags, as well as sunflower seeds. That's where he got the money to buy the tractor.

'I left in 1979 on the 6th January. When I went I left another woman behind. That was his last wife. I left my children because I could see no other way out of it.

'My husband gave me R10 a month. I was supposed to buy everything for my children and myself. I couldn't manage. So I said good-bye. In the same way his first wife left him. And we left the young wife. But she'll also leave. She's got four children. But she'll leave too. In the six years the new wife was there she had four children. Only one died.

'Last week I went to see my children. They are really suffering now. At least when I was there I used to buy some things with the kitchen money. I used to get second hand clothes from whites. Now that I'm not working there's nothing I can do for them. At the time when I was working I used to send them clothes at Christmas.

'I sit at home because I can't get registered, and they suffer. Because they have no shoes and they have to walk to school their feet are cracked. That is the greatest poverty of my life — my children. But the eldest is all right. He's now working at Bronkhorstspruit. He got a job in Standerton with LTA, a construction company, and was transferred to Bronkhorstspruit. I went to try to find him to ask for money but I couldn't find him.

'When I left my husband I went to look for a job and I found one in Piet Retief in the Eastern Transvaal, working in the houses of men who were making the dam. In Piet Retief they refused to register me. This was in 1982.

'I worked for one woman for nine months. During that time the police arrested me and locked me up again and again. My missus would get me out.

'They kept saying I must go back to Standerton. I kept saying, back to what in Standerton? — I have no mother, no father. My father died in 1962 and my mother in 1982. And so I had to leave and I began to search for a place. So I went to look for my grandmother.

'So I came to Driefontein. I thought I could find a place to live, which I could have as an address and get registered. By luck I found my grandmother. I now live with her. I've been here for a year now.

'But the problem is I still can't get a contract and permission to work. So we haven't got money. I am really struggling. Now I'm really platsak [broke] because I went to visit my children and that finished me. If I could just get registered I could get a job easily, because there are jobs.

'There is only one in the family who is all right now. That is my one sister who now lives in Soweto and is married. There were ten of us, and eight lived. The rest of us are not married anymore. We have all really suffered. One sister lives in Standerton and she's got a house. But she has no children. She has nobody. Her two children died.

'My other sister is still in the kitchens in Standerton. She managed to bribe a pass. She bought a pass. So she's working. You can buy it from any white who will write a letter to say you were born on his farm and left it.

'But you get caught. Many of the whites have already been caught. Because once they've caught the white he betrays you. Then they put you in jail. There are lots of people who have tried it and some have succeeded. When you get evicted from Standerton you get evicted to KwaNdebele [bantustan north of Pretoria].

'What happened to my father in the end was that his young wife had a lover, and she and her lover killed him and left him in the forest.

'When we heard he had died I knew that was the end. Before that I always used to think that no matter how poor I was I could go back to my father. His place on the farm is now lost. His father was born there, and his father's father. My father's wife's lover was arrested because he was found with my father's pass. The case was heard in Standerton and he got seven years.

'Yes, I've had a hard life. It all started because my father deserted my mother in 1948 when I was seven years old. My father got another young wife and my mother went off with me and my brother.

'It was because of that we had to work. She really suffered for us. Working in the kitchens was a new thing. In those days we used to get mielie meal and eggs and would trade for sugar and things.

'In the time that I lived with my mother I thought and thought of a way to change things. I came up with getting married. I thought by getting married I would get my own place. So I tried it and it was terrible. So I left. And until today I've never solved that problem.

'So today I'm living here with my grandmother — the mother of one of the many brothers in my father's family.

'My main problem is still the pass. What I want is permission to work anywhere — not just in Piet Retief or somewhere. In Wakkerstroom if you can get a pass you can work in Jo'burg or Sasol — of course you can't go to Natal, but Jo'burg is good enough.'

JOHANNA MASILELA

Let Me Make History Please

from *Vukani Makhosikazi* ed. by J. Barrett, A. Dawber, B. Klugman, I. Obery, J. Shindler, J. Yawitch (1985)

Johanna Masilela was born in 1916 in the Vereeniging district where her father was a sharecropper.

'They called it Hokieslagt ... it was a farm. It was Willem Petoor's, an Afrikaner. My mother and father were working on the farm. He used to get many bags of mielies. They shared the products they grew. The farm was the boer's [farmer] farm, but he gave us land too — we'd share.'

As a child Johanna 'helped' at the farmer's house. Her father was a sharecropper. So he had to let the farmer use his family as workers. Johanna worked in the 'boer' house until she was eight years old and sent to school. When she was very young she became disabled.

'When I got crippled my mother was out working clearing the crops. That day I was left with my aunt and my mother's grandmother. We used to have fowls, pigs and oxen. We had a lot of pigs. Big pigs! My aunt 'abbad' me — tied me to her back — but then she got on top of the pig like a horse. Then when the pig said 'Hrruggh' I fell. I was small, about three years.

'When my mother came back, she found me crying, but they didn't tell her what happened, frightened perhaps that she might hit my aunt. So the foot swelled up slowly until at last they told her. You know in those days doctors were not too experienced. In any case it shrank. But I could not walk because I walk on my toes all the time.'

In time Johanna learned to walk well enough to make the long walk to school each day.

'It was a long distance from the place where we lived to where we attended school. Yes, so I used to walk with my crippled foot. And sometimes my father used to take me by horse cart and fetch me when it was raining or when it was very cold.'

Johanna was the eldest of four children, two brothers and a sister.

After she had been at school for a few years her family moved to Evaton outside Vereeniging where, until the 1950s freehold title was available to Africans.

'My father bought two stands when he felt we were working hard and were staying too far from school. My mother told him it was no good any more. She could no longer work. At the farms you work hard, yes. They were getting old then so we moved. We went to Evaton, nearer the school we attended.'

In 1927 Johanna was very ill and could not attend school. 'I got very sick. My neck and legs were full of sores. I couldn't walk. And then I went to hospital at Driefontein. They called it Thembisa Hospital at that time. I went there in November 1927 and I was there until March 1928.'

Johanna only attended school until the age of sixteen. After passing standard six she left school and stayed at home helping her mother.

In 1932 she left Evaton and went to live with her uncle in Sophiatown. She worked as a domestic servant in Mayfair, a suburb of Johannesburg.

'That's all I could do, because I only passed my standard six. I could work because I was brought up working. So there was nothing that could defeat me. You could only tell me to do this, do this, do this, and I used to do it.

'And funnily, I never got nice easy jobs. I used to get hard-working jobs. Scrub the floor, polish everything, washing, ironing, cooking, you know everything. But I could manage to do that, even with my foot. And if I got a job and wanted to leave, they didn't want me to go because they knew I was hard working.

'In 1937 I got a job at Melrose working for Mrs Sinclair. And there I got a very nice job because I was a baby-minder. That child was Shelley. I used to care for her. Sometimes her mother used to just leave and go to Durban and leave me with the child and the granny. Because she knew I knew everything about the child.

'That child used to be like my child. Because she never used to bother me. If the child was sick I phoned the doctor and the doctor came, treated the child and I nursed the child until she was well.

'It's where I got that experience of caring for children. I knew in the morning what I must do for the child. And I got to know if you are with a child you must know how to talk to a child, make speeches for her to laugh, read books and so forth. Everything, bath her, wipe the napkin clean. Must be clean, yes.

'Cook for the child. Until she could feed herself a little bit and while she eats I'm also eating, making speeches for her to laugh, so that when she laughs she eats more than when she's just quiet.

'Sometimes I had to go and take a blanket and go and sleep next to her so that she can see me and then she can start sleeping. And when she was asleep I would go out to my room. It was nice, I enjoyed it. It gave me very good experience.

'But Newlands was nearer Sophiatown. I thought, let me work in Newlands to be nearer home, so I can go home every day to see my husband. I used to do a lot of washing too. After giving one madam her washing, I'd go to the other one and wash. The following day I start ironing.'

Johanna's first child was born in 1940, the second in 1944, the third in 1951 and last in 1956.

'When I got pregnant I left the first job. Until I felt all right, then I worked and after that I used to leave the job, get the baby, and after two months, I start working again.

'I put the baby on my back and I used to let her sleep under the table where I was working, perhaps ironing. When she wasn't sleeping, she would go to the kitchen or out into the yard. The child I used to take with me to work was my second boy. The oldest one stayed with my mother in Evaton. I left him with my mother from when he was about six months.

'They didn't mind when I brought my children to work, my Europeans didn't. You know if you're a hard worker she must get soft. Because she knows that what you are doing is freeing her. But if you are lazy then she will notice everything, and she will say, 'You come with your children, you waste my time. You're caring for your child, you don't do my job. The thing that must be very important is the work.

'In 1957 Sophiatown was removed. They moved us to Meadowlands in Soweto. We didn't like it. You know, getting a new place which you're not used to, you think you're going to suffer. Because Sophiatown was near town you could take a bus. That time it was pounds, shillings and pence. Take a tickey [two and a half pence], go to town, tickey back. We thought it was going to be very far if we have to go to the station and travel by train. But then it just happened that we forgot about that Sophiatown removal.

'But I couldn't work in Johannesburg. I was too far. So I would go and buy fruit in the Indian market and come and sell fruit. In 1959 I got a job doing ironing in Empire Road, Parktown [Johannesburg suburb]. So I used to go once a week and leave that young one with my neighbour. The elder one would come back from school, bring the brother, so I'll find them at home.

'When we came in this house in Dube I had to do something else. A friend of ours was a teacher. They had a baby and he came to me and asked me where I was working, so I said, 'I'm ironing in Empire road.'

'Then he said, "Can't you look after my baby? Just tell me what that madam is paying you for doing her ironing. I will pay you more!" And I thought how can an African like myself say he can pay me money? I talked to my husband and he said, "Ag just try it."

'So I left the ironing and I started caring for that child. Now the gate was open. Every day I got somebody else who wanted me to care for their child.

'Had it not been for these children, where would I be now? The mothers bring their children in, they fetch the children and take them. It's not for me to travel by train.

'Right now I can't board a train because of my leg. I can't lift it high. I can't even get into these kombies [minibuses]. I can get into a car because a car is flat.

'Now where will I get that work? So I used to enjoy it. They used to help me, because if you're gnarled, your life is no more good. And you still see you're earning something. Can't you say thank God. Those children, they took me as their real mother. Because they don't know their mothers. They used to see their mothers late in the afternoons. I was the mother.

'But since 1983 I'm tired, I'm tired, you know. My leg is getting tired, paining sometimes. The muscles must have a rest. I've worked too hard. I'm crippled. With my leg it just becomes loose, as if I don't feel it. Sometimes it gets cool and sometimes it's hot.

'Since 1981 it started feeling like this. So I think I must give it a rest. I've been standing too long with it and doing hard work. I must say, thank God he has kept me standing with one foot all these years.

'When you are sick, each time a child cries you feel miserable. So I don't want to feel like that. I'm no longer in my same mood. Even if I see a child I could help by doing something, but I have no patience to stand up. When your whole body's tired you become cruel, so it's not nice. A child needs a very good care and you must be broadminded, have a nice feeling.

'All these years I've been so nice and I've enjoyed doing it. Now when I see it's no good I don't want it. I don't want to have children because I see now I haven't got patience any more. But I used to have a nice life, a very nice life.

'So I've left my history somehow. I'm happy that I've got somebody who will introduce me. Let me make history please. Johanna Masilela. My number is 827.'

JAYAPRAGA REDDY

Friends

from *On The Fringe Of Dreamtime And Other Stories*(1987)

She stretched her limbs languorously. Every morning she was gripped by this same reluctance to move and so acknowledge another new day. She could hear the children as they prepared for school in a frenzy of disorganized activity, bickering and slamming doors. At last, the front door slammed and the usual welcome silence descended upon the house. Sadhana sighed and prepared to luxuriate for another hour in the lulling warmth of her bed.

She never emerged before nine. Mornings were always the same. Suren slid out of bed around six and was gone by seven. Then the children awoke and clattered about the place. In the early days of her marriage, Suren used to like her to be up seeing to things. But after her last child, he stopped expecting it.

The door opened and Asha burst into the room. She clambered onto the bed and engulfed her in a tight hug. Sadhana received the embrace passively. At five, the child was a bundle of energy.

'I want tea,' she demanded.

'Just now, when Ma gets up,' Sadhana temporised.

'But I'm thirsty!' the child persisted.

She shut her eyes and feigned sleep. But the child's voice, loud and insistent, was intrusive and she rose indolently.

As she slipped into a gown, she studied herself in the mirror. After eleven years of marriage and three children, her figure was gone, she concluded ruefully. Only her skin was still smooth and youthful. Anyway, what did it matter? Suren hardly noticed her these days. Last night, she recalled his half-hearted love making. Why had he even bothered, she wondered bitterly. Her wedding anniversary ruined by his lack of interest and enthusiasm.

She turned away. She mustn't dwell on these things. There were so many things she didn't want to think about. Her mother's voice echoed in her mind.

'You let him get away with too much! His duty is to see to you and your children, not to other women!'

'But he gives me everything,' Sadhana had pointed out.

'Everything? What's everything when there's no love?' the old woman had retorted.

The kitchen was in a mess. The bread and milk were uncovered. Someone had spilled tea on the table. Oh well, Bessie would clear up. Vaguely, she was aware of her singing as she made the beds. Outside in the yard, Phumza, her four-year-old daughter sat quietly. Asha ran out to her, glad for her company.

'Drink your tea first,' Sadhana called out sharply.

Really, did Bessie have to bring her everyday? She was making a habit of it. At first, it had been just once or twice a week. Her excuse being that there was no one to look after her. How had she managed all these days? Her mother, Bessie explained, had been living with her. But now she had returned to the farm. At first she hadn't minded, for Asha seemed to enjoy the child's company. But now she viewed the friendship with mixed feelings.

She watched them through the window, chasing a ball, laughing and carefree. It wasn't good for her to mix too much with the child. She might pick up something. Really, she must have a word with Bessie about it. She noticed that these days Bessie too was getting fancy ideas. Like wanting her child to dress like Asha. Once, when Asha had been dressed in a new frock all ready to go out, Bessie had asked, 'Missus, where did you buy that dress?'

Sadhana had hesitated before answering. 'It's very expensive.'

'Never mind. I pay slowly,' Bessie had answered simply.

'There are shops ... where you can get good clothes at a bargain,' Sadhana reminded her.

'I got one child. Sometimes I must buy her good things,' Bessie had said quietly.

The nerve of the woman! Good things indeed! She gave her the name of the shop, but added, 'Buy her something different. It mustn't look like Asha's.'

Bessie had given her a strange, unfathomable look before replying loftily. 'The shops are for everybody.'

She found one cold roti and a bit of mushroom curry which she used as a filler on the unleavened bread. 'Come and have your tea. It's getting cold,' she called.

The child complied instantly, more out of thirst than obedience.

Phumza stood on the doorstep and watched her friend swallow her tea. Sadhana carried her rolled roti and tea into the lounge.

She moved to the television set. There were five new films for her to watch. She selected a cassette and read the brief outline. Ah yes, it was the Hema Malini film so popular at the moment, she noted with satisfaction. She inserted the tape and curled up on the settee, preparing herself for three hours of sheer indulgence.

She nibbled her roti absently and became vaguely aware of the children as they moved to the front garden. But her concentration shifted to the screen. Rich man woos beautiful girl and wins her. After the marriage loses its romance, she becomes a mere chattel in his hands. How true, Sadhana thought feelingly. All men were the same. They used you for a purpose and then discarded you.

Through the patio door, she caught a glimpse of the children playing hopscotch.

The story was good and she identified with the heroine's problems.

Her attention was momentarily distracted when Asha ran in and curled up beside her. She watched the film for a while. Grown ups were so boring! But her mother watched with complete absorption.

'I'm hungry,' Asha said.

But Sadhana was caught in the drama and did not heed her. Asha tugged at her sleeve impatiently. 'I'm hungry!' she wailed.

Sadhana held out her half eaten roti. 'Have this,' she said absently.

The child flung the proffered roll on the floor in a fit of temper. Sadhana slapped her sharply on her hand and called Bessie to clean up the mess.

'Go and play outside. You are worrying me for nothing!'

The child withdrew to a corner of the settee, sullen and rebellious.

The heroine was now undergoing the pain of disillusionment, stripped of joy and bereft. The husband realized in time that he had been deceived into believing the worst of her. So slowly she was emerging from a world of darkness and loneliness. How sad it all was, and yet how beautiful! But in reality men were worse. She brushed her eyes and prepared for the finale.

She did not notice the child slip away.

Outside the world was warm and beautiful. Phumza looked expectantly as her friend emerged onto the verandah. She carried a doll, a new one with frilly clothes and hair plaited and tied with pretty ribbons. She eyed the doll wistfully. But Asha made no move towards her.

Phumza remembered the day she went shopping with her mother. While being dragged through the bazaar, they had passed the toy section. Phumza had hung back, enthralled by the fascinating array of toys.

Especially the large lifelike doll with a blue dress and golden hair. She was drawn irresistibly towards it. For a long while she had stood there, yearning for possession and knowing the futility of such a wish. When Bessie found her after a frantic search, she had dragged her off. Phumza listened to her mother's scolding, and locked away her secret desire.

Now she watched her friend undo the doll's plaits and felt the same desire surface. Asha looked up and met her eyes. She read the unspoken yearning and felt something stir and uncoil within. When it broke loose she did nothing to restrain it. Suddenly she grabbed the doll by the hair and flung it to the ground. Phumza watched in frozen horror as she trampled it viciously. She felt the pain go through her and stab her. She got up and ran to stop her.

'No! No!' she cried.

But she went on, heedless. She tried in vain to stop her, but Asha pushed her savagely. The doll lay with its face cracked and head broken. Suddenly her anger spent, she hurled the doll in a corner.

From within, Sadhana was vaguely conscious of the noise and called out absently,

'Asha, play quietly.'

Asha scowled and went back indoors. Phumza hesitated uncertainly. Then she stooped and picked up the battered doll. She cradled it gently and ached for its bruises. She went to the back verandah where her mother kept things in a shopping bag. She took out her mother's doek and eased the doll onto her back in the manner of generations of African mothers.

The film was reaching its happy ending. Sadhana felt Asha's impatient tug on her sleeve. 'I'm hungry!'

'Sit down. I'll make you something,' she said.

Asha sat on the carpet and watched the figures moving on the screen. How she hated that screen! Her mother sat before it for hours, forgetting her and disregarding her needs. She longed to smash it, like how she had smashed the doll. She twisted the lace on her nightie and imagined the picture shattering and those endless talking figures dying.

Sadhana returned with a plate of scrambled egg and bread and plonked it before the child. 'Eat that and don't worry me,' she warned.

At the sight of the unvarying egg, her appetite palled. She pushed the plate away. Sadhana shrugged, indifferent to the child's mood. 'Eat that! There's nothing wrong with it.'

She inserted another tape and settled back. She would give the children an egg each when they got home from school. That way she needn't cook till four, in time for supper.

She reached for the plate. The egg was now cold and tasteless.

'I don't know why you waste food,' she berated the child. 'The trouble is you have too many good things.'

She took the rest of the uneatable mess back to the kitchen.

Phumza was on the back verandah, swaying contentedly, the doll on her back. Asha followed her mother into the kitchen. The sight of Phumza so at home with the doll, brought all her frustrations and ill temper to the fore. With a swift movement, she ripped the doll off her back. She clutched it tightly. They stood there regarding each other tensely. Phumza involuntarily grabbed the doll's leg. She clung to it mutely. Asha tried to wrench it away. A little tussle ensued.

'My doll!' she asserted grimly.

But Phumza held on. Bessie emerged with a bucket of wet washing. Her eyes took in the scene quickly. She spoke quietly but firmly.

'Give it back my child,' she said in Xhosa.

Phumza looked at her mother in disbelief.

'But she broke it and threw it,' she pointed out.

'Never mind. Give it back. It's still hers.'

The unfairness of it all! Reluctantly she relinquished her hold. She turned and followed her mother to the washing line, her heart numb, feeling as crushed as the doll.

From within, Sadhana observed the scene with detached amusement.

ZOË WICOMB

When The Train Comes

from *You Can't Get Lost In Cape Town* (1987)

I am not the kind of girl whom boys look at. I have known this for a long time, but I still lower my head in public and peep through my lashes. Their eyes leap over me, a mere obstacle in a line of vision. I should be pleased; boys can use their eyes shamelessly to undress a girl. That is what Sarie says. Sarie's hand automatically flutters to her throat to button up her orlon cardigan when boys talk to her. I have tried that, have fumbled with buttons and suffered their perplexed looks or reddened at the question, 'Are you cold?'

I know that it is the act of guiding the buttons through their resistant holes that guides the eyes to Sarie's breasts.

Today I think that I would welcome any eyes that care to confirm my new ready-made polyester dress. Choosing has not brought an end to doubt. The white, grey and black stripes run vertically, and from the generous hem I have cut a strip to replace the treacherous horizontal belt. I am not wearing a cardigan, even though it is unusually cool for January, a mere eighty degrees. I have looked once or twice at the clump of boys standing with a huge radio out of which the music winds mercurial through the rise and fall of distant voices. There is no music in our house. Father says it is distracting. We stand uneasily on the platform. The train is late or perhaps we are early. Pa stands with his back to the boys who have greeted him deferentially. His broad shoulders block my view but I can hear their voices flashing like the village lights on Republic Day. The boys do not look at me and I know why. I am fat. My breasts are fat and, in spite of my uplift bra, flat as a vetkoek.

There is a lump in my throat which I cannot account for. I do of course cry from time to time about being fat, but this lump will not be dislodged by tears. I am pleased that Pa does not say much. I watch him take a string out of his pocket and wind it nervously around his index finger.

Round and round from the base until the finger is encased in a perfect bandage. The last is a loop that fits the tip of his finger tightly; the ends are tied in an almost invisible knot. He hopes to hold my attention with this game. Will this be followed by cat's cradle with my hands foolishly stretched out, waiting to receive? I smart at his attempts to shield me from the boys; they are quite unnecessary.

Pa knows nothing of young people. On the morning of my fourteenth birthday he quoted from Genesis III . . . in pain you shall bring forth children. I had been menstruating for some time and so knew what he wanted to say. He said, 'You must fetch a bucket of water in the evenings and wash the rags at night . . . have them ready for the next month . . . always be prepared . . . it does not always come on time. Your mother was never regular . . . the ways of the Lord . . .' and he shuffled off with the bicycle tyre he was pretending to repair.

'But they sell things now in chemists' shops, towels you can throw away,' I called after him.

'Yes,' he look dubiously at the distant blue hills, 'perhaps you could have some for emergencies. Always be prepared', and lowering his eyes once again blurted, 'And don't play with boys now that you're a young lady, it's dangerous.'

I have never played with boys. There were none to play with when we lived on the farm. I do not know why. The memory of a little boy boring a big toe into the sand surfaces. He is staring enviously at the little house I have carved into the sandbank. There are shelves on which my pots gleam and my one-legged Peggy sleeps on her bank of clay. In my house I am free to do anything, even invite the boy to play. I am proud of the sardine can in which two clay loaves bake in the sun. For my new china teapot I have built a stone shrine where its posy of pink roses remains forever fresh. I am still smiling at the boy as he deftly pulls a curious hose from the leg of his khaki shorts and, with one eye shut, aims an arc of yellow pee into the teapot. I do not remember the teapot ever having a lid.

There is a lump in my throat I cannot account for. I sometimes cry about being fat, of course, especially after dinner when the zip of my skirt sinks its teeth into my flesh. Then it is reasonable to cry. But I have after all stood on this platform countless times on the last day of school holidays. Sarie and I, with Pa and Mr Botha waving and shouting into the clouds of steam, Work Hard or Be Good. Here, under the black and white arms of the station sign, where succulents spent and shrivelled in autumn grow once again plump in winter before they burst into shocking spring flower. So that Pa would say, 'The quarters slip by so quickly, soon the sun will be in Cancer and you'll be home again.' Or,

'When the summer train brings you back with your First Class Junior Certificate, the aloe will just be in flower.' And so the four school quarters clicked by under the Kliprand station sign where the jewelled eyes of the ice plant wink in the sun all year round.

The very first lump in my throat he melted with a fervent whisper, 'You must, Friedatjie, you must. There is no high school for us here and you don't want to be a servant. How would you like to peg out the madam's washing and hear the train you once refused to go on rumble by?' Then he slipped a bag of raisins into my hand. A terrifying image of a madam's menstrual rags that I have to wash swirls liquid red through my mind. I am grateful to be going hundreds of miles away from home; there is so much to be grateful for. One day I will drive a white car.

Pa takes a stick of biltong out of his pocket and the brine in my eyes retreats. I have no control over the glands under my tongue as they anticipate the salt. His pocket-knife lifts off the seasoned and puckered surface and leaves a slab of marbled meat, dry and mirror smooth so that I long to rest my lips on it. Instead my teeth sink into the biltong and I am consoled. I eat everything he offers.

We have always started our day with mealie porridge. That is what miners eat twice a day, and they lift chunks of gypsum clean out of the earth. Father's eyes flash a red light over the breakfast table: 'Don't leave anything on your plate. You must grow up to be big and strong. We are not paupers with nothing to eat. Your mother was thin and sickly, didn't eat enough. You don't want cheekbones that jut out like a Hottentot's. Fill them out until they're shiny and plump as pumpkins.' The habit of obedience is fed daily with second helpings of mealie porridge. He does not know that I have long since come to despise my size. I would like to be a pumpkin stored on the flat roof and draw in whole beams of autumn's sunlight so that, bleached and hardened, I could call upon the secret of my glowing orange flesh.

A wolf-whistle from one of the boys. I turn to look and I know it will upset Pa. Two girls in identical flared skirts arrive with their own radio blaring Boeremusiek. They nod at us and stand close by, perhaps seeking protection from the boys. I hope that Pa will not speak to me loudly in English. I will avoid calling him Father for they will surely snigger under cover of the whining concertina. They must know that for us this is no ordinary day. But we all remain silent and I am inexplicably ashamed. What do people say about us? Until recently I believed that I was envied; that is, not counting my appearance.

The boys beckon and the girls turn up their radio. One of them calls loudly, 'Turn off that Boere-shit and come and listen to decent American music.' I wince. The girls do as they are told, their act of resistance deflated. Pa casts an anxious glance at the white policeman pacing the actual platform, the paved white section. I take out a paper handkerchief and wipe the dust from my polished shoes, a futile act since this unpaved strip for which I have no word other than the inaccurate platform, is all dust. But it gives me the chance to peer at the group of young people through my lowered lashes.

The boys vie for their attention. They have taken the radio and pass it round so that the red skirts flare and swoop, the torsos in T-shirts arch and taper into long arms reaching to recover their radio. Their ankles swivel on the slender stems of high heels. Their feet are covered in dust. One of the arms adjusts a chiffon headscarf that threatens to slip off, and a pimply boy crows at his advantage. He whips the scarf from her head and the tinkling laughter switches into a whine.

'Give it back ... You have no right ... It's mine and I want it back ... Please, oh please.'

Her arm is raised protectively over her head, the hand flattened on her hair.

'No point in holding your head now,' he teases. 'I've got it, going to try it on myself.'

Her voice spun thin on threads of tears, abject as she begs. So that her friend consoles, 'It doesn't matter, you've got plenty of those. Show them you don't care.' A reproachful look but the friend continues, 'Really, it doesn't matter, your hair looks nice enough. I've told you before. Let him do what he wants with it, stuff it up his arse.'

But the girl screams, 'Leave me alone', and beats away the hand reaching out to console. Another taller boy takes the scarf and twirls it in the air. 'You want your doekie? What do you want it for hey, come on tell us, what do you want it for? What do you want to cover up?'

His tone silences the others and his face tightens as he swings the scarf slowly, deliberately. She claws at his arm with rage while her face is buried in the other crooked arm. A little gust of wind settles the matter, whips it out of his hand and leaves it spread-eagled against the eucalyptus tree where its red pattern licks the bark-like flames.

I cannot hear their words. But far from being penitent, the tall boy silences the bareheaded girl with angry shaking of the head and wagging of the finger. He runs his hand through an exuberant bush of fuzzy hair and my hand involuntarily flies to my own. I check my preparations: the wet hair wrapped over large rollers to separate the strands, dried then swirled around the head, secured overnight with a nylon stocking, dressed with vaseline to keep the strands smooth and straight and then pulled back tightly to stem any remaining tendency to curl. Father likes it pulled back. He says it is a mark of honesty to have the forehead and ears exposed. He must be thinking of Mother, whose hair was straight and trouble-free. I would not allow some unkempt youth to comment on my hair.

The tall boy with wild hair turns to look at us. I think that they are talking about me. I feel my body swelling out of the dress, rent into vertical strips that fall to my feet. The wind will surely lift my hair off like a wig and flatten it, a sheet of glossy dead bird, on the eucalyptus tree.

The bareheaded girl seems to have recovered; she holds her head reasonably high.

I break the silence. 'Why should that boy look at us so insolently?' Pa looks surprised and hurt. 'Don't be silly. You couldn't possibly tell from this distance.' But his mouth puckers and he starts an irritating tuneless whistle.

On the white platform the policeman is still pacing. He is there because of the Blacks who congregate at the station twice a week to see the Springbok train on its way to Cape Town. I wonder whether he knows our news. Perhaps their servants, bending over washtubs, ease their shoulders to give the gossip from Wesblok to madams limp with heat and boredom. But I dismiss the idea and turn to the boys who certainly know that I am going to St Mary's today. All week the grown-ups have leaned over the fence and sighed, Ja, ja, in admiration, and winked at Pa: a clever chap, old Shenton, keeps up with the Boers all right. And to me, 'You show them, Frieda, what we can do.' I nodded shyly. Now I look at my hands, at the irrepressible cuticles, the stubby splayed finger-nails that will never taper. This is all I have to show, betraying generations of servants.

I am tired and I move back a few steps to sit on the suitcases. But Father leaps to their defence. 'Not on the cases, Frieda. They'll never take your weight.' I hate the shiny suitcases. As if we had not gone to enough expense, he insisted on new imitation leather bags and claimed that people judge by appearances. I miss my old scuffed bag and slowly, as if the notion has to travel through folds of fat, I realise that I miss Sarie and the lump in my throat hardens.

Sarie and I have travelled all these journeys together. Grief gave way to excitement as soon as we boarded the train. Huddled together on the cracked green seat, we argued about who would sleep on the top bunk. And in winter when the nights grew cold we folded into a single S on the lower bunk. As we tossed through the night in our magic coupé, our fathers faded and we were free. Now Sarie stands in the starched white uniform of a student nurse, the Junior Certificate framed in her father's room. She will not come to wave me goodbye.

Sarie and I swore our friendship on the very first day of school. We twiddled our stiff plaits in boredom; the *First Sunnyside Reader* had been read to us at home. And Jos. Within a week Jos had mastered the reader and joined us. The three of us hand in hand, a formidable string of laughing girls tugging this way and that, sneering at the Sunnyside adventures of Rover, Jane and John. I had no idea that I was fat. Jos looped my braids over her beautiful hands and said that I was pretty, that my braids were a string of sausages.

Jos was bold and clever. Like a whirlwind she spirited away the tedium of exhausted games and invented new rules. We waited for her to take command. Then she slipped her hand under a doekie of dyed flour bags and scratched her head. Her ear peeped out, a faded yellow-brown yearning for the sun. Under a star-crammed sky Jos had boldly stood for hours, peering through a crack in the shutter to watch their fifth baby being born. Only once had she looked away in agony and then the Three Kings in the eastern sky swiftly swopped places in the manner of musical chairs. She told us all, and with an oath invented by Jos we swore that we would never have babies. Jos knew everything that grown-ups thought should be kept from us. Father said, 'A cheeky child, too big for her boots, she'll land in a madam's kitchen all right.' But there was no need to separate us. Jos left school when she turned nine and her family moved to the village where her father had found a job at the garage. He had injured his back at the mine. Jos said they were going to have a car; that she would win one of those competitions, easy they were, you only had to make up a slogan.

Then there was our move. Pa wrote letters for the whole community, bit his nails when he thought I was not looking and wandered the veld for hours. When the official letter came the cooped-up words tumbled out helter-skelter in his longest monologue.

'In rows in the village, that's where we'll have to go, all boxed in with no room to stretch the legs. All my life I've lived in the open with only God to keep an eye on me, what do I want with the eyes of neighbours nudging and jostling in cramped streets? How will the wind get into those back yards to sweep away the smell of too many people? Where will I grow things? A watermelon, a pumpkin needs room to spread, and a turkey wants a swept yard, the markings of a grass broom on which to boast the pattern of his wing marks. What shall we do, Frieda? What will become of us?' And then, calmly, 'Well, there's nothing to be done. We'll go to Wesblok, we'll put up our curtains and play with the electric lights and find a corner for the cat, but it won't be our home. I'm not clever old Shenton for nothing, not a wasted drop of Scots blood in me. Within five years we'll have enough to buy a little place. Just a little raw brick house and somewhere to tether a goat and keep a few chickens. Who needs a water lavatory in the veld?'

The voice brightened into fantasy. 'If it were near a river we could have a pond for ducks or geese. In the Swarteberg my pa always had geese. Couldn't get to sleep for months here in Namaqualand without the squawking of geese. And ostriches. There's nothing like ostrich biltong studded with coriander seeds.' Then he slowed down. 'Ag man, we won't be allowed land by the river but nevermind hey. We'll show them, Frieda, we will. You'll go to high school next year and board with Aunt Nettie. We've saved enough for that. Brains are for making money and when you come home with your Senior Certificate, you won't come back to a pack of Hottentots crouching in straight lines on the edge of the village. Oh no, my girl, you won't.' And he whipped out a stick of beef biltong and with the knife shaved off wafer-thin slices that curled with pleasure in our palms.

We packed our things humming. I did not really understand what he was fussing about. The Coloured location did not seem so terrible. Electric lights meant no more oil lamps to clean and there was water from a tap at the end of each street. And there would be boys. But the children ran after me calling, 'Fatty fatty vetkoek.' Young children too. Sarie took me firmly by the arm and said that it wasn't true, that they were jealous of my long hair. I believed her and swung my stiff pigtails haughtily. Until I grew breasts and found that the children were right.

Now Sarie will be by the side of the sick and infirm, leaning over high hospital beds, soothing and reassuring. Sarie in a dazzling white uniform, her little waist clinched by the broad blue belt.

If Sarie were here I could be sure of climbing the two steel steps on to the train.

The tall boy is now pacing the platform in unmistakable imitation of the policeman. His face is the stern mask of someone who does not take his duties lightly. His friends are squatting on their haunches, talking earnestly. One of them illustrates a point with the aid of a stick with which he writes or draws in the sand. The girls have retreated and lean against the eucalyptus tree, bright as stars against the grey of the trunk. Twelve feet apart the two radios stand face to face, quarrelling quietly. Only the female voices rise now and again in bitter laughter above the machines.

Father says that he must find the station master to enquire why the train has not come. 'Come with me,' he commands. I find the courage to pretend that it is a question but I flush with the effort.

'No, I'm tired. I'll wait here.' And he goes. It is true that I am tired. I do not on the whole have much energy and I am always out of breath. I have often consoled myself with an early death, certainly before I become an old maid. Alone with my suitcases I face the futility of that notion. I am free to abandon it since I am an old maid now, today, days after my fifteenth birthday. I do not in any case think that my spirit, weightless and energetic like smoke from green wood, will soar to heaven.

I think of Pa's defeated shoulders as he turned to go and I wonder whether I ought to run after him. But the thought of running exhausts me. I recoil again at the engery with which he had burst into the garden only weeks ago, holding aloft *Die Burger* with both hands, shouting, 'Frieda, Frieda, we'll do it. It's all ours, the whole world's ours.'

It was a short report on how a Coloured deacon had won his case against the Anglican Church so that the prestigious St Mary's School was now open to non-whites. The articles ended sourly, calling it an empty and subversive gesture, and warning the deacon's daughters that it would be no bed of roses.

'You'll have the best, the very best education.' His voice is hoarse with excitement.

'It will cost hundreds of rands per year.'

'Nonsense, you finish this year at Malmesbury and then there'll be only the two years of Matric left to pay for. Really, it's a blessing that you have only two years left.'

'Where will you find the money?' I say soberly.

'The nest egg of course, stupid child. You can't go to a white school if you're so stupid. Shenton has enough money to give his only daughter the best education in the world.'

I hestitate before asking, 'But what about the farm?' He has not come to like the Witblok. The present he wraps in a protective gauze of dreams; his eyes have grown misty with focusing far ahead on the unrealised farm.

A muscle twitches in his face before he beams, 'A man could live anywhere, burrow a hole like a rabbit in order to make use of an opportunity like this.' He seizes the opportunity for a lecture. 'Ignorance, laziness and tobacco have been the downfall of our people. It is our duty to God to better ourselves, to use our brains, our talents, not to place our lamps under bushels. No, we'll do it. We must be prepared to make sacrifices to meet such a generous offer.'

His eyes race along the perimeter of the garden wall then he rushes indoors, muttering about idling like flies in the sun, and sets about writing to St Mary's in Cape Town.

I read novels and kept in the shade all summer. The crunch of biscuits between my teeth was the rumble of distant thunder. Pimples raged on my chin, which led me to Madame Rose's Preparation in mail order. That at least has fulfilled its promise.

I was surprised when Sarie wept with joy or envy, so that the tears spurted from my own eyes on to the pages of *Ritchie's First Steps in Latin*. (Father said that they pray in Latin and that I ought to know what I am praying for.) At night a hole crept into my stomach, gnawing like a hungry mouse, and I fed it with Latin declensions and Eetsumor biscuts. Sarie said that I might meet white boys and for the moment, fortified by conjugations of *Amo*, I saw the eyes of Anglican boys, remote princes leaning from their carriages, penetrate the pumpkin-yellow of my flesh.

Today I see a solid stone wall where I stand in watery autumn light waiting for a bell to ring. The Cape south-easter tosses high the blond pigtails and silvery laughter of girls walking by. They do not see me. Will I spend the dinner-breaks hiding in lavatories?

I wish I could make this day more joyful for Pa but I do not know how. It is no good running after him now. It is too late.

The tall boy has imperceptibly extended his marching ground. Does he want to get closer to the policeman or is he taking advantage of Father's absence? I watch his feet, up, down, and the crunch of his soles on the sand explodes in my ears. Closer, and a thrilling thought shoots through the length of my body. He may be looking at me longingly, probing; but I cannot bring my eyes to travel up, along his unpressed trousers. The black boots of the policeman catch my eye. He will not be imitated. His heavy legs are tree trunks rooted in the asphalt. His hand rests on the bulge of his holster. I can no longer resist the crunch of the boy's soles as they return. I look up. He clicks his heels and halts. His eyes are narrowed with unmistakable contempt. He greets me in precise mocking English. A soundless shriek for Pa escapes my lips and I note the policeman resuming his march before I reply. The boy's voice is angry and I wonder what aspect of my dress offends him.

'You are waiting for the Cape Town train?' he asks unnecessarily. I nod.

'You start at the white school tomorrow?' A hole yawns in my stomach and I long for a biscuit. I will not reply.

'There are people who bury dynamite between the rails and watch whole carriages of white people shoot into the air. Like opening the door of a birdcage. Phsssh!' His long thin arms describe the spray of bird flight. 'Perhaps that is why your train has not come.'

I know he is lying. I would like to hurl myself at him, stab at his eyes with my blunt nails, kick at his ankles until they snap. But I clasp my hands together piously and hold, hold the tears that threaten.

'Your prayer is answered, look, here's Fa-atherrr', and on the held note he clicks his heels and turns smartly to march off towards his friends.

Father is smiling. 'She's on her way, should be here any second now.' I take his arm and my hand slips into his jacket pocket where I trace with my finger the withered potato he wears for relief of rheumatism.

'No more biltong, girlie,' he laughs. The hole in my stomach grows dangerously.

The white platform is now bustling with people. Porters pile suitcases on to their trolleys while men fish in their pockets for sixpence tips. A Black girl staggers on to the white platform with a suitcase in each hand. Her madam ambles amiably alongside her to keep up with the faltering gait. She chatters without visible encouragement and, stooping, takes one of the bags from the girl who clearly cannot manage. The girl is big-boned with strong shapely arms and calves. What can the suitcase contain to make her stagger so? Her starched apron sags below the waist and the crisp servant's cap is askew. When they stop at the far end of the platform she slips a hand under the edge of the white cap to scratch. Briefly she tugs at the tip of her yellow-brown earlobe. My chest tightens. I turn to look the other way.

Our ears prick at a rumbling in the distance which sends as scout a thin squeal along the rails. A glass dome of terror settles over my head so that the chatter about me recedes and I gulp for air. But I do not faint. The train lumbers to a halt and sighs deeply. My body, all but consumed by its hole of hunger, swings around lightly, even as Father moves forward with a suitcase to mount the step. And as I walk away towards the paling I meet the triumphant eyes of the tall boy standing by the whitewashed gate. Above the noise of a car screeching to a halt, the words roll off my tongue disdainfully:

Why you look and kyk gelyk,
Am I miskien of gold gemake?

MARGARET ROESTORF

The Very Quick Man

from *The Dog Of Air* (1987)

... tell you, when I saw you, I thought that something had happened before ... but it came after.

... happened like this.

I was in a peasant village in a country where I couldn't speak the language. I was watching a hill. They were farming on top of its high plateau. An accident seemed imminent. Unlikely, I thought, in this country where the wagons are slow and the oxen that pull them halt long before that deep drop.

A moment later a big old grey Ford truck came rushing forward with a man with grey hair at the steering wheel. I watched it rear up and then sink down the cliff and land hot and heavy.

The village ran forward ... even the houses seemed to move closer, but the old man shook himself.

The Very Quick Man was not dead.

He lay on the veranda of his bamboo house. His eyes closed and his two big hands on top of the blankets. In the way that women understand me, I looked around, saw no one, and took one big hand, led it to the top of my bikini pants, and in.

Some reaction. He fondled, but his eyes didn't open.

He must have sensed something was amiss, because slowly the lids lifted.

His surprise. He grunted like a pig, and then farted like one and pulled me on to him.

With signs I cautioned him. He was on his veranda. His wife — the whole village might walk by.

Being a woman, I felt the urge to go back. I knew that he couldn't get up, so I had to go to him. Excusing myself more and more often from the archaeological dig I led his hands into many new places — strange species that we women are; always watching the street and always watching him, for we know what men are thinking by the way they move next to us and on us.

I think by this time I had healed the old grey Ford truck scar in his mind. Just a little. I could see his eyes come alive each time I arrived. But if they had come alive the whole village had died. It was too quiet. I decided to check for holes in the bamboo lattice.

My surprise. They all stood, old and dressed in black, gums smiling, gums gaping, fingers nudging, all silent. The elders obviously had the privilege for the children and the young villagers stood silently at the back, watching the old people, also silent.

MAUD MOTANYANE

Two Minutes

from *Sometimes When It Rains* ed. by Ann Oosthuizen (1987)

Tosh and I were an odd pair; she was tall and thin, and I was short and plump. People called us the big and small twins, or B & S for short. In very many ways we were different, and yet there was something strong that bound us together. We stood out like sore thumbs from the rest of the girls, who were adventurous and full of pranks. They were wild, while Tosh and I tried to lead a life as pure as possible.

It is twenty years since I last saw Tosh, and I feel guilty that I have not been back to see her. I am sure she is plagued by the same guilt. We made a vow many years ago, and we promised to keep it whatever happened. We crossed each other's hearts and spat on the ground as we promised.

'Strue's God, my friend, if I ever do it I will come back and tell you.' There was only one 'it' that little girls in a convent school could promise not to get themselves involved in. According to Sister Marietta, the matron of the convent, boys came second after witches and ghosts as the deadliest poison for little girls. It could take less than two minutes for a boy to ruin a girl's entire life, she said.

The Little Flower Girls' Hostel formed part of a huge mission station founded by Catholic missionaries at the turn of the century. Most of them were of European origin, but over the years the mission, set in the village of Asazi in Natal, had become a fully fledged community, producing its own breed of African nuns and priests from the surrounding villages.

Sister Marietta was a mouse-like creature of German origin. Armed with a Bible and a strict Catholic upbringing, she was determined to save the whole African continent from death and destruction. Her biggest challenge while at The Little Flower was to keep the girls away from the evil clutches of men. Old Marie, as the girls referred to her, made it her business to slot in her anti-male propaganda whenever she could. Her best performances were a day or two before we broke up for the school holidays. She seemed to think that a good dose of lecturing would protect us from the menacing world outside.

She marvelled at the story of a boy who once cast a spell on a girl by simply looking at her. The girl, she said, had trusted her own worldly strength instead of asking for protection from the Virgin Mary. The boy had looked at the girl, the story went, and, without him saying a word, the girl had felt weak. So weak was she that, of her own accord, without the boy even propositioning her, she asked him to 'please kiss me and carry me to the bush'.

'I need not tell you what happened in the bush,' the nun would conclude.

As a rule, anyone who was caught eyeing the boys, whether in church, in class, or in the street, was punished severely. Ten bad marks in Sister Marietta's black book was the highest number one could get at a go, and they indicated the seriousness of the crime. As a result, trying to avoid boys and not being seen with them in a lonely place became our biggest challenge at The Little Flower.

'They will take you and use you, leaving you an empty shell,' Sister Marietta would say, indicating with her hand how a girl would be tossed away as something useless. So ominous was the prospect of being thrown away as a useless shell that Tosh and I would spend long nights discussing ways and means to avoid being subjected to that kind of treatment. Although we did not admire Sister Marietta personally, the idea of being sinless and celibate appealed to us a great deal. Often our night sessions would end with us saying the rosary together, asking for forgiveness for sins we had never committed.

Anastasia, Tasi to her friends, was the most popular girl at The Little Flower. While the rest of the girls loved and admired her, Tosh and I despised her. She dressed in the best fashion clothes, and had all the answers to life's problems. A dark person by nature, Tasi relied on skin-lightening cream to make her skin look lighter. So light was her face at one stage that her ebony hands looked borrowed next to it. Somehow her ears never got lighter, no matter how much cream she used on them. They stuck out like little appendages above her oval face. Tosh and I laughed about her ears behind her back. We did not dare do so in her presence. Tasi's tongue was much too scathing.

'I wonder how Old Marie can be so knowledgeable about matters of the flesh when she has never been involved in them,' Tasi would say mockingly. 'She must be displacing her own fears and using us to fight her own inward physical desire. Celibacy ... what nonsense. Old Marie must be jealous of our freedom. After all, *we* never sent her to tie herself to a life devoid of male pleasure.'

Tasi had quite a following, and her bed, which was at the corner of the hundred-bed dormitory, became the girls' rendezvous. This was where all subjects ranging from politics to sex were discussed. Tasi owned a small transistor radio, and often her gang would convene at her bed to listen to the 'Hit Parade'. This had to happen behind Sister Marietta's back because to her, love and rock 'n roll constituted mortal sins. Often the music-listening session would end in a row, with the participants arguing about the lyrics of a song, or which song had been number one on the 'Hit Parade' the previous week.

It was at the rendezvous that the anti-missionary politics were discussed. As far as Tasi was concerned, the missionaries, and that included Sister Marietta, had left Europe because of frustration, hunger and poverty. 'Under the guise of Christianity, they came to save us. Save us from what? When they themselves are guilty of racism and bigotry?' Tasi would ask, pointing at the stone building in which the black nuns were housed.

The Little Flower was not immune from the country's racial laws, which decreed that blacks and whites live separately. The white missionaries were clearly a privileged class. They lived in a glass building at the top of the hill, while their black counterparts were housed in a stone and brick building at the bottom of the hill. It looked more like a cave than a hut and, because of the density of the trees around it, it was cold and dark in winter.

Politics was a sacred subject at The Little Flower, and Tasi was the only one who openly challenged the racism of the convent. 'If they were like Jesus, they would be defying the laws of the country,' Tasi would say angrily. When Tasi questioned the school principal at assembly one day, we feared that she would be expelled from school. She was not. Instead she was fobbed off with an 'it was not the policy of the church to get involved in politics' statement, and asked never to bring up the subject again. That did not deter Tasi. She continued to question and attack what she termed inexcusable behaviour from the people of God.

It was at the rendezvous that a perfect plan for smuggling letters was hatched. As a rule, letters sent in and out of the convent were read and censored by Sister Marietta. Incoming parcels were opened too, and every little gift considered to be too fancy for life in a convent school was kept, and not given to the owner until we broke up for the school holidays.

Love story books were banned from the library, and any pages with kissing couples, or people holding hands, were either cut out or blocked with paper. The same applied to movies. Scenes which were remotely sexual were edited out of the movie. We were allowed to watch *The Sound of Music* in my matric class. The movie was so butchered that when I saw it again a couple of years later, it looked completely new.

The smuggling of letters to and from the boys' side took place during morning mass. As the heads bowed down in silent prayer after holy communion, letters would be thrown across the aisle dividing the boys' from the girls' pews. The little pieces of paper, which for some reason were called schemes, would fly like missiles right above the nuns' heads.

One day a scheme which was thrown from the girls' to the boys' side landed right in the lap of Sister Marietta. Her face lit up with glee as she pocketed the letter, waiting for the perfect moment to pounce on the culprit. By the time she did, the school was buzzing with the news of the person who had been found with a scheme. Most of us were not sure who it was, but we were sympathetic because we knew what this would mean.

I had always suspected Sister Marietta to have a mean streak, but I never thought her capable of doing what she did with Thoko's letter. Of course Thoko's boyfriend denied any association between them, so she had to face the music alone.

Not only was the letter read to the whole school, it was sent home to her parents, with a letter instructing them to arrive at the school to reprimand Thoko 'or else she will be asked to pack her things and go'.

I could not understand how a private thing such as a letter could be read to the whole school. That convinced me that Sister Marietta was downright malicious, doing that kind of thing to a nice girl like Thoko. Though remote, the thought of becoming a nun had often crossed my mind. What made me hesitate, however, was my mother's deep and sincere wish that I become a nurse. She would have been disappointed if I had gone the way of celibacy. Old Marie made the decision for me. Her reaction to Thoko's letter dashed my wish of ever becoming a nun. I was disgusted.

Tasi teased Thoko for having allowed herself to be caught with the letter. To her it was a big joke, and her friends laughed heartily when she described how foolish Thoko had been.

'There are only two rules,' Tasi said jokingly, 'it is either you keep away from trouble, or get involved, but be smart enough not to get caught.'

Tasi always boasted about how she and her boyfriend Michael smooched right under the nose of the Virgin Mary. She was referring to the statue of Mary on the lawn outside the school's courtyard. For those who had guts like Tasi, the grotto was a perfect lovers' nook.

More than once I heard Tasi tell the story of how she and Michael had climbed into one of the church towers. 'We stood there kissing to the chime of the bells next to us, while the priests heard confessions in the church below. Old Marie herself was playing the organ!' Tasi boasted. 'We did not get caught. What fool has any business to be caught?'

The stigma of being a boy's love followed Thoko until she left The Little Flower. She was banned from going to the movies on Fridays, and all the newcomers were warned that she was a bad influence. With the interesting parts censored out of all movies, Thoko didn't miss much, but it was the boring evenings that drove her nuts.

Thoko's every mistake became a big issue. She was ostracised by the rest of the girls who feared reprisals from Old Marie. As punishment for an offence Thoko was made to clean the local graveyard. It was not so much the hard work which caused grave-cleaning to be regarded as the most severe form of punishment. According to African culture graves are sacred ground where children are not allowed unless they are there to bury a very close relative such as a brother, a sister, or a parent. When Old Marie sent Thoko to dig round the graves for the second time, Tasi suggested we send a delegation to her to protest, and to make it clear what our tradition was regarding being in the cemetery.

'It is a bad omen, and shows no regard for our culture,' Tasi had protested. Although the delegation was given a hearing, their arguments were dismissed as primitive and unchristian, and Thoko was sent to clean up the graves a third and a fourth time. Such punishment was meted out to various other people, but Tasi vowed she would rather pack her bags and leave The Little Flower than dig round the graves. As if to avoid a confrontation, Old Marie never gave her the grave-digging punishment, robbing the girls of a chance to witness a showdown.

Once Sister Marietta embarrassed Thoko by pulling out the hem of her dress, saying that her dress was too short. As a rule, dresses had to be an inch above the knee. Thoko's must have been slightly more than an inch. The poor girl had to walk around with a funny dress the whole day because Sister would not let her change into another. It was her way of punishing her for, according to her mind, trying to be attractive to the opposite sex. But trying to make Thoko unattractive was an impossible task. Besides her God-given beauty, Thoko had natural style which made her look good with or without a torn hem. She looked elegant even in her gym slip, and Sister Marietta hated her for that. So intense was her hatred that she was forever looking for a reason for her to be expelled from school. 'You will dig the graves for a week, or pack your things and leave The Little Flower,' became the nun's familiar cry whenever Thoko did something wrong.

Tosh and I were both eighteen when we left The Little Flower. As we hugged and said goodbye, we renewed the vow we had made so many times before. If we ever slept with a boy, we would write or telephone to say we had finally fallen. I do not know exactly what motivated Tosh to make that vow. But for me, it was Thoko's experience that pushed me and forced me to make that decision. If a love letter could elicit so much hatred and anger, I thought to myself, then surely boys must be a real threat to girls. I sincerely believed that there would be no place for me in the world if I ever fell into the trap which every man around had set to catch me. As Old Marie said, 'The world will spit at you.'

Twenty years have passed since I last saw Tosh. I did not try to find her after my first encounter with a man. I did not feel the urge to write to her that I had finally fallen. To my mind, it had not happened. I remember the incident very clearly. It was on the couch in my mother's own lounge, not even in the bush as Sister Marietta had warned. Because he was Catholic like me, I trusted Sipho more than I would have trusted an ordinary boy. Somehow, I thought he knew the same rules that I knew.

He pleaded with me and told me it would not take long. He fondled my breasts and kissed me all over. I still cannot say whether the feeling was pleasurable. It was as though a cold and a warm shiver went through my body at the same time. I heard two voices, that of Sipho in one ear pleading with me that 'it won't be long', and Sister Marietta in another, warning 'it will take two minutes'. I saw myself being discarded like an empty shell and the whole world spitting at me.

Suddenly I fought like a little monster to push Sipho away. It was too late. I heard him take one deep breath and the act was over. It was exactly two minutes. I pulled myself together and walked out of the door, leaving Sipho sitting on the couch. When I walked away from him, I also walked away from the fact that he had made love to me. As far as I was concerned the incident had not happened. How could I admit that I had been used?

I have had a lot of sexual encounters since that day on my mother's couch. I am married now with two children; still I have not made love to a man. Sister Marietta never told me that there would come a time when being in a lonely place with a boy would be a right and a safe thing to do. So every private moment I have spent with a man has been wrong, and something I have to be ashamed of. Even as I go to bed with my husband every night, Sister Marietta's voice rings in my mind. 'He will take you and use you and throw you away like an empty shell.' When she drummed those words into my innocent mind, she tied a knot that I am not unable to undo.

How can I give myself on a platter to a person — a man — who will con me and leave me spent and useless? As I pull myself away from each sexual act, I feel used and unclean. A sense of guilt and emptiness comes over me. Often I have felt the urge to go back to The Little Flower, lock myself into a confessional with my priest, and say, 'Father, I have sinned. I have slept with a boy.'

I have not gone back to Tosh to tell her that I have broken the vow we made so many years ago. I have slept with none of the men I have made love to, none of the men I have met over the past twenty years. Maybe one day I will be able to untangle the knot in my heart and mind. I will be able to say to a man, 'Let us eat together from the sexual pot, let us share the pleasure equally.' I will not write to Tosh. No, not until I reach equality with my men. Tosh has not written either. Could it be that she is plagued by the same anguish, or is she still pure?

PNINA FENSTER

Dreams Of Golden Beauty

from *The Vita Anthology Of New South African Short Fiction* ed. by M. Leveson (1988)

(The title of this story comes from a Joni Mitchell song)

It's as if we've turned into tropical fish — swimming together througł the lush currents of darkness in his room. And the darkness tastes ol mouth and smells of brandy and is full of secret sounds. And in the darkness we sway and dive and splash and then, like flapping fish, come gasping up for air. 'Do you like it?' he asks. And I hear his body — slip-slap, slip-slap, slip-slap. 'Turn over now,' he says. And I hear his breatł — sucking the darkness in, sighing the darkness out. 'Did you like it? ask the stars above the streetlights. I stand at the bus stop, wrapped up ir my new blue coat, blowing icy, white billows. 'Did you like it?' ask the sleepy houses slipping past the rattling seats of the last bus home. 'Dic you like it?' ask the gate and the garden and the front door key. 'Did yor like it?' ask the pots and pans in the kitchenette. And I look at the Botticelli posters above my bed, and dream of golden beauty. I can only afford to visit him once a fortnight. In between, I work, watch TV, pain my nails. He isn't cheap, you know. That was the first thing he told me when I phoned. But I couldn't wait for ever. Especially if I didn't go tc parties or meet men at work. Especially if strangers at the bus stoj turned their faces away from my smile.

I found his number in the newspaper. 'Discreet', it said. 'Body massage — women only.' And even if he isn't cheap, he knows what want. 'Leave the money in the vase, and come lie with me on the bed,' he tells me. And I feel the blood catch in my throat. Then he closes my eyes with his fingers, and starts to touch and stroke and kiss. 'Do you like it, he asks. And my thin blotched face slips away into the darkness. 'I love you,' he says. Somewhere inside me, a bird calls.

'Two waxes, a pedicure, a facial, a massage and another facial at thre

›'clock. You'd better skip lunch,' says Mrs Foster. And I wonder if she ‹nows that I know what it is. And that I liked it just as much as other vomen do. All the more because I waited so long. His room is black and mells of brandy. But in the drunken darkness, I feel desired. He touches ny body, the way he's touched a dozen others. And with that touch, I oin the club of all the other women who have danced and flirted and ›een loved by men. Perhaps my face will change now that I've been ouched. The thought leaps inside me like a heartbeat. All through the alon, the smell of melting wax clouds the air.

Mrs. Foster's salon has mauve, shot-taffeta curtains and gold pots of ubber plants. The walls are painted the colour of candy-floss — sweet nd silly. In the front, there are clean, glass-topped tables with imported nagazines and display cabinets for perfume and make-up. In the back, here are narrow passages with doors on either side. Behind the doors — ecrets! And all along the passages and in all the secret rooms — mirrors nd pictures of women. The women in the pictures smile as they watch ne work. 'Be pretty,' they say. 'Pretty is easy. It comes in a tube, in a ar, in a brush, in a bottle.' But the mirrors spit my face back at me. Long nd thin, with small, slit-eyes and lumpy, blotched skin.

'Don't you worry,' said Mrs Foster, when I first came to work for her. I'm sure we can do something with you. Peel your skin once a week and ix your hair up nicely. Soon you won't recognise yourself. What ›eautiful hands you have! From now on, you must take care of them. 'aint your nails every evening and watch that you don't chip them.'

For six months, Mrs Foster peeled and plaited, pinned and curled. And he never docked it off my pay. But pretty never came. 'Do you have a ›oyfriend?' my first client asks. Usually, I shake my head. But today, I mile. 'I met him last week,' I tell her. 'You look like you're in love,' she aughs. I catch my face in the mirror. It's blushing. She wants to know vhat he does. 'He has a flat in town, he ... he's a salesman.' My neck eels hot. 'He's very good looking — Mediterranean, with dark eyes and ong eyelashes.' 'Bet lots of women are after him then!' she teases. We're going steady,' I tell her. 'It was love at first sight.'

Pretty, sings the song on the radio. Pretty, pretty, pretty, pretty. I vrap my client's hair in a pink towel. And I began to scrub and smooth. I ›olish her chin and cheeks. She leans back in the chair, closes her eyes. You're so good,' she sighs. I shape her brows — pick and pluck. 'Don't eave it on too long,' she cautions as I spread dye onto her eyelashes. 'hen I file her nails. 'Love' sings the song on the radio. 'Pretty love,' my lient hums. Her nails gleam orange. Her face is as smooth and pale as nilky moons. I look at my lap. It's full of cotton wool, files and nail clippings. Down below, I see her feet floating like waterlilies in a bowl c soapy water.

Every evening after bussing home from work, I sit in front of the T' set with a tray of tea and a box of muesli rusks. TV land is full c shampoo. Shampoo, deodorant, bunches of flowers and neat, brigh people in neat, bright clothes. I watch men kiss Morgan Fairchild as paint my nails. She has a new man every week. I have a new colour ever evening. I keep the bottles inside a shoebox — pouting plum, gossame peach, roaring red, iridescent opal, midnight rose and tangerine.

'Go to parties, or join a club,' my mother tells me. 'You'll never mee anyone if you sit at home watching TV. You're almost 37.'

'Girls like me don't meet people at parties,' I want to tell her. 'Yo have to be pretty to do that.'

Once at a high school function, a boy asked me to dance. His frienc started to laugh. So he crept into a corner, and left me standing alone i the middle of the room.

On Monday morning, during prayers, I heard the other girls gigglin and whispering to each other. 'He put his hand under my bra', 'He want to go all the way', 'He's going to take me to the movies on Saturday a ternoon!' And words — they had so many mysterious word Smooching, getting off, waiting for the curse, two-timing and goin steady.

'You can't go on like this,' my mother says. 'Three boxes of rusks week and fried eggs with tomato sauce every morning. Positive thinkin and inner strength — that's what men are looking for nowadays. I know I read a magazine article about it. Beauty that comes from within. That the thing that really counts.'

I watch Morgan's face on the TV screen — red lips, tipped-up nos and swirling blonde hair.

'There's someone I have to phone,' I say, thinking of the feeling human flesh. But my voice disappears in the violins and drums of the T programme. Outside, the wind crushes the branches against th window. Inside, something starts to howl. Somewhere in between Morgan Fairchild lifts her fox fur collar around her neck, turns toward the camera and smiles.

KEFILOE TRYPHINAH MVULA

The Naked Night

from *Women In South Africa From The Heart* (1988)

It was during the month of February in 1985 when it happened. I was sixteen years old. I had a trim figure. I was of middle height and my complexion was a good shade of brown.

To most people I was an ordinary girl. I belonged to a Christian family of seven children. The Pitsieng's. We lived in Moroka, which is also known as Rockville. The house was the usual type of four-roomed one. It's appearance left one cold and miserable.

Mama was a house-wife, daddy didn't want her to work, although he was earning peanuts as a night-watchman.

Though I went to church every Sunday, I hated the sight of it. Whenever I see it, I feel like cursing. Of course, I had to swear, because it was only a building where the worshippers held their services.

The Sunday school teacher, my parents and my class-teacher used to bore me. Love, loyalty and respect were all they could talk about.

I was coping well with my lessons at school. Though I had never failed, I wasn't the most intelligent pupil. There were some I couldn't beat, but usually I rated among the first and second class pupils.

Like most girls, I had received love proposals from guys of my age and some were several years my senior. Some I loved, some I didn't, but since I didn't know what is expected when one is in love, I had to reject the proposal and set myself free. One cannot commit oneself to an unknown game.

For others life was fast and easy, but for me it was slow and hard.

I longed to live freely. To go places and meet new faces. Unfortunately my lifestyle differed from my family. Daddy had declared a curfew within the house, that all children should be at home at 17.00 (hrs) in the evening.

He chose my friends, those he liked were only church members' children.

During those days I thought of my relatives. Would life be any better if I went and stayed with them? I wondered. My conscience stopped me from doing that. Truly, I shouldn't, because Dad would come after me and convince the very people of how stubborn and lacking in good behaviour I am. I imagined him saying, 'If Lucy cannot respect me, how can she respect you?' I realised that the innocent people would have to refuse my request.

What puzzled me, was my soft-spoken elder sister who was bashful and agreed to every inconvenient rule daddy declared. She seemed to be satisfied and lived happily, while I seemed to live in misery and despair. I didn't bother to discuss anything with her because I regarded her as ignorant. She had only churchgoers as friends. This left my heart with an unsatisfied yearning.

Home was some kind of hell. I wanted to be free from them and to be happy. I only found happiness outside home.

School was the best place to be. I had two friends who were both my class-mates. They were Nonkululeko and Shirley. Nonkululeko stayed in Pimville, a few kilometres from us. Shirley and I were located in the same area. It took minutes to reach Shirley's home from mine. Our social stature ranged thus, Shirley belonged to an upper class family Nonkululeko from the middle one and I, from the lower class.

Though our personality and interests differed, we treated one another with sisterhood and true love. I didn't wish to be like them, and they did not wish to be like me. There is no reward for regretting who you are.

One evening the bishop visited us. It was cold. The wind was blowing forcefully.

We were all at home, five were in the kitchen, warmed by the heat from the coal stove. Thandi, my elder sister and I were sitting on a three-seater sofa in the other room. She was sitting on the left corner of the sofa while I was sitting on the right. There were two other sofas. One was placed in front of the wall. The other was placed at the right side of the wall facing the left one where there was a side-board. In the middle was a dining table.

We heard them talking in the kitchen. Daddy invited the bishop to come inside the room where we were seated. I began to shiver and have cramps all over my body.

He sat on the sofa facing us, daddy sat on the other one.

'Hello, Mr Pitsieng, I had forgotten that you've got two lovely girls' he said to Dad.

'How are you girls?'

This was the moment I had long been waiting for. The moment to ignore him. The moment of dishonouring him, and the moment of lowering him. There was no need to answer him since he didn't really care about my health.

'We are well Moruti,' (We are well, our Priest) Thandi replied. I stared at him, how did he know what frame of mind I was in? In good or bad health, perhaps he sensed that I was unwilling to talk to Moruti.

He nodded then asked. 'And you Lucy?' Had he known how I felt, he would not have bothered to ask. I glanced at him wondering if my eyes were not like those of a dragon.

The room was filled with silence as they were all waiting for my response. Their eyes on me. I remained quiet and immovable. He couldn't hide his uneasiness. Finally he managed to ask again. 'Are you in deep thought Lucy?'

I stared at him with a look as serious as death. I realised that daddy was embarrassed, while Thandi was more or less disgusted. Daddy called my name calmly, but I didn't bother to give him a damn look. Thandi sighed.

'I think she's ill brother.' Moruti said to Dad. 'I doubt it. Are you Lucy?'

It was as if I was a statue.

These two men were just the bulls I had long wanted to put in their place.

Mama interrupted by bringing in tea for three. The bishop suggested that they pray for me than bless the tea. I nearly laughed while they prayed. This would have annoyed daddy greatly.

When they finished, Thandi went to the kitchen. Mama sat on the middle seat next to me. She asked me to go to the kitchen. I left the room quite aware that I had irritated them all.

After the bishop left, he called me. He held the sjambok in his right hand. The sight of it encouraged me to be more stubborn, more hostile. Rather to hurt them. It consoled me.

'Lucy, you have disappointed me, you have embarrassed me greatly, therefore I'll give you five lashes.'

There was no need to inform me. Since when had he informed me whenever he had whipped me? It is because I showed no sign of emotion when he did that I would never answer. I would just keep quiet.

Mama was preparing the evening meal while others were witnessing the action. I folded my arms when the eighth lash had whipped my soft skin. I thought it was the end of the lesson because he had thrown the sjambok away, only to discover that it was the beginning of another one.

He sent me down with a fist which would have challenged an opponent inside the ring. He knelt down, setting himself comfortably so that he could practise four more fists onto the punching-bag which was my face.

I heard Tshepiso, the little one shouting at mama to help. 'Mama please come and see, blood from the eyes, blood from the nose. She is dying.' She was crying.

'Tjhee ntate ho lekane.' Mother said. 'It is enough.'

It was too late, he had already kicked me on the jaw and between the legs.

The house was filled with noise. Darkness captured my senses.

When life came back, I realised that everyone except Dad was there, and was looking at me as if I were a stranger.

While I had fainted, they had washed and dressed me. My head was aching painfully. Knowing that pain-killer pills were unavailable, I decided to rest. Although my face was swollen, the cut under my left eye could be seen clearly.

Our sitting room was a bedroom by night where Thandi and I slept. I didn't like to disturb Thandi's peaceful night, so I switched off the light.

Nothing, but the quietness and darkness consoled me. I reached the conclusion that I would commit suicide, for if my own father hated me, who's going to love me? If he didn't care, who's supposed to? I have long endured, long pretended. I didn't want to live as a stranger any longer. I only wanted my soul to rest.

It was about 2:15 am when I went to the kitchen. I switched on the light. Pulled out the drawer of a kitchen-cupboard and picked out the longest knife we had.

I was about to push it slowly into my stomach when our eyes met. He came near me, his eyes burning with fire, and I knew he would satisfy himself and kill me, knowing I wouldn't cry or scream.

His next step towards me was the one fatal mistake he made. I knew it was him or I. Automatically I pushed the knife with great force into his stomach. For the first time I heard him roar like a dying lion. He fell down on his knees with the knife buried in him.

Many questions arose. I saw blood, a corpse, a coffin, policemen, funeral procession, I smelt a jail cell.

And I was alone standing there, helplessly facing the naked night.

FARIDA KARODIA

Something In The Air

from *Coming Home And Other Stories* (1988)

'By God, we'll get them both this time. You make bloody sure of it or so help me it'll be your head on the block!'

Her father's study door was slightly ajar on Sunday evening when Elsie heard his angry outburst. Startled she stopped midway up the stairs, her attention drawn by the sound of her father's voice raised in anger. She peered over the bannister but could not see into the study to identify her father's visitor. She dallied on the stairway, audaciously listening in on the rest of the conversation.

'Marais sent a message that Bezuidenhout will be crossing the border this Friday. Apparently the young Indian is very deeply involved in this whole scheme,' her father told his visitor.

'We only have five days, then,' a male voice replied.

'*Ja*. But we will be waiting for them right here,' her father said. 'If the worst comes to the worst . . . shoot the *donders*, but remember one thing. I want Bezuidenhout alive.'

Her father, Faanie van Staaden, was not only the local sergeant of police but also worked with the Special Branch Forces involved in tracking down terrorists and political agitators who tried to make their way to and from the Botswana border a hundred miles to the north.

For Faanie van Staaden it was generally all the same — dead or alive. The one exception was in the case of Daan Bezuidenhout, a once respected Afrikaner lawyer who was at the top of the Special Branch's list of wanted men. Moscow trained, Bezuidenhout's speciality was urban terrorism. And Faanie wanted him alive.

'To think that the *coolie* grew up in town right under my nose and I didn't know what he was up to,' her father said, almost unable to believe that he could have been so negligent.

He had never cared much for Indians and made no bones about it. In his estimation they were a treacherous bunch, too smart for their own good. 'The country would have been a lot better off had the government put them all back on a boat to India, in 1948,' he used to say.

Elsie crept up the stairs to her room. The word *coolie* brought back so many associations. She wondered if the Indian referred to in her father's conversation was the same one she had met when she was about eleven years old. A fuzzy image of a lanky boy with black hair came to mind and for a while, as she prepared for bed, she struggled to recall his name. Eventually just as she was dozing off it came to her.

On Tuesday morning Elsie reluctantly drove into town. Her father had taken the jeep and her mother's small car was quite inadequate for carrying a load of any kind. The only vehicle at her disposal, therefore, was the old *chorrie* lorry. Her father who generously brought home the supplies on a Monday afternoon was too busy to do so that week, and since Elsie was home from boarding school he instructed her to pick them up from Faurie's General Store in town. She would not have minded, had he not been so gruff and off-hand with her and her mother.

He was always too busy, she thought resentfully, as she climbed into the truck for the twenty-mile drive into town. Even when she was a child, she and her mother hardly ever went anywhere because even at that time her father was preoccupied with terrorists and troublemakers.

The town which was located close to one of the Bophuthatswana territories and, not far beyond that, to Botswana, where many of the terrorists were given refuge, was of strategic importance. As a consequence Sergeant Faanie van Staaden enjoyed a prominent role in the community.

Jackson, one of the farm labourers, accompanied her to load the bags of flour, mealie-meal, samp, sugar and other supplies for the week. Instead of riding in the front with the *klein Missies,* he stood in the back, choking on the dust kicked up behind them, hanging on for dear life as the lorry with its broken suspension bucked like a cantankerous old horse.

It was a slow, dusty ride along the ten miles of corrugated farm track. The old lorry strained to the top of each hill as though it would rattle to pieces. Eventually they reached the main road, much of which had been tarred to facilitate the movement of troops all the way to the border.

Crawling along at a snail's pace, Elsie's mind meandered all over the place, but her thoughts returned to the Indian boy, on her mind so much since Sunday when she had overheard her father's conversation. She recalled when they met during that school break about ten years ago. She was about eleven and the boy, Rashid, about fifteen.

The schools had closed on a Friday and normally by Monday she was already bored silly. At that time they still lived in the *dorp*. It was the period just before her father bought the farm, *Vreugde*. Life became a little more interesting when they moved to the farm but she always retained the same dread of Sundays.

In the *dorp* they were boring lethargic days, waiting for something interesting to happen, a futile expectation in those days because the children were not to be seen or heard while the adults took their afternoon nap. Afterwards when the adults awakened, the children had to sit quietly on the *stoep* listening to the drone of voices while the grown-ups discussed the two popular subjects of the day: farming and politics.

She was always thankful when Sundays were over; wished away in the hope that Monday would present better possibilities. She remembered how she had lazed around the house on that first Monday morning of the school holidays ten years ago, driving her mother to distraction with all her questions. Finally in the afternoon when Sinnah van Staaden could no longer stand having her daughter underfoot, she told her to play outside.

Encouraged by her mother, Elsie went off that afternoon in search of adventure. At the far end of town her feet automatically turned towards the river, following the pathway along the bank; poking at the clumps of bushes with her stick because the one thing she dreaded most was coming unexpectedly upon a snake.

Eventually Elsie arrived at the old weir. At first glance it appeared to be deserted. Disappointed she was about to turn back when she spotted the tall, lanky, youth. He was fishing, his bare feet planted on a smooth river stone, trousers rolled up below his knee, exposing dark, roughened calves. On the rock beside him was a small plastic pail.

Fishing was not one of her favourite pastimes. It was boring to wait around for some dumb fish to bite, and the thought of squeezing a worm onto a hook filled her with revulsion. She watched idly. There was an air of aloof detachment about him like someone who had built a wall between himself and the rest of the world. He did not see her until she was standing right beside him.

'What are you doing here?' she demanded sharply. This was her spot and she was resentful of the invasion by this stranger.

Startled, he almost lost his balance. His dark eyes, reddened by the sun, glanced down at her in irritation.

Her eyes as she watched him, were full of frank curiosity. 'Who are you?' she asked. Then before he could answer she demanded: 'What are you doing here?'

He tilted his head slightly and with an indulgent smile, as though speaking to a child, replied: 'My name is Rashid. I'm fishing, can't you see?'

The condescension in his tone made her retract the friendship she had so cautiously offered. 'I know you're fishing. Do you think I'm stupid or something?' she snapped, using the same tone with which her father addressed the Blacks. 'Where do you come from?'

He inclined his head towards town.

'Are you from the *coolie* shop?'

At first he was taken aback then he laughed at her insolence. But when he discovered an absence of malice in her expression he began to understand something his mother had told him one day when he came home angry and indignant about being insulted by one of the Afrikaners in town.

'They're ignorant, Rashid, sometimes they're like frightened little children. Leave them alone. They don't know any better. We mustn't get mad, we must teach them the right way. Show them that we are even better than them,' his mother said.

'What's so funny?' asked Elsie, offended by his laughter.

'You are. You *Boere* are so ignorant.'

'Don't you call me a *Boer*!' she cried stamping her foot.

'Well don't go around calling me a *coolie*.'

'But you are one,' she said in a small voice, a little unsure of herself now.

'No,' he said. 'It's a bad word.'

The wind had come up, rippling the calm surface of the water, sweeping her hair across her face so that it got into her mouth and made her sputter.

'You don't call me *coolie* and I won't call you *Boer*. Is that a deal?'

She studied him for a moment, her dark blue eyes intelligently considering his proposition. Finally she offered her silence as tacit agreement, and asked instead: 'What kind of fish have you caught?'

He grinned and shrugged. 'I don't know what they're called. They're just fish,' he said, reaching into the bucket and bringing out a small, flat silver fish which he offered to her in the palm of his land. 'Lots of bones though. My mother doesn't like them because of that.'

The wind died down again and for a moment he concentrated on his fishing. She stood a little to the side and behind him, watching him reel in the fish.

'You eat lots of carrots, hey?' he teased, turning his head slightly to glance at her over his shoulder.

'What do you mean?' she demanded, her brows coming together defensively. But she knew what he meant. Everyone teased her about her hair.

'Your red hair,' he grinned.

Elsie resented his remark. He was being forward and she didn't like that. She wanted to hurt him with words of her own and when none came to mind, except *that* word, she retreated, marching off in a huff.

But the next day she returned again. He was there. Every day of that week Elsie stopped by the old weir, and on each occasion she learnt a little more about him. He told her that he was at school in Jo'burg and that like her, he too was on holiday.

During the first few days she stood on a rock behind him peering over his shoulder while he fished, stepping back as he cast his line into the deep end; then with her hands carefully clasped behind her back, closing in to share the excitement when he had a bite.

Sometimes while they waited she prattled on, asking many questions. The knowledge that he was an outsider who had come home for the holidays, created a bond of sorts between them. The fact that he was Indian seemed of no further consequence and in the ensuing days no reference was made to either of the offensive words.

He spoke hesitantly about his family and she told him a little about hers. She discovered that they were both *only* children, his older brother having died several years before. Being an only child was one more thing that they had in common. He told her that their house was behind the store.

Elsie confessed that she had never been to the store.

'You should come one day,' he said.

Elsie slowed down to avoid a large bump in the road where the tar had heaved up and remembered so clearly the good feeling she had had at the end of that week when she and Rashid had become firm friends. It had nothing to do with the fact that she'd had no one to play with because all her friends had gone away for the holidays.

On the following Monday when she returned to *their* spot, he was not there. Thinking that he might have been delayed, she waited and when he still did not come, she went looking for him at the store. She did not go in though. Instead she peered through the window, catching a glimpse of his parents. But of him there was no sign.

On the following Wednesday, after having gone to their spot on three successive days without finding him, she returned to the store. This time she went inside on the pretext of buying some sweets. His mother was there, dressed in a yellow sari.

There was a peculiar odour that drifted into the shop from the house. The smell of spices and sandalwood was unfamiliar to her. How could she have known that it was the smell of curry and incense?

'Where's Raasit?' she asked his mother, after she had made her small purchase.

His mother smiled, amused by her question. 'Rashid has gone back to school, my dear,' she said.

That was the last time Elsie had gone into the store. The following year her father had bought the farm, *Vreugde*, twenty miles out of town and she was shipped off to boarding school. She had not seen or heard anything further about him until the day she overheard her father's conversation.

Near the town the sun-baked earth changed to fields of bleached grass and stalks. She hit a pot-hole in the road and the lorry bounced on its worn springs. The jar drove her head against the roof, she cursed loudly and slowed down.

Peering into the mirror, she saw that Jackson, who had been standing up against the cab, had not fared too well either.

'*Stadig, klein Missies*! Slow down!' he cried, thumping the roof of the cab. Fortunately he had braced himself against the safety-bar in the back of the lorry, and after being bounced into the air had landed on his feet, slightly winded but unhurt.

Elsie reached the outskirts of the town. Then on a sudden impulse turned off onto the back road which passed by the Indian store. It was still there just as she remembered it; the little snub-nosed building set back from a sandy road. The same blue sign proclaiming 'G.M. Trading Co.' hung from the side, a little more battered than it used to be. She wondered as she saw this what the initials G.M. stood for.

The ground in the front of the building was worn smooth; so was a footpath which cut across a field of mealies to the location. The heat had bubbled the paint which had cracked and peeled away exposing the many layers beneath.

Chained to the bars of the long window which almost reached the ground, were several metal trunks of the variety commonly used by African travellers. Beside the entrance to the store was a stack of three-legged iron pots used for cooking in the open. Bunches of billy cans hung from the door like Christmas decorations.

An assortment of metal signs were stuck to the outside walls like postage stamps, each advertising a product. One of these signs showed a cheerful black face holding up a bottle of Coca Cola; another, an African man with glossy hair proffering a tin of pomade. Directly below this was another sign with a picture of a contented baby, its well-being attributed to the tin of Lactogen in the foreground. At the far side was yet another sign with the picture of a light-skinned African woman who had placed her trust in a jar of Metamaphosa cream.

Elsie drove by slowly straining to peer inside, but the merchandise hanging from the doorway obscured her view. She brought the old lorry to a shuddering halt about three hundred yards past the store then carefully backed up to the door.

'Wait here,' she told Jackson as she lowered her sandalled feet to the ground.

In the store two counters at right angles demarcated the public area. It seemed that little had changed since the time she had stopped here in search of Rashid. A few cheap watches waiting to find a new home, lay face upwards on the top shelf in the glass display case. Behind this counter was a clutter of merchandise thrust haphazardly into the shelf space. The other counter contained sweets and jars of colourful beads.

Elsie recognised Rashid's mother. Although her face was still relatively smooth and unlined, her black hair was peppered with grey. The yellow sari looked familiar too, perhaps a little faded, the frayed fringe forming balls of tangled thread.

For a moment she wondered what Rashid had done after leaving school. She was almost tempted to ask his mother but changed her mind. She remembered him telling her that he needed to be free of a small town and all the restraints it held for him. Johannesburg was where 'it' was happening. Years later, when she was in high school, she discovered what he had meant by 'it'.

The woman watched her, a little suspiciously at first. Elsie could see her hesitation, could see that she expected her to retreat. But instead of hurrying away, Elsie dallied, examining the contents of the showcase, trying to decide how she should respond to the woman's questions.

Ayesha Moola surreptitiously studied the newcomer. There was something vaguely familiar about the girl's face, especially the red hair, but at that moment she couldn't place her. Ayesha adjusted the sari over her shoulder. The corner of her mouth twitched into a half-smile as her glance settled on the young woman. Because it was not usual for Whites to wander into the store, a dozen speculative thoughts ran through her mind. Amidst these an alarm went off.

Ayesha knew only that her son was participating in a dangerous mission which involved the fugitive, Daan Bezuidenhout. The mere thought of the danger he faced filled her with dread. So many freedom fighters had been killed by the police in this area. It was too dangerous. When her son had visited the previous week, she had begged him not to go. Finally when all else failed, she had offered some unsolicited advice, albeit in a circumspect manner.

'You know, Rashid,' she said. 'If I were going to smuggle someone important across the border, someone like a white person for instance, I would put some brown stuff on his face and tie a turban around his head like a Sikh. That way I could say he was my father's brother, or something like that, you know.'

Rashid said nothing. Not a word of denial or approval or anything like that. All he did was exchange glances with his father.

The next day with heavy heart, she had watched him getting into his car for the drive back to Johannesburg.

'What do they know about the difference between a Sikh, Moslem or Hindu? What do you think, hey Goolam?' she had asked her husband over breakfast that same morning, her glass bangles jangling as she gestured with her hands.

Goolam had merely shrugged and had continued with his breakfast, but she could see that he too was full of anxiety.

There was something in the air. Ayesha could feel it. It was nothing she could articulate, just a vague nagging premonition which had put her on edge.

She studied the white girl. Perhaps it was the duplicating machine. Could it be that someone knew about the machine concealed behind a panel in the kitchen wall?

The Afrikaners in town didn't worry much with them and so sometimes people from the 'Congress'* would come and go without raising suspicion; but lately the police had been watching the store and asking questions. It was a big worry for her and it also made for a lonely life because the others had been warned to stay away. Now no one came any more and it was strange for her not to be cooking and entertaining a steady stream of people.

'Good morning,' Elsie said in Afrikaans. She smiled a little nervously, as she began to realise that it was a silly idea to have come here. Why should she care about them? Rashid was probably one of those who laid land mines which killed innocent people. In her opinion they deserved what they got. But it was a little difficult to envisage the young boy with his dark laughing eyes cast in such a ghastly role.

Ayesha still uneasy, was relieved when at that moment her husband entered the store through the side door. He came to an abrupt halt in the doorway when his glance alighted on Elsie.

In a quiet, even voice with one brow arched, he addressed his wife in Gujarati. She responded in the same language. He smiled at Elsie.

'Good morning,' Elsie said.

'Good morning,' Goolam replied. Still smiling he made a comment to his wife in Gujarati again. The smile never left his face as he peered short-sightedly at Elsie. He was short, robust and balding. The shirt buttons were straining to contain the excessive bulge of his belly which ballooned over his belt.

'You must be the new lady teacher in town,' he said.

Elsie did not reply. Instead her glance was drawn to the two large curry stains on his shirt. He waited, but she gave no explanation.

'I was just saying to Abdul,' Ayesha spoke up, 'you look so familiar.' She paused, studying Elsie. 'Doesn't she look familiar Goolam? Who are you, my dear?'

'My name is Elsie and I am on holiday,' she muttered, her tone discouraging any further questions.

'Oh,' Ayesha said, lapsing into awkward silence.

She had a smooth round face with dark eyes which were strangely haunting. The pendant hanging from a gold chain was trapped in the cleavage of her full breasts, thrust up voluptuously by the tight, white calico bodice she wore beneath her sari. When she raised an arm to adjust the fold of sari on her shoulder, her glass bracelets clinked against each other.

'My wife must be mistaken. You know, she was just telling me she remembers a young girl with your hair colour coming into the shop a long time ago. Sometimes, you know, our memories are not what they ought to be. Huh, Ayesha?' he ventured, breaking the silence and giving his wife an affectionate grin.

'I was so sure, Goolam. But you are right. I must be mistaken.' Her hands flicked in gestures while she spoke, the steady clink of her bracelets punctuating her words.

She placed her hands on her hips and studied Elsie, the elusive memory struggling to surface. Her dark intelligent eyes flicked back and forth, not wishing to offend the white woman again by being too direct.

'I want to buy some of my supplies from you,' Elsie said.

'I thought you were on holiday,' Ayesha said with alacrity.

'It's not for me.'

'I'm just asking because the white people don't buy from us. They go to Faurie's,' Ayesha continued, exchanging glances with her husband.

'Ayesha, my dear. We must not look a gift-horse in the mouth. The lady must have her reasons for not wanting to patronise Faurie's, he said, glancing at Elsie for confirmation.

Elsie nodded.

'Who did you say you were visiting?' Ayesha asked.

'I didn't.'

'Oh,' Ayesha said flustered, distractedly moving the watches around on the top shelf in the showcase.

'I need two bags of flour, a bag of mealie-meal . . .'

'Do you have a list?' Goolam smiled apologetically for interrupting.

'Here it is,' Elsie said, handing it to him.

He passed the list to his wife who expertly scanned it. 'We'll have it ready for you in a jiffy. Would you like a cool drink?' she asked. Although she was polite there was an aloofness about her, born of her earlier suspicions.

Elsie nodded. 'I'd like that ... You could add it to my list and also one for Jackson. He's sitting in the lorry.'

'Of course. We'll call him in,' Ayesha said, directing the comment at her husband, who went outside.

Goolam returned with Jackson who stood to one side, nervously wringing his cap. Ayesha's smile, however, as she handed him the cool drink was reassuring.

'You can sit down on this chair if you like,' she said to Elsie.

'Don't worry about me,' Elsie replied. 'I'll take a look around.'

When the supplies were ready, Goolam helped Jackson to load the lorry while Elsie settled the bill with Ayesha.

'I hope you'll come again,' Ayesha said as Elsie prepared to take her leave.

'I will.' She sniffed. 'What is that smell?' she asked curiously.

Ayesha's eyes widened in amusement. 'Curry,' she said. 'That's what we eat. It's really very good, you should try it sometime.'

'I don't know much about it,' Elsie protested.

'The next time you come in, maybe you'll want to try some. What do you think Goolam?' She smiled at her husband and turned her attention back to Elsie. 'Let me know. Are you coming in at the same time next week? I'll cook *roti* as well and you can sample a little bit of India,' she called gaily. Ayesha was a different person; quite buoyant now that she had shed her earlier reservations.

'Thank you,' Elsie said.

'Come again,' Ayesha called from the doorway.

Elsie climbed into the lorry and started the engine.

'What a lovely young girl. Who was she, Goolam?' Ayesha asked, returning to the store.

'Faanie van Staaden's daughter,' he said.

'How do you know that, Goolam?' she asked, her voice thin and quivery with apprehension.

'I spoke to Jackson.'

Ayesha's hand flailed behind her, searching for a chair as her knees weakened.

'*Marshallah*! Goolam, I thought I knew her from somewhere and all the time you were telling me I was wrong,' she said in a voice that was barely above a whisper. 'What will we do now?'

Outside Elsie turned off the engine and sat hunched over the steering wheel. In her mind's eye she saw the woman's guileless dark eyes as she invited her back for a meal. Then she had a fleeting image of Rashid, the young boy, lying dead in the *veld*, a lock of hair fallen across his brow.

She had lied about her identity. Why? she wondered. Why hadn't she told them who she was? For a moment she was torn by indecision. Then quite abruptly she made up her mind. Since the trap was set for Wednesday, there would still be enough time to warn their son. Elsie climbed back out of the lorry watched by the surprised Jackson, and hurried back to the store.

MIRIAM TLALI

Mm'a Lithoto

from *Footprints In The Quag* (1989)

Paballo sat on the hard bench in Park Station, Johannesburg railway concourse and thought regretfully of her marriage. She did not know whether to stay out of Musi's life for ever. At that moment, she wished she could bid him and his people goodbye and face her future alone.

She looked once more at the bundles of clothing which lay in front of her and wondered whether her once-blissful marriage had been irretrievably lost. Her feelings were shreds of unrelated emotional impulses. One moment she felt like crying at the top of her voice, and seconds later she knew that she did not care. She told herself that in the midst of all the traffic she had at last found peace of mind. That she had finally managed to tear herself away from the unhappy circumstances which made up her married life was an accomplishment she would never regret. Yet at the same time, the pain of estrangement stabbed at her heart, especially when she looked into the innocent unsuspecting face of her three-year-old son, Mzwandile.

Paballo's teenage niece — Mahali — sat next to her, looking at the passing commuters and commenting on the latest fashions girls of her age were wearing. She had rattled on incessantly, trying her best to wrest the attention of her aunt away from the sordid experience they had both been through. They had had to grab clothes, wrap them up into 'lithoto' (bundles) and leave her aunt's home unceremoniously. Where would it all end, she wondered? All she knew was that she would follow her long-suffering aunt to wherever she ventured.

Paballo whispered into Mahali's ear so that the other waiting passengers would not hear. She said, 'Mahali, I have to go to the ladies' room. Just remain with the child and look after the bundles. Keep counting them.' The urge to visit the toilet had suddenly made her aware of the many people around and the pungent smell which emanated from the rows of closed doors and the impatient faces of the women who were awaiting their turns.

When she returned, Mahali looked at her with a smile. She had already thought of a solution to their problem. Before Paballo had squeezed herself into 'her place' on the bench, Mahali stammered, 'I know what we shall do, Aunty. Before it becomes too late for us to find a place ... "A re e o kopa boroko ha Nkhono Mm'a-Letia".'

'How *can* we?' Paballo asked, raising her shoulders in despair.

Mahali could not understand. She always found Grandmother Mm'a-Letia smiling and happy to see them whenever they went visiting there. She wondered why her aunt was hesitant to go to her house and 'ask for sleep'.

With an earnest face, Paballo asked Mahali, 'Are you aware just how much Aunt Mm'a-Letia struggles in the house of hers, Mahali? Ever since her daughter Letia died, she has had to raise her two granddaughters and grandson besides caring for Thabo her own son. The two granddaughters are the only ones who sometimes help her with some money; but those two men — Thabo and Keletso — just do not bother. There are only four small rooms like ours, and there are already five adults sleeping there. How shall we all squeeze ourselves and our luggage in there?'

Mahali thought of Thabo and Keletso. She nodded, remembering the 'names' by which they were known to the youth in the township. Thabo, known as 'Bra Tabs', was in fact her 'uncle' in the extended family tree; and Keletso was popularly known as 'Keltz'. How ugly these names became when they were distorted! Mahali shook her head, remembering that according to custom, *she* would have to regard her Uncle Thabo as 'Malome-mo-ja-lihloho' (the one who is answerable to all her life's 'affairs', who has to carry out all the ritual requirements as prescribed). How would these 'lost' couldn't-care-less, yet valuable and irreplaceable members of the extended family cope when *their* turn came?

Paballo realised that she had to 'educate' her niece, lest she be 'lost' like so many of her generation. 'Mahali, you must know all your relatives so that one day when you cannot find happiness and success in your matters, you know where to "run to". It is important for you to know that you are not alone, that you are never an "orphan". There is always someone in the "family" who is under obligation to "stand" by you. These are your people, your own flesh and blood. They cannot turn away from their duties no matter how irresponsible they may be. It is their blood that counts.'

'Yes, Aunty. But how are we to work together when we never even meet? Look, I had even forgotten that there are such people at Grandma

Mm'a-Letia's. Whenever we go visiting there, they are never there. In fact I've always thought that they live somewhere far away. Even on Sundays we never find them. Are they aware that sometime in the future when some of us have "matters" to be dealt with, they'll have to live up to the demands of custom? Do they know these rituals at all?'

'It is just that things are so much more difficult to organise, Mahali. They *are* aware of these "laws" because the elders always "preach" about them. The word is not the finger, it does not go and come back, it stays ... "Lentsoe ha se monoana, ha le e e le khutla", you know that, don't you. Just like I am telling you all these things, "tomorrow" you'll be telling your children, those who come after you. If we throw away our rituals we are as good as dead. No one can succeed in destroying us if we know ourselves and those "laws" that our ancestors have left us with.

'When their turn comes, people like your Uncle Keletso will realize that *they* too will never find peace and their "affairs" will never succeed because their "duties" are not fulfilled. The spirits of the ancestors will never set them free. They will be bound to abide by the "rules". You must realise that they are being tossed around by difficulties which they encounter. "Ba thefuloa ke lifefo tsa bophelo." But of course that does not mean that they have to give in to problems. It is their duty to fight them. Aunt Mm'a-Letia is also not without blame because she allows these young people to trample over her. What she should do is to insist that they respect her. She should not allow them to toss her around. Perhaps it is because she is getting on in years and they know that their other elders are far away and unable to come and "speak to them". It is high time someone from our uncles and big-Fathers straightened them up. They are like carnivorous animals which move at night. They hunt for places where they can find something to drink. Then they stumble home to Mm'a-Letia's when the biting early winds force them to find a place where they can cuddle. When they wake up hungry, they open empty pots and beg, or even demand food from 'Mm'a-Letia. Big men expect their elderly grandmother and mother to feed them — it's wrong! How can we now go to add on to Aunt Mm'a-Letia's problems, Mahali? How can we ask for sleep at her place? Mind you, she would never turn us away because it is also her "duty" to welcome me when I "come crying" to her according to custom and blood, but really, I feel for her "mosali-moholo oa molimo". She is my mother's own sister.'

'Does Grandma Mm'a-Letia feed such big men from her lousy pension money?'

'Yes, she does. If it were not for the help she gets from her granddaughters Grace and Neo they would really starve. Grace is a nurse-aid at Baragwanath Hospital and Neo has a clerical job in town.

'If we go there, there'll be nowhere for us to sleep. Chairs and tables would have to be packed in some corner to make room for us. We would perhaps have to sleep in the kitchen. But even then, the little space in the kitchen is virtually a passage as you know. Everyone going out or coming in walks through the kitchen. It means they'll have to jump and hop over us. I shall never find sleep. And I have to wake up and go to work in the morning and leave you to look after Mzwandile. It means that you'll have to stay away from school. You'll have to go to school some time in the day and report to the Principal that you had to look after the child. We shall have to say that you had to take "Zwandie" to the clinic, what shall we do? I cannot stay away from work because we need the money.'

Paballo thought silently for a while and shook her head vigorously. She muttered, 'No Mahali, we cannot go to Aunt Mm'a-Letia's place, we can't. She has her hands full. Her own son Thabo — your uncle — drinks heavily. What if he should trip over us and fall? Imagine what would happen if he fell on little Zwandie? And Keletso seems to have taken after Thabo too. He must be thinking it is "manly" to go about doing nothing but drinking all day and night. Those two never even help to do chores around the house. They are not even ashamed to see old Mm'a-Letia struggle to do the garden with her "arthritis" and everything.'

'No Aunty, I can see that we cannot go and "ask for sleep" there. What shall we do?'

Paballo thought seriously. She was just about to say something when she stopped abruptly, winced and twisted her face. Mahali noticed her aunt's distorted face and snapped uneasily, 'What's wrong, Aunty?'

Unmistakable. She sat poised, as if listening. It was the first signal, the early quickening of the new life within her. It was a disturbing sensation. Prior to the events of the past hours which had led to her leaving her home unexpectedly, not a minute had passed when she did not remember that she was pregnant once more. The devastating confirmation she had received from the clinic doctor had left her confused and uncertain whether to rejoice or to cry.

With the additional responsibility of caring for another baby she would have to stop working. Being at work at certain hours of the day granted her the very-much-needed break to be away from the stress and strain of being with her in-laws, the inevitable outcome of sharing her small house with them. Their unconcealed hostility towards her clouded her mind day and night. What shattered her even more was the fact that Musi, her husband, had not received the announcement that they were expecting another child enthusiastically either. She remembered that she was now eighteen weeks pregnant and that the 'signals' she was now feeling would develop into violent kicks as time went by, never giving her time to forget that she should prepare for a new life.

Paballo felt even more alone. The ground over which she was resting seemed to have shifted away, leaving her hanging over a ghastly chasm. She should have known better, she thought bitterly. Deep in her heart she was reprimanding herself ... "Leoto ha le na nko; ha le nkhelle." The foot does not have a nose; it does not smell out. The foot carries you even to the thresholds of your enemies. It even takes you and deposits you at the very edge of a precipice and you can watch helplessly as you dangle and your hopes for survival are sinking into the depths of despair.

It was Mahali who broke the uneasy silence. She spoke softly so that the people around would not hear. She said, 'Honestly, if one day I should marry, I'll insist that my in-laws live in their own house far away from my husband and me, honestly. If they force matters and come to where I am, I'll leave them and get another house.'

Her aunt was a little annoyed at what Mahali had said. She retorted, 'You really speak like a child, Mahali. You think it's easy for a woman like myself (or a man, for that matter) just to bolt out when it is tough and get yourself another place. What about the law? What about the whole set-up of locations and superintendents and black-jacks and the waiting lists and so on? Besides, under the law, I would have to get my husband's permission. What if he should refuse, even if there *was* "another place or house" as you say?'

'Of course he would refuse because he is not having any problems putting up with his people. *I* would leave him immediately, honestly, Aunty.'

'What about your children: what would you say to them? You are able to talk like that because you are now old enough to understand what is happening. What about Zwandie here, for instance? Even now as we are sitting here he understands nothing. He has already asked so many times when we are going back home.'

'I am sorry, Aunty, if what I said offended you. I suppose I do not understand, just like Zwandie.'

Mahali excused herself and moved in the direction of the stench, where some women were waiting in an unending queue to go in the toilets. She stood there shaking her head. The whole thing of marriage and in-laws and houses and laws and superintendents was all too confusing and annoying at the same time. What does being a woman mean to everybody, to the laws anyway, she wondered, tears of remorse filling her eyes. With the back of her hand, she wiped the tears away and was thankful that she was a good distance away from her aunt.

Mahali sat next to her aunt and said nothing. Paballo gave her a bank-note which she had dug out of her purse. 'Just go and buy us two more cold drinks. You know what I like ... lemonade.' Of late Paballo had been drinking virtually gallons of the stuff. 'Buy yourself one too if you like.'

Mahali smiled and shook her head. She remarked, 'I've been drinking too many Cokes, Aunty; I'd like something to eat — a hamburger. Don't you feel like eating something? You never ate anything since this morning when we arrived here. We were all looking forward to having a good Saturday lunch meal with that soup as an "introduction". The soup was smelling so good. Those herbs and bayleaves we added into it really smelt good and inviting. I couldn't wait to taste it ... and then it happened ... everything was spoilt.'

As Mahali left for their refreshments, her aunt reminded her, 'Don't buy any more ice-creams for Zwandie, Mahali. He has already had too many of them. Get him something to eat too.'

She did not want to speak nor remember what had happened before she and her niece had left the house with the bundles on their heads. She felt a little uneasy and ashamed. What did anyone in their street who had seen them carrying bundles on their heads, like old Sophiatown washerwomen, think, she wondered. No matter how much she tried, her mind clung on to those moments like a nightmare. She had tried hard to dispel those thoughts about her quarrel with Musi. It was striking to her what little provocation it took of late to get them bickering at each other. He seemed so much more impatient, and ready to take her to task more than ever before. Is it true, she wondered, that 'monna o hlalisoa mosalie,' that when a woman is expecting a baby, her husband feels a certain aversion towards her, and that he usually finds himself unable to do anything about it? But the quarrels and bickering started long, long ago when Zwandie was only a baby. In fact she could even trace them to when they started living under the same roof with his people. The removals of his parents from the farm Klipgat in the northern Transvaal had forced them to come to their son in Soweto. Musi could not bear to stand by while his elderly parents were being shunted around from one bare veld to another.

Paballo recalled Musi's loud clanging offensive voice echoing through the kitchen that morning. It seemed to hit the rafters above, then knock against the iron roofing and bounce back to her with the momentum and thunder it gathered as it traversed through space. He bellowed at her. '... And can someone tell me just why that damned pot of soup keeps boiling away? For goodness' sake why can't someone dish out for my parents anyway?'

He had not even bothered to find out how she had struggled to get the food in the pots in the first place. She had had no time to think clearly.

All she knew was that she had to go out of their lives once and for all! Is that why the old women sit and tell you to 'giny'ilitye', swallow the stone, when you get married? That you as a woman should overlook whatever unpleasant and painful things happen to you in marriage and bear it all out like a soldier, she wondered. 'Well I just could not go on taking it any more,' Paballo mumbled to herself. 'It just does not matter how much you sacrifice, they always regard you as a "ngoetsi", "makoti" — something with no feelings like a stone!'

Mahali had yet another brain-wave. She was excited and smiling when she made the suggestion. She snapped, 'What about Kwa-Thema, Aunty? We could go to Ntate-moholo Tsitso's place. The last time, we "ran" to his place, didn't we?'

'That's far away in Springs. And that was only possible because I was on leave at the time when we quarrelled with Musi and he drove me away. I've thought of it too; but then I have to come to work here in Johannesburg every morning. It's not possible Mahali . . . very expensive too. Uncle Tsitso is in fact "Malome-mo-ja-lihloho", my eldest maternal uncle who has to make decisions on matters concerning my welfare.'

'Ntate-moholo Tsitso is not aware that you are still having all these problems; that we still run around having to "look for sleep" with "lithoto" balanced on our heads. Or have you ever written to him to tell him that things still have not changed?'

Mahali shook her head. She added sadly, 'What hurts most is that at the time, it was decided by Musi's people that they would pay the "fine" of an ox imposed on them by my people for "ill-treatment" and for Musi's audacity in driving me out of my own house. That fine was never paid, and now we're back to square one.'

'Ao! It was never paid? I was too young to understand but I never asked because as youngsters one is not allowed to probe and question affairs of elderly people. Now what is the use if in-laws do not respect the rulings of the people? It means that anything can happen to you as "ngoetsi". What shall we do now, Aunty?'

Paballo reflected for a while and replied, 'I was just thinking that because it is already becoming late and the traffic of commuters is increasing, and because we have these bundles to carry, we must go back to Soweto.'

'Back to Dube and those people, Aunty, back to your house?'

'No, Mahali. Let's go to my brother — your Uncle Mpempe in Molapo township. He will help me sort everything out. I did not want to upset him because he gets quite irritated seeing me "looking for sleep" all over the place because of what happens between me and Musi. But now I have nowhere to go to at the moment. I have to find some place. We must find a place to sleep. Zwandie is tired and sleepy.'

It was a relief to Mahali that her Aunty had finally made a decision. She immediately picked up Zwandie from Paballo's lap and strapped him on her own back. She suggested, 'OK, Aunty, I'll take Zwandie and two bundles and you can take the rest.'

Paballo was thankful for Mahali's nearness and for her very understanding and considerate nature. Deep in her heart, she prayed that her niece should not meet with the kind of problems she was now experiencing. As she bent down to pick up her two bundles, she could already feel inside her the discomfort caused by the additional 'bundle', and the tightening of the muscles in her groin. She sighed and whispered, 'Let's go.'

By the time Mahali and Paballo got off the bus at the 'Pietersburg' stop on the outskirts of Rockville township, it was dark. With the help of a few sympathetic passengers, they managed to roll the bundles through the narrow passage, out of the bus and on to the gravel pavement.

The smell of smoke from the chimneys and the grey dust raked up as the vehicles sped along Vundla Drive hit their nasal passages. They did not notice the silvery moon above, across whose face clouds of smog were drifting and playing hide and seek. They trudged along anxiously.

It was important that they keep moving because it was becoming late. Paballo heaved the one big bundle and deposited it on the crown of her head so that her neck jerked backwards. She steadied herself by keeping her legs astride. For the first time since she and Mahali had taken to the street, tears of bitterness flooded her eyes and she wished that her parents were still alive. Had she truly been reduced to a mere lingerer carrying bundles of clothing balanced on her head, she wondered. Never in her whole life did she even dream that such a thing would happen to her.

From the noise coming through the open windows of Mpempe's house, it was evident that they had many visitors. It would not be good behaviour for the tear-stained face of a woman to appear suddenly before a rowdy, jovial 'crowd'. The two women hesitated. Paballo, in her feminine wisdom, stepped aside at the gate and beckoned Mahali to follow her. In the shadowy protection of the hedge fence, they relieved themselves of the bundles and wiped their sweaty brows. Roars of laughter mingled with yells of female voices punctuated an incoherent chorus of music and ululating. Paballo felt uneasy that her own sadness would immediately transform the exaltation of her brother's 'family' into dejection. This was not to happen; she would make sure of that. She whispered to her niece, 'Mahali, you go in and call Mpempe. Be careful not to attract the attention of the visitors. Make sure that no one overhears you. Tell him that I'm here. Tell my brother that I would like to speak to him.'

An hour later, Mpempe knocked impatiently on the front door of Paballo's house. His sister and Mahali looked at each other, an atmosphere of uncertainty preying on their minds. They stood quietly and waited with the bundles still balanced on their heads. All Mpempe wanted was to resolve the whole matter of what he called 'the repeated degradation of his sister'. This time he had come to confront his brother-in-law man to man!

It was Musi's father who opened the door. The three went into the house and stood at the door. Mpempe, suppressing his anger, informed the old man that he had come to see Musi. He impatiently explained the purpose of his 'visit'. All the old man could say was, 'Musi left early in the afternoon. He said that he was going to look for his wife.'

His eyes rested on Paballo's face for a while. The three put the bundles on the floor almost simultaneously. Mpempe sighed uneasily as he went through the whole process of explanation. All he wanted was to settle the matter with his brother-in-law *once and for all*, he emphasised. The old man, on the other hand, implored him to have the whole matter deferred to a later time 'when the elderly people on both sides can resolve the matter'.

There was no point in trying to speak to these old people, Mpempe felt, shaking his head. They will hold on to the stumps of a tree even when leaves are long squashed dead and the branches are only dry twigs.

'Tell your son that he has had a very narrow escape,' Mpempe murmured into the face of the bewildered old man.

Somehow Paballo knew that the planned meetings would never take place. All her uncles were now too ill or too old to deal effectively with Musi's people. She knew that she was back to square one. Her brother had assured her that he would settle the matter man to man. That she saw as her only hope. It was becoming more and more difficult to work things 'our way' — the respectable traditional way.

Mahali sat down and transferred Mzwandile on to her lap. He was fast asleep and untouched by all that was happening. For him it had been a long, long day of drifting from pillar to post.

Mpempe shook his head and left. He would certainly be coming again, he said. Paballo looked around at the furniture and wondered whether she would ever find happiness within the walls of that dreary match-box. The bundles looked like objects which did not belong to the surroundings. She wondered why she had agreed to come back at all. But where would she have escaped to, she asked herself.

The old man looked at Mahali and the child and smiled uneasily. He said, 'Mahali, put Mzwandile to sleep and take the bundles back into the bedroom. Let us all go to sleep.'

Inside the old people's bedroom, Paballo's mother-in-law sat with bated breath, waiting for her husband to come and inform her of what had happened. You never know what young people can do when they are angry, she said to herself. The old man entered and shut the door behind him. He smiled broadly and whispered into his wife's partially deaf ear, 'Thank God they are back. Where would we get all that money to pay another fine? Another ox!'

Exactly four-and-a-half months later, Paballo gave birth to a bonny baby girl. Musi's people named her Mm'a-lithoto, mother of bundles ... yet another of Paballo's bundles of joy.

BESSIE HEAD

The Lovers

from *Tales Of Tenderness And Power* (1989)

The love affair began in the summer. The love affair began in those dim dark days when young men and women did not have love affairs. It was one of those summers when it rained in torrents. Almost every afternoon towards sunset the low-hanging, rain-filled clouds would sweep across the sky in packed masses and suddenly, with barely a warning, the rain would pour down in blinding sheets.

The young women and little girls were still out in the forest gathering wood that afternoon when the first warning signs of rain appeared in the sky. They hastily gathered up their bundles of wood and began running home to escape the approaching storm. Suddenly, one of the young women halted painfully. In her haste she had trodden on a large thorn.

'Hurry on home, Monosi!' she cried to a little girl panting behind her. 'I have to get this thorn out of my foot. If the rain catches me I shall find some shelter and come home once it is over.'

Without a backward glance the little girl sped on after the hard-running group of wood gatherers. The young woman was quite alone with the approaching storm. The thorn proved difficult to extract. It had broken off and embedded itself deeply in her heel. A few drops of rain beat down on her back. The sky darkened.

Anxiously she looked around for the nearest shelter and saw a cave in some rocks at the base of a hill nearby. She picked up her bundle of wood and limped hastily towards it, with the drops of rain pounding down faster and faster. She had barely entered the cave when the torrent unleashed itself in a violent downpour. Her immediate concern was to seek sanctuary but a moment later her heart lurched in fear as she realized that she was not alone. The warmth of another human filled the interior. She swung around swiftly and found herself almost face to face with a young man.

'We can shelter here together from the storm', he said with quiet authority.

His face was as kind and protective as his words. Reassured, the young woman set down her bundle of sticks in the roomy interior of the cave and together they seated themselves near its entrance. The roar of the rain was deafening so that even the thunder was muffled by its intensity. With quiet, harmonious movement the young man undid a leather pouch tied to his waist. He spent all his time cattle-herding and to while away the long hours he busied himself with all kinds of leather work, assembling skins into all kinds of clothes and blankets. He had a large number of sharpened implements in his pouch. He indicated to the young woman that he wished to extract the thorn. She extended her foot towards him and for some time he busied himself with this task, gently whittling away the skin around the thorn until he had exposed it sufficiently enough to extract it.

The young woman looked at his face with interest and marvelled at the ease and comfort she felt in his presence. In their world men and women lived strictly apart, especially the young and unmarried. This sense of apartness and separateness continued even throughout married life and marriage itself seemed to have no significance beyond a union for the production of children. This wide gap between the sexes created embarrassment on the level of personal contact; the young men often slid their eyes away uneasily or giggled at the sight of a woman. The young man did none of this. He had stared her directly in the eyes, all his movements were natural and unaffected. He was also very pleasing to look at. She thanked him with a smile once he had extracted the thorn and folded her extended foot beneath her. The violence of the storm abated a little but the heavily-laden sky continued to pour forth a steady downpour.

She had seen the young man around the village; she could vaguely place his family connections.

'Aren't you the son of Ra-Keaja?' she asked. She had a light chatty voice with an undertone of laughter in it, very expressive of her personality. She liked, above all, to be happy.

'I am the very Keaja he is named after', the young man replied with a smile. 'I am the first-born in the family.'

'I am the first-born in the family, too', she said. 'I am Tselane, the daughter of Mma-Tselane.'

His family ramifications were more complicated than hers. His father had three wives. All the first born of the first, second and third houses were boys. They were altogether eight children, three boys and five girls, he explained. It was only when the conversation became more serious that Tselane realised that a whole area of the young man's speech had eluded her. He was the extreme opposite of the light chatty young woman. He talked from deep rhythms within himself as though he had invented language specifically for his own use. He had an immense range of expression and feeling at his command; now his eyes lit up with humour, then they were absolutely serious and in earnest.

He swayed almost imperceptibly as he talked. He talked like no one she had ever heard talking before, yet all his utterances were direct, simple and forthright. She bent forward and listened more attentively to his peculiar manner of speech.

'I don't like my mother', he said, shocking her. 'I am her only son simply because my father stopped cohabiting with her after I was born. My father and I are alike. We don't like to be controlled by anyone and she made his life a misery when they were newly married. It was as if she had been born with a worm eating at her heart; she is satisfied with nothing. The only way my father could control the situation was to ignore her completely ...'

He remained silent awhile, concentrating on his own thoughts. 'I don't think I approve of arranged marriages', he said finally. 'My father would never have married her had he had his own choice. He was merely presented with her one day by his family and told that they were to be married and there was nothing he could do about it.'

He kept silent about the torture he endured from his mother. She hated him deeply and bitterly. She had hurled stones at him and scratched him on the arms and legs in her wild frustration. Like his father he eluded her. He rarely spent time at home but kept the cattle-post as his permanent residence. When he approached home it was always with some gift of clothes or blankets. On that particular day he had an enormous gourd filled with milk.

Tselane floundered out of her depth in the face of such stark revelations. They lived the strictest of traditional ways of life, all children were under the control of their parents until they married, therefore it was taboo to discuss their elders. In her impulsive chatty way and partly out of embarrassment, it had been on the tip of her tongue to say that she liked her mother, that her mother was very kind-hearted. But there was a disturbing undertone in her household too. Her mother and father — and she was sure of it due to her detailed knowledge of her mother's way of life — had not cohabited for years either. A few years ago her father had taken another wife. She was her mother's only child. Oh, the surface of their household was polite and harmonious but her father was rarely at home. He was always irritable and morose when he was home.

'I am sorry about all the trouble in your home', she said at last, in a ofter, more thoughtful tone. She was shaken at having been abruptly olted into completely new ways of thought.

The young man smiled and then quite deliberately turned and stared t her. She stared back at him with friendly interest. She did not mind is close scrutiny of her person, he was easy to associate with, comfort-ble, truthful and open in his every gesture.

'Do you approve of arranged marriages?' he asked, still smiling.

'I have not thought of anything', she replied truthfully.

The dark was approaching rapidly. The rain had trickled down to a fine rizzle. Tselane stood up and picked up her bundle of wood. The young nan picked up his gourd of milk. They were barely visible as they walked ome together in the dark. Tselane's home was not too far from the hill. he lived on the extreme western side of the village, he on the extreme astern side.

A bright fire burned in the hut they used as a cooking place on rainy ays. Tselane's mother was sitting bent forward on her low stool, lis-ening attentively to a visitor's tale. It was always like this — her mother vas permanently surrounded by women who confided in her. The whole tory of life unfolded daily around her stool; the ailments of children, vomen who had just had miscarriages, women undergoing treatment for arren wombs — the story was endless. It was the great pleasure of 'selane to seat herself quietly behind her mother's stool and listen with ascinated ears to this endless tale of woe.

Her mother's visitor that evening was on the tail end of a description f one of her children's ailments; chronic epilepsy, which seemed eyond cure. The child seemed in her death throes and the mother was ust at the point of demonstrating the violent seizures when Tselane en-ered. Tselane quietly set her bundle of wood down in a corner and the onversation continued uninterrupted. She took her favourite place ehind her mother's stool. Her father's second wife, Mma-Monosi, was eated on the opposite side of the fire, her face composed and serious. Ier child, the little girl Monosi, fed and attended to, lay fast asleep on a leeping mat in one corner of the hut.

Tselane loved the two women of the household equally. They were oth powerful independent women but with sharply differing per-onalities. Mma-Tselane was a queen who vaguely surveyed the ingdom she ruled, with an abstracted, absent-minded air. Over the 'ears of her married life she had built up a way of life for herself that illed her with content. She wa reputed to be very delicate in health as fter the birth of Tselane she had suffered a number of miscarriages and eemed incapable of bearing any more children. Her delicate health was source of extreme irritation to her husband and at some stage he had

abandoned her completely and taken Mma-Monosi as his second wife
intending to perpetuate his line and name through her healthy body.

The arrangement suited Mma-Tselane. She was big-hearted an
broad-minded and yet, conversely, she prided herself in being th
meticulous upholder of all the traditions the community adhered to
Once Mma-Monosi became a part of the household, Mma-Tselane di
no work but entertained and paid calls the day long. Mma-Monosi ra
the entire household.

The two women complemented each other, for, if Mma-Tselane was
queen, then Mma-Monosi was a humble worker. On the surface, Mma
Monosi appeared as sane and balanced as Mma-Tselane, but there wa
another side to her personality that was very precariously balanced
Mma-Monosi took her trembling way through life. If all was stable an
peaceful, then Mma-Monosi was stable and peaceful. If there was an
disruption or disorder, Mma-Monosi's precarious inner balance regis
tered every wave and upheaval. She hungered for approval of her ever
action and could be upset for days if criticised or reprimanded.

So, between them, the two women achieved a very harmoniou
household. Both were entirely absorbed in their full busy daily round
both were unconcerned that they received scant attention from the ma
of the household and Rra-Tselane was entirely concerned with his ow
affairs. He was a prominent member of the chief's court and he divide
his time between the chief's court and his cattle-post. He was rich i
cattle and his herds were taken care of by servants. He was away at hi
cattle-post at that time.

It was with Mma-Monosi that the young girl, Tselane, enjoyed a fre
and happy relationship. They treated each other as equals; both enjoye
hard work and whenever they were alone together, they laughed an
joked all the time. Her own mother regarded Tselane as an object t
whom she lowered her voice and issued commands between clenche
teeth. Very soon Mma-Tselane stirred in her chair and said in tha
lowered voice: 'Tselane, fetch me my bag of herbs.'

Tselane obediently stood up and hurried to her mother's livin
quarters for the bag of herbs. Another interval followed during whic
her mother and the visitor discussed the medicinal properties of th
herbs. Then Mma-Monosi served the evening meal. Before long th
visitor departed with assurances that Mma-Tselane would call on her th
following day. Then they sat for a while in companionable silence. A
one stage, seeing that the fire was burning low, Mma-Tselane arose an
selected a few pieces of wood from Tselane's bundle to stoke up the fire.

'Er, Tselane', she said, 'your wood is quite dry. Did you shelter fro
the storm?'

'There is a cave in the hill not far from here, mother' Tselane replied. And I sheltered there.' She did not think it was wise to add that she had heltered with a young man, a lot of awkward questions of the wrong ind might have followed.

The mother cast her eyes vaguely over her daughter as if to say all was n order in her world; she always established simple facts about any natter and turned peacefully to the next task at hand. She suddenly deided that she was tired and would retire. Tselane and Mma-Monosi vere left alone seated near the fire. Tselane was still elated by her enounter with the young man; so many pleasant thoughts were flying hrough her head.

'I want to ask you some questions, Mma-Monosi', she said, eagerly.

'What is it you want to say, my child?' Mma-Monosi said, stirring out of a reverie.

'Do you approve of arranged marriages, Mma-Monosi?' she asked, arnestly.

Mma-Monosi drew in her breath between her teeth with a sharp, issing sound, then she lowered her voice in horror and said:

'Tselane, you know quite well that I am your friend but if anyone else eard you talking like that you would be in trouble! Such things are ever discussed here! What put that idea into your head because it is toally unknown to me.'

'But you question life when you begin to grow up', Tselane said defenively.

'That is what you never, never do', Mma-Monosi said severely. 'If ou question life you will upset it. Life is always in order.' She looked horoughly startled and agitated. 'I know of something terrible that once appened to someone who questioned life', she added grimly.

'Who is this? What terrible thing happened?' Tselane asked in her urn agitated.

'I can't tell you', Mma-Monosi said firmly. 'It is too terrible to menion.'

Tselane subsided into silence with a speculative look in her eye. She nderstood Mma-Monosi well. She couldn't keep a secret. She could lways be tempted into telling a secret, if not today then on some other ay. She decided to find out the terrible story.

When Keaja arrived home his family was eating the evening meal. He irst approached the women's quarters and offered them the gourd of nilk.

'The cows are calving heavily', he explained. 'There is a lot of milk and can bring some home every day.'

He was greeted joyously by the second and third wives of his father who anxiously enquired after their sons who lived with him at the cattle post.

'They are quite well', he said, politely. 'I settled them and the cattle before I left. I shall return again in the early morning because I am worried about the young calves.'

He avoided his mother's baleful stare and tight, deprived mouth. She never had anything to say to him, although, on his approach to the women's quarters, he had heard her voice, shrill and harsh, dominating the conversation. His meal was handed to him and he retreated to his father's quarters. He ate alone and apart from the women. A bright fire burned in his father's hut.

'Hullo, Father-of-Me', his father greeted him, making affectionate play on the name Keaja which means I am eating now because I have a son to take care of me.

His father doted on him. In his eyes there was no greater son than Keaja. After an exchange of greetings his father asked:

'And what is your news?'

He gave his father the same information about the cows calving heavily and their rich supply of milk; that his other two sons were quite well. They ate for a while in companionable silence. His mother's voice rose shrill and penetrating in the silent night. Quite unexpectedly his father looked up with a twinkle in his eye and said:

'Those extra calves will stand us in good stead, Father-of-Me. I have just started negotiations about your marriage.'

A spasm of chill, cold fear almost constricted Keaja's heart.

'Who am I to marry, father?' he asked, alarmed.

'I cannot mention the family name just yet', his father replied, cheerfully, not sensing his son's alarm. 'The negotiations are still at a very delicate stage.'

'Have you committed yourself in this matter, father?' he asked, a sharp angry note in his voice.

'Oh yes', his father replied. 'I have given my honour in this matter. It is just that these things take a long time to arrange as there are many courtesies to be observed.'

'How long?' Keaja asked.

'About six new moons may have to pass', his father replied. 'It may even be longer than that. I cannot say at this stage.'

'I could choose a wife for myself,' the son said, with deadly quietude. 'I could choose my own wife and then inform you of my choice.'

His father stared at him in surprise.

'You cannot be different from everyone else', he said. 'I must be a parent with a weakness that you can talk to me so.'

Keaja lowered his eyes to his eating bowl. There was no way in which he could voice a protest against his society because the individual was completely smothered by communal and social demands. He was a young man possessed by individual longings and passions; he had a nervous balance that either sought complete isolation or true companionship and communication and for a long while all appeared in order with him because of the deceptive surface peace of his personality. Even that evening Keaja's protest against an arranged marriage was hardly heard by his father.

His father knew that he indulged his son, that they had free and easy exchanges beyond what was socially permissible; even that brief exchange was more than all parents allowed their children. They arranged all details of their children's future and on the fatal day merely informed them that they were to be married to so-and-so. There was no point in saying: 'I might not be able to live with so-and-so. She might be unsuited to me', so that when Keaja lapsed into silence, his father merely smiled indulgently and engaged him in small talk.

Keaja was certainly of marriageable age. The previous year he had gone through his initiation ceremony. Apart from other trials endured during the ceremony, detailed instruction had been given to the young men of his age group about sexual relations between men and women. They were hardly private and personal but affected by a large number of social regulations and taboos. If he broke the taboos at a personal and private level, death, sickness and great misfortune would fall upon his family. If he broke the taboos at a social level, death and disaster would fall upon the community.

There were many periods in a man's life when abstinence from sexual relations was required; often this abstinence had to be practised communally as in the period preceding the harvest of crops and only broken on the day of the harvest thanksgiving ceremony.

These regulations and taboos applied to men and women alike but the initiation ceremony for women, which Tselane had also experienced the previous year, was much more complex in its instruction. A delicate balance had to be preserved between a woman's reproductive cycle and the safety of the community; at almost every stage in her life a woman was a potential source of danger to the community. All women were given careful instruction in precautions to be observed during times of menstruation, childbirth and accidental miscarriages. Failure to observe the taboos could bring harm to animal life, crops and the community.

It could be seen then that the community held no place for people wildly carried away by their passions, that there was logic and order in the carefully arranged sterile emotional and physical relationships between men and women. There was no one to challenge the establishe order of things; if people felt any personal unhappiness it was smothere and subdued and so life for the community proceeded from day to day i peace and harmony.

As all lovers do, they began a personal and emotional dialogue tha excluded all life around them. Perhaps its pattern and direction was th same for all lovers, painful and maddening by turns in its initial insec urity.

Who looked for who? They could not say, except that the far-wester unpolluted end of the river where women drew water and the forest where they gathered firewood became Keaja's favourite huntin grounds. Their work periods coincided at that time. The corn had jus been sown and the women were idling in the village until the heav soaking rains raised the weeds in their fields, then their next busy perio would follow when they hoed out the weeds between their corn.

Keaja returned every day to the village with gourds of milk for hi family and it did not take Tselane long to note that he delayed an lingered in her work areas until he had caught some glimpse of her. Sh was always in a crowd of gaily chattering young women. The memory o their first encounter had been so fresh and stimulating, so full of unex pected surprises in dialogue that she longed to approach him.

One afternoon, while out gathering wood with her companions, sh noticed him among the distant bushes and contrived to remove hersel from her companions. As she walked towards him, he quite directly ap proached her and took hold of her hand. She made no effort to pull he hand free. It rested in his as though it belonged there. They walked o some distance, then he paused, and turning to face her told her all he ha on his mind in his direct, simple way. This time he did not smile at all.

'My father will arrange a marriage for me after six new moons hav passed', he said. 'I do not want that. I want a wife of my own choosin but all the things I want can only cause trouble.'

She looked away into the distance not immediately knowing what sh ought to say. Her own parents had given her no clue of their plans fo her future; indeed she had not had cause to think about it but she did no like most of the young men of the village. They had a hang-dog air a though the society and its oppressive ways had broken their will. Sh liked everything about Keaja and she felt safe with him as on that storm afternoon in the cavern when he had said: 'We can shelter here togethe from the storm ...'

'My own thoughts are not complicated', he went on, still holding o to her hand. 'I thought I would find out how you felt about this matter. thought I would like to choose you as my wife. If you do not want t choose me in turn, I shall not pursue my own wants any longer. I might even marry the wife my father chooses for me.'

She turned around and faced him and spoke with a clarity of thought that startled her.

'I am afraid of nothing', she said. 'Not even trouble or death, but I need some time to find out what I am thinking.'

He let go of her and so they parted and went their separate ways. From that point onwards right until the following day, she lived in a state of high elation. Her thought processes were not all coherent, indeed she had not a thought in her head. Then the illogic of love took over. Just as she was about to pick up the pitcher in the late afternoon, she suddenly felt desperately ill, so ill that she was almost brought to the point of death. She experienced a paralysing lameness in her arms and legs. The weight of the pitcher with which she was to draw water was too heavy for her to endure.

She appealed to Mma-Monosi.

'I feel faint and ill today', she said. 'I cannot draw water.'

Mma-Monosi was only too happy to take over her chores but at the same time consulted anxiously with her mother about this sudden illness. Mma-Tselane, after some deliberation, decided that it was the illness young girls get when they are growing too rapidly.

She spent a happy three days doctoring her daughter with warm herb drinks as Mma-Tselane liked nothing better than to concentrate on illness. Still, the physical turmoil the young girl felt continued unabated; at night she trembled violently from head to toe. It was so shocking and new that for two days she succumbed completely to the blow. It wasn't any coherent thought processes that made her struggle desperately to her feet on the third day but a need to quieten the anguish. She convinced her mother and Mma-Monosi that she felt well enough to perform her wood gathering chores. Towards the afternoon she hurried to the forest area, carefully avoiding her companions.

She was relieved, on meeting Keaja, to see that his face bore the same anguished look that she felt. He spoke first. 'I felt so ill and disturbed', he said. 'I could do nothing but wait for your appearance.'

They sat down on the ground together. She was so exhausted by her two-day struggle that for a moment she leaned forward and rested her head on his knee. Her thought processes seemed to awaken once more because she smiled contentedly and said: 'I want to think.'

Eventually she raised herself and, with shining eyes, looked at the young man.

'I felt so ill', she said. 'My mother kept on giving me herb drinks. She said it was normal to feel so faint and dizzy when one is growing. I know

now what made me feel ill. I was fighting my training. My training has told me that people are not important in themselves but you so suddenly became important to me, as a person. I did not know how to tell my mother all this. I did not know how to tell her anything yet she was kind and took care of me. Eventually I thought I would lose my mind so I came here to find you . . .'

It was as if, from that moment onwards, they quietly and of their own will had married. They began to plan together how and when they should meet.

The young man was full of forethought and planning. He knew that, in terms of his own society, he was starting a terrible mess; but then his society only calculated along the lines of human helplessness in the face of overwhelming odds. It did not calculate for human inventiveness and initiative. He only needed the young girl's pledge and from then onwards he took the initiative in all things. He was to startle and please her from that very day with his logical mind. It was as if he knew that she would come at some time, that they would linger in joy with their lovemaking, so that when Tselane eventually expressed agitation at the lateness of the hour, he, with a superior smile, indicated a large bundle of wood nearby that he had collected for her to take home.

A peaceful interlude followed and the community innocently lived out its day-by-day life, unaware of the disruption and upheaval that would soon fall upon it. The women were soon out in the fields, hoeing weeds and tending their crops, Tselane among them. She worked side by side with Mma-Monosi, as she had always done. There was not even a ripple of the secret life she now lived; if anything, she worked harder and with greater contentment. She laughed and joked as usual with Mma-Monosi but sound instinct made her keep her private affairs to herself.

When the corn was already high in the fields and about to ripen, Tselane realised that she was expecting a child. A matter that had been secret could be a secret no longer. When she confided this news to Keaja, he quite happily accepted it as a part of all the plans he had made, for as he said to her at that time: 'I am not planning for death when we are so happy. I want that we should live.'

He had only one part of all his planning secure, a safe escape route outside the village and on to a new and unknown life they would make together. They had made themselves outcasts from the acceptable order of village life and he presented her with two plans from which she could choose. The first alternative was the simpler for them. They could leave the village at any moment and without informing anyone of their intentions. The world was very wide for a man. He had travelled great distances, both alone and in the company of other men, while on his hunting and herding duties. The area was safe for travel for some distance. He had sat around firesides and heard stories about wars and fugitives and hospitable tribes who lived far away and whose customs differed from theirs. Keaja had not been idle all this while; he had prepared all they would need for their journey and hidden their provisions in a safe place.

The second alternative was more difficult for the lovers. They could inform their parents of their love and ask that they be married. He was not sure of the outcome but it was to invite death or worse. It might still lead to the escape route out of the village as he was not planning for death.

So after some thought Tselane decided to tell her parents because, as she pointed out, the first plan would be too heart-breaking for their parents. They, therefore, decided on that very day to inform their parents of their love and name the date on which they wished to marry.

It was nearing dusk when Tselane arrived home with her bundle of wood. Her mother and Mma-Monosi were seated out in the courtyard, engaged in some quiet conversation.

Tselane set down her bundle, approached the two women and knelt down quietly by her mother's side. Her mother turned towards her, expecting some request or message from a friend. There was no other way except for Tselane to convey her own message in the most direct way possible.

'Mother', she said. 'I am expecting a child by the son of Rra-Keaja. We wish to be married by the next moon. We love each other . . .'

For a moment her mother frowned as though her child's words did not make sense. Mma-Monosi's body shuddered several times as though she were cold but she maintained a deathly silence. Eventually, Tselane's mother lowered her voice and said between clenched teeth:

'You are to go to your hut and remain there. On no account are you to leave without the supervision of Mma-Monosi.'

For a time Mma-Tselane sat looking into the distance, a broken woman. Her social prestige, her kingdom, her self-esteem crumbled around her.

A short while later her husband entered the yard. He had spent an enjoyable day at the chief's court with other men. He now wished for his evening meal and retirement for the night. The last thing he wanted was conversation with women, so he looked up irritably as his wife appeared without his evening meal. She explained herself with as much dignity as she could muster. She was almost collapsing with shock. He listened in disbelief and gave a sharp exclamation of anger.

'Tselane', Mma-Monosi said, earnestly. 'It is no light matter to break custom. You pay for it with your life. I should have told you the story that night we discussed custom. When I was a young girl we had a case such as this but not such a deep mess. The young man had taken a fancy to a girl and she to him. He, therefore, refused the girl his parents had chosen for him. They could not break him and so they killed him. They killed him even though he had not touched the girl. But there is one thing I want you to know. I am your friend and I will die for you. No one will injure you while I am alive.'

Their easy, affectionate relationship returned to them. They talked for some time about the love affair, Mma-Monosi absorbing every word with delight. A while later Mma-Tselane re-entered the yard. She was still too angry to talk to her own child but she called Mma-Monosi to one side and informed her that she had won an assurance in high places that no harm would come to her child.

And so began a week of raging storms and wild irrational deliberations. It was a family affair. It was a public affair. As a public affair it would bring ruin and disaster upon the community and public anger was high. Two parents showed themselves up in a bad light, the father of Tselane and the mother of Keaja. Rra-Tselane was adamant that the marriage would never take place. He preferred to sound death warnings all the time. The worm that had been eating at the heart of Keaja's mother all this while finally arose and devoured her heart. She too could be heard to sound death warnings. Then a curious and temporary solution was handed down from the places. It was said that if the lovers removed themselves from the community for a certain number of days, it would make allowance for public anger to die down. Then the marriage of the lovers would be considered.

So appalling was the drama to the community that on the day Keaja was released from his home and allowed to approach the home of Tselane, all the people withdrew to their own homes so as not to witness the fearful sight. Only Mma-Monosi, who had supervised the last details of the departure, stood openly watching the direction in which the young lovers left the village. She saw them begin to ascend the hill not far from the home of Tselane. As darkness was approaching, she turned and walked back to her yard. To Mma-Tselane, who lay in a state of nervous collapse in her hut, Mma-Monosi made her last, sane pronouncement on the whole affair.

'The young man is no fool', she said. 'They have taken the direction of the hill. He knows that the hilltop is superior to any other. People are angry and someone might think of attacking them. An attacker will find it a difficult task as the young man will hurl stones down on him before he ever gets near. Our child is quite safe with him.'

Then the story took a horrible turn. Tension built up towards the day the lovers were supposed to return to community life. Days went by and they did not return. Eventually search parties were sent out to look for them but they had disappeared. Not even their footmarks were visible on the bare rock faces and tufts of grass on the hillside. At first the searchers returned and did not report having seen any abnormal phenomena, only a baffled surprise. Then Mma-Monosi's precarious imaginative balance tipped over into chaos. She was seen walking grief-stricken towards the hill. As she reached its base she stool still and the whole drama of the disappearance of the lovers was re-created before her eyes. She first heard loud groans of anguish that made her blood run cold. She saw that as soon as Tselane and Keaja set foot on the hill, the rocks parted and a gaping hole appeared. The lovers sank into its depths and the rocks closed over them. As she called, 'Tselane! Keaja!' their spirits rose and floated soundlessly with unseeing eyes to the top of the hill.

Mma-Monosi returned to the village and told a solemn and convincing story of all she had seen. People only had to be informed that such phenomena existed and they all began seeing it too. Then Mma-Tselane, maddened and distraught by the loss of her daughter slowly made her way to the hill. With sorrowful eyes she watched the drama re-create itself before her. She returned home and died.

The hill from then onwards became an unpleasant embodiment of sinister forces which destroyed life. It was no longer considered a safe dwelling place for the tribe. They packed up their belongings on the backs of their animals, destroyed the village and migrated to a safer area.

The deserted area remained unoccupied until 1875 when people of the Bamalete tribe settled there. Although strangers to the area, they saw the same phenomenon, heard the loud groans of anguish and saw the silent floating spirits of the lovers. The legend was kept alive from generation to generation and so the hill stands to this day in the village of Otse in southern Botswana as an eternal legend of love. Letswa La Baratani. The Hill of the Lovers.

GLADYS THOMAS

The Promise

from *Ten Years Of Staffrider* ed. by A.W. Oliphant and I. Vladislavic (1989)

I, Maria Klaasen, came from the Swartland to this city. I remember when it all happened so suddenly on that beautiful farm-fresh morning. I was busy making the morning mieliepap for the children who were hungry and restless. Beta was lucky to be at school still, and so was little Mannetjie, my baby brother, the apple of my father's eye. Mama worked over at the big house as a housemaid.

When I think back I remember her often saying, 'You're not going to be no maid, Maria. You've got your Standard Six and you are a smart girl. You're going back to school as soon as Mannetjie is bigger.'

To return to school became my only wish! I often prayed to God to help me. Papa worked in the fields, leaving at four o'clock every morning. On that particular morning I was woken by the clanging sound of the labourers' spades.

I remember that the atmosphere was tense between Mama and Papa. I overheard her say, 'Where do we go from here? You know you cannot do any other work except work in the fields. Even if you had grown up in the big house and your mother had been their maid like me, our days here are numbered. It cuts no ice! Why must your mouth always run away with you when you're drunk?'

'But it's the truth.'

'I know it is the truth. But these people don't like it!'

It all happened the previous Saturday when the 'Oubaas' took the farmworkers on their monthly outing to the dorp. The children would run around and the wine flowed freely. The teenagers preferred the cinema and had to hike back at night to the farm. Wives would sit and breast-feed their babies unashamedly while the men had a good time in the small country bar. The young girls would do the shopping and be on the lookout for rummage sales. I remember the town square being packed on these outings with babies' bare bums and mothers with their exposed breasts; the rummage sales, purchased meat and groceries, and drunk men urinating in the side streets. Who cares, they seemed to think we were away from the farm for a holiday.

That morning Papa got drunk and started swearing at the passing whites. Said they're all a lot of slave-drivers and told them to look at our women in their rags and at the near-naked babies. Someone shouted that he needed a soapbox and the people laughed at the suggestion.

One of the neighbouring farmers quietly went over to the Hotel and called out the 'Oubaas' who came rushing out, red up to his ears. He took Papa by the scruff of his neck and threw him into the truck and shouted at him, 'Sit op jou gat totdat ons huistoe gaan, verdomde donner.' Papa struck his head against the side of the truck and I was so upset at the punishment meted out to him that I stood crying near the truck until we moved off.

When we arrived back at the farm the 'Oubaas' asked the others to hold Papa, but they pretended to be too drunk and attempted to stumble off to their shacks. He called them back and told them to see what would happen to people who liked to make political speeches. He called his son, who had returned recently from army training, to help hold Papa. My mother pleaded with the 'Oubaas' but he was determined to use his whip.

'Hy praat nie op so 'n manier van die dusvolk nie!'

'Asseblief, Oubaas,' my mother pleaded.

'Wat gaan aan in jou gedagtes? Ek neem vir julle dorp toe en hy wil politiek praat!'

The whip came cracking down over my father's back. After I don't know how many strokes, the children became hysterical. He stopped finally with the sweat streaming down his face, told us that it was his teatime and walked back to the big house. The other workers, by now sober, carried Papa inside and I washed his face.

Mama had to go back to the old house to serve tea to the 'Oubaas'. It was then that I made my decision to get the hell out of there and move to the city. I kept on patting the wet facecloth over the wrinkled face and tried to cheer him up.

'I'll read for you tonight, Papa.'

'I'll be all right, child,' he said softly.

My mother always brought reading matter from the big house: magazines, with beautiful fashions that I dreamt of wearing, and other books. At night I would lie between them and read in the candle-light: love stories, fiction, articles, anything that happened to take Papa's fancy. He and Mama liked to listen to the stories that I read them and he often remarked that he never dreamt that one of his children would one day be able to read and write. He looked real proud during our reading sessions.

'Go to sleep now, Papa, so that the swelling can go down.'

'What do you think of me, Maria?'

'I love you, Papa.' I closed the door and went to feed the chickens and look for Beta who had run away when she saw the whip.

The following morning the children ate their mieliepap and Beta left for school which was miles away from the farm. Mannetjie was having his afternoon nap and I was washing napkins. I looked down the road opposite our shack and saw a car approaching. That road, I was told, would take you all the way to Johannesburg. While hanging up the napkins I saw the big silver car stop near our shack. A man and a woman got out and walked towards me. She wore a flowing sari of floral chiffon and he a safari suit, just like those the friends of 'Oubaas' wore when they came to visit on Sundays.

She was smiling in a very friendly way and asked my name. I told her, and she asked if I would like to come to Cape Town to help her. She explained that they owned a large supermarket near the city and needed help. She asked if she could speak to Mama. I told her that Mama would be back soon and that Papa would be coming for his bread and coffee soon as it was almost lunch time. I took them inside and she sat down on the old wooden chair in our little kitchen while he stood with arms folded, looking around. He said, 'Look, we have no time to waste. Get done with your business quickly as we have a long journey back and you know what happens when I'm not at the shop.'

Finally I had to call Mama and tell her what the people wanted. At first she was adamant: 'Not on your life. You're not leaving here.' I begged and pleaded with her to let me go. Mama greeted them and they told her about the help they needed. She offered them tea but he refused. She said she could do with a cup. Papa came in from the fields and the man told him about their proposition for me. Papa didn't agree either, saying that the City was wicked and that I was only seventeen.

'I promise we will look after her and let her finish her schooling. That's a promise,' he said. Papa showed interest at this suggestion and enquired, 'But how can she go to school and work?'

'There are many schools in our area. She can go to night school. I promise we will treat her like one of the family.'

'I like her,' the woman said. 'Don't stand in her way. You won't regret it.'

Papa finally agreed and the man gave him twenty rands which he could not resist. God, how he must work a whole month for that sort of money!

While Mama was weeping silently, Papa asked, 'Do you rather want her to spend her young life here on this fucking farm like me? Since my childhood I've worked for them. Come now, it's best for her.'

'She can come home once a month, that's a promise.'

'I'm only glad that she can go to school. Look after my girl!' Mama assented.

I got into the big silver car and after all the goodbyes we slid away from the farm which I haven't seen again. For a long while I could still hear Mannetjie crying for me. I really loved that child with his chubby cheeks. I sat back in the car and thought my whole life was going to change and silently thanked God. I prayed to Him to keep my family safe, and that there would be no more whippings. We drove on what seemed to be an endless road while the two in the front seats spoke about their friends, their new houses, and about new schemes to make more money.

We arrived at a large house with a shopping complex attached. I read the name 'Allie's Supermarket' written large across the front of the building. It looked grand with all the good fresh fruit displayed on the pavement and the pretty dresses in the windows. I thought that I would get a smart dress like those that I had seen in the magazine back home. He came round to her side and opened the car door for her. She told me that this was their shop. I stood on the pavement not knowing what to do. 'You go round the back and I'll come to show you around soon. Go through the big gate.'

I carried my case through the back gate and came face to face with a huge Alsatian dog. At first I wanted to scream with fright but I talked to him softly. 'Hello, boy. Hello, hello boy.' The dog wagged his tail and followed me to the back door. I sat on my case and waited and waited and became hungry. The dog remained sitting at my feet. The yard was wet and cold and the broken cement patches formed puddles of water. Their were fruit boxes piled high. They smelled mouldy. I looked at my surroundings and felt like crying when I heard footsteps coming down the lane.

A man appeared with a heavy bag on his back. After he put the load down I saw his tall, black and handsome figure. He came towards me and said, 'Hello. You're coming to stay here?'

'Yes,' I whispered, the tears stinging my eyes. He saw this and became very sympathetic.

'Don't cry. What is your name?'

'Maria,' I answered and started weeping again. He took out a clean white handkerchief, as white as his strong teeth, and his lovely smile disarmed me. I wiped my tears shyly.

'Don't cry. I'll help you.' We heard footsteps approaching.

'Ben! Where the fucking hell are you?'

'Coming, baas. I was drinking water.'

'Now shake your arse, man,' the voice said angrily.

Ben wiped his face with the handkerchief which was now wet with my tears.

To pass the time I patted the dog and spoke to it. As Ben walked off he said, 'That's funny. That dog doesn't like strangers but he likes you.'

I sat in the wet yard for what seemed hours. Eventually she came out. 'My God, child! I was so busy behind the counter. Come, I'll show you your room. Here we are. This is not the farm so see that you keep it clean.' When she left I wanted to shout to her that I was hungry but she had disappeared.

It was a dull tiny room with a single iron bed, and a fruit box with a vase on it. I hung my jacket on a wire hanger and it was obvious that someone had lived here recently. She returned and said that Ben would have to sleep in the fruitshed. 'Can't trust those kaffirs. Come to the kitchen and eat something. You must be starved. My mother runs the house and she'll give you supper. What standard did you pass at school?'

'Standard Six, Missis.' Immediately I thought, here comes the shop assistant job and the night school. I felt relieved and glad as I entered the kitchen for my first meal in the city.

In the large American kitchen on a small table in the corner stood a plate of curry and a mug of tea. The food was strong but I was hungry. I sat looking around the big tiled kitchen with cupboards all matched in colour, like in the books back home.

The two teenage girls of the family came into the kitchen. They were about my age. One was so fat that she even had droopy cheeks and I could not see her neck. They walked past me as if I didn't exist, and opened the fridge, taking two bottles of cool-drink and opening them next to the table where I was eating. What a luxury, I thought, for the only cool-drinks I knew of came from a packet of powder that makes ten glasses. We only had the drinks on Sundays and I remember Mannetjie gulping down one glass after another, hoping to fill his stomach to last till next Sunday, the little glutton!

The girls drank half of the bottles and dumped them on the main table. Their grandmother asked them to clear the dinner table but they walked out grumbling, 'That will be the day,' and 'We've got homework to do.' The fat one opened the fridge again and I peeped inside and was amazed by so much food and drink. Only the whites had fridges like this one back home on the farm. We used to keep our food in a gauze wire cupboard which hung on a tree outside.

'Come, girl. I haven't got all night.'

I said grace and thanked the old lady.

'Here's the dishcloth. You can dry the dishes for me,' the old lady said in a frustrated voice. 'I don't know why they did not bring two girls. Expect me, with my old body, to be busy all day.'

I went on with the dishes.

'You're going to work in the shop. There's a lot of shoplifting going on lately. But they could've brought another girl to help me.'

I remembered the twenty rands which Papa could not resist. I bade her goodnight after I had finished the dishes and went through the wet yard to my room with the dog following me. Ben saw me passing and brought me a candle. I thanked him and asked him for something to read. He brought me the *Sunday Post*. The dog whined at the door until I let him in. I felt homesick when I read the depressing news of how people lived in Johannesburg. I dropped off to sleep with the newspaper in my hands.

The next morning I awoke to someone calling my name. 'Maria! Maria! Come, get up. Come clean the girls' shoes. You *must* wake up earlier. The girls must get to school in time.' The word school reminded me of her promise.

I sat at the back door cleaning their shoes which they took from me without even a thank you or a nod. My mind strayed to the previous night and to the cool-drinks which they had wasted.

Ben passed me with brooms and buckets and called me over to him.

'I hear you must stand guard for the day.'

'What does that mean?' I enquired.

'While I pack all the goods outside you must stand there and watch if anyone steals. There are a lot of people passing by. This is a busy area what with all the schools and bus terminus and station nearby.'

'You mean I must stand there all day and just watch if people steal?'

'They trust no one,' Ben replied knowingly.

Every morning thereafter, after a mug of hot coffee and bread, I would wash off the pavement. Ben had his section and I had mine. Buckets of soapy water were splashed over the pavement and then swept down the gutter. Then I was posted in front of the shop, begging people to come in to see the 'bargains' inside. I also had to look out for shoplifters. I hated every moment of this work. Some days the sun blazed down so fiercely that I felt faint. I watched with envy the girls from the different schools passing in the afternoons, wondering when I would be sent to school.

She fetched her daughters from school in the afternoon. They would get out of the big silver car and bang the doors shut. Running past me they would rush to the icecream counter inside the shop and come out licking large pink icecreams or suckers. Sometimes I felt hungry and tired but lunch often was just left-overs.

Sometimes Ben would pass me a sweet secretly and whisper, 'Don't let them see you eat.' He always came to talk to me or to give me something which he had taken in the shop without them noticing. I shall always remember him carrying the heavy sugar bags on his back.

One afternoon he came over and said, 'You look pale. Are you sick?'

'Yes,' I said, embarrassed.

'Don't let them see you cry like that. What is the matter?'

'My stomach is cramping so,' I replied.

He disappeared into the shop and after a while returned with a pack of sanitary towels. The blood had started to run down my legs. I was so grateful to him. I had to go inside the shop to ask permission to go to the toilet.

'Yes, and don't be long,' he said.

After I had cleaned myself up I walked back to the cursed job, watching people. If people stole they must be hungry, I reasoned. Standing in that busy street and watching everyone going somewhere. That night I felt so sick that I fell down on the bed into a deep sleep. I was sure that I was suffering from sunstroke. The dog slept in his usual place and I dreamt about Papa, Mama, Beta and Mannetjie. I was woken by a faint knocking at my door. I knew immediately it was Ben and I was glad of the opportunity to speak to someone again.

'Come in, Ben,' I said softly.

'How're you feeling now?'

'Fine, thanks. What is the time? You're still up? I've slept already.'

'Eleven o'clock. I had to pack the shelves in the shop. During the day it is too full of people.'

'They pay you well, Ben?'

'Not a damn. Here's a chocolate for you. Have it.'

'Thanks. You must be careful, Ben. I don't like these people. They'll send you to jail even for a chocolate bar.'

'I know. I want you to have it. I'm going to look after you.'

'I'm not a child, Ben.'

'Who cried like a big baby today?' he laughed. 'Why did you come to this place?'

'I thought it better than the farm and she promised to send me to high school. I want to learn more, Ben. That's why I came.'

'My girl, you won't even reach a schoolgate. These people don't keep their promises.'

After that night he came every evening and I loved him when he kissed me. He was so big and strong. We spoke about how much we loved each other and he even said that I was as pure as a lily. He always brought me little things from the shop. One night he brought me lipstick and mascara and held the mirror for me to make up my face. I was as thrilled as he for that was the first time I had used make-up. I knew I looked attractive and was shy when he said, 'Hell, you are beautiful.' That night we made love for the first time and fell fast asleep, oblivious of the danger of being found together. Later he woke me and said that we must get the hell out of that place.

'We can't get away from them, Ben. Don't talk about my family. I will have to learn to forget about them. I've got no money even to go and visit them. Besides, she doesn't let me off, even on Sundays.'

One night after a long day in the sun, I washed and got to bed early. He came in and pulled open the blankets and looking at my body he said, 'I've never seen such curves.' We laughed and read the newspaper.

'I must wake up at four o'clock tomorrow. It's market day and that man mustn't find me here. He asked me today why you never catch anyone stealing.'

'Must I say people steal if they don't? Don't worry, I'll wake you Ben.' Then we fell asleep but our happiness was short-lived. The next morning we were woken to loud banging at the door.

'Come out of there, kaffir! And you, farm-bitch. Get out this minute. You can both go back to where you come from.'

We jumped up and dressed in a hurry. Ben looked worried.

'Don't worry,' I said kissing him and peeped through the window. It was still dark and the stars were still glowing brightly. The yard lights were on when we came out of the room.

'Pack your things and go,' he commanded.

'Where can we go?' Ben asked.

'You had time to think of that before.'

When we left he searched our bundles and locked the yard gate behind us.

'You can collect your papers at the Bantu administration,' he sneered through the gate. 'You know what *that* means!'

We walked out of that cold wet yard into the misty dawn like two thieves. The lights in the huge house were still not switched on. The dog followed us as we walked towards the station. We avoided the main road because of the patrolling vans. We had no papers and the bundles made it obvious that we were now vagrants. We sat cuddled up, shivering with cold in the waiting room, hoping that the Railway Police wouldn't find us.

When the first train came along I said, 'Ben, where do we go from here?' He replied that he had friends at the Epping vegetable market and that I must wait for him on Cape Town station. I said that I would miss the dog and wondered if he wouldn't be killed by a car before he reached home or whether that damp yard wouldn't eventually claim him. Ben reassured me, saying he would get me a dog when we had a place to stay. I knew that those two fat girls would not feed the dog. Even in the train I was still worried about the dog. It was then that Ben realised that he had left his passbook in his white jacket, in the fruitshed.

'I don't want to see that man again. Let the book rot there! I hate that book!'

We reached Cape Town and Ben said I should wait for him until he returned from Epping. I sat till lunch time thinking, what if he doesn't come back? Where will I get money to go back to the farm? I watched the throngs of people coming and going. They all looked so serious; everybody seemed to know where they were going. I wished I was one of them.

Ben finally returned soon after lunch time. I saw from his worried face that his journey had been in vain. He bought a packet of fish and chips and we ate hungrily.

'I found nothing. The shanties were all numbered last week; the people are afraid of taking in others for fear of having their homes bulldozed.'

We roamed the streets of Cape Town day after day, sleeping in servants' rooms at night. Ben knew a lot of people, friends he had made when he used to come to Cape Town to the wholesalers for Allie's Supermarket. Days turned into months and we moved from place to place until we met his friend, Lucas. He pitied us as he felt we were so young. 'To live like this! I stay near the mountain. Come and live with me,' he told Ben.

We arrived at the mountain home which was just a large hole like a cave, with mattresses on the floor, but it was clean. 'This is better than the streets,' Ben said. That night Ben asked me if I'd rather go home to the farm or live there with him like this. Because I loved him I told him that I couldn't leave him. There were many others who lived like us. Outcasts of the city. Lucas had lost his wife a while back and I was accepted as the lady of the house.

One day while I was busy cleaning out our hole, making the beds and sweeping, Lucas came to tell me that they had arrested Ben. 'I expected something like this to happen,' he said.

'But why?' I asked unbelievingly.

'Pass! He's got no papers!' Lucas replied.

I wept for a long time but I am still waiting for him. I lay down on the mattress and sobbed my heart out. Rita, one of the friends I came to know tried to comfort me. 'All right, my girl. Don't cry. Come let's have a drink.' I followed her and got drunk for the first time.

I lay on the grass in a drunken stupor and hated the nauseous feeling of everything revolving around me. In my drunken dream I saw his outstretched arms reaching for me: 'Ben, Ben? You've come to take me away from here?' Instead a fist smashed into the side of my face and the pain confused and alarmed me. I opened my eyes but could not focus properly nor could I lift my arms, which seemed so heavy, to protect myself. Vaguely in the distance I was sure I heard Rita's high-pitched sensual laughter. I shouted for assistance in the direction of her voice but received no answer.

Then I realised that the figure standing over me was not Ben's. He hit out at my face again. As I slipped into unconsciousness, I felt him tearing at my underwear and his heavy weight on me muffled my screams. No one heard or cared.

MAUREEN ISAACSON

I Could Have Loved Gold

from *Fair Lady* (28 March 1990)

Dad talked about gold all the time. Gold standard and shares and world market and creating work for the masses. The intonation of his voice acted as a soporific on mother and her already pale countenance and air of absence further dissolved. My little brother Jonathan would dip his middle finger into the butter and my aunt would yawn. But sometimes she'd say something and the two would hiss like prize bantams in a sparring match.

Into the spotless order of our Houghton mansion, Aunt Sal would bring the smoke and jazz of the streets of Sophiatown. It was in her walk and in her talk and in her eyes. She vibrated with the sax of Kippie Moeketsi and the huskiness of Dolly Rathebe and all the musos she heard there. As soon as dad got going, she'd lose that bluesy cool; she'd talk and move fast, like a train chasing its own steam.

'Do you know what happens in the gold mines? About the hostels where there's no place for loving and precious little money to show for it when the miners do get back to their families?'

Dad would swell up with argument and a watery silence would envelop mother. It seemed that this dissension was irrelevant in the face of having an Anglo magnate husband who swathed her in nine carat this and twenty two that.

She wore it burnished in her ears and round her neck, her wrists and waist and in her teeth. Her eyes were dull with it, with easy living and the loneliness of dad being away so often.

Aunt Sal adored Jonathan and me. Whenever one of us felt sad she'd say that nothing stays the same and she'd sit with us until it went over. She'd tell us stories; it was only through her that we ever got to hear of cottages in woods and baskets to be taken to grandmothers and people like Rapunzel letting down their hair. She told her own version; with syncopated rhythm and high drama.

Dad believed in facts. When he did tell us stories they would invariably be about gold.

'The Incas of Peru,' he said, 'believed that the tears of the sun fell in golden drops. They wore huge golden circles in their ears, just like the wooden ones the Nguni natives wear in South Africa.'

'If you're going to tell kids something, make sure it's useful', he said. He told us tales of ancient Roman gold mines. He talked about gold leaf death masks, thin as gossamer, used by the early Greeks and said that gold was civilized; it was something to believe in. It had changed his life. 'I don't make it big through fairy stories. Nor jazz for that matter,' he said.

Aunt Sal laughed at the way my parents listened to the sounds of Elvis Presley and the Everly Brothers, when there was all that going on just around the corner. My parents weren't interested in what was going on round the corner, and told friends that Aunt Sal had a basic problem that made it necessary for her to go into the 'Natives', world.

She brought us Glen Miller records and blues and 'marabi'; the sounds of the shebeens and we'd dance until we dropped. It gave mother a headache, she would say, then she'd go and lie down. Once I heard Aunt Sal say to mother, 'You weren't like this before, Sarah', and mother said 'Well now I am.'

I was at primary school at the time, and my experience of the world was limited to our Houghton mansion, our many servants and mother's golden unhappiness.

She remained passive and inert, it was as if she'd been alchemised into some mystical substance, and was no longer with us. She looked into mirrors for a long time and I wondered what she was thinking; if she was thinking. She was always around, but I missed her.

We waited for Aunt Sal's jazz; she brought us records of Miriam Makeba, the Haarlem Swingsters and Zig Zag Zakes. 'I bring you the Bantu Men's Social Centre special,' she'd say then she'd roll up her red trousers and she'd rumba and samba and talk about the way people lived in the townships.

'Eight people live in a house the size of this kitchen, minus the breakfast nook, no kidding.'

I couldn't really see how they did it. It all seemed so strange to me, like some foreign country somewhere.

I spent hours playing with mother's jewelry and holding it up to the sun to see what dad meant when he talked about the purity of gold, the essence of it. I studied the gold plates and vases he brought back from his travels and encased in glass, the gold-bound books and thought about being as good as gold and silence being golden. I would have loved gold if it wasn't for Aunt Sal.

When I think about the mansion now, maid-polished and ordered it echoes with a drab silence. Into the odorless shine, Aunt Sal sped; alive with the fumes and stains and conversation of nights in shebeens. Crazy with tales of dark side-streets where gangs of men with American clothes and accents flicked knives and tongues. Talking about the way these guys would ruin concerts and break up cosy evenings in shebeens.

'Aren't you scared?' I asked.

Then the corners of her mouth lifted slightly and turned and the green of her eyes deepened and she took a draw of her cigarette. She said nothing, but I often saw that expression after that.

It was the expression she got when she talked about music and about a friend of hers called Albie. Although I never met him I knew exactly how he walked, hand in one pocket, cigarette dangling; hat cocked, because Aunt Sal would show us. Albie played piano and sang in one of the shebeens where Aunt Sal had her heart torn apart by the blues of Snowy Radebe and the late-night throb and 'bebababerop' she came home singing. It was where she drank the home-brewed spirit 'skokiaan', a bout of which Aunt Sal said could knock your head right across the nation.

'Hardly suburbanite stuff', she said.

My parents' friends were other mining magnates and their wives and sometimes Jonathan and I would be allowed to join them for dinner. It was the only time mother would come alive. On such occasions, Joseph, who cleaned the floors and served at table would wear a white jacket with a diagonal sash, red as a wound.

The wives would ask us how we were enjoying school and if we liked our teachers and what our friends' names were, then they'd talk to each other about clothes and hair and Italian gold collars with streams of half-point diamonds and say things in very hushed tones. The men would talk loudly and clearly about gold exports and foreign exchange and balance of payments and South Africa's economic role in the world.

Mother said that our cook Sanna was a genius at whatever she turned her hand. She cooked Fish Soup Basquaise and Lamb Charlotte to perfection. Mother loved to surprise the guests with treats like black truffles in Italian rice, fresh foie gras or water-melon in glazed wine. Imported white wines were a favourite; their chill glistened from generous crystal glasses.

One such evening, just as mother was saying 'Children, don't you two think you should be getting to bed now?', Aunt Sal burst in.

'No thanks, I've eaten,' she said, and 'How do you do? how do you do?' to everyone and kissed Jonathan and me. The wives touched their half moon gold earrings and chunky bracelets and stared at Aunt Sal.

Suddenly, without warning, she shouted: 'Yaabo! Yaabo!' Everybody stopped talking and father said, 'C'mon Sal, not now.' Then she smiled and said 'That's what the small boys shout when the police come near the home-brewed beer in the townships.'

'Sal . . .' said Dad.

'They keep it in tins underground and cover them with sand and wet sacks — it's illegal to brew beer because of the liquor prohibition for blacks, you know. When the police come they pierce the tins and everyone runs away before they can be arrested.'

'Have some wine, Sal' dad said.

'Thanks. Very nice, what vintage?'

' '49.' Dad looked relieved and everyone relaxed and started talking again. Jonathan pinched me and giggled.

'Mm, very nice wine,' Aunt Sal said again. 'Nothing like Twala.'

'Twala?' asked a magnate's wife.

'Yes, Twala. It's the stuff they give black mineworkers. A kind of non-alcoholic beer, rich in vitamin B.'

Mother wiped the corners of her mouth with her serviette. Father breathed audibly. Then that steam-train speed got hold of Aunt Sal and there was no stopping her.

'Twala, loudspeakers, heat and unbearable noise — that's what you get when you work on the mines.'

One of the magnates said: 'Do you know what you're talking about? To what do you think the country owes its wealth? Has it ever occurred to you that the industry provides work for people? The Natives love the mines. They even call Johannesburg "Egoli", which means "City of Gold". South Africans have a damn lot to thank the people who discovered gold and the mining corporations for.'

'Egoli safoot!' said Aunt Sal. 'A city built on cheap mineworker-sweat, what do you know about their lives?'

'The mines provide employment.' He was rigid.

'Okay, so what about the danger they work with, poison fumes, fires, accidents, and the rockbursts and all the people that get killed?'

'Safety measures . . .' started the magnate. He was red-cheeked and everyone seemed to have forgotten their food.

'Don't tell me about safety and about us having the deepest mines and not being able to compare with the rest of the world, I know that argument. I'm talking about people's lives!' Aunt Sal's voice quavered.

'Well so are we. We're providing people with an opportunity to eat, people who would otherwise starve.' The magnate was redder.

'What do you know? Have you been there? Have you ever heard of faction fights? Have you ever seen the way they fight amongst themselves? Everyone knows they'd kill each other if we didn't put a stop to it!'

Aunt Sal said nothing.

Mother called Joseph to clear the plates and bring in the chestnuts and poached pears.

'It's way past your bedtime, you two,' she said to Jonathan and me. So we left the table and hid in the passage to see if anything more would happen. It didn't.

My parents didn't refer to that evening again and neither did Aunt Sal, but Jonathan and I went over and over the way the red-cheeked magnate who'd shouted at Aunt Sal had never known that there was a piece of lamb lodged in his beard all the while. And how his wife, the one who asked us how school was, had cut up three tomatoes into a million tiny pieces throughout the conversation.

After that Dad and Aunt Sal didn't talk to each other for a while. She visited when he was away. The ice thawed slowly and things returned to normal for a while.

One day she came in, eyes heavy as clay. She wouldn't say what was the matter but I knew it had something to do with Albie. 'Has he gone away?' I asked her. 'Don't talk about it', she said.

The shebeens and the bioscopes and the dancehalls were empty, she said. 'The jazz don't sound and the blues make me cold inside instead of warm and I want to be at home, waiting, in my little tower, to let down my hair.'

But as she believed that things never stay the same, she smoked and drank into shebeeny nights, waiting, becoming thin and ashen, a shadow of her silent older sister.

Time edged along slowly. Aunt Sal's misery encircled her, etching a darkness around her eyes. It weighed down the air. She smoked fifty cigarettes a day, and another twenty at night. She coughed all the time.

Then she decided to go and live in London. She promised to send for us when we were old enough. She left us in the mansion with a distant father who stored gold rings and earrings and promises in a safe for my coming of age.

He left us, finally, with a weight as heavy as a gold bar, and the price we had to pay for his contribution to world economy. He left us with a mother whose sheen was fast fading. She said less than ever, now that Aunt Sal had gone.

JOAN BAKER

Undercover Comrade

from *South* (Feb. 1–7 1990)

My kitchen sink, installed about 40 centimetres below the window sill, affords me an ideal look-out point.

The flimsy curtain, artistically draped, transforms the window into a two-way mirror. A very exploitable feature.

I have watched many an unwanted visitor turn from the unresponsive doorbell. This strategy saves me time when I have none to spare, and leaves sensitive feelings intact.

Bill's expression is screened as he approaches the house in the evening.

Forewarned, I arranged my face into a disarming smile to dispel the frown from the cloudy face he brings home from work. It sets the evening on a smooth sociable course.

The credit belongs to the window, or rather, to the unknown architect. Through his innovation, our kitchen window is not stuck on the rear end of the house like a glazed anus gasping domestic smells into the back-yard.

Today, however, the blank window predicted disaster. I stared desperately through it, as if to conjure up the flesh and blood images of Raymond and Diane, by some hocus-pocus means.

Where the devil could those two be?

Putting my faith in the numerous magazine articles I have read, on the telepathic powers of positive thinking, I applied it without success. All day has been spent monitoring the short stretch of road between the corner and the front gate.

It was a quarter to five. Bill was due home at five. He was never early, nor late.

For God's sake children ... come home ...

Anxiety stimulated by imagination, the images in my mind overpowered my whole being.

I heard Diane's screams, it pulled at my scalp, mummee ... mummee her cries hammered at my temples. My imagination went a notch further, to drag me through the angry littered streets.

Raymond was being beaten up by two burly policemen. I distinctly heard the dreaded wheeze in his voice as he called out to Diane to run.

Please God don't let him have an attack out there.

The prayer was uttered aloud and of its own accord. The sound of my own voice released me from the clutches of my self-inflicted torment.

The asthma pump lying on Raymond's bed aggravated my concern. There were seven unticked minutes left. I turned from the sink to lift the lid from the pot. The sight of the meat in the Irish stew made my stomach lurch. I fled to the bathroom, lifted the toilet seat then vomited into the bowl. Feeling calmer after rinsing my mouth, I sweetened my breath with toothpaste.

Then I flushed away the tension that came from my insides. Bill stood in the doorway, 'What's wrong with you?' he asked in lieu of his usual monosyllabic greeting.

'Oh! it's nothing, must be something I ate,' I lied glibly.

'Where are the children?'

'Oh! they're at the church hall, with the youth.'

'Good, that will keep them away from the rioting riff-raff.'

You see, a voice in my head said, sometimes it pays to lie.

He removed the Argus from his sports bag, carried it to his favourite chair in front of the TV, to wait for his customary cup of tea.

'Maybe it would be a good idea if they stay off the streets until things settle down,' he addressed me from the lounge.

'Aagh shurupp, before I spit in your tea,' the voice said.

I carried his tea to him, the cup rattled on the saucer. 'Thanks,' he said into the newspaper, without looking up.

There it was again, the voice. 'He knows something's amiss, something that could jeopardise his peace and quiet'.

There were no unwashed dishes. I let some water into the sink, put two tea towels in it, then rubbed at it slowly to resume my vigil without arousing suspicion. Every passing or approaching figure that came into view tightened the already tangled network of nerves in my stomach.

I cross-examined myself mentally, was it courage or the lack of it that stopped me from joining my neighbours earlier today? Maybe I should have attached myself to the crusade.

Single-handedly, each parent virtually frog-marched their shame-faced off-spring home, after plucking them from the playgrounds and classrooms.

I heard the dry crackle of the newspaper, accompanied by the slapping sound, as Bill performed the ritual of folding the newspaper back to its bookstall condition.

The sound made a statement, supper could not be delayed any longer. I abandoned my trumped-up task at the sink. A last desperate look rewarded me with the sight of Raymond and Diane as they swooped around the corner.

Laughing and gesticulating, they raced each other to the gate. It was a photo finish. Side by side, using their hips for battering rams, they exploded through the gate without bothering to unlatch it.

Both looked up at the kitchen window, then smiled at the invisible sentry. They knew I was watching them.

In the same unruly fashion they burst into the house, with an untidy tangle of arms and legs. When confronted with Bill's glare, they came comically to attention. Still at attention, Raymond wheezed a soft 'good evening, dad'.

'Evening, daddy,' Diane echoed.

'Evening.' He scolded them for being late for supper. 'Sorry, daddy,' they said in unison. It sounded rehearsed.

They were waiting for the real fireworks. 'And another thing.' They froze.

'Next time don't you two enter this house like hooligans. Well-bred children take a pride in their homes.' They were about to dismiss themselves, when he spoke again. Here it comes, they thought. 'I told your mother to keep you two off the streets while all this rioting is going on.'

Relieved, they slunk past me to the bathroom. I didn't look up from the sink. The relief on my face could too easily be taken for condonation. Raymond puffed out his cheeks, then deflated them in a dramatic sigh. Diane caught him as he drooped his shoulders, and buckled his knees, preparing to fall into a theatrical swoon.

The performance was for my benefit. In my refusal to be mollified, I ignored them.

The sound of their voices, and the giggles drifting from the bathroom, extended an unrefusable invitation to eavesdrop. I heard them sympathising with their friends, (now referred to as comrades) for the humiliation they suffered at the hands of their mothers.

'Ray, do you realise that mummy did not squeal on us?'

'Yaah, she may not know it, but she's in the struggle.'

'You mean she's a comrade?'

'Yaah, she's an undercover comrade.'

The corners of my mouth were out of control. It twitched, and bullied my cheeks into a smile. I ducked into the kitchen, drew the blind between the window and the curtain, then I ladled the stew into serving dishes.

The voice was more gentle this time, 'Look at you,' it said. 'You are just as mixed up as the stew, neither this nor that.'

I blocked out the voice to make room for my own thoughts. It led to a path in between. I was caught between two children who had outgrown me, a husband whom I had outgrown, and a voice in my head that was stirring up a revolution in my heart.

NOORIE HAMMOND

An Act Of Love

from *The AWA Collection* (1989)

I remember waking up with the sun's rays touching my face gently as if coaxing me to open my eyes. It was hard to believe that I had been sleeping for a whole day and night. I felt good, ready to face the intricacies of life which had overcome me in the past ten months and which culminated into utter chaos in the last three months.

The year was 1980, the era of advancement in almost every field from science, medicine, computers to women's lib and the sexual revolution. The generation gap had become somewhat smaller compared to the 60s and 70s, people seemed more susceptible to new ideas and change. This was the new era, where freedom was the password. Yet, there I was lying, listening to the stifled sobs of my mother, which filtered into my room, from across the passage, having to make a decision which would certainly hurt the people I loved.

A decision that would be tearing me away from the loved ones; a decision which meant leaving my home town. How I loved the hillsides which I climbed when just knee high, and the cold waters of the river in which we swam on scorching summer days as children; and the old huge trees, hundreds of years old, which were always there, like guardians. All these things were part of me, an invisible skin, which I would have to tear from myself, should I decide to marry the man I love. Should such an everyday occurrence as marriage have to affect my life in such a big way?

Yes, unfortunately it would, because in this era of the 80s we here in the Northern Cape town of Vryburg, and everywhere else in South Africa, still stood in the dark ages, where marriage between the different races was an ugly word, unmentionable, avoided and a criminal offense. Oh yes, we were ahead in most aspects of life, yet the most basic aspect of humanity had been left behind to corrode in the hearts of people, to breed hatred amongst one another because of the colour of one's skin. Alas, the gap between black and white was growing even larger to the extent that each group feared the other even more. And as fear grew it swallowed love like a shark swallows everything else it can devour, then spews out the remaining dirt and rubbish.

The Immorality Act as it was called was the dirt, and to be caught under the Immorality Act was an act of shame to both black and white people of this country. This vicious Act forbade one to love another of a different skin colour. One was placed into sections from superior to inferior, where degradation and shame were the mantle and inner strife and conflict the core. How sad that man could implement such acts against man, not against beast or alien but against his own species, man.

'Apartheid' had not reared its ugly head in my direction yet; it was there of course; I was born into it, and was raised by the norms of the system, and lived by the rules of the system, but that had not bothered me. I was like almost everyone else in any South African city or town. I had accepted the system! I am Indian. A race group which had been allotted to me, my late grandfather having come from India, yet if I would be sent to live in India, I would be a complete foreigner. I have never been there. Of course I've been taught what the climate is like there, where it is situated, what crops they grow and how many times a year it rains. Yet not having lived there, I do not know the people, I do not know of their struggle to survive, nor do I hear the pulsating of their hearts, or see them laugh or hear them cry or know what makes them angry or happy; neither do I know their way of life.

Oh, yes, I am proud of my heritage, we still practise the Indian way of life, but are we truly like the Indians born and bred there? Do we qualify to be called Indians? We speak English and Afrikaans in our schools, so the Indian language is seldom used; most of us dress in the Western style, we live in westernized houses; would I truly know India? Would it not be more appropriate to be called African?

I am an African, we all are; we the children of this earth, this very earth that fed us with its crops; these very rivers that provided the water we need to survive, this very earth whose valleys and mountains I have in my heart. This is the land I was raised in. I know its people, I know what makes them sing, I can feel what goes on in their hearts and know what they are longing for. Yet we were placed into groups of White, Indian, Coloured and Bantu, and the term 'African' was forgotten.

No longer did we belong to the land, we were given sections of the land, each group in its own section, the boundaries were not to be transgressed, and the fear grew. Yet when I first saw Peter, it was not as if I was crossing the boundary. He was just there; young, vital, good-looking with a heart of gold. He was also White!

I knew it was taboo getting involved with a White man, yet as time went by the colour of his skin did not matter to me, nor did it matter to him. We were just two young people, with so much to do, and so much to talk about that it had slipped our minds that we had crossed the boundary. We had reached out to each other so imperceptibly, and had wandered into each other's lives and all that goes with it, without noticing. Our days were filled with laughter like any other couple in love, and life was great.

Whenever I invited him to my family, I would jerk back into reality. Yes, I would realize that I had crossed the boundary which was taboo; I had done the unspeakable and shame was my punishment. Gone were the carefree days, and all I could feel was guilt, as if I had committed a treacherous crime. I could not understand that something that made me feel so good and happy could be considered as a crime. My mother looked at me with such great sadness. Maybe she could foresee what lay ahead. She loved me, and did not want me to be hurt. Also, as Peter was White, she did not trust him. All the years of living closely with only one's own race group had made her suspicious of Whites. It was all right to work for them, but when it came to loving them that was unacceptable!

Whenever Peter was around at my home, the atmosphere would grow tense, and I would feel cold and afraid. Our neighbours were no different, and they would whisper, and smile sarcastically. I could feel that they were ridiculing me. I tried to break free from this bondage I had with Peter, but to no avail because he wanted to go on seeing me. Thus, on and on went our meetings, this time furtively, but these meetings were not the same as before, we were no longer just a couple in love, but fugitives in the dark, alone, hanging onto each other now more than ever before, the bond growing stronger; we were not afraid. My mother's fear that we would be caught for contravening the Immorality Act soon came to pass.

One evening during our secret meetings, Peter's car parked on a dark side road, we were rudely stormed upon by bright torch lights pressed against the windscreen of his car. I was so afraid, and could hardly discern what the shouting was all about, we were screamed at, the car was surrounded by men, some in uniform and others in civilian clothes. The car doors were flung open, and we were hustled out. The cooldrink in my hand fell onto my skirt, I was soaked. My skirt clung to my legs which made me feel naked to the eyes of everyone surrounding me.

I stood there, shivering in the cold June night, their lights blinding me. All I could hear and see were the ugly voices of faceless people; giant shadows hovered over me and I felt myself being shoved into a police van. I called out to Peter, but obviously he was already being pushed into the police car nearby. My words of protest that we had done nothing wrong fell onto deaf ears, and my sobs drowned their words of scorn and defamation which were hurled at me. After what seemed like an eternity, the police van stopped and the harsh noise of grating locks was all I heard. I found myself in a small brightly lit room, all alone and so afraid. I could not stop trembling.

A man wearing a white coat entered. I did not know what was happening. What was this all about? What were they going to do to me? He looked at me with the coldest eyes I have ever seen, and then announced that he was a state doctor. Then it dawned on me (the utter degradation I felt at that moment was insurmountable) he was going to examine me. I remembered that to arrest one under the Act, there had to be evidence of sexual intercourse and the fact that we had not, did not make any difference. The degradation was there, the dirt was there and no matter what the result of the examination, I felt cheap and used. Of course I would not go to jail, but something more precious had been damaged. All the self-esteem I had, had been brutally ripped off from me by these so-called self-respecting law enforcement officers; they who were there to protect us. Was the criminal actually the victim?

Thereafter, I was free to go. It was past midnight as I walked the lonely gravel roads, which led to my home. Only after 2 hours did I see from afar, monotonous rows of street lights which lit up the Indian township. The roads were strangely quiet, with only the barking of dogs which echoed into the stillness of the night. A few cars passed, some slowed down, others stopped to offer me a lift which I dared not accept as I saw the leering glances of men eager to satisfy the cravings that went on in their distorted minds. I thought of Peter all the way. Where was he? What did they do to him? I dared not inquire from them at the police station. I was afraid, and all I wanted to do at that moment was get as far away from them as possible, for the longer I stayed close to them the more my self-respect dwindled.

My mother was waiting for me in the lounge. The lines on her face showed even deeper. Suddenly she looked years older. I could not forgive myself, I was responsible for this. The moment I saw her like that I knew that I must make amends. I had to make amends, and bring our life back to the way it was, but I wondered if it would ever be the same again. Words were not necessary, she knew what must have happened, I did not have to explain. I went straight to my room. The rest of the night was spent tossing and turning. I promised myself that I would never see Peter again because we did not belong together.

The next morning I received a telephone call from Peter. He was frantic, he could not come and see me after he was released as he suspected that they would follow him. At least they had told him that they had let me go home. He wanted to see me now more than ever.

He was a fighter, unlike myself; this incident was not going to scare him off. Thus, the promise I had made to myself only the night before, was soon forgotten and out meetings continued . . .

I became bolder and angrier. It was an anger against those faceless shadows, the state doctor, my family, myself and the world.

We were more careful now, and our meetings were confined to the homes of friends. Our feelings towards each other grew more intense, and I wondered if it would have been the same if we were in another country, another time or maybe of the same race group. The tension between my family and I grew worse. We spoke to one another, yet only with meaningless words. We laughed but it was laughter not from the heart; we cried silently, and did what we had to do automatically, like robots, while deep in our hearts we wept bitterly.

Months went by like this, wasted months of pain and fear and hatred as the country focused on more important issues of the world. And one read of the dramatic changes taking place in our society, and more opportunities open to all the people of South Africa, and the economic stability prevalent here, and the gold price rising, and the New Zealand rugby team being invited to play here. Thus showing that we were even being accepted internationally; and as I read all this in every newspaper, day after day, after day, I was horrified to discover that the most important issue of all, human freedom, in a small dorp like Vryburg had been cast aside.

Was I perhaps wrong? Had I chosen the wrong path? Was degradation after all due to me? Was it only we that felt this way? Was my family the only family affected in this way? Or were there many like us those hundreds of people I meet in the street every day on my way to work; those hundreds of apathetic faces what were they hiding deep down inside? Were their actions also automatic like ours? I could not be sure.

My friend had gone on holiday and had left us the keys to her flat. At last we would be able to be utterly alone, without the fear of being hustled out of the car. We would meet in a cozy, warm place with four walls around to blot out the fear and suspicion which were our shadow. We would be rid of all shadows, the real ones and the ones that lurked inside of us. To us privacy was just a word. We did not know the meaning of being in private. We did not know what it meant to hold each other without having someone peering at us from the dark or talk to each other without having someone or other barge in or be able to sit together in utter serenity without the fear of looking over each other's shoulder.

Now we could be alone to love each other normally, where love and respect was the only real thing around and self-esteem could be uplifted again.

It was in the early hours of the morning, as we lay in each other's arms, content and overflowing with love for each other, when a harsh voice accompanied by a loud banging on the door cut through the mellowness of the moment like a sharp knife, which twisted into my gut. I shuddered, but lay there, unable to talk or move. I just lay there as Peter jumped up quickly threw on his clothes and said that he would go out by the back window, while I opened the front door. They would not know that he was there. In a moment he was gone. I still lay there, I could not move. All at once two men had come into the bedroom, I pulled the covers right up to my face, but the manner in which they stared at me made me feel that they could see right through those covers, my body and soul felt bare before them. Then they were interrupted by shouts from outside, and I knew they had caught Peter. They ran outside as well, leaving me to grab my clothing and get dressed. When I reached the front door, I saw Peter being driven away in a police van. I saw the caretaker of the building swiftly move away. He was one of my people. Had it now reached the stage where brother would betray brother? Was the system succeeding in actually destroying the good in man?

We were thus arrested and spent three months in prison; three long months of agony; not only for myself, but for all those I held close to my heart. Yet this time I did not feel ashamed or guilty, I just knew that we had not done anything wrong, and that it was not a crime to love each other. Those three months brought new ideas to me, made me think a great deal, and all the hatred that had built up in me had disappeared. I wondered if Peter felt the same. What did prison do to him? I hoped that it did not destroy the goodness in him. I knew that if the two of us as well as my family could keep the love in our hearts and destroy the fear, many others would do likewise; and change, real change in a society so blinded by prejudice, would be inevitable for now I knew that love was greater than hatred.

The last seven days, were real days. Peter, my family and I spoke to one another with real words, and the true feelings in our hearts came to the surface, and our weeping was no longer silent; and our anger was no longer with ourselves; and as our laughter and tears echoed, I also heard the joyous laughter of a million others.

PONKIE KHAZAMULA

I Won't Be Moved

from *One Never Knows* ed. by Lindiwe Mabuza (1989)

The old woman straightened her body, stood upright and blinked at the setting sun. Motionless and silent, she looked at the crimson haze that suffused the windy horizon. Far beyond, dominating her view, towered the proud building that graced the sky. In the late afternoon sky, this elegant structure was swathed in a profusion of flaming red, as the setting sun splashed its rays on the gleaming glass walls. The surrounding buildings, which completed the rest of the Sandton City complex, were now slowly melting into the gathering shadows. Her eyes roved over to the broad high way a few hundred metres before her. All she could see were convoys of vehicles speeding in opposite directions.

'It's not coming, today,' she murmured to herself. Her eyes, full of forlorn hope, were fixed on the highway nonetheless. Her reverie was broken by a ruffling sound next to her. Looking around, she saw a scrawny dog rummaging a neatly packed card-board box. *'Voetsek!'* She cried. The dog scampered off, stopping at a short distance, refusing to move further.

'Voetsek!' She repeated. The dog refused to move. The old woman picked up an old dirty bottle and threw it at the dog. The dog ducked, stood firm and bared its teeth. The old woman became angry and restless. In one hand she held a stick. Choosing her way carefully through the rubbish around her, she advanced towards the animal. On nearing it, she lifted the stick high. Before she could strike, the dog jumped aside and barked at her.

'Voetsek!' 'Voetsek!' came voices from another direction. Two little boys, waving sticks, came running towards the dog. The dog refused to budge. One of the boys hurled his stick at it, and hit it on the ribs. It let off a loud, sharp yelp. Whining in pain, it ran off.

'Did it bite you, Ouma?' they asked of the old lady.

'No. She was trying to pinch from the box,' the old woman replied.

Looking around the dumping ground, she said to the boys: 'It's getting late. The butchery truck is late today. We can't wait.'

'Did you get anything, Ouma?' asked one of the boys.

'Yes. Bless the Lord. I found a few slices of brown bread and a lump of ham. The slices are a bit musty though. And you?'

One of the boys was holding a rumpled parcel. He looked uncertainly at it.

'Well, I found some cookies,' he said, handing them over to the old woman.

'Hmmm,' she mumbled as she looked at the parcel.

'You are lucky that dog did not grab the bread and ham, bless you. I don't know what we would have had for supper tonight,' she said.

'Ouma,' called one of the boys.

'Yes,' she answered.

'I am getting cold. May I have your shawl, please?'

'Yes, you may. Let us go. It's getting late and colder.'

She unwrapped the shawl from her waist and wrapped it around the boy's shoulders. She picked up the box from the ground and put it on her head. Flanked by the two boys, she trundled across the dumping area.

A fetid stench rose from the surrounding rubbish and permeated the air. Cans, bottles, tins, ash; and somewhere nearby the rotting carcass of a dog added its horrid smell to the reeking air.

The old woman and the two boys trudged on. Darkness was gaining. A blanket of dull grey smoke swept from the ghetto. From the dumping ground a wide view of the ghetto was available.

Throughout the ghetto, curls and coils of smoke could be seen, snaking their way into the darkening sky, as hundreds of chimneys and braziers were set in operation. This blanket of smoke created an artificial darkness.

The ghetto streets were riddled with potholes; small furrows zigzagged across the streets. One had to tread carefully. As usual, the street lights were not on this evening.

The old woman and the boys plodded on. Presently, they came upon an open area littered with debris. The place was filled with broken bricks, tin cans, bottles. In the middle of this evidence of past human occupation stood a ramshackle tin shack. As though in bold defiance of the rampant destruction around it, in open challenge to the raging winter wind, the shack stood rigid and resolute like a sentinel of hope in the face of adversity. On reaching the shack, the old woman opened the door and they all crept in. She put the box on the table and struck a match, lighting a candle.

'Pump the primus stove, Pule,' she ordered.

One of the little boys put the primus stove on the table and set it burning. Soon, both boys were huddled around the softly whirring stove. The old woman put a dish on the table and started transferring victuals from the box to the dish.

'Really, I don't know. I really don't know anyway, the Lord knows best,' the old woman was murmuring to herself, her lips barely moving.

'Did you say something, Ouma?' asked one of the boys.

'No, just talking to myself.'

'Ha, ha, ha, Ouma. How can one talk to oneself?' He was putting the back of his hand to his mouth, trying to hide his laughter.

'Yes, I have noticed that Ouma talks to herself at times. Sonny says his grandpa does as well,' added the other boy.

'Well, it's very funny,' persisted the other, beside himself with laughter.

'All right Pule, stop your nonsense. Everybody to the table. The food is ready,' said Ouma.

Pule stood up and brought a bowl of water for all to wash their hands in.

'Let's ask for grace,' said Ouma.

The three of them stood by the table as Ouma recited the short prayer. After the prayer, they sat down at table and started with their supper. After a while one of the boys spoke:

'Ouma,' he said.

'Yes, Jabu,' the old woman replied.

'Early this afternoon, while you were away at church, a car called here,' Jabu continued.

'A car?' Ouma asked as she went on eating.

'Yes, Ouma. The driver and his companion asked for you.'

'Me? What on earth!' Ouma put the morsel back on the plate and looked at Jabu.

'I thought we had no relatives,' It was Pule again.

'Oh, I am sorry Ouma,' Pule apologised as he went about collecting the dishes from the table.

'Carry on Jabu.'

'I told them you were in church. The young lady said she'll come back tomorrow.'

'Did they say why they wanted to see me?'

'No, Ouma.'

'Oh well, we'll see when she comes,' said Ouma, her brow creasing into a frown.

Giving her dish to Pule, she wiped her hands and mouth with the towel in the wash basin. She took out of her pocket an old worn-out leather purse. She extracted and examined coins, looked hard at the purse and shook her head.

'Ouma.'

'Yes, Pule.'

'Who goes to school tomorrow?' He was busy washing the dishes.

'I think it's Jabu, is it not?' Ouma replied.

'But I missed two days last week, Ouma,' protested Pule, who was the younger.

'Oh yes. You were ill, by the way.'

'Let him go Ouma, I'll go the other week,' said Jabu who was drying the dishes.

'Is the uniform washed and ironed, Jabu?' asked Ouma.

'Yes, Ouma, it is.'

'Be careful when you have the uniform on, Pule. Don't put stones and bottle caps in your pockets. It is all you have, both of you.'

'I understand, Ouma,' replied Pule.

'Jabu, tomorrow you'll be helping me at Kwa-Mathikithwane. Remember, it's Friday. We must be there before lunch . . .'

The knocking on the tin-sheet door grew louder. Finally the door was opened, and Ouma found herself face to face with a young woman. She was well-dressed, wrapped in a woolen overcoat, her hands in brown leather gloves. In her right hand she had a black attaché case. In the other hand hung her handbag.

'Oh, good morning,' Ouma said, eyeing the stranger closely.

'Good morning,' she replied. 'I'm sorry to disturb you on so cold a morning.'

'Don't bother. I was still cleaning. Do come in.'

The young woman, standing in high-heeled boots, had to bend slightly as she went into the tiny shack.

'You'll excuse this disarrangement of things,' Ouma continued, as her hand swept the room, indicating the disorder of benches and table.

'No, I do not mind indeed.'

Ouma set about arranging the table, the benches, the primus stove and other odds and ends. Putting a bench next to the table, she offered the young woman a seat. The tiny room, save for the two chairs, the table and the bed, was virtually empty. The clean cement floor was not yet dry from scrubbing. There was no source of heat in the room. Flattened sheets of cardboard were stuck on the corrugated iron walls. However, these means could not keep out the severe chill from outside. The room was bitterly cold.

The young woman put her case and handbag on the table. As she sat down on the bench, she drew her coat closer to her body and her skull-cap down to her ears. Reluctantly, she took off one glove, took out a handkerchief and blew her nose into it. Having wiped her nose, she put her handkerchief back in the bag and quickly hid her hand in the warmth of her glove. Being light in complexion, her nose took on a reddish hue. As she sat there, huddled and gently rocking on the bench, the nose looked like a tiny, bobbing signal.

'You're cold my child,' Ouma said to her.

'Sho-o-o. It is cold! They say it has snowed as far as Standerton,' she said. The nose bobbed a signal.

'What puts you in these parts in this terrible weather, my child?' asked Ouma.

'Work. Work, Ouma. They call you Ouma, don't they?'

'Yes. I have grandchildren, so I suppose I should be called Ouma,' she said, her hollowed cheeks melting into a gentle smile.

The young woman bent her knee-length-booted legs, drew her coat closer and opened the attaché case. She took off her gloves, and rubbed her hands together. She then took out some papers from the case and spread them on the table. Finally, she said: 'I have been sent by the Welfare people to you, Ouma.

'You see, Ouma,' she went on, 'the local authority has requested us to come and speak to you. To make you, ... to help you understand some of the directives they have been sending to you.'

'Such as ... ? I am listening, my child.'

The young woman looked up from the papers, looked at Ouma, and back at the papers.

'Well, they tell us that they have been telling you to leave this area, but you refuse ...' she paused. Ouma, sitting on the other side of the table, kept quiet. The young woman went on:

'The local authority says you're forcing it to take drastic action, something they very much wish to avoid.'

'Where am I supposed to go, they say?'

'Well, you'd be resettled somewhere like everybody else.'

'But why must I leave this area? My roots are here. My husband is buried here. My relatives are buried here. My friends are here. I want to die here. Be buried here ...'

'I see that Ouma, but you have no alternative. These people can be cruel, believe me.'

'I'm sorry my child. I won't leave. As for their cruelty ... I'd sooner expect mercy from a hundred mambas.'

The tiny red signal bobbed again. The young woman cupped the palms of her hands and put them to her mouth. She blew a steady stream of breath into the cup.

'... from Sophiatown. Then it was Evaton. The next was Lady Selbourne. Now it's Alexandra. What's next?' Ouma was going on. The old, thin cotton dress was all she had on. Yet, the anger rising in her voice seemed to heat her tiny, thin body. The two vertical lines on either cheek cut deep furrows in her ebony skin. The little eyes, black and normally misty with misery, were sharp and flashing sparks of defiance and anger.

'... living in a hell-on-earth,' she said bitterly. 'We can't even die in peace. Nor rest in peace.'

The young woman rested her elbows on the table, raised her arms, and opened the palms, buried her face in them. Presently, she heaved a long sigh, then went back to her papers.

Outside, the wind raged furiously. The shack's loose tin sheets rattled madly at this vicious assault. Soon, there could be heard a patter of feet, then voices, excited voices. And suddenly the door burst open.

'Ouma, Ouma,' the voices pierced the chilly interior of the shack.

'Close the door!' cried Ouma.

After the door was closed, Pule and Jabu stood next to it, panting and wide-eyed. Pule held some exercise books in his hand. He was dressed in a short-sleeved nylon shirt, torn in the stomach area. He had nothing on underneath. He was also dressed in black shorts, tied at the waist with an old neck-tie. He was bare-footed. They looked cautiously at the stranger.

Finally, Jabu's young face flashed with excitement as words tumbled out of his mouth:

'Ah, Ouma, this is the *Ousi* I told you about.'

'Hello boys,' the young woman smiled at them.

'Hello.'

'Hello.'

'Are you from school already?' she asked, looking from one to the other.

'Yes,' replied Pule. 'The morning session is through.'

She was about to ask Jabu the same question when he said:

'*Ousi*, is that your car outside?'

'Yes,' she replied.

'You drive it yourself?' inquired Pule.

'Yes. I do.'

'A-a-ah' exclaimed Jabu, 'I thought only white ladies could drive.'

'She must be smart,' added Pule, winking at Jabu.

The young woman started collecting her papers from the table. She piled them neatly and put them into the case.

'Ouma,' she said, 'I have to go now. But I'll come back soon. I do not know when. But it will be soon.'

She stood up and opened her handbag. Extracting two one-rand notes, she said to the boys:

'Here boys, this is one rand for each of you. You'll buy yourself some fish and chips and other things at school.'

The boys looked at the money and made no effort to take it.

'Please keep your money,' Ouma said, speaking so low she could barely be heard. 'Accepting money from strangers is forbidden in this family. Sorry to hurt your feelings, but this rule must be observed.'

'Oh, I see,' said the young woman. She put back the money in the bag. 'I must go now. Goodbye, Ouma. Goodbye boys.' She left.

'Pule,' Ouma said, 'I believe we have some coal left. So prepare the brazier towards sunset. Jabu, get the box. We must be early today. It's Friday. Everybody will be rushing to Kwa-Mathikithwane. There is no time to lose.'

'Do you think the butchery truck will come today, Ouma?' asked Jabu.

'It must come. It's Friday.'

You cannot miss the dumping grounds, or, as the ghetto residents call it, Kwa-Mathikithwane. The first street cutting Alexandra from west to east separates this ghetto from the dumping ground. Standing at the corner of Ouma's street, 6th Avenue, you can see, on the right side, a huge mound of ash. On getting closer, you see that the mound contains every conceivable peace of junk. Milling all over the junk area are people of all ages. Every one of them, one way or another, is busy probing into the ashen ground. Women, children, men, dogs, cats mingle as they rifle through the junk for various objects: food, clothing, utensils, coal, bones, cloth. All of them are covered with a grey film of ash, as though in readiness for some ritual. Not far from this dump is a sign in bold letters: 'Sandton Municipal Area. No UNAUTHORISED dumping allowed.'

Tins and metal clank; bottles tinkle; smoke of ash rises to the sky; people shout at one another; dogs bark and growl as they quarrel with human beings over discarded food; cats miaow wildly; all sorts of vulgar words and obscenities flow hither and thither as people swear at the top of their voices. Even fights are a common occurrence. It is a bitter struggle for survival.

The big yellow truck appeared on the highway. Somebody on the dumping ground cried: *'Iyeza.* It's coming!' Everybody stood erect, and looked towards the highway. The big yellow truck swung off the highway into a dirt road leading to the grounds. As it lumbered on the dusty gravel road towards the dumping area, the people formed two parallel columns, as though forming a guard of honour for this distinguished guest. As the truck moved into the guard of honour, the crowd chorused in unison: *'Woza, Woza, Woza!* Ho-o-o-! Ho-o-o-! Driver Ho-o-o-!' The truck came to a halt. A man in a white dustcoat splattered with blood jumped out. He called to the driver: 'O.K.' The truck was a big Mercedes Benz with a red canopy on which was written, in huge black letters, SANDTON MEAT SUPPLY.

The driver started operating the levers. The canopy rose steadily and came to rest at an angle of about 40 degrees. Its doors swung open, and it began to disgorge its contents. And then followed a vicious scramble as men, women, children, dogs and cats fought over the precious contents from the truck. In a few minutes all was over. Only a whimpering dog was left lapping some scraps of bloody sawdust from the ground.

'Ouma,' cried Jabu, 'I found some bones.' He handed Ouma the bones.

'Good. That's my boy,' said Ouma as she gathered the bones into the box.

'They are pork bones too. How lucky you are. At least we'll prepare soup tonight.'

'Is that all for today, Ouma?'

'Yes, let's go ... It's getting late. I have a few cents. We must get some potatoes and onions.'

The soft pink petals dilated gently in the feeble sun. All over, the isolated apricot trees were in full bloom. Their pink flowers deceptively radiated warmth: deceptively, because although the apricot trees bespoke spring, there was nothing warm about the weather. Weather reports noted the heavy snowfalls on the Drakensberg Range. The reports further indicated that it was very unusual for snow to fall in August. As usual, this snowfall sent shivers across the hinterland of South Africa. So that you found an anomalous situation: fruit trees gaily greeting spring, while on the other hand a blistering chill swept the country.

But then everything is anomalous in South Africa.

Ouma's shack was in the shade of a large apricot tree. The shack's roof was blanketed with fallen pink petals of apricot flowers. Time and again, the wind sent them scattering in the neighbourhood.

The small dark-brown Datsun stopped opposite Ouma's shack. The young lady with the bobbing red nose stepped out of the car. She was wearing dark-brown knee-length boots, a dark-brown woolen overcoat, dark-brown hand gloves and a dark-brown skull-cap — all to match her dark-brown Datsun. Her overcoat was knee length, and it was tightly wrapped around her body. She was carrying her attaché case and her handbag. After locking the car she jumped the furrow of dirty water and landed on a spread of kikuyu grass. Cutting through the kikuyu was a thin footpath leading up to Ouma's shack. She walked up the foot path. Halfway she was greeted by the stench of a rotting dog. With her left hand she covered her nose to shut off the foul smell. However, the handbag swayed to and fro, and she was forced to remove her hand from her nose.

She stopped to survey the area. To her right was the single men's hostel. This monstrosity was four storeys high and was Ouma's only neighbour within a radius of half-a-kilometre. To her left, about three paces away, she could see the ribcage of a dead animal, the carcass swarming with little yellow worms and flies buzzing noisily around. Then taking her eyes off this sight she looked at the ghetto spread before her. Instantly she felt revolted. The clutter of tin shacks, dilapidated buildings, dirty streets, — this sight ... She wondered. Had she seen it in a newspaper? Yes, it occurred to her, it had been in the previous month's Johannesburg *Star*. A white reporter had described this ghetto as 'a festering sore on a healthy body.' Oh yes, that was the wording. This is it.

But 'a healthy body?' ... I'll be damned! For all I care, she continued reflecting, this body is riddled with festering sores, all oozing puss. A sick, sick, rotten-sick, body.

'*Kena, kena*. Come in,' called a voice. The door opened and the young woman walked in. The whole family was in. A little brazier was glowing in the centre of the floor. Jabu and Pule were sprawled on the floor, paging through a picture magazine. Ouma was busy sewing an old khaki shirt. The atmosphere was cosy and homely. The young woman felt cheered.

'*Dumelang*. Good day,' she said.

Dumela', replied Ouma.

'*Dumela Ousi*,' chorused the boys.

'How's everybody?' she went on.

'We are fine. How are you in this cold weather, my child?'

'I'm okay, Ouma. Thank you.'

'Anyway, we have had colder weather before, and it always passes. This will pass,' said Ouma.

'But this is August. We are supposed to be having spring now,' the young woman continued, as though protesting.

'*Ousi* did you come in your car?' asked Jabu.

'Yes, I did.'

'Thieves around here steal cars in the wink of an eye. Don't you want us to go and guard your car?' asked Pule.

'Oh no, I don't mind,' she replied. 'Here is the key to the door.' She handed them the key.

'Don't you go and mess around in that car,' Ouma warned them.

'No, no, Ouma, we won't,' they said, shooting out of the shack. The young woman seated herself on the bench next to the table. She opened her case and took out some papers, which she carefully spread on the table.

'How's your health, Ouma?' she inquired.

'Not very good. Not good at all. But I do manage.'

The young woman looked at the papers before her. She coughed, a slight cough. Finally, she looked Ouma squarely in the face.

'Ouma, I am sorry. I have bad news for you,' she said.

'Don't worry my child. Do your work. I have heard a lot of bad news in my lifetime. This won't make any difference.'

'Ouma, your case has become urgent. The local authorities say they cannot reason with you anymore. They have decided that you are going to be forced out of this area. They say you are blocking the hostel project that should be started very soon. Really, Ouma, you must try to understand.'

'I won't be the first person they are dumping in the street. Nor will I be the last. If the authorities really care about people's welfare, why destroy their homes? Why break families? Indeed why destroy families? They should be improving and rebuilding this place. What guarantee does one have that one won't be moved again from wherever one is being shunted to?'

'But Ouma, look at the matter this way ... You are old and sickly. What will happen to these little boys after you are dead? What will their future be?'

'Those are my grandchildren!' Ouma's voice had a strange, menacing quiver as she said this. 'They go wherever I go. They stay wherever I stay. I vowed to my dying daughter, their mother, that I'd keep them. Please don't bring them into this matter. They are my business, and mine alone. I won't be moved!'

There was a long silence.

A thin wind ululated outside. A solitary dog barked somewhere in the neighbourhood. Some two birds trilled in the apricot tree, gaily welcoming spring.

The young woman straightened her hands before her and laid them flat on the table, palms down.

She sighed. Then, in a soft, constricted voice, compressing her lips as if holding back tears, she said: 'I'm sorry, Ouma, I am really sorry. I don't like what's happening to you, or anybody, for that matter. Oh ...' She paused, issuing a sharp short cry, 'It's inhuman!'

'No, no, my child,' said Ouma in a very soothing tone. 'Don't be upset. It is the law, their law. You are just doing your work.'

As though she had composed herself, the young woman continued: 'Ouma, have you heard of the Save Alexandra campaign?'

'No, I have not.'

'Well, this is a body which was formed recently by a number of citizens here. They say that one of the examples that gives them courage to fight is your resistance. I must indicate to you, Ouma, that this is one of the reasons why the authorities are becoming so harsh with you.'

The man was of average height and well built. He walked with a firm step as though nursing a limp. As he came upon the hostel he stopped. He looked at the building with intense curiosity. It was as though he was counting the windows. He walked on. When he reached the empty area surrounding the hostel he stopped. He turned around and carefully surveyed the area around him. Again he looked at the hostel. He looked at the empty property adjoining the hostel. For a long time he stared at the vacant lot. He was disturbed by the screeching sound of metal grazing the gravel. He turned round to find a wheelbarrow full of vegetables neatly stacked in different compartments as though in a stall. This mobile vegetable stall was operated by an old man clad in dirty rags. The clothing was so tattered that it was difficult to tell what the rags had been originally. The old man took out a piece of cloth from his pocket and wiped his face. Blinking continually, he said to the man:

'Are you lost mister? Or looking for something?'

'Well - er - I've been wondering . . . is this 6th Avenue?'

'Yes, it is.'

'Where can I find No. 39?'

'This is No 39 - was - No. 39,' the old man declared, pointing at the vacant lot in front of them.

The man's face registered disbelief. The old timer, noting this reaction, continued: 'All the houses in this area were demolished and the people packed away. Looking for anybody in particular?' He spat on to the ground. 'Yes, I am,' the man said, and proceeded to describe the person he wanted.

'Oh! That's Ouma. She stays in that little tin house,' he pointed at the shack.

'Thank you.'

'Aren't you going to buy Ouma some vegetables? The poor thing needs them!' the old timer said, with a wink in his left eye. Before the man could answer, he was already wrapping some vegetables in an old newspaper.

The man paid for them and started towards the shack. The sun was setting and darkness was slowly creeping in. He knocked on the tin door.

A boy's voice cried out from inside: 'Kena.' As he entered he stopped a bit and hovered a moment over the threshold. There was a candle lit in the room, which was still in semi-darkness. Ouma was sitting at the table sewing by the candle light. There were wisps of faint carbon monoxide fumes emanating from the dying coal in the brazier. The man came forward and stood in the middle of the room, exposing himself to candle light.

'*Dumelang*,' he said.

'*Dumela*,' Ouma said, returning the greeting. Jabu and Pule were huddled next to the dying brazier.

'How's everybody at home?' the man went on.

'We are fine, thank you. How are you? Please have a seat,' said Ouma.

The man drew a nearby bench and sat at the table, opposite Ouma, placing the little package of vegetables on the table.

'We are just wondering when this cold spell will be over. It's causing us so much illness,' Ouma continued lightheartedly. She went on with her sewing. After some time the man said: 'Well, the weather people say we must expect an extended winter. It won't last long though.' Ouma was about to pierce the shirt with the needle in her hand when she stopped abruptly. The hand fell limply on the sewing resting on her lap. She looked up at the stranger. It seemed as though she was having difficulty in focusing. Finally the face in the candle light fell within her full view. The sewing fell to the floor as the face registered in Ouma's consciousness. She raised one hand to cover her gaping mouth. However, it was too late. The sharp, subdued cry was out already.

'Jo-o-o. Jo-o-o-!! Jo-o-nna-we-e-e!' Her face fell into the palms of her hands. She shook convulsively.

'*Mohlolo! Mohlolo-o-o-!*' The old woman sobbed uncontrollably. The man stood up and walked up to her. He took her tiny body into his arms. The old woman wept on, in sharp, piercing spasms.

'They ... they said ...' Ouma uttered between gasps,' ... they said you were dead. Fell over a high wall or something ...'

'They lied, the bastards! They merely wanted to break your heart. It's all right now Ouma. Don't worry. Don't worry,' the man pleaded.

'Oh, my God. Bless the Lord. *Ke tla robala. Oho, ke tla robala.* At last, I'll be able to rest,' she said in low tones.

The young woman parked her small dark-brown Datsun at the usual spot. Yet she did not get out immediately. Her gloved hands holding the steering wheel firmly, she rested with her forehead on her wrists. She sat in that position for some time. Finally taking a long breath, she opened the door and stepped out into the raging chilly wind. Deliberately, mechanically even, she locked the door, and jumping the furrow with the dirty water, went on to Ouma's shack. She was walking with a slight stoop, as though deep in thought, as indeed she was.

Finally, as she raised her head to see better, she stopped abruptly and gasped: 'Oh my God!' and told herself: 'I'm too late. They have already acted.'

Outside Ouma's shack were some people. Six to be exact. There was the stranger who had arrived the night before, an old man and two elderly women wrapped in shawls. Jabu and Pule were basking in the morning sun. They were leaning against the shack. Next to the shack were several belongings of Ouma's. Her bed, table, two benches and some pots. All were bundled together, as if in preparation for a journey. The young lady came upon the little group. One old woman spoke something to Ouma's visitor. Then the stranger walked over to the young woman.

'Good morning,' he said.

'Good morning,' she replied, eyeing him curiously.

'I understand you are the social worker who is handling Ouma's case?' he inquired.

'Yes, I am,' she affirmed.

'To start with, I'd like you to know that Ouma has passed away. She died this morning,' he said in a solemn tone.

'Oh dear,' she cried. 'Oh no! I'm from the local bureau, and came to warn her that they were going to evict her today.'

'Don't worry. Everything is under control,' he said.

'Who are you? A relative?' she asked.

'Yes. Ouma was my aunt,' he replied.

'I thought Ouma had no relatives.'

'She thought so herself. I've been on Robben Island, for the past 15 years. I was convicted during the post-Sharpeville trials. They lied to her and told her I was dead. The bastards.'

'These poor boys . . . ?' she asked, pointing at Jabu and Pule.

'I'll take them with me. They'll be okay,' he replied.

'Oh, what a brave woman. A brave old woman. Noble, courageous, principled, strong. What an honour to have met someone like her!'

'She will be buried at home . . .'

Biographies

BAKER, Joan
Born in Wynberg in 1934 and attended school at Battswood. Presentl living in Mitchells Plain. A mother of four, she started writing in 198 and is a member of the Congress of South African Writers.

BYRON, Mary
Born in 1870 in Scotland and married Brigadier J.J. Byron who served i the Anglo-Boer War. After the war they settled in the Orange Rive Colony. She published two volumes of poetry: *A Voice From The Vel* (1913) and some years later *The Owls: A Book Of Verses*. A collection c short stories and sketches, *Dawn And Dusk In The Highveld*, appeare in 1931. Died in 1935.

CLAYTON, Cherry
Born in 1943. Lectures in English at Rand Afrikaans University. Cc edited an anthology of interviews with South African women writer: *Between The Lines* (1989) and edited an anthology of critical essay: *Women And Writing in South Africa* (1989). Currently working on photographic biography of Olive Schreiner. Poetry, fiction and critic writing published in journals and anthologies.

FENSTER, Pnina
Born in Johannesburg in 1959 and studied for a B.A. at Wits Universit and later Graphic Design. Worked as barmaid, waitress and journalis Presently writes weekly 'Fenster on the World' column for the *Sunda Times*.

GORDIMER, Nadine
Born in 1923 in Springs. A foremost writer of fiction in English today

ducated at local schools and the University of the Witwatersrand. Pub-
cations include seven collections of short stories and eight novels. The
hort story collection, *Friday's Footprint*, won the W.H. Smith Literary
ward in 1961, *A Guest of Honour* was awarded the James Tait Black
Memorial Prize in 1973, and in 1974 she shared the Booker Prize for *The
Conservationist*, which was also winner of the French international
ward, the Grand Aigle d'Or. Her books have received widespread
ritical acclaim and won numerous other literary prizes including the
Malaparte Prize from Italy, and the Nelly Sachs Prize from West Ger-
many. In 1981 she was awarded the Scottish Arts Council's Neil Gunn
ellowship. She lives in Johannesburg.

GOUDVIS, Bertha
orn in 1876 in England and came to South Africa in 1881. Lived in
outh Africa, Southern Rhodesia and Moçambique, working as a
otelier and journalist. In 1949 she published a novel, *Little Eden*, and in
956 a volume of short stories, *The Mistress Of Mooiplaas And Other
tories*. She also published a play, *The Aliens*, in 1936. Died in 1966.

HAMMOND, Noorie
orn in 1950 in Kimberley. Studied for a year at the University of
Durban. Is presently a secretary at the University of Bophuthatswana.

HEAD, Bessie
orn in Pietermaritzburg in 1937, the daughter of a wealthy white
woman and family's black stable hand, after her mother had been ad-
nitted to a mental hospital. Worked as a journalist in Johannesburg and
Cape Town. In 1964 she left South Africa on an exit permit and lived
lmost half her life in Serowe, Botswana, where she died in 1986. Her
works include three novels: *When Rain Clouds Gather* (1972), *Maru*
1972), *A Question of Power* (1974). She also published an anthology of
hort stories, *The Collector Of Treasures* (1977), and a book of social his-
ory, *Serowe, Village Of The Rain Wind* in 1981. An historical novel, *A
Bewitched Crossroad: An African Saga* appeared in 1984, and recently a
osthumous collection of short stories, titled *Tales Of Tenderness And
Power* (1989) was published.

HOUSE, Amelia
orn and brought up in Wynberg in South Africa. Studied at the Uni-
ersity of Cape Town. Emigrated to England in 1963, where she studied
rama and acted. In 1972 she emigrated to the United States. Has pub-
shed poetry and critical essays in the United States, South Africa, and

France. Published *Checklist of Black South African Women Writers i English* (1980).

ISAACSON, Maureen
Born in Johannesburg in 1955 and studied at Wits University. Lived fo three years in Sweden. Worked as a copywriter, journalist and re searcher on *The Fifties People of South Africa* and *The Finest Photo from the Old Drum*. Currently working on a collection of her shor stories.

JONSSON, Elizabeth N.
Born in Durban in 1898. Influenced by her artist mother, she studied ar at the Technical College in Durban and later at Heatherley's Art Schoo in London. Short stories, articles and poems published in English American and South African newspapers and journals. Her stories ar collected in *The Silver Sky And Other Stories* (1974?). Published tw prose commentaries *Futility Farm* (1958) and *Cross-stitch Footprint* (1969). Died in 1983.

KARODIA, Farida
Born and raised in South Africa. Emigrated to Canada in 1969 afte teaching in Johannesburg and Zambia. In Canada she wrote several radi dramas for C.B.C. while teaching. She is currently a full-time writer Her first novel, *Daughters Of The Twilight*, was published in 1986 an was a runner-up for the Fawcett Prize. Her short story anthology *Coming Home And Other Stories* was published in 1988.

KHAZAMULA, Ponkie
Born in Alexandra Township. Was studying law at the time of th Soweto uprising in 1976, whereafter she left South Africa. Currentl studying French and Portuguese.

LESSING, Doris
Born in Persia (Iran) in 1919 of English parents. Moved with her parent in 1925 to a farm in Southern Rhodesia (Zimbabwe). In 1949 she lef Salisbury, after a hectic time of radical political involvement, to live i London. The following year her first novel was published, *The Grass I Singing* (1950), which was followed by others. Publications also includ three collections of short stories and numerous essays and reviews Among other literary honours she received the Society of Author' Somerset Maugham Award and the Prix Medici.

MACPHAIL, E.M.
Born on the farm in 1922 in the vicinity of present day Soweto, and lived in small towns in the Transvaal and isolated parts of the bushveld. Work published in South African and North American literary magazines. Was awarded the 1987 CNA Award for English Fiction for her novel *Phoebe & Nio*. In 1989 her collection of short stories, *Falling Upstairs*, was reprinted.

MASILELA, Johanna
Born in 1916 in the Vereeniging district where her parents were share-croppers. Worked in the white farmer's house until the age of eight, when she was sent to school. Disabled at a very young age, she continued attending school until the age of sixteen. She has worked as a domestic worker for whites and later took care of the children of black families.

MAZIBUKO, Anna
Born in 1944. Worked on farms and in white households from the age of 12 years, moving from job to job in search of money for her children. In 1983 she settled in Driefontein in the Eastern Transvaal, a community which is threatened with removal in terms of government resettlement policy.

MHLOPHE, Gcina
Has published poetry, a children's book, *The Snake With Seven Heads* (1989) and a play, *Have You Seen Zandile* (1989). She is an accomplished actress and is currently Resident Director at the Market Theatre in Johannesburg.

MILLIN, Sarah Gertrude
Born in Lithuania in 1889, but lived mostly in South Africa. Her publications include seventeen novels, including *God's Stepchildren* (1924); biographies, autobiographies and histories. Between 1944 and 1948 she published a six-volume diary about Hitler's war. In 1957 her short story anthology, *Two Bucks Without Hair And Other Stories*, was published. Died in 1968.

MOTANYANE, Maud
Born in Nigel, near Johannesburg. Studied Library Science at the University of Zululand, and later journalism. Worked for *The Post* and *The Star*. In 1983 she was chosen as a fellow of the World Press Institute, St. Paul, Minnesota and spent several months travelling in the United States. She is a member of the African Writers' Association and is currently editor of *Tribute* magazine.

MVULA, Kefiloe Tryphinah
Born in Mapetla, Soweto in 1967. Received education at Khotso Lowe Primary School and later Mabewana Higher Primary School. Wrot matric at Sekano Ntoana High School in 1988.

PALESTRANT, Ellen
Born in 1943 and lived in Johannesburg, where she ran a hydroponi farm. Also worked as a remedial teacher and television script writer. novella and short stories with a psychological emphasis was published i 1983 under the title *Nosedive And Other Writings*. In 1987 she emig rated to America.

REDDY, Jayapraga
Born in Durban in 1948. Published a collection of short stories, *On Th Fringe Of Dreamtime and Other Stories* (1987). Her plays and storie have been broadcast by the BBC and SABC. Confined to a wheelchai she is a full time writer.

ROBERTS, Sheila
Born in Johannesburg. Received schooling in Potchefstroom. Complete a doctoral dissertation on the novels of Patrick White. Has worked as typist and teacher. Currently Professor of English at the University Milwaukee-Wisconsin in the United States. Received the Oliv Schreiner prize for her first collection of short stories, *Outside Life Feast* (1975). In 1983 a second anthology of short stories, *This Time C Year*, was published. She also published three novels and poetry and tw books of literary criticism, including essays on women writers, *Still Th Frame Holds* (1986).

ROESTORF, Margaret
Lives and works in Maraisburg, five kilometres from where she grew u Has worked as apprentice sangoma, journalist, diamond marker an waitress. She has published two poetry collections and *The Dog Of A* (1987), a collection of tales and paintings, launched in conjunction wit her second one-person art exhibition.

SCHREINER, Olive
Born in the Eastern Cape in 1855. With little formal education sh worked as a governess on farms in the Karoo and wrote fiction as well a polemical essays. In 1883 her well known novel *The Story Of An Africa Farm* was published. Apart from other writings, she also wrote eigh short stories and twenty-six allegories or dreams. These were publishe

in *Dreams* (1890), *Dream Life And Real Life* (1893) and *Stories, Dreams and Allegories* (1923). Schreiner lived in Europe from 1881 to 1889, whereafter she returned to South Africa. In 1920 she died in Wynberg, Cape.

SELLO, Doris
One of the few women writers who had a story published in *Drum* magazine during the 1950s.

SMITH, Pauline
Born in 1882 and grew up in the Oudtshoorn district. Became acquainted with the Little Karoo and its people as a child, while accompanying her father, a doctor, who visited the sick and dying by cart. In 1985 she was sent to boarding-school in England. In 1909 she met Arnold Bennett who encouraged her to publish her writing. Her collection of short stories, *The Little Karoo* (1925) was followed by a novel, *The Beadle*, then *Platkop's Children*, a collection of stories about children. After Bennett's death she wrote his biography, *AB* (1933). Died in 1959.

THOMAS, Gladys
Born in the Cape in 1935 and living at Ocean View, her plays, short stories and poems reflect on the social problems of South Africa. An anthology of protest poetry, *Cry Rage*, co-published with James Matthews, has been banned in South Africa. Her first three plays won a literary competition organised by *Post* newspaper in 1989. Her creative writing is published in newspapers and journals. A collection of her writing will be published shortly.

TLALI, Miriam
Born in Doornfontein, Johannesburg in 1933 and grew up in Sophiatown. Studied at Roma University in Lesotho but was forced by increasing financial difficulties to leave prior to graduation. Returning to Johannesburg, she worked as a clerk and typist in a furniture and appliances store, which provided the material for her first novel *Muriel at Metropolitan* (1975). *Amandla!* followed in 1980, but was banned in South Africa. The ban has recently been lifted. In 1984 she published a prose collection titled *Mihloti*. An anthology of short stories, *Footprints In The Quag* appeared in 1989. She now lives and writes in Soweto.

WICOMB, Zoë
Born in the Cape Province in 1948. After completing an Arts Degree at the University of the Western Cape, she left for England in 1970 to study

English Literature at Reading University. Currently living in Nottin gham, where she teaches English, Black Literature and Women' Studies. Also an active member of the Nottingham Anti-Apartheid Movement. Published one short story anthology, *You Can't Get Lost In Cape Town* (1987).

ZWI, Rose
Born in Mexico in 1928, but lived most of her life in Johannesburg where she was involved in publishing. Recipient of the 1982 Oliv Schreiner Prize for prose for her novel *Another Year In Africa* (1980). She traces the experiences of a South African Jewish family in her thre novels, including *The Inverted Pyramid* (1981) and *Exiles* (1984). Emig rated to Australia in 1988.